I0632953

The Conqueror of Death

IN THE SAME SERIES

The Conqueror of Death
and Other Stories
from *La Science Illustrée*

translated, annotated and introduced by
Brian Stableford

A Black Coat Press Book

English adaptation and introduction Copyright © 2013 by Brian Stableford.

Cover illustration Copyright © 2013 Yoz.

Visit our website at www.blackcoatpress.com

ISBN 978-1-61227-230-6. First Printing. December 2013. Published by Black Coat Press, an imprint of Hollywood Comics.com, LLC, P.O. Box 17270, Encino, CA 91416. All rights reserved.
Except for review purposes, no part of this book may be reproduced or transmitted in any form or by any means, electronic or mechanical, including photocopying, recording, or by any information storage and retrieval system, without permission in writing from the publisher.
The stories and characters depicted in this novel are entirely fictional. Printed in the United States of America.

TABLE OF CONTENTS

Introduction

Literary genres are not created *ex nihilo*; they are woven together from pre-existent threads that consequently seem to have been leading toward them, fated to entwine. Thus, when Hugo Gernsback invented "scientifiction," trailing it in *Science and Invention* before founding *Amazing Stories* in 1926, he formed a deliberate compound, selecting what he considered to be exemplary works from the oeuvres of Jules Verne, H. G. Wells and Edgar Allan Poe, and adding in what he thought to be relevant components from the contemporary American pulp magazines, including works by Edgar Rice Burroughs, A. Merritt, Ray Cummings, Austin Hall and Homer Eon Flint, which had themselves taken some inspiration from earlier writers, including H. G. Wells and H. Rider Haggard. A generation before then, however, in the 1890s, the editor of the French popular science magazine *La Science Illustrée*, Louis Figuier—who had been privileged a generation before that, to have exercised a highly significant influence on Jules Verne's *Voyage au centre de la Terre* (1864; rev. 1867; tr. as *Journey to the Centre of the Earth*)—made a concerted effort to define and delimit a genre of *roman scientifique* [scientific fiction], using that rubric to head a series of *feuilletons* that ran in the magazine from 1888 to 1905.

To some extent, Figuier's project ran along the same lines as Gernsback's. Jules Verne was, inevitably, one of the central exemplars he employed in formulating his notion of what "scientific fiction" ought to be like, and in selecting exemplars from Verne's extensive canon, he would undoubtedly have had the same works in mind as Gernsback—except, of course, that copyright problems and the fact that his readers would already have been familiar with the works in question prevented him from reprinting them, whereas Gernsback did not let such niceties stand in his way. Although Wells had not yet begun producing his "scientific romances" when Figuier began his project, as soon as the relevant works began to appear in French translation, Figuier began featuring them in his *feuilleton* series, and did so on a prolific scale for some years, continuing for some while even after the prestigious literary magazine *Le Mercure de France*, also began printing Wells translations—including some of the same ones—in some quantity.

The one source to which Figuier had no inspirational access was, of course, the American pulp fiction that did not begin to appear in any profusion until sometime after his own experiment had concluded, and a handful of French precursors of that distinctive kind of interplanetary action-adventure fiction that were produced after the turn of the century also arrived too late for inclusion, so it remains a matter for conjecture as to whether Figuier would have been enthusiastic to accommodate them. As things turned out, that component of American "scientifiction," which was soon relabeled "science fiction," became such an important aspect of the genre as to be considered by many fans of the genre to be central and essential, although it remained peripheral to the British tradition of scientific romance that developed in the wake of Wells and the French tradition that survived Figuier's abandonment of his *feuilleton* series. In fact, the label Figuier used effectively died with his *feuilleton* slot, Alfred Vallette never having consented to adopt it for its own generic experiments in the *Mercure*, which were also soon interrupted, presumably because both editors realized that the genre did not have enough reader support to make it commercially worthwhile to continue its development.

That absence of exemplars of interplanetary adventure fiction was not, however, uncompensated. Figuier had other exemplars to draw upon, which gave rise to a significant thread of his *roman scientifique*, but which remained virtually unechoed in Gernsbackian science fiction. Alongside the work of Jules Verne, in the 1860s, several other writers participating in a significant crusade to popularize science had dabbled in various fictional formats, experimenting with different methods of trying to exploit narrative methods to dramatize scientific materials and subtle ways of intruding scientific information and perspectives into conventional narratives. The leaders in that enterprise were Camille Flammarion and S. Henry Berthoud, both of whom produced a good deal of what they thought of as "scientific fiction," but most of which bears little resemblance to what eventually acquired the label of "science fiction." Both writers produced occasional items of what might be called, in a broad sense, "speculative fiction," but both were very wary of basing their speculations on the imaginative extrapolation of present-day technologies to produce images of hypothetical future technologies.

That reluctance seems surprising to us, because we are so accustomed to the strategy, but in the 1860s, it was seen as hazardous and controversial in its propriety; Jules Verne would probably have done a great deal more of that kind of speculation had he been given free rein, but his publisher, Jules Hetzel—who, unusually, had him under contract—did his level best to rein in that aspect of Verne's work, encouraging him to concentrate primary of supposedly-naturalistic tales of exploration and adventure. Flammarion's imagination was far more-reaching than Verne's, but when his reaching mechanisms ventured beyond mere dreaming, they drew almost exclusively on the astronomer's enthusiasm for "spiritism" (the French equivalent of the Anglo-American spiritualism) rather than his understanding of technology. The devoutly Catholic Berthoud was skeptical about spiritualism and reluctant even to use dreaming as a visionary ploy, and the vast majority of his manifold attempts to alloy science with narrative involve naturalistic narratives in which the characters encounter unusual phenomena or encounter the various tribulations that he considered to be routinely associated with scientific endeavor.

These two kinds of precedents were not very copiously extrapolated by other writers, and cannot really be said to have prompted subgenres in the manner in which "Vernian fiction" became a distinguishable and fairly prolific subgenre, but they were not without influence. Figuier seems to have been skeptical about spiritism and only allowed it to serve a peripheral role in one or two of the stories he included in his feuilleton series, but he was certainly sympathetic to the strategy of writing conventional narratives whose story-value was similar to that of popular fiction in general, but whose characters become involved with unusual phenomena or have occasion to employ the scientific method to perfectly possible situations in ingenious and intriguing ways. Henry Berthoud was still alive in 1888 but was very old and no longer active as a writer, or Figuier well might have approached him to contribute to his series, and some of the authors he did invite or take up were of a similar stripe.

The situation of Figuier's fledgling genre was further complicated by the fact that the term *roman scientifique*, which had been used by critics and commentators in connection with Jules Verne's works, had also been previously used to describe fiction of a very different sort: the strictly-defined "Naturalism" for which Émile Zola offered a formal manifesto, which claimed to draw upon scientific perspectives in its analyses of human behavior and motivation. For the most part, Zola confined his "scientific" analyses to such phenomena as alcoholism and religious fanaticism, although one instance of the supposed taint of the Rougon-Macquart blood was the obsessive data-gathering of *Le Docteur Pascal* (1884), whose experimental endeavors also give rise to a bizarre elixir of life. That novel brought Zolaesque "roman scientifique" much closer in its concerns to the many hypothetical studies of obsessive scientific endeavor developed in fictional form by Henry Berthoud, who had little else in common with Zola.

Figuier did not include Zolaesque fiction in his feuilleton series, sticking almost entirely to the norms of popular fiction and avoiding literary pretentions, but he was sympathetic nevertheless to works that were "naturalistic" in a more elementary fashion, and published a number of works that would not be considered, in retrospect, to be "proto-sciencefictional," although they were not out of keeping with many of the popularizing endeavors that Henry Berthoud described as "fantaisies scientifiques" [scientific fancies], of which he published a four-volume set in 1861-2 (some samples of which are included in the Black Coat Press Berthoud collection *Martyrs of Science and Other Victims of Devilry and Destiny*).[1] Inevitably, whether they were influenced by Berthoud or Zola—or, conceivably, both—several of Figuier's writers also developed a marked interest in the psychology of science and its occasional bizarre attributes.

In selecting stories from the *Science Illustrée feuilleton* series for inclusion in my previous anthologies, I generally picked out those whose themes and narrative strategies bear the most resemblance to what is now considered as typical of science fiction. Inevitably, therefore, the present collection, which completes the set of short fiction from the series currently available on *gallica* and other on-line sources (the later items in the series remain unavailable, presumably because the relevant issues are missing from the Bibliothèque Nationale's run of the periodical) is biased in the other direction. Although it includes one item that is thoroughly "sciencefictional" and others that are marginal in that respect, it also includes some that belong to a curious gray area of an "alternative scientific fiction" that was eventually dropped from the typification formed by the American genre. Figuier must either have selected them from submitted material or specifically commissioned them, so they were obviously in conformity with his notion of what *roman scientifique* might or ought to be, and might therefore be considered especially interesting in terms of their equivocal status in modern eyes.

One writer who became a regular contributor to Figuier's series, who is of particular interest in this context, is Camille Debans (1834-1910), who contributed seven stories to the series in all, four of which are reproduced here: "Histoire d'un

---

[1] Black Coat Press, ISBN 978-1-61227-229-0.

tremblement de terre" (26 November 1892-24 December 1892; tr. as "The Story of an Earthquake"), "L'Île en feu" (15 April 1893-20 May 1893; tr. as "Fire Island"), "Un duel à vapeur" (13 April 1895-25 May 1895; tr. as "A Steam Duel") and "Le Vainqueur de la mort: chronique des siècles à venir" (25 November 1895-30 November 1895; tr. as "The Conqueror of Death"). The other three are unavailable at present. The first three of the four stories listed are interesting not merely in differing from the sciencefictional method robustly featured in the fourth, but in being interestingly different from one another.

"Histoire d'un tremblement de terre," like many popularizing endeavors by Flammarion and Berthoud, masquerades as an item of non-fiction presented in narrative form in the interests of dramatization, although it is a work of fiction whose careful use of real places and false dates are tactical exercises intended to create a sense of verisimilitude. "L'Île en feu" similarly undertakes to provide a graphic description of a dramatic natural phenomenon, but is much more drastically fictionalized in its use of ironic melodrama and the striking exoticism of its climax. "Un duel à vapeur" is even more ironic in tone, and owes a considerable debt to the American tradition of "tall stories" developed by such writers as Mark Twain and Bret Harte, but its central motif appears to have been borrowed from an episode in Albert Robida's classic Vernian parody *Voyages très extraordinaires de Saturnin Farandoul* (1879; tr. as *The Adventures of Saturnin Farandoul*[2]). The futuristic "La Vainqueur de la mort" is much more obviously sciencefictional to the modern eye, but its tone is not so very different from that of "Un duel a vapeur" and it is solidly based in the particular strand of Henry Berthoud's work that examines the supposed psychology and social tribulations of scientific genius, and is surely influenced by Berthoud's work in that vein.

---

[2] Black Coat Press, ISBN 978-1-934543-61-0.

Debans is not significantly reputed as a proto-science fiction writer for any of the work he published outside *La Science Illustrée*, although one of his novels is entitled *Boissat chimiste* [Boissat, Chemist] (1892) and the first three stories translated herein were reprinted, along with other items of a broadly similar kind, in his collection *Les drames à toute vapeur* [Dramas at Full Steam] (1898). As the first story by Debans that Figuier published appeared in the magazine late in 1892, it might well have been the publication of *Boissat chimiste* that prompted the editor to approach the author for contributions, which he continued to use at approximately annual intervals.

Two of the other authors represented herein contributed considerable quantities of other material to the *feuilleton* series. The first is Alphonse Brown (1841-1902), author of "Les Tribulations d'un pêcheur à la ligne (21 August 1891-21 November 1891; tr. as "The Tribulations of an Angler"), whose novel *Une Ville de verre* (1890-91; tr. as *City of Glass*[3]) and novelette "Les insectes révélateurs" (1889; tr. as "The Tell-Tale Insects") have been previously translated, the second in the Black Coat Press anthology *Nemoville*.[4] Brown had been well-known for some time before Figuier launched his feuilleton series as a "Vernian" writer, and had became a stalwart of the Vernian periodical *Le Journal des Voyages*, so he was a natural recruit to Figuier's cause, but it is significant that the three stories that Figuier published are all considerably less fanciful than Brown's early Vernian romances; although the novel is a Vernian fantasy of exploration it contains no drastic technological extrapolation, and the two shorter narratives are tales of everyday life in which scientific knowledge comes to play a significant role in the strategies of the characters.

The second author who published other work in the series was Paul Combes (1856-1909), alias "C. Paulon," the author of "Les Mines D'or de Bas-Meudon" (12 February

---

[3] Black Coat Press, ISBN 978-1-61227-023-4.
[4] Black Coat Press, ISBN 978-1-61227-070-8.

1898-28 May 1898), two of whose short stories are translated in *Nemoville*. Combes was a well-known author under his own name, where he had some reputation as a lightweight naturalist of a moderately literary stripe, and did, in fact, reprint the novella translated herein as a book under his own name, where it presumably passed for a naturalistic comedy without any difficulty.

One of the other two authors represented here, Émile Gautier (1853-1937), author of "*Le Désiré*, première traverse d'un bateau sous-marin" (31 December 1892-18 January 1893; tr. as "*Le Désiré*"), was the editor of *La Science Illustrée*'s chief imitator and rival, *La Science Française*; he ran a similar feuilleton series of his own for some years, although he never contributed to it under his own name, and might not have done so at all. He did, however, collaborate with a celebrated ex-head of the Sûreté, who signed his works "Goron," on *Fleur de Bagne*, a long feuilleton novel published in *Le Journal* in 1901, which is an interesting hybrid of crime fiction and *roman scientifique*; that too has been published in translation by Black Coat Press as *Spawn of the Penitentiary*.[5] The marginally-sciencefictional story included here is a similar experiment in genetic hybridization, adding an element of scientific romance to a light-hearted mixture of methods and themes conventional in contemporary popular fiction written with female readers in mind—a rare ploy in *roman scientifique*, although Henry Berthoud had been a contributor to women's magazines.

The remaining inclusion in the present collection, "Les huit cents doubloons de Springfield" (1 December 1894- 2 February 1895; tr. as "Springfield's Doubloons") was by-lined Georges Price, the signature employed on all his books and magazine stories by Ferdinand-Gustave Petitierre (1853-1922), who had published books of various sorts before publishing this novelette in *La Science Illustrée*, but afterwards diversified into Vernian fiction with sufficient determination

---

[5] Black Coat Press, ISBN 978-1-61227-137-8.

to become something of a specialist, although he also wrote two non-fiction books about railways, reflecting another interest that he evidently shared with numerous contributors to Figuier's periodical.

Price's Vernian romances, which routinely feature significant components of *roman scientifique*, include *Les trois disparus du Sirius* [The Three Missing Men of the *Sirius*] (1896), its sequel *Les Chasseurs d'épaves* [The Wreck-Hunters] (1898) and *La mine d'or infernale* [The Infernal Gold-Mine] (1920), the last-named being one of two items illustrated by Albert Robida. As with "La Vainqueur de la mort," "Les huit cents doubloons de Springfield" has strong and striking affinities with Henry Berthoud's accounts of scientific obsession and its social and psychological costs and dangers. That remained a central theme of French *roman scientifique* long after the label had faded into the historical background, to a greater extent than in British scientific romance, and a much greater extent than in American science fiction and its eventual bastard imitations, and is one of its most interesting features.

With one exception, all the stories included herein were translated from versions available on *gallica*, although I used the versions contained in the Debans collection *Les Drames à plein vapeur* published by A. Mame in 1898 and the one-volume reprint of *Les Mines d'or de Bas-Meudon* published in 1903 by Librairie d'éducation nationale rather than the serial versions in *La Science Illustrée*, for the sake of convenience. The exception is the translation of "Le Vainqueur de la mort," which was taken from the undated Apex "Periodica" edition of a reprint of the serial contained in *Les Romans Célèbres*, again for the sake of convenience.

Brian Stableford

Alphonse Brown: *Tribulations of an Angler*
(1891)

Nothing is more elegant, charming or graceful than our local river. To describe the agricultural landscapes through which its capricious meanders flow would require the pen of George Sand or André Theuriet, the two writers most expect in depicting nature and making us love it. That river has nothing banal about it, and although it does not flow through any famous region or water and important town, it excites the admiration of tourists who take vacations in the locality, by the fertility of the plain through which it runs, by the beauty of its banks, and by the picturesque quality of the hills, sometimes crowned with feudal ruins, around the gentle slopes of which its green-tinted waters wind.

Here and there, profoundly upstanding rocks, speckled with moss, cleave the bank and cause eddies in which wisps of straw, dead leaves and all the other tiny wrecks that follow the watercourse swirl and are swallowed up.

If Plutus had lavished his favors on my modest person, I would have hastened to acquire some land bordering on my beloved river in order to live there as a philosopher and a sage. What God had pitilessly refused me, alas, he had accorded to other mortals, and among them was Vincent Champignol, a retired haberdasher who had become, thanks to his private income, a petty agriculturalist and a keen angler.

An angler!

At the mere pronouncement, I can see mocking smiles parting all lips and hear the more or less witty gibes that are incessantly repeated with regard to fanatics of the hook. Oh, my God, an angler is not always what vain people think; there are depths of sentiment within him, refined by solitude, long reveries and multiple contemplations of nature.

When he had sold his shop in order to live in the country, Vincent Champignol had devoted himself entirely to agriculture and made every effort to become a fervent follower of Olivier de Serres,[6] a worthy rival of Mathieu de Dombasle, de Gasparin[7] and the greatest landowners in France. But the sacred fire was lacking. One is born a peasant; one does not become one. He tried hunting, but having sworn many times over to massacre all the hares and partridges in the canton, he so often came back empty-handed from his cynegetic excursions that he sacrificed a splendid game-bag and a superb almost-virgin Lefaucheux[8] to the great St. Hubert. Then he thought of fishing.

The river ran through the depths of his property, and brought him enjoyments and intoxications untroubled by provocative irritations. The water scintillated in dazzling oscillations beneath the caresses of the sunlight and sometimes radiated gleams as rapid as lightning flashes. There were agile bleak, massive carp, yellow-tinted barbels and gluttonous pike in pursuit of prey, skimming the breeze-stirred wavelets with their dorsal fins. The slope of the bank was so cluttered with brambles, vine-stocks, ivy, honeysuckle and other climbing plants whose names I forget that one might have believed, with a little imaginative effort, that one were seeing the tangle

---

[6] Olivier de Serres (1539-1619) was the author of *Théâtre d'Agriculture* (1600), which became the textbook of French agricultural practice for more than a century, and founded "soil science."

[7] Mathieu de Dombasle (1777-1843) was a significant agricultural pioneer who founded a school of agriculture near his home town of Nancy and invented an improved plough. His contemporary Adrien de Gasparin, Comte de Vaucluse (1771-1862), the son of a member of the Convention, had a political career himself, but remains more celebrated as the author of a significant agricultural textbook.

[8] Casimir Lefauncheux (1802-1852) was the most famous French gunsmith of his era.

of lianas and formidable interlacement of sarmentous vegetation characteristic of the forests of the New World. Beneath the somber foliage snaked a narrow, primitive path unknown to the profane, ending at a rocky point on which had grown—God knows how!—a thicket of bitter-scented alder bushes, a clump of reeds and a single stunted willow.

It is impossible to imagine a more discreet and picturesque hideaway. On the opposite bank the view was blocked by a curtain of poplars whose slender trunks were reflected in the current, like enormous boa constrictors forever in movement. And to animate that scene, reed-warblers, sedge-warblers, elegant wagtails and chattering blackbirds were perpetually coming and going within and without the dense foliage, casting their most joyful notes and their most cheerful songs to all the winds. Sometimes, a blue streak would fly through the air like a shooting star and disappear into the obscurity of some crack masked by lacy ferns; that was a kingfisher seeking a quiet shelter in order to devour a freshly-caught fish.

The spot pleased Vincent Champignol. One morning, he installed himself there bravely, equipped with a rod and line, basket, landing-net and other accessories indispensable to any angler who takes his art seriously. No one is unaware that certain special manuals declare that angling is an art to be ranked alongside poetry, music and painting, if not above them.

At first, the former haberdasher did not manifest the fervor and zeal that distinguish neophytes of all kinds. Having only a short step to take—which is to say, to cross the towpath and descend the hidden path—to reach the edge of the water, he went nonchalantly to the retreat, did not stay long, cast a distracted eye on the cork, attached his rod to some twig, and went home, abandoning to hazard the care of catching a fish on a hook often deprived of its bait. Little by little, however, and especially after the few catches that are always epoch-making in the splendors of angling, what had been only an amusement became a passion.

Then he spent hours, and then half-days, and finally entire days with his arm extended, his eyes fixed on the float, in all seasons and all weathers, stoically receiving the sun's rays full in the face and enduring diluvian downpours. Soon, he did not hesitate to take of his shoes and socks, roll up his trousers to the knees and take prolonged foot-baths in order to increase the range of his line. Henceforth, he was an angler, a true angler, and he was able to repeat to the echoes of the bank Correggio's famous "*Anch'io son pittore*."[9]

Vincent Champignol and I were almost the same age, and quite good friends. During my daily strolls along the bank, I often ran into him. After having exchanged a cordial greeting and a vigorous handshake, we chatted. Our conversation scarcely varied. Between ourselves, we discussed the probable perturbations of the atmosphere, the temperature and limpidity of the water, and conditions favorable for fishing. When Champignol had made some important catch, however, it was impossible to put a brake on his loquacity. He counted emphatically the innocent ups and downs of his battle against the "denizens of the deep," and embroidered them, as befits every angler or hunter of merit, with a few lies that would have disconcerted the astonishing Monsieur de Crac himself.[10] Finally, he put his arm in mine and, if it was morning, invited me to lunch, or if it was evening, to dinner.

Although I am no gourmet, and the gratitude of my stomach does not incite me to the slightest flattery. I must say that one ate well at Vincent Champignol's, and I had many good times at his table. It's true that the reception was enhanced by the amiability and perfect manners of Madame Champignol and Mademoiselle Laure Champignol. They lav-

---

[9] This saying, apocryphally attributed to Antonio Allegri, alias Correggio, on seeing Raphael's St. Cecilia in Florence (which he never actually visited), translates as "I, too, am a painter."

[10] The central character of Charle Lecoq's comic opera *Le Testament de Monsieur de Crac* (1871), which spawned imitative sequels by other hands.

ished all sorts of kindness upon me and always welcomed me with demonstrations of esteem and amity, which tickled my self-respect agreeably.

Madame Champignol was an excellent and worthy woman, an accomplished housekeeper, modest and unpretentious in spite of her wealth, living for her husband, whose manias she excused, and her daughter, whom she cherished as only true mothers can. Laure Champignol could not have been cited as one of those accomplished beauties who turn all heads and speak to all hearts, but even so, she was genteel, gracious and possessed of a simplicity that had its seductiveness. When I have added that she had pretty eyes, slightly curly dark hair, an intelligent forehead, pink lips and perfect teeth, there will be nothing missing from the sketch I am making of that charming individual. I shall not stress her moral qualities and her attractive character. Well brought up and adequately educated, she talked well and knew how to listen. Although there was a slight hint of saintly Touch-Me-Not about her, which suited her delightfully, one divined that she had a fundament firmness about her that scarcely admitted compromise. Thus, I often murmured between my teeth: "There's an Agnes who has claws under her velvet paws."

One evening in summer, I met Vincent Champignol on the towpath. In accordance with the custom of most anglers, he was rigged out like one of Callot's beggars and was carrying his rod triumphantly in his left hand, while his right hand held a fine bundle of fish, in the middle of which I distinguished a bream weighing between 1200 and 1500 grams.

"You're in luck!" he cried, as soon as he saw me. "You know the proverb: whoever has a bream in his pond can give a friend a feast; but one feasts even better when the bream is out of the pond and ready to be handed over to the cook."

I excused myself, on the pretext of certain business affairs that were summoning me to town, and that I wanted to get home early, but Vincent insisted tenaciously.

"Bah!" he said. "You're a bachelor and your time is your own. My wife and daughter will be delighted to have your company this evening. Then again, one doesn't always have the opportunity to at a bream as fine as this one…and so fresh! I'll simply say this: Nanette will prepare us a meal fit for a king."

So many judicious arguments seduced me. I accepted the invitation in order not to disoblige Vincent, who would have been very annoyed if he had not been able to find any listener, apart from his family and servants, disposed to celebrate his glory. Was that fault not excusable in an angler doubling as an Amphitryon?

As usual, the dinner was one of the best, and Nanette, a cook renowned throughout the neighborhood, prepared the bream in a superior fashion. Needless to say, I congratulated the chef warmly, and then my host, whose skill had given me a meal worthy of the gods. Nanette smiled agreeably, and Vincent gave free rein to his loquacity.

"Can you imagine, my dear chap," he said, "that this slut"—he meant the bream—"led me a merry dance before being caught. First of all she's finicky, turning around the bait with a veritable disgust. By the movement of the cork, I deduce that the fish is a good size, and desires something other than the boiled wheat garnishing the hook. 'You'll be served what you want," I murmured. Quickly, I baited the hook with an earthworm with a color and vivacity bound to create a desire to taste it. I cast the line, and *bang!*—down goes the float. I reel in immediately, and feel something like an electric shock in my arm. My bream is caught…unfortunately, the line's a trifle weak and I feel some apprehension about its solidity. It's necessary to tell you, my dear fellow that my intention was to fish for small fry rather than *the big one*, and I hadn't taken all my precautions. The bream writhed and thrashed like a demon in a font, and manifested a violent desire to escape. I understood her tactics…you can't fool an old hand like me…and instead of lifting her out I drew her gently toward the bank. She resisted, the minx, and got back into the open water two or three times; I brought her back, and finally grabbed her with the landing net. The fight lasted a good ten minutes, but the victory was mine..."

"And thanks to your talent, sagacity and patience," I hastened to put in, to interrupt the verbiage, which was wearying us somewhat, "we're devouring the *optima spolia* of the victory."

My reflection was found to be very apt; it served as a transition to a conversation that was often renewed. With a great deal of tact, Laure Champignol pretended to be very interested in the historical facts that had rendered the *optima spolia* of the Romans famous, and when I had cited Acron, king of Caenina, killed by Romulus; Lars Tolumnius, king of the Veii, killed by Cornelius Cossus; and Viridomarus, king of the Gauls, killed by Marcus Claudius Marcellus, the conversation became less pedantic, and generalized in the thousand trivia that often give it all its charm.

I don't know how or why the word "marriage" came to fall from my lips. It had the effect of a bucketful of cold water unexpectedly thrown over people who were already freezing. Madame Champignol had a coughing fit; Laure blushed so deeply as to make a poppy envious; Vincent looked at me with a slightly bewildered astonishment. I was trying to explain my blunder, and repair it, if it arose from tactlessness on my part, when the master of the house said to me, in a familiar fashion: "Joker! You know something..."

"Me?" I said, utterly surprised.

"Come on, admit it...talk at your ease. A marriage isn't a mystery, damn it!"

"I can assure you that I'm unaware..."

"Bah! You aren't unaware of anything. After all, why hide something that will soon be published? We're marrying Laure."

"Oh!"

"We're marrying Laure to Félix Grandin. You know Félix, the son of Gaspard Grandin, who has the draper's shop in the High Street."

"My heartiest congratulations," I murmured.

23

"My word!" Vincent Champignol put in, with a dry chuckle. "I've caught a lot of fish in my time, but never one as big as that. Do you know that Grandin's giving his son a dowry of 150,000 francs? What do you think of that catch? Truly, it'll be a rich marriage..."

Vincent had let his tongue run away with him; he did not win the approval of his wife or his daughter. By their expressions, I gathered that the announced marriage scarcely made them smile...

"The marriage is only at the stage of negotiation," Madame Champignol added, "and I don't see why we should be preoccupied with it before a complete agreement has been reached."

"Grandin and I are in agreement," Vincent insisted, stubbornly, "And the marriage will be made...soon."

I deduced that the weather was getting stormy—which is to say that one of the conjugal tempests that sometimes trouble the closest of marriages was about to blow up—and that my presence was becoming awkward. I withdrew.

Madame Champignol accompanied me to the door in order to say to me, covertly: "I need to talk to you. Be good enough to come tomorrow while my husband is fishing. My daughter's future and happiness are at stake. I'm counting on you."

"I shall obey, Madame."

While tipping my hat one last time I had the time to examine Laure's face. Her features remained impassive, but her dark eyes were alight with ardent gleams.

"Good!" I murmured. "Her claws are beginning to show..."

The next day, while Vincent Champignol was pestering "the aquatic gentry" I presented myself at his house. Having given me a cordial welcome, Madame Champignol cut directly to the reasons that had driven her to talk to me in private.

"You're too good a friend of the family," she said, "for me not to explain myself frankly and for me to hesitate about asking you for a favor."

"I'm entirely at your disposal, Madame."

"Yesterday, a fortuitous circumstance revealed to you a subject of keen preoccupation for us all. Seduced by the wealth of the Grandins, my husband thought he was ensuring Laure's happiness by arranging, unknown to us, a marriage...of money. To be sure, my husband is the best of men, and an excellent father, but when he has caressed an idea for some time, when a conviction gets into his head, he becomes obstinate, and finds it difficult to let go of resolutions he has made."

"That fault," I observed, "is typical of most anglers."

"That's the peril—the veritable peril—we're in, and I'm telling you in order to beg you to help us avoid it."

"How can I hope to obtain what has been refused to you?"

"My husband holds you in high esteem. He'll listen to your advice. It's necessary to demonstrate to him that this marriage is impossible and that money alone is not a sufficiently powerful factor on which found the happiness of a domestic hearth...although songs proclaim the contrary."

"That argument is quite specious, Madame, and I dread that it will only exert a distinctly secondary leverage on Monsieur Champignol's resolution."

"You're right. Although I'm reluctant to speak ill of my neighbor, there are circumstances when silence is culpable, especially on the part of a mother. I've known Félix Grandin for a long time, and I'm convinced that he'll be a detestable husband. Spoiled by unthinking parents who've told him over and over again that he's rich and that nothing in the world can prevent him from indulging himself and abusing his life, he leads a deplorable existence, scornful of everything that does not reflect opulence, brutalizing himself in pleasures, and mocking al the sound traditions that are the guarantees of the future in mirage."

"That picture is very dark, Madame, and..."

"No, no; don't think that I'm obeying the paltry sentiments that are the inseparable companions of slander." And the worthy woman added: "In me, the mother-in-law is not yet born. Will she ever be? I feel enough affection in my heart to love my daughter and the man who will become my son equally. Félix Grandin hides his faults—not to say his vices—beneath a varnish of elegance and a decorum that attracts the admiration of the naïve, but I'm not deceived by it. In any case, women have a clairvoyance that is completely lacking in men. My husband is dazzled too, fascinated by the allures of milord Félix, and it's up to you to disillusion him."

"And Mademoiselle Laure...?" I asked.

"Laure doesn't want to be Madame Félix Grandin...and I cannot associate myself with my husband in making our daughter unhappy."

"Well, Madame, I shall fulfill the mission you have confided to me as fully as you desire...but what if I don't succeed?"

"Be brave! And remember that you have faithful allies."

I promised to deploy all sorts of admissible means to vanquish Vincent Champignol's resolution. The task was difficult; I had no illusions about that, for the well-known patience of anglers is closely akin to obstinacy, and gives them an inertia capable of resisting all intrepidity.

How many curious and pleasant monographs had I read? And all of them, without exception, enviously celebrated the stoicism and the stubbornness of the heroes of the maggot: qualities that frightened me now because they loomed up before me, as inexorable as fatality, in opposition to my designs. It was almost with terror that I recalled the following observations:

An angler must combine calmness, patience and resignation; three qualities—I should say three virtues—that seem incompatible with the ardent passion that consumes him. Look at him, with his feet in the water, the nape of his neck devoured by the sun, his hands and face harassed by mosquitoes;

he does not flinch; as motionless as a boundary-marker, with his arm extended and his eyes glued to a cork that fascinates and magnetizes him, he waits anxiously for a quiver to give him a sign of life. Do not speak to him; he will not answer; or rather, he will answer you in a low voice, with some monosyllable that means to say, politely—for he is very polite—"Go away; leave me alone." Only the cork has the right to speak to him, and then only by signs.

Come back in two hours; he is still there, in the same position; angler and cork are mummified, and when nightfall forces him to pack up his baggage, he returns home placidly. He rarely gets a bite, and it is marvelous to see the stoicism with which the crestfallen angler, incapable of discouragement, replaces the maggot that the malign gudgeon has just eaten off the barb of his hook, and continues that maneuver until dusk, chasing away the daylight, puts an end to the unequal combat in which the man, always vanquished, returns the next morning to recommence his new and infallible defeat.

Defeat! Now it was me who feared it, remembering that Vincent Champignol was a man to pursue the execution of his decisions with the tenacity of a Mohican. Nevertheless, I reproached myself for my hesitations, and when the time came I made the decision to commence the attack and to fall upon the enemy. "To vanquish without peril, or triumph without glory," I recited with the poet, in order to excite my courage—and I went down incontinently to the water's edge.

A strong breeze was shaking the tangled vegetation leading down to the hiding-place. Vincent didn't hear me coming. I surprised him in the middle of detaching his hook, which had caught on a bramble—an inconceivable error for an experienced angler. Thus, it was in a murderous humor that he greeted me, without any great expenditure of courtesy.

"Oh, it's you," he said. "My word, I wasn't expecting you!"

"Believe me, I wouldn't disturb you if an urgent and imperious reason hadn't obliged me to speak to you for a few moments."

"Good God, what's it about? Wait a minute…and above all, don't speak too loudly…you'll frighten the fish. Damned hook…it's stuck to this accursed branch…good! It's free…it wasn't so difficult. Some new bait, and I'll be all ears."

Vincent cast his line methodically, with a gesture that he attempted to render both noble and graceful.

"Hazard," I went on, "has informed me about the imminent marriage—or, rather, the marriage plans—relative to Mademoiselle Laure, and I feel that it's my duty to warn you about the rumors…the nasty rumors circulating with regard to Félix Grandin…"

"What are these rumors, if you please?"

"They claim that Monsieur Félix is not a well-behaved man, that he leads a dissolute existence, and…"

"Shhh! Shhh! I had a bite, damn it! If you hadn't spoken, I'd have caught a nice fish. Go on—I'm listening…"

"They say, moreover, that he's a thoroughly bad lot and will end up devouring the paternal fortune."

"Who's *they?* When one makes accusations against someone, it's necessary to be precise."

"The public in general—everybody, in sum, is in agreement in saying that Félix Grandin is a debauchee, and that the woman he marries will be the chief victim of his passions."

"Come, come, my friend, turn the handle you're holding—I know this song, damn it! Félix is now what we once were…he's young, he's taking advantage of his youth. When you were twenty-five, didn't you have fun? Personally, I don't mind admitting that that I had fun—a lot of fun…an enormous amount of fun…which doesn't prevent me from being an honest man and an excellent husband…"

"But you didn't amuse yourself in the same way as Félix Grandin…"

"Oh damn! That's another one I've missed…damn it! I believe you're frightening the fish, and you'll be the cause of my going home empty-handed…"

"Please," I said, impatiently, "leave the fish where they are and listen to me. It's a matter of your child's future, and I think that consideration far outweighs those that it pleases you to invoke in order to prevent me from speaking."

Vincent raised his head and forgot himself to the point of losing sight of his cork.

"Don't go on," he said to me. "I understand how difficult your situation is. I can see that you're an 'envoy extraordinary,' and I can't hold it against you. Do you think that I'm acting lightly and that I don't know how to strive for my daughter's happiness? Félix Grandin is a charming young man, perhaps something of a fop, but a god enough fellow. If one judges young men by the peccadilloes and indiscretions that are virtually part and parcel of youth, none of them would be worthy of marriage. Women get alarmed about trivia, silly things they laugh about later, when time and experience have ripened heir reason. It isn't possible for me to desire or find a more suitable son-in-law than Félix Grandin…and Laure will marry him no matter what."

This parental and matrimonial tirade was pronounced in a tone that neutralized my determination to do Madame Champignol's bidding. I was especially humiliated to find that our artillery had been unmasked at the very beginning of the battle, and that it only remained for me to retreat in good order. Even so, I made one further attempt.

"Come on," I went on. "What if you're mistaken, and Laure's inclinations are in another direction…if she doesn't love Félix…"

"She will love him…"

"If you inflict an incurable wound on her heart…"

"Ah! At last! I've got one…"

And the excited angler pulled a small barbel out of the water. Either because the backward movement of the line was too precipitate, however, or because the fish was poorly hooked, it came loose and fell back into the river.

What curses! What wrath! No blast of wind was ever unleashed in the bosom of a tempest with greater fury. No thunderbolt ever burst with as much violence in the midst of the sinister rumblings of a storm. I alone was guilty. Why was I meddling in an affair that was none of my concern? I was frightening the fish. What a disastrous idea it had been for me to come! I'd brought the evil eye with me. To miss such a nice catch! And for idiotic quibbles! Did one need permission to marry a daughter?

"I swear by God," he continued, with concentrated rage, "that Laure will marry Félix Grandin, and I'll never permit her to fall for a good-for-nothing, an art student, a dauber, a sign-painter who'll let her die of poverty and starvation..."

I listened in bewilderment. The plot was thickening.

In Vincent Champignol's tone there was all the scorn and ferocious disdain of a bourgeois for an artist who has not yet *arrived*.

An artist! There was an artist in the woodpile!

Why hadn't Madame Champignol warned me, thus leaving me disarmed before her husband, as he yielded to all the extravagances of spite? Mentally, however, I excused the poor woman, thinking that intimate considerations that were none of my business had forced her to be discreet and reserved.

But who was the fortunate mortal sufficiently favored by fate to merit the sympathy of the Champignol ladies and attract the aversion—or, rather, the hatred—of Vincent Champignol? In our small town I knew only three amateur painters and two photographers, all devoid of the aureole, the ideal quality that sometimes seduces romantically-inclined young women. Of the five individuals in question, moreover, three were married and the two other confirmed bachelors. It was not in that society that I ought to seek for the new Juliet's Romeo.

I withdrew, slightly disappointed, casting a farewell and rather dry "Good luck" in Vincent's direction. The latter had already calmed down, though, and he shook my hand effusively.

"Don't hold it against me," he said. "You caught me at a bad moment. I was annoyed by the memory of a family argument. Then again, I've drawn an absolute blank. I don't have my usual self-composure—the fish are running away from me. When I'm alone, I'll get my revenge. *Au revoir!*"

All the fatherly affection had disappeared beneath the egotism of the angler!

I continued my walk, reflecting sadly on the unexpected vicissitudes of existence, and embarrassed by the inept role that I had just played. What was I going to say to Madame Champignol? Would not confessing my discomfort allow her to suppose that I was apprehensive of doing her bidding and was retreating from the task she had imposed upon me? And yet, the morning breeze was so fragrant, the summer heat so frank, the countryside so beautiful; the insects and the birds were celebrating the joy of living with so much enthusiasm that the unwelcome impressions in my mind were erased one by one, and my thoughts came gradually into harmony with the splendid landscape that was unfolding before my eyes.

I believe—God forgive me!—that I even rhymed a few lines and that an Alexandrine strophe was elaborated in my mind. While versifying, and seeking to avoid a hiatus that would hinder my poetic eloquence, I arrived at a clump of acacias providing a profusion of cool shade. I was about to sit down and devote myself to the dulcet *forniente* so beloved by the favorites of Apollo when, to my great surprise, I heard someone speak my name.

A man of about twenty-seven, with a masculine bearing, distinguished features and a proud gaze was standing before me, respectfully. He had a sketch-pad in his hand, on which I could make out a drawing of the location that surrounded us, and in the distance, the Champignol house, with its appearance of a Swiss villa, and the veranda on which Madame Champignon and her daughter loved to devote themselves to some embroidery work or read the newspapers that they received regularly.

Aha! I thought. *Can this be anyone but the Prince Charming that no one mentioned to me?*

The unknown brought me out of my embarrassment by saying: "Excuse me if I take the liberty of interrupting you. I'm assured that you can give me some assistance in…a most delicate affair, and I'm coming to you…at one time, you were an acquaintance of my father's, and I dare to hope that you might do me the honor of taking an interest in me. I'm Julien Tafforel."

"Julien Tafforel! Dr. Tafforel's son?"

"Yes."

"My God! That name brings back memories. Your father and I were more than acquaintances—we were true friends. He had such a generous heart, there was so much nobility in his character that the most indifferent individuals felt attracted to him.

"Oh, Monsieur, how glad I am to hear you say that..."

Julien Tafforel furtively wiped away a tear that had formed beneath his eyelid and offered me his hand cordially. It was all so natural, so rapid and imprinted with an emotion so sincere that I formed the highest opinion of the tall young man, whose solicitations I understood.

And for a few moments, I invoked the past.

Dr. Tafforel, a college friend, had been the providence of the region, and many people retained grateful memories of him. And yet, good fortune had not been with him. Married to a wife he adored, he had lost her after a few years of marriage. His child remained to him, and he left no stone unturned to give him an excellent education. There, at least, he received some satisfaction, for the child was intelligent and learned quickly. But the good doctor was not to see the results of his effort and sacrifice. One night, summoned to the bedside of an invalid whose home was several kilometers away, he harnessed his trap and departed. Whether because the night was too dark or the horse bolted, his carriage was found the next day, overturned by the roadside. Tafforel was badly hurt; his skull was fractured.

Julien was then fourteen or fifteen years old. What had become of him since? The doctor's modest fortune comprised an annual income of 1,800 francs and a small property with a rustic house whose revenues were much reduced. Presently, the property and the house, also situated on the bank of the river, were let to a "fish farmer," a former mariner known as Père Benamer. It was known that Julien Tafforel had been taken in by his father's sister, who lived in Paris, and after that, no one gave him any further thought. Had I even been aware that he still inhabited this vale of tears and misery?

Side by side, the young man and I walked along the river bank, and a few minutes of conversation confirmed my first impressions. Without it being necessary to solicit "confidences," we understood one another very quickly and chatted with casual ease.

"Come on," I said, "how did *this* come about?"

"*This* was caused by a sprained ankle," Julien replied, in the same tone. "About two months ago, I remembered that I was a property-owner, and decided to take advantage of the spring to visit my domain, knowing that it was surrounded by pretty landscapes and that I wouldn't be wasting my time, for I'm a painter…I forgot to tell you that I'm a painter…"

"I know that—go on…"

"The country pleased me…there were genuine treasures to be gleaned. The nature of the Midi is so beautiful, so rich, so varied in hue! Père Benamer gave me two rooms, diabolically furnished but perfectly lit. I asked for no more. Immediately, I set to work, going hither and yon, sometimes absenting myself for days at a time—in sum, leading the nomadic life, full of the unexpected, that has so many charms for the artist. You see, Monsieur, that I have employed my vacation well and am worthy of the second medal that my works brought me at this year's salon."

"Oh! You have a second medal—very good, and so much the better!"

I rubbed my hands joyfully, for, in my opinion, the metal planted the "dauber" five hundred feet underground. It was a powerful argument to combat Champignol's prejudices.

"One evening," Julien Tafforel continued, "I was coming back home, laden with all the impediments I take with me on my excursions. I was rather badly dressed and I must have looked like a stray clown. At the corner of the path leading to my house, I perceived two women. One of them, the younger, was sitting on a pile of stones and whimpering in pain. I went to them and offered my services. It was one of those thousand misfortunes, one of those little accidents, that always happen unexpectedly. While out walking, after a false step, a sprain had occurred, and the young woman appeared to be suffering intensely.

"Well—one goes to war when needs must! I was alone. Except for me there was no possible assistance. Madame Champignol and your servant picked Mademoiselle Laure up and we clip-clopped to my domicile. I'm not the son of a physician for nothing, and artists know a heap of remedies that work marvelously. Madame Champignol took her daughter's shoe and sock off and I saw the daintiest, the pinkest...well, Cinderella didn't have such a foot..."

"Oho!" I said. "What enthusiasm!"

"I'm giving you my impressions as an artist. I immediately brought a large bowl full of fresh water and prepared a curative compress with camphorated eau-de-vie, which perfumed my apartment. I placed it myself, with a dexterity worthy of an experienced medical student. For at least five minutes, I held that foot in my hand, rubbing it gently, scarcely brushing it with my fingers, so fearful was I of reviving the pain occasioned by the sprain.

"When the suffering had diminished, the two women cast an investigative glance around them, and paused on a few paintings hanging on the wall.

"'Is it you, Monsieur, who painted all these pretty pictures?' *she* asked.

"I nodded my head. Oh, I'm not mistaken. Before those canvases, into which I had put all my inspiration, in which I had faithfully reproduced nature while trying to discover its most poetic aspects, *she* experienced those elevated sentiments

34

which remove all banality from admiration and reveal noble souls.

"What can I add? They left. Then they came back to thank me. I sought to see *her* again. And when I saw her, it seemed that life was passing into my brushes and that my colors harmonized, identifying with I don't know what unknown, which plunged me into an ecstasy from which I never wanted to emerge...and little by little, my heart went out to *her*...but I'm becoming as sentimental as a romance, and I must be making you laugh."

"No, no," I replied, squeezing the brave lad's heart. "One doesn't laugh at the skylark, nor the nightingale, when they sing their songs of love; on the contrary, one listens to them with a religious silence."

"I've learned that Monsieur Champignol has rejected me, and I've come to you..."

"I've seen Monsieur Champignol this very morning and catechized him as best I could, but I ran into resistance, and a stubbornness I hadn't expected."

"From where does his aversion to me stem?"

"Oh, you great innocent. You don't have much money and you're a painter."

"But my paintings are appreciated and I'm beginning to earn money. I'll wager that Monsieur Champignon thinks I'm looking for a dowry. Let him keep his dowry. The future belongs to the valiant. Without boasting, I affirm that I am one of them..."

"Does Monsieur Champignon know you?"

"He has never seen me."

"Perfect. Are you determined to attempt anything to be worthy of Mademoiselle Laure?"

"Yes."

"You know that Monsieur Champignol is a fervent angler."

"So I've been told."

"Well, it's necessary to make use of his passion—or rather, his obsession—to win him over and get him on your side."

"I don't understand."

"Listen to a little true story, and try to profit from it."

"I'm all ears."

"Monsieur de Salvandy, one of Louis-Philippe's ministers, was a keen angler. He knew the best spots, and when his functions left him a little leisure time, he devoted himself ardently to his favorite pleasure. The chroniclers of the era claim that he was prouder of catching a good fry-up than of his successes in the Chambers. Is it more difficult to catch fish than humans? Who can tell? A frequent petitioner studied his minister and kept careful watch on him. He became convinced that Monsieur de Salvandy was fond of a particular place...the *good spot*. Almost all anglers are superstitious. And every morning, as soon as rosy-fingered dawn parted the gates of the Orient, he took possession of it. The first day, the Minister was irritated; the second day, His Excellency was more violently irritated; the third day..."

A burst of sonorous laughter interrupted me.

"I know your story," Julien Tafforel exclaimed, gaily. "To get rid of the intruder—or, rather, a redoubtable competitor, Monsieur de Salvandy gave him a well-paid position...a long way away."

"That's right. What moral do you deduce from the anecdote?"

"What, that it's necessary for me to take up angling? To poach on Monsieur Champignol's preserves?"

"Exactly."

"But I'll turn him against me even more. He'll get angry with me, and imagine that I'm mocking him, and he'll never consent to accept me as a son-in-law."

"Tut tut! Try..."

"It's impossible for me to maintain my *incognito* for long, and once Monsieur Champignol knows who I am, he'll understand that I'm playing with him and feel a sharp resentment toward me."

"Don't you understand, you big baby, that the painter will disappear before the angler. It won't happen overnight...Monsieur Champignol will be vexed to begin with, and look at you darkly, because a competitor is always unwelcome—but he'll form a better opinion of your character. For many bourgeois, a painter is still a kind of phenomenon, who does not share the morals, the tastes or the habits of other mortals, whereas an angler is a pearl among men, the living symbol of calm and resignation, the incarnation of ingenuity and candor. Is it possible to desire a better son-in-law? If you're clever, within a week, Félix Grandin will be sunk; Monsieur Champignol will be singing your praises, declaring that you're the foremost painter of the era, and that you alone—take my word for it—are worthy to aspire to his daughter's hand."

"Truly, that would be a surfeit of happiness."

"Try, then."

"When should I set to work?"

"Tomorrow."

"Well, until tomorrow."

After a last handshake, Julien left me.

While retracing my steps, I smiled at the singular idea that had germinated in my brain, and the awkward position in which I was going to put Vincent Champignol. The latter's anger, stubbornness and conceit merited a lesson. I found a thousand good reasons to excuse the planned mischief, and that evening, when I had an opportunity to see Mademoiselle Laure, I whispered to her: "I've seen him. He's worthy of you."

"Does he not have a great heart and a chivalrous character?" Laure replied, without anxiety.

"Yes. He wants to be worthy of you, and for that, he'll attempt..."

"For God's sake, don't let him run any risk because of me."

"Don't worry; he won't be in any danger."

"That's reassuring. Can I do anything to help?"

"Later."

"Tell him that, whatever happens, I'll never marry Félix Grandin—that I'm my father's daughter and I have a will of my own."

"There are the claws extending," I murmured.

We parted, she thinking about some romantic adventure in which the exploits of Amadis would pale by comparison with those of her "fiancé," me to sleep without anxiety or remorse, in spite of my dark designs.

The following day, immediately after lunch, I went to see Julien Tafforel. His house, about half a league distant from the Champignols', was almost completely hidden in a dip in the ground formed by an old ravine. It looked to be in danger of collapse. The walls, cracked in places, were no longer vertical; large patches of roughcast that had fallen off left the gradually-disintegrating bricks and mortar bare. On the other hand, there was such a profusion of bushes and climbing plants around it that, from a distance, it resembled an enormous clump of verdure negligently thrown on the ground.

On the roof, damaged by bad weather, pigeons were cooing and sparrows chirping, intoxicated by the sunlight. To one side, chickens were scratching the ground and cackling, while several ducks were paddling gravely at the edge of a pond alimented by the continual sweat of a bank that limited it. In sum, the habitation, inelegant as it was, ought to please an artist like Julien Tafforel, or a philosopher, such as its tenant seemed to be.

I found the painter in the midst of preparing his brushes and colors. He intended to work on a painting whose sketch had been completed several days ago.

"Well," I said, "this is how you follow my prescriptions. Laure is getting away from you and you're only thinking of yourself."

"But my dear Monsieur," Julian Tafforel replied, "I've carried out your orders to the letter."

"Come on, tell me about it."

"This morning, very early, I installed myself in Monsieur Champignol's 'spot' and fished with the patience of a angel. Naturally, I caught nothing, since my line was innocent of hooks and only comprised a poor bit of string attached to a hastily-cut reed. I hadn't had time to buy fishing equipment. Nevertheless, it was urgent to persuade the enemy that it was a formidable apparatus."

"Monsieur Champignol must have made fun of you."

"Not at all! I had taken a few little precautions. When one isn't strong, it's necessary to be cunning, as the saying has it. I had gone to the market in order to buy two or three kilograms of fish, which I had ostentatiously scattered at my feet. When Monsieur Champignol appeared, he uttered a cry of surprise, darted a rapid glance at my 'catch' and retired, grumbling. I held firm and didn't budge. He came back twice, and twice he found me there, as if rooted to the ground..."

"Well played!" I exclaimed. "Your intelligence has resources that are a guarantee of success in attaining your objective."

"Here's my famous catch—a miraculous catch," Julien Tafforel continued.

A mighty burst of laughter swelled my chest and abdomen. In the plateful of fish that the painter set before my eyes, I distinguished salt-water species mingled with freshwater species.

"Oh!" I said, still laughing. "Wretch—your catch is a veritable salad, which must have scandalized Monsieur Champignol."

"Really?"

"Yes, of course. How do you expect him to take seriously a fisherman who catches in a river fish that are only found in the sea?"

"Oh, if that's all it is, I'm not worried. Monsieur Champignol was so upset and vexed that he didn't pay any great attention to what I'd caught. Do you think he'd be concerned about the origin of fish scattered on the grass? I could have had sardines in oil or pickled herrings that he'd have imagined I'd just caught. Who can tell whether he might not have supposed that I was experimenting with bait that attracted new species?"

"Go on," I continued. "I observe with pleasure that you're neither short-sighted nor naïve. The future is yours. You'll succeed, if you hold firm...and for some time."

"Have no fear on that subject."

"Most of all, don't rest on your laurels. An angler is like the peasants that Victorien Sardou put on stage in *Nos Bons villageois*. Notions of property take on a new and surprising meaning in him. The river is *his* river, the place he occupies on its bank belongs to him by right of choice. He creates for himself an area of exploration in which any mere mortal who intrudes thereupon immediately becomes an enemy. As for the fish, they have been put into the bosom of the waters for his greater pleasure, and no one except him has the right to take possession of them. I won't mention the dose of obstinacy and egotism that enters into his character. Don't you remember the amazing event recently reported by all the newspapers? A young clerk went swimming in the Couesnon and drowned, not without struggling and calling for help. Twenty paces away was an angler, an excellent swimmer, but he had a bite. The moment was too psychological for him to try to save a human life. When that impassive witness was interrogated about the accident, he reported that he had experienced..."

"Remorse, no doubt?"

"No, an acute annoyance, because the desperate movements on the drowning man were stirring up the water and disturbing it..."

"But your anglers are savages."

"Some are."

"Is Monsieur Champignol one of them?"

"Oh, you're asking too much of me. If he's good, it's up to you to seduce him. If he's wicked, it's up to you to tame him."

"When a man is the father of a young woman like Mademoiselle Laure, he can't be bad."

What reply was possible? Don't lovers always see everything through rose-tinted spectacles? Don't talk to them before a marriage about the ridiculousness of a father-in-law or the shrewishness of a mother-in-law. They won't believe you. The aureole with which they have surrounded their fiancée covers everything close to her with its dazzling reflections.

I had not only come to talk about fishing, but also to see. I wanted to observe Julien Tafforel's talent for myself—that is to say, to convince myself that I was dealing with a true artist and not a servile copyist. My examination satisfied me fully. The few canvases I looked at very attentively proved to me that my new friend had a very clear sentiment of nature and understood its least-known charms. Following in the footsteps of our great Millet, he knew how to identify individuals and landscapes by means of felt impressions, and to reject the conventions and apparatus of color employed by painters who seek to flatter. A kind of soft and gentle harmony radiated from his works and explained the success of his painting "In the Wheatfields," which had won him a silver medal at the latest Salon.

Julien Tafforel received my compliments and approval without false modesty. He was fully conscious of his merit and did not take refuge behind those restrictions which, in spite of their apparent humility, reveal vanity and complacency.

"And what do you think of this one?" he asked, lifting up a piece of calico covering a painting.

I saw the portrait of Laure Champignol—a portrait painted from memory, but ravishing, superb and bursting with life.

"And it's a man like you that Monsieur Champignol refuses as a son-in-law?" I exclaimed, enthused. "We have to prevent him from committing that…stupidity."

"I'd like nothing better, to be sure."

"Well then, prepare…"

"My brushes?"

41

"No, your lines and bait. And tomorrow, without fail, be at your post."

"I'll be there."

"No hesitation, no weakness. The fisherman must be worthy of the painter."

"He will be."

"And now, have courage!"

"I shall."

The following day, Julian Tafforel, clad in a long gray smock, wearing a vast battered panama hat, decked out like a highwayman, took possession of Vincent Champignol's spot, fishing with a brand new rod and line prepared by old Benamer. For three days he repeated that maneuver; for three days, he arrived first on the terrain. He even caught—what a miracle!—a few fish...and the beginning of a sunstroke that had no serious consequences.

I would need the verve of Ariosto, the immortal author of *Orlando Furioso*, to give worthy credit to the wrath of Vincent Champignol. At least twenty times he descended to the hidden location, and he always found *his* spot occupied. What imprecations, execrations and abominations fell from his lips! He inveighed with extraordinary violence against those who did not respect the sacred rights of property; he accused heaven, the mores of the epoch and the government of producing and tolerating vagrants, starvelings who had no other resource but to catch a few fish in order to subsist; he regretted not possessing the monstrous privileges of the aristocrats of the Middle Ages, in order to exterminate all the poachers on land and water who pullulate in this world.

I laughed covertly, for I took great care not to reveal my schemes. Even the Champignol ladies, weary of the former haberdasher's irritation, were beginning to get annoyed with the threadbare and scurvy unknown who permitted himself, insolently, to occupy a place that no one had ever disputed with Vincent Champignol, and which really belonged to him, since he had been going there on a daily basis for five years.

The Grandins were country neighbors of the Champignols, and Félix Grandin, encouraged by the warm welcome of the man he regarded as his future father-in-law, made numerous visits. Needless to say, Laure received him with a cold reserve, but without wounding him. He arrived on one occasion at the moment when Vincent Champignol was fulminating against the wretched fisherman who was "stealing" his fish.

"Do you know who that animal is?" he said to me. "Does anyone know where he comes from? And the authorities permit it! If I were a magistrate, he'd already have been expelled, the good-for-nothing vagabond, the scoundrel who has no respect for anything. Once, a price was put on the head of men who hadn't committed a quarter of the crimes that rogue must have committed. Taking my spot! Occupying it for four days! Can you imagine that? And the gendarmes haven't arrested the vagabond! And lightning hasn't struck him down! Everything's upside-down in today's world. But that's how we're governed!"

Félix Grandin made a gesture à la Nicolas[11] and twirled his moustache, which he wore very long. "Can't one citizen be brought to book?" he said, animatedly. "I'll take charge of it personally. If he doesn't obey my injunctions and disappear immediately, I'll bring you his ears, Monsieur Champignol."

The handsome Félix left us and headed for the river in the manner of a moor-slayer. After an absence of a quarter of an hour he came back, rather crestfallen. Not only did he not bring back the ears of the stubborn angler, but he had been roundly abused and threatened with being thrown in the water like a bundle of dirty laundry.

"Instinctively," Julien Tafforel told me, later, "I understood that it was my rival who was shouting at me and giving me an order to decamp as quickly as possible. I replied hotly

---

[11] Perhaps the painter Nicolas Charlet, who delighted in images of arrogant military men, rather than the more famous Nicolas Poussin.

and invited him to come down to me in order that he might obtain the benefits of a forced bath. He preferred to withdraw, threatening me with the rigors of the gendarmes and all the other subaltern representatives of authority. Five or six thoroughly Parisian *zuts* informed him as to the dread he inspired in me."

Nevertheless, that slightly shameful retreat won Félix Grandin warm felicitations. By design, Vincent Champignol praised his courage and temerity, while addressing violent invective to the mysterious fisherman whom no one knew, and who had suddenly surged forth, unceremoniously taking other people's spots.

The next day, Vincent Champignol preceded his adversary on to the battlefield. When Julien Tafforel arrived he manifested neither surprise nor resentment. With the composure of a consummate practitioner and a wise slowness, he prepared and baited his hooks, and cast his line beside the haberdasher's.

The adversaries finally found themselves together and battle was about to be engaged! For a good hour they did not take their eyes off their floats and did not say a word. Neither had a bite.

"It's disappointing," said Vincent Champignol, finally. "One can't catch anything...and yet this was once the best spot on the river."

"Which is why," Julien Tafforel said, "I've caught more than twenty kilos of fish here in a few days." He was lying brazenly, but intentionally, to excite acute regrets."

"Twenty kilos!" said Vincent Champignol. Since you've been here, I've been watching you from the corner of my eye, and I've observed that you don't know anything about fishing..."

"Really! And from what club have you come, to judge with so much authority? Is there an Academy of Anglers, and are you its permanent secretary?"

"Leave the stupidities there. You have a floating line, but you're taking it out of the water all the time as if you were fishing with a dangling line. Is it knowing one's business to act like that?"

"Everyone fishes as he likes. Probably, if you hadn't come to disturb me, I'd already have a good fry-up."

"What! But it's my spot you're occupying."

"Your spot? Excuse me! Where are your title-deeds? Show them, so that we can see whether the notary has stamped them. Your spot! Why should it be yours rather than mine? I'm here, I'm staying...and I'm going to keep coming back."

"I can have you removed."

"You think so?"

"I think it's an unspeakable infamy. I've been coming here for five years, and no one has ever dared to trespass on my rights."

"There's a first time for everything. I won't abandon this spot until I've depopulated the river. And that'll take a minute or two, won't it?" And Julien Tafforel made a rather irreverent gesture.

That was too much. Vincent Champignol left, swearing that he would make himself respected, and that he would not surrender his prerogatives as a longstanding occupant to a badly-dressed stranger, a peasant who probably had no hearth or home. That made him angry, and it was far from the outcome for which I had hoped. But, remembering that Cupid is a sly god who overcomes all obstacles, I maintained my habitual calm.

That evening, when I saw Julien Tafforel, I received a volley of reproaches. The plan was going awry, and it was all my fault. Monsieur Champignol was very annoyed and would never compromise.

"A little patience," I replied. "We're only in the first act of the comedy that's in performance—wait for the denouement; and, as in the majority of comedies, you'll see that it will end with a marriage."

"Monsieur Champignol is out of patience."

"So much the better. After the tempest comes the calm, and every skillful pilot knows how to take advantage of it."

Since the world began, people have claimed that love works miracles, but I'm almost certain that it has rarely transformed an artist into an angler, especially an ichthyologist. I omitted to mention that Julien Tafforel was studying fish, aided by voluminous textbooks of natural history and pisciculture, La Blanchère's[12] *Dictionnaire de pêche*, two or three manuals of angling and a few popular works "for the use of laymen."

The pupil was admirably prepared for these new studies, for his father, having intended to make a physician of him, had strive to develop scientific tastes in him that work in the studio had not extinguished. He surprised me enormously when, I don't know why, he listed for me without the slightest hesitation the different orders comprising the bony and cartilaginous fishes.

Firstly:

The Acanthopterygians (perches, gurnards, mackerels, etc.)

The abdominal Malacopterygians (carps, barbels, gudgeon, tench, pikes, herrings, breams, etc.)

The apodal Malacopterygians (eels, conger-eels, electric eels, etc.)

The Lophobranches (seahorses, etc.)

The Plectognathi (porcupine-fishes, sunfishes, puffer-fishes, etc.)

Secondly:

The Acipenseridae (sturgeons, etc.)

The Selachians (sharks, saw-fish, rays, dogfish, etc.)

The Cyclostomes (lampreys, hag-fish, etc.)

I shall not list the sub-orders, for I frankly declare that although Julien Tafforel could find his way through that labyrinth, I got lost easily therein, and could never retain the barbaric names with which he flayed my ears.

---

[12] The ichthyologist Pierre Moulin du Coudray de La Blanchère (1821-1880).

My surprise increased when I observed a few changes in the painter's slightly primitive furniture. Instead of the pine dresser, I noticed five inverted bell-jars supported by iron tripods. They were three-quarters full of clear liquid in which fish of various species were frolicking.

"They're my aquaria," Julien Tafforel told me.

"They're very well-installed," I replied.

At that moment, old Benamer came in, carrying an earthenware pot. "Monsieur Julien," he said, in his hoarse voice, "I've cast the net a few times on your behalf. I've only caught bleaks and gudgeons—but that's for bait, and this evening, if my luck's in, I'll catch you some barbels, carp and eels to garnish your bells. Where shall I put my pot?"

"Leave it in that corner. Thanks, Père Benamer. Until this evening."

"Bonjour, Monsieur Julien, and company."

The fisherman withdrew.

"You see," Julien Tafforel continued, "one is never knowledgeable when one only studies I books. Like art, science requires something other than theories. A chemist isn't really a chemist until he's spent long hours in the laboratory. If I'm studying fish *in anima vili*, it's to get to know them better, to familiarize myself with their habits…and to be better at catching them. That way, I'll learn how to vanquish Monsieur Champignol and will be able to show myself worthy of an adversary who…"

"Yes, yes," I interjected, "you'll become a great angler, before God, men…and a person I can't name."

In order not to be forestalled, the painter lay in ambush at dawn in the hidden spot and waited patiently for Vincent Champignol to come. The latter arrived at about five o'clock, with a cheerful expression that testified to the liveliest satisfaction. When he perceived Julien Tafforel he could not suppress a start of surprise, and exclaimed: "Have you spent the night here, then?"

"Yes."

"Then you're acting like a vagabond."

"That's possible. Not everyone in the world can be a rentier."

"Good God, what infamy!"

And the haberdasher withdrew, red with anger, not daring to admit that he feared the unknown man whose manner had nothing engaging about it and who replied in such a cavalier fashion when criticized.

Meanwhile, curiosity had been keenly excited by the impertinence of the "stranger" who had been able to discover Vincent Champignol's favorite spot and had taken possession of it without the slightest scruple. Everyone wanted to examine him at close range, including the Champignol ladies, and Nanette, who was desolate to see her stove devoid of fish to fry for several days.

We headed for the river with the tread of people preparing to penetrate into a cave filled with ferocious animals, and went stealthily down the path leading to the hidden place. Finally, we perceived the dogged fisherman...

With a mechanical gesture he raised his line and projected it forwards with a flick of the wrist whose dexterity I had to admire.

"You call that fishing!" Vincent Champignol whispered to me, in an indignant tone.

In sum, the painter produced a rather unfavorable impression, and I judged that his accoutrement was not doing him any favors. His back was turned to us and it was impossible to make out his face, hidden by the drooping brim of a huge straw hat.

I looked at Laure. Oh, she wasn't deceived for a moment. She had recognized her Romeo and, utterly red, utterly astonished and radiant with joy, she bit her handkerchief to hide the emotion she was feeling. She darted a glance at me more significant than the most eloquent speech and rapidly crossed the distance that separated her from Julien Tafforel.

"You! What, it's you?" said Laure Champignol, accosting Julien Tafforel.

"Yes, it's me," the painter replied. "Me, who has found no better way to get close to you than to disguise myself as a fisherman. Oh, Mademoiselle, I feel that I'm capable of great deeds to show myself worthy of you."

"Do you think you'll succeed dressed like that?" replied the young woman, smiling. "Especially by exasperating my father?"

"Monsieur Champignol doesn't want a painter. Perhaps he'll accept an angler."

"Shh! They're coming..."

"Don't give me away—I'll continue fishing..."

Having become impatient, Vincent Champignol did indeed arrive—but hazard took charge of resolving the difficulties of a situation that might have been embarrassing. At that solemn moment, Julian Tafforel got a bite, and triumphantly pulled out of the water a perch fifteen or twenty centimeters long. He seized it carefully because of the spines on its dorsal fin and presented it to Laure more proudly than if it had been a rich and magnificent jewel-case.

"Yes, Mademoiselle," he said, without being disconcerted, already sensing Vincent Champignol's breath on the back of his neck, "it's a perch. The perch is the most beautiful fish in our rivers. Admire the gleam of its black-striped coat, the magnificent golden color of the irises of its eyes, the dark red of the ventral and anal fins, like a child's lips. But don't trust appearances. The exterior is deceptive, and our fish is a glutton of extraordinary voracity. It hurls itself brutally on anything that appears to it to be prey, even on animals stronger than itself, and even those of its own species..."

Vincent Champignol listened, exceedingly surprised, and even somewhat appeased by a conversation revolving around one of his favorite themes.

"Undoubtedly, Mademoiselle," the painter continued, "you know that the majority of predatory animals are solitary. Well, the perch is an exception to that rule. It gathers in groups to idle at the surface of the water. At the slightest alert, it disappears into a hole serving as a common refuge for all its fellows. If there are forty or fifty fish in that hole, one can catch them all one after another. That suggested the following reflection to Izaak Walton, the first author to write about angling: 'They resemble miscreants and criminals, who are not frightened, although their companions are perishing before their eyes.' 'I don't like that comparison very much,' added Dr. Jonathan Franklin. 'I'd prefer to attribute that composure and courage to a sort of oath that they have made to live and die together.' As for me, Mademoiselle, I don't accord such fine sentiments to perches, and I imagine that fear is the principal cause of their immobility..."

"Oh, where did you get all that from?" exclaimed Vincent Champignol, suddenly intervening. "Are you by chance a fisherman—a veritable fisherman?"

"How do you think Monsieur has learned so many curious things about fish, if he does not keep company with them?" Laure replied, marveling at the success that Julien Tafforel's speech had obtained.

"I've been fishing for a long time," the latter replied, with an imperturbable aplomb, "and for me there's no greater pleasure in the world."

"Oh, very good, very good!" exclaimed the former haberdasher, his frown having vanished. "Why didn't you explain sooner, damn it? I would have been delighted to fish in concert with you. I'm quite certain that, even if you know the history of fish better than I do, you don't know more about catching them."

"You think so?"

"I challenge you."

"I accept. Until tomorrow, here?"

"So be it—until tomorrow!"

Fearing that Madame Champignol might recognize her daughter's suitor and give him away, I gave the signal to retreat. We went back to the towpath.

That evening, the painter confided his plight to me; he feared the consequences of his inexperience, his awkwardness, and, most of all, Vincent Champignol's mockery, probably followed by his anger, indignation and scorn.

At that moment, Père Benamer passed close by, carrying a net on his shoulders. I called to the old man, and, without entering into long details, told him about the impending contest.

"It's indispensable," I told him, "that you give Monsieur Julien a few fishing lessons…and that Monsieur Champignol doesn't catch any fish."

"Have no fear," the farmer replied. "Monsieur Julien will soon be fishing like a man…like me, in fact! And as for that toff Champignol, who has eaten at least a thousand écus'-worth of fish, I'll throw myself all the way to the river-bed if he catches a single tiddler as stout as a piece of string. Have no fear—I'll keep watch, and very slyly. It's a cunning man who can put one over on Père Benamer."

My man was at the pitch I wanted, and I knew that the confidence I had in him would not be misplaced.

To begin with, he caught Vincent Champignol red-handed in a felonious act. It is true that the rules of combat had not been determined and that each adversary was free to any expedients he thought fit, but like the *deus ex machina* in ancient comedies, Père Benamer took responsibility for equilibrating the chances—or, even better, destroying them all. At about ten o'clock in the evening, roaming in his boat in the vicinity of the terrain on which the two adversaries were to clash, he perceived the former haberdasher in the process of ground-baiting—which is to say, throwing a certain quantity of nourishment into the water in order to attract large number of fish to the exact spot where he intended to cast his line. The method was not precisely criminal, but it would put Julien Tafforel at such a disadvantage that his defeat became inevitable.

The farmer waited patiently, and at midnight, he agitated the water with a gaffe, stirring up the bed, lifting up the sand and mud, disturbing the tufts of water-weeds, and doing everything in his power to frighten the fish and drive them away. As soon as day broke, he recommenced the same maneuver, only withdrawing after having acquired the certainty that the spot was ruined, and the conditions deplorable for fishing.

The two adversaries were not long delayed in arriving. Need I say that I had been appointed judge and witness of the great deeds that were about to be accomplished, and that it was up to me to award the palm to the victor? The lines were deployed, measured as if they were fencing-foils, baited and thrown into the water on the command: "*En garde*, Messieurs! Let battle commence!"

An hour passed, and nothing bit.

Vincent Champignol's face, initially cheered up by the assurance of victory, gradually darkened, while Julian Tafforel's retained an absolute impassivity.

A second hour went by. Nothing bit. The former haberdasher became impatient; he checked his hooks feverishly in order to assure himself that the bait had not fallen off.

"It's very surprising," he said to the painter, "that neither you nor I have caught anything yet."

"There are days like that," Tafforel replied.

"It astonishes me, for..."

Vincent Champignol stopped on the brink of the confession. He wanted to profit from his petty felony, but not to divulge it. However, he did not understand the penury of fish at all. Never—absolutely never—had he gone for more than a quarter of an hour without catching anything at all, especially when the preparations left nothing to be desired.

"I think the contest will have to begin again," I said, "and there won't be a victor or a loser today."

"How do you know?" replied Vincent Champignol. "The day's not over yet."

"Isn't it at the last moment," Julien Tafforel put in, "that the fate of battles is decided?"

At all costs, I wanted to break the silence that had reigned for two long hours—a silence that weighed upon us all and did not help my plans at all. I knew that Julien Tafforel was a fine conversationalist, and would win Vincent Champignol over if he had the liberty to express himself without constraint. At any rate, he had been perfectly positioned since daybreak, and a significant wink reminded him that he had other things to do than stand there eternally with his arms extended and his gaze fixed on a cork.

"Do you think, then," he said, "that one can become an excellent angler without a long apprenticeship?"

"It's probably a matter of intuition," I replied.

"No," said Vincent Champignol, "one can only master this art after long practice."

"Oh, this *art!*" I said, pulling a face, almost scornfully.

"The name has no effect on the thing," Julian Tafforel went on, in a tone of conviction. "If angling has had its detractors, it has also had its panegyrists. It's almost as old as the world. Primitive humans, living in lacustrian cries, devoted themselves to it ardently. Moses, the prophet Amos and many other individuals praised the contemplative life of line-fishing. Jesus Christ chose his disciples among simple fishermen who were not always deploying their nets, and Saint Peter, our illustrious patron, must have thrown a perfidious hook into the sacred waters of the Jordan or Lake Tiberius on more than one occasion."

"We have ancient titles of nobility," said Vincent Champignol, smiling, "but I confess that I don't know them."

"And yet," Julien Tafforel continued, "an angler worthy of the name must be very intelligent, if not very knowledgeable. He needs to know the natural history of the fish that frequent the regions in which he operates, as well as that of the insects and worms that serve him as bait. Every species of fish, a zoologist observes, requires a different alimentation according to the seasons, the locality, the time of day and other circumstances. A bait that has proved its efficacy in one part of the day will be offered in vain a few hours later to the animal's sensuality."

"That's true."

"Humorists thought that they were saying something witty when they defined angling as a rod and a line with an idiot at each end. Walter Scott was one of those idiots. He loved fishing passionately and devoted entire days to it. He confessed that he owed his best inspirations to that calm and tranquil exercise, which permits the intelligence to wander in the blue while the water flows slowly by, the eye rests on picturesque scenes and the fish are teased by cleverly-prepared bait.

"Not to mention the enjoyment experienced by the angler when he achieves some beautiful catch and delights himself in advance with the tasty flesh that a skillful hand will prepare on the stove or in the fish-kettle. There's nothing better than a fish fried in batter, or lightly boiled, a matelote or an eel in tartar sauce."

"Ah, Monsieur Champignol, you must have been born Roman."

"Why? Because I like fish?"

"Certainly. Do you not know that the masters of the world preferred fish to anything else, and never shirked any expense to procure the most delicate species."

And Julien Tafforel told us, with a stunning brio and sparkling verve, about the gastronomic follies of the Romans. He cited Asinius Celer, who paid eight thousand sesterces for a single mullet, and Callidorus, who sold one of his slaves for thirteen thousand sesterces in order to buy a barbel weighing four pounds—which attracted violent abuse from Martial: "Wretch, that's not a fish, it's a man—yes, a man—that you're devouring!"

The Romans astonished Vincent Champignol with their passion for certain fish. Did they not have immense fish-ponds constructed at great expense, in which they place the most sought-after species? Licinius Murena, Lucius Philippus, Quintus Hortensius, Hirrius, Lucinius Crassus, Vedius Pollio and Lucullus, the vanquisher of Mithridates, were noted for their prodigalities and the fabulous wealth they consecrated to the maintenance of their artificial ponds. The last-named had a mountain pierced in order to bring water to one of his fields, and did not appear, according to Varro, to cede anything to Neptune in his empire over the fish.

I shall not mention the bizarre caprices of some citizens of the Eternal City for the red mullet, the moray eel and the dorado. Quintus Hortensius, the rival of Cicero, Antonia, the daughter of Drusus, and Licinius Crassus, the friend of Caesar, wept when their moray eels died. The last-named was more afflicted by the loss of one of his fish than he had been by the death of one of his three children.

Julien Tafforel concluded that excursion into the historical domain by relating a fact cited by Seneca. The emperor Tiberius received a mullet weighing four and a half pounds; he put it up for auction, certain in advance that it would be bought by Apicius or Octavius, two celebrated gourmands. He was not mistaken. Octavius bought it for five thousand sesterces, which is the equivalent of nearly a thousand francs in our money.

"If you continue, gentlemen," I said, ironically, "it isn't one of you who'll claim such a benefit today."

At that moment, a dead carp passed by, belly up, drawn by the current. Naturally, it became the object of a conversation in which I learned many interesting things. For me, and probably for Vincent Champignol, the carp was only a vulgar cousin of the goldfish, having very recommendable qualities in the eyes of a cook. The painter surprised us with the curious details he gave us regarding that gallinaceous inhabitant of our rivers.

"The carp," he told us, "is originally from Asia Minor; it recommends itself by its tasty flesh. The Romans appreciated the fish, and in the time of Pliny they received them at great expense in pond-boats expressly constructed for that purpose. It is claimed that they were introduced into the rivers of northern Europe at the beginning of the sixteenth century by the burgrave Casper von Nostitz or the Englishman Peter Marshall, a gentleman from Plumstead in Sussex. It's undeniable that Peter Oxe acclimated them on Denmark in 1560. However, the carp had been mentioned long before the sixteenth century in documents of which every angler possesses a copy. In 1258 a royal decree designated it by the name of *Carpeau*. The *Book of St. Albans*, published by Wynkyn de Worde in 1486, containing several serious treatises compiled by Lady Julian Barnes, prioress of the convent of Sopwell, says that "it is a delicate fish." In 1328, one the occasion of the coronation of Philippe de Valois and Jeanne de Bourgogne, the city of Reims offered the royal couple a feast in which two thousand six hundred and nineteen carp featured."

"Where the devil did you get all that?" exclaimed Vincent Champignol, full of admiration. "You're a well of science, and it's a pleasure to listen to you."

"The carp will astonish you even more," Julien Tafforel continued, entirely disposed to display his knowledge before an approval that he sought. "I won't talk about its longevity, its extraordinary fecundity or its mores, with which everyone is familiar. Have you ever noticed its mouth?"

"Of course! It's a mouth similar to those of all freshwater fish."

"Don't be deceived; its lips are protractile—which is to say that they form an organ of prehension somewhat reminiscent of the lower extremity of an elephant's trunk. To nourish itself, the fish digs into the sand or mud and introduces a certain quantity into its mouth by means of its membranous lips. As you can imagine, the carp, which grows fatter almost visibly, is not a geophage and is not content with impure mud. By means of a still-inexplicable mechanism of *exglutition* it expels the sand it has swallowed, conserving every last fragment of the nutritional elements contained therein."

"It's quite probable," I put in, "that it crushes the aliments, and that those whose hardness is not excessive are masticated..."

"It has no teeth."

"You're doubtless joking..."

"No, of course not! At least, it has no teeth in its mouth. They're placed in its throat. Nourishing itself almost exclusively on vegetable matter, and especially grains, the cyprids have no need to bite and tear. They need a machine for crushing and pounding, and they have one. Their pharynx presents an improved grinding instrument comprising five large teeth implanted on each side, in the inferior pharyngeal bones; slightly behind and above is an enameled disk, a sort of anvil held by the bones of the skull, which assists in the crushing of aliments."

"Well," said Vincent Champignol, "I've caught and eaten many a carp, and yet I'd never suspected that."

"Because you've only researched fishing as a pastime and not as a subject of serious study. But let's not leave the carp while there's so much more to say on the subject. Do you know, Messieurs, that some 'fish-farmers' have succeeded in domesticating it? They respond to the voice of the person who distributes a supplement of nourishment in their ponds, and even allow themselves to be caressed. But the Dutch have done better; they extract a carp from the water and fatten it.

"They envelop the carp in damp moss and wet grass, and keep it in a slightly dark place where the temperature is constant. A basket serves as a cage—or, better, as a poultry co-op—and several times a day a maidservant comes to 'stuff' it, as is done to geese in Toulouse, chickens in Mans or ducks in Picardy. She introduces cooked grains into their mouths, curdled milk, bread steeped in wine and pastes composed of flour, bran and milk. After three or four weeks, the animal reaches a point at which it is worthy to appear on a table and flatter gourmet palates."

Julien Tafforel chatted for a long time in this fashion, and was able to make us forget that we were on the river's edge precisely to add a new chapter to the natural history of fish of Lacépède or Valenciennes.[13]

---

[13] Étienne, Comte de Lacépède (1756-1825) continued the Comte du Buffon's massive *Histoire naturelle*. Achille Valenciennes (1794-1865) worked with Georges Cuvier on a 22-volume *Histoire Naturelle des Poissons* (1828-1848).

Vincent Champignol leaned toward me and said: "My adversary is a learned man. I wouldn't be astonished if he came from a good family."

"That's also my opinion," I replied.

"Does no one know his name?"

"I'll try to find out. He'll be very clever if he succeeds in hiding it much longer."

As it got warmer and the two fishermen caught absolutely nothing—for good reason—I proposed that the contest should be adjourned. Vincent Champignol pulled a face, for he had desired a less indecisive battle. However, he said to me: "What tribute will the loser have to pay?"

"It's quite simple," I said. "He'll invite us to dine at his home…on fish caught here." And, leaning toward the former haberdasher, I added swiftly: "You'll be the victor and your antagonist won't be able to escape the obligations imposed. Thus we'll discover his domicile and his name."

"That suits me!" Vincent Champignol replied.

"What do you think of the new conditions?" I asked Julien Tafforel.

"I accept them without any argument."

"Since you're in agreement, then, start again."

But the sacred fire was to longer there. Ennui and lassitude, occasioned by the heat, caused favorable ears to heed my renewed proposals for an adjournment.

"You'd do better," I said, "to fish at dusk. Experienced practitioners have often told me how propitious the evening hours are for fishing. Either because the fish, wearied the sun's rays, become more alert in the coolness, or because they desire to eat before going to sleep, they go hunting, and hurl themselves gluttonously on prey placed within range."

"That's true," said Vincent Champignol. "I've observed that many times."

I was very happy with this approval, for it was admirable suited to a plan that had just popped into my head, and which ought to assure Julien Tafforel of a striking victory. It was therefore agreed that the combat would recommence that evening, and that the "dead" would be devoured at the expense of the vanquished, in his home, the following day.

You will remember that the spot of which Vincent Champignol was fond was limited by a rocky point covered by a willow, and elder, a few bushes and a dense reed-bed, whose final plants were in contact with the water. That vegetable ensemble formed a massive clump in the middle of which a man might hide without being seen by a living soul. No shelter was surer or more discreet, especially when the daylight faded and the night was advertised by opaline tints in the sky.

I gave my instructions to Père Benamer. The latter gave me his characteristic "have no fear" expression, and, glad to play a good joke on Vincent Champignol, he hid himself among the reeds at six o'clock in the evening, carrying a watertight cask filled with fish taken from his reserves. I informed Julien Tafforel of my intentions, and recommended him to leave as much of his line in the stream as possible.

"Père Benamer will draw it to him," I said, and attach a fish to it. For you, and for you alone, they'll bite."

I soon overcame Julie Tafforel's scruples by talking to him about his "fiancée" and the necessity to surprise Vincent Champignol and make him marvel, in order to extract from him a consent that still threatened to be a long time coming.

At the fixed time—which is to say, half past six—the two antagonists were side by side, and cast their lines. I had arranged things, of course, for he painter to be in proximity with the reed-bed and that his line would be drawn by the current past the little promontory where Père Benamer was hidden.

"I've got one!" Julien Tafforel cried suddenly, after a long silence.

He brandished his line, at the end of which a barbel of three hundred and four hundred grams was agitating desperately.

Vincent Champignol grimaced, but he was polite. "First strike to you," he said, bowing.

The former haberdasher concentrated al his attention on his float, of which he did not lose sight for an instant. Immediately, Julien Tafforel brought his line out again. Now he had a tench weighing at least half a pound.

"Oh, this is too much!" cried Vincent Champignol, impetuously. "I'm catching nothing and you're catching everything. There's some trickery behind it..."

"There's skill," I said.

"Get away! Are you trying to put one over on an old water-rat like me? The tench is a bottom-dwelling fish, not an open water fish."

"Where did I pull it out from, though?" said Julie Tafforel.

"There are probably several species of tench," I said, "and I've seen many fisherman catching them while out walking."

"It's never happened...to me."

"What does that prove? You haven't baited for tench, that's all."

"And has the Monsieur baited for tench and barbel at the same time?"

"That's his business. I can only observe the results of the contest, not verify the hooks. Isn't each of you free to bait as he pleases?"

During this conversation, which I gladly spun out in order to gain time, the daylight was fading and the dusk intensifying.

From then on, the catches succeeded one another relentlessly. Every time the line fell into the water it was retracted with a fish, whether a tiddler or a large specimen. Barbel, bleak, chub, bream, carp, gudgeons, etc. piled up in the basket. Julie Tafforel accompanied each of his prizes with an ironic reflection or a facetious remark. I amplified in complimentary terms and deliberately exaggerated the results obtained.

Finally, Vincent Champignol exploded like a bomb. His wrath overflowed in statements punctuated and emphasized by a violent spite.

The final stroke, the veritable killer punch, was landed by Père Benamer. Still hidden, he was listening to the discussion with all the more jubilation, he confessed to me the following day, because it was an oblique compliment to him. When he heard mention of the honesty and frankness necessary to any individual combat, he abandoned his redoubt, went back up to the towpath and came to join us as if he were just chancing to pass by.

"Bonsoir everyone, and the company. Excuse me if I'm disturbing you. Don't worry about me. I saw that someone was fishing here. The fishing must be good."

"Not bad. Look at everything that's been caught. There's at ten kilos of fish." And I showed him the basket, full to the brim.

"Christ! What fish, my lads! That's not small beer...but that Monsieur Champignol's a sly one—a trickster, a filibuster—isn't he? I saw him here yesterday evening, putting down ground-bait—and there! He must have thrown a good three francs' worth of nourishment hereabouts to fatten the fish. It no longer astonishes me that the fish came to rendezvous here to get themselves caught—but that's not honest, Monsieur Champignol; it puts too many trumps in your hand against the poor aquatic animals..."

"What were you saying, then, about stratagems, secrets and preparations?" I said, in a slightly scandalized tone.

"So what," replied Vincent Champignol, "if I threw in a few grains of hemp and wheat? It's scarcely me who's profited from it."

"Then again," added Julien Tafforel, moved to pity by the embarrassment of his future father-in-law, "it's permitted. The most authoritative treatises on fishing recommend that preparatory operation."

"That's as may be—but not when one's competing with an honest and trusting adversary..."

"Anyway," exclaimed Vincent Champignol, exasperated by my reasoning. "having baited for me, haven't I baited for him?"

"That's the truth, as true as there's a sun to light the world for us!" concluded Père Benamer, giving me a slight nudge with his elbow.

The old farmer loaded the basket of fish on his shoulders and went back up to the towpath with us. Understanding that his role was a trifle ridiculous, and that he would only render himself shabby and odious by persisting, Vincent Champignol put a brave face on things and said: "I spoke out of turn...I've been beaten hands down. You'll grant me a return match, won't you?"

"Of course," I replied, "when the expenses of the war have been paid."

"Oh, I won't go back on my word, Messieurs—you're invited to dinner at my house...with your fish."

"We wouldn't miss it for the world," said Julien Tafforel. Then, with charming good grace, he added: "Monsieur, adversaries ordinarily shake hands on the field of combat, in order to demonstrate that all rancor is banished from their hearts. Would you permit me to shake your hand?"

"With pleasure."

A cordial handshake was exchanged. Julien Tafforel went away, carrying his rod and line, which Vincent Champignol contemplated admiringly.

The Champignol ladies strongly suspected that Julien Tafforel's victory was due to some unusual maneuver, but they did not interrogate me and submitted without protest to a situation that fulfilled their secret desires. Moreover, Vincent Champignol too accepted his defeat philosophically and spoke about his competitor in laudatory terms.

The most thankless part of the task that I had imposed on myself was about to commence, and it was not without some apprehension that I prepared finally to name Julien Tafforel. However, after a good night's sleep, I felt rested and well, ready to brave Vincent Champignol's wrath.

When I arrived at his home I was quite astonished to encounter Gaspard Grandin and his son, the handsome Félix, there. They too had been invited to eat "our" fish. Counting in advance on a victory that he believed to be certain, the former haberdasher had invited them in order to celebrate his glory more pompously and to find obliging adulators of his profound science and skill. I confess that the encounter displeased me and embarrassed me, but, determined to burn my boats, I asked for a few minutes private conversation with Vincent Champignol.

"Do you know something?" he asked me.

"Your vanquisher is named Julien Tafforel."

Vincent Champignol bowed his head, prey to a sharp annoyance, and reflected for a few seconds.

"I wouldn't want to be reckoned a rude man," he said, "and yet, I can't receive this...Julien Tafforel. Please present my excuses to him."

"Me? Never..."

"What can I do, then?"

"Keep your word."

"Did you know that my adversary was Julien Tafforel?"

"Yes. If I kept silent about his name it was because I saw that you had taken against him without any good reason. Is he not a man of honor, and the most accomplished angler imaginable? Does that not give you sufficient guarantees regarding the equilibrium of his character and the perfect weighting of his faculties? Such a man could not be other than an excellent husband."

"I don't deny it, but one frankness calls for another. I have engagements with the Grandin family; I've made promises...and you'll understand my difficulty."

"One can find a thousand means to break off an engagement so slightly advanced."

"It's impossible for me to withdraw."

Laure passed nearby and I called to her. "Your father," I said to her, "intends you to marry Félix Grandin."

"Me! Marry that horror! Never!"

It is astonishing how rapidly everything that does not suit young women is transformed into a horror.

The response was clear and categorical. Now the claws were unsheathed.

"Go on," said Vincent Champignol, with a moderation I had not expected on his part. "Let Monsieur Tafforel be introduced when he arrives."

"Here he is now."

Transformed by an irreproachable and tasteful costume, the painter arrived, all smiles, and we bowed with the urbanity that reveals a good education.

"Messieurs," said Vincent Champignol, "may I present the foremost angler of our era!"

Our Amphitryon, although assiduous and very polite to his guests, seemed rather preoccupied. Like Buridan's ass, he was torn between the two suitors who aspired to his daughter's hand. Ought he to impose his paternal authority no matter what the cost, or allow Laure to follow her own inclinations?

At dessert, he cheered up. We went into the drawing room to take coffee. The conversation took on a more relaxed and informal tone, which broke through the polite reserve by which we were restrained. Julien Tafforel was even able to insinuate himself into Vincent Champignol's good graces with regard to a fine eel that was swimming nonchalantly in an aquarium installed by a window.

"Well, Monsieur," asked the former haberdasher, "would it be possible for you, who know so much about fish and catch them so well, to give us some information about the eel, which is certainly the most mysterious animal in our watercourse?"

"It's more confused than mysterious," Julien Tafforel replied, "for certain scientists have overcomplicated the question of the eel and divided up its species infinitely. Eels, it's true, have a history as glorious as the red mullets, dorados and morays that we talked about at length during the Homeric combat that Monsieur Champignol and I engaged in, weapons in hand. The Greeks and the Romans held them in high esteem; the Sybarites exempted those who fished for them from all taxes. They were often he guests of sacred fountains, sand were then decorated with valuable gems; magnificent pendant earrings were attached to their gills. They were regarded as divine by the Egyptians, and the priests forbade their flesh to the common people. The poet and physician Nicandre threw considerable discredit on them by maintaining that they became poisonous to eat when they came into contact with vipers."

"And that," I murmured, "is how slander does considerable injury to the finest things."

"Eels offer one very curious particularity," Julien Tafforel continued, "which has probably contributed to rendering them the object of certain superstitions. At the extremity of the caudal vein they have a 'lymphatic heart.' Many fishermen know that, and when they want to kill them without submitting them to any apparent mutilation they bite their tails forcefully. That extreme sensitivity of the eel had been observed without it being attributed to the cause I have just indicated. It is, in fact, sufficient to pass a finger lightly over the fleshy part of the tail to provoke rapid writhing movements and convulsions, even when it is almost deprived of life."

"That's something else I never suspected," said Vincent Champignol.

"Do you want me to talk about the extraordinary endurance and vitality of eels? They're found everywhere, in turbulent running water, under waterfalls, in stagnant waters, marshes and ditches. They undertake long voyages and have no fear of venturing on to land. They sometimes travel long distances crawling like snakes, taking advantage with an admirable instinct of wet ground and grassy terrain abundantly moistened by dew. As they only set out *en route* during the darkest nights, that curious migration has been contested, but thousands of facts have demonstrated its exactitude. During their excursions they live on worms, snails, larvae and insects, and even a few vegetables for which they have a certain predilection. Not everything is beneficial, however, and if they eat too much they are often afflicted by a malady known as 'white stains,' white leads to rapid deterioration and sometimes to death."

"Are eels oviparous or viviparous?" I asked, wanting to display a measure of ichthyological knowledge myself.

"The answer is rather embarrassing, because scientists are not in accord regarding the reproduction of this fish, which presents so many singularities. The ancients believed that it was born in mud, thanks to fragments of its body that it detached by rubbing itself against hard objects. However, it's almost proven now that eels are oviparous—which is to say that they reproduce by means of eggs, and that they deposit their spawn at the mouths of rivers, in littoral pools, almost everywhere that fresh water mingles with salt water. At any rate, every year, in spring, thousands and millions of little eels, known as elvers, travel upstream in compact masses, disseminating at length all the way to the sources. It's certain that eels only reproduce in the sea, or at least in close proximity to the sea, but that fresh water is indispensable for them to grow. They therefore travel up rivers and streams, where they resemble threads, and come downstream again when they are adults, in order to ensure the survival of the species. It is in accordance with these facts that fishermen in the lagoons of Commachio in Italy had organized an entire system of canals and basins permitting them to catch considerable masses of eels long before naturalists, Spallanzani in particular, had described their mores and habits."

"Which proves," I added, sententiously, "that observation and experiment are very valuable."

"A few moments ago," said Vincent Champignol, "you mentioned numerous species of eels; however, all those I've caught resemble this one."

"There's no shortage of varieties," the painter replied, "and with their mania for classifying everything infinitely, scientists will invent them if they don't exist. Lacépède distinguished the Acérines, the Pimperneaux, the Guiseaux, the Verniaux; Blanchard listed the broad-nosed eel, the medium-nosed eel, the oblong-nosed eel and the long-nosed eel; Valenciennes added the flat-nosed eel. I'll spare you the black, grey, brown, yellow and green eels—I'd never finish."

66

"It's a pity," said Vincent Champignol, "that the eel, which is a delicious fish when it has passed through Nanette's heads, doesn't bite a line more readily."

"That's because you don't know how to fish for eels at the right time. It's alleged that they remain in hiding during the day and only quit their shelter, mud or deep hole during the night. And it's also necessary for the night to be very dark, without the slightest moonlight; add to that obscurity stormy weather and a little thunder."

"Thank you, but I sleep at night and only fish in daylight."

Félix approached Julie Tafforel and said to him: "Permit me to congratulate you, Monsieur. Your lecture on eels is admirable!"

"I'm delighted to have taught you something, Monsieur," the painter replied, standing up straight. "Nevertheless, I forgot to cite a proverb to which the eel has given rise."

"Which one, if you please?" asked Félix Grandin, with a certain arrogance.

"That the harder one grasps them in the hand, the slipperier they become...and finally escape."

"Oh, that's very true!" said Laure, spontaneously.

"Well," I said to the former haberdasher, when we found ourselves alone, "what impression has Monsieur Tafforel made on you?"

"He's a charming young man, converses well, is good company, with a certain zest..."

"Of course. He's an angler!"

"That's true—and he's good at it!"

Vincent Champignol did not hide the excellent opinion that he had of Julien Tafforel. On the other hand, he returned to his engagement with the Grandins and explained all the difficulties preventing him from breaking it.

"Don't worry," I said. "I know someone entirely disposed to help you."

"Who's that?"

"Mademoiselle Laure..."

Vincent Champignol could not overcome his hesitation, however, and while declaring that Julien Tafforel was a charming fellow, he did not decide in his favor—or, rather, made no decision.

As you can imagine, we had not accepted a return match or renewed our miraculous catch. The painter, moreover, often absented himself in order to work and dared not come as often as he would have liked. In his moments of leisure, he fished—or rather, trained with Père Benamer, who, always devoted to the "cream" of landlords, prepared good lines for him, and instructed him as to how to bait them in accordance with the time and the place. Soon, he acquired a certain skill, and dared to compare himself with Vincent Champignol. Three or four times, he fished in his company, and was able to hold his own.

Almost invariably, he broke the monotonous silence of the angling with instructive recitations and notions of natural history that amazed the former haberdasher and put a strong dose of esteem for his young companion into his heart. The later offered to paint a portrait of him casting his line at his favorite spot, with specimens of all the fish that lived in "his" river at his feet.

The proposal was accepted, but in order not to start the evil tongues that are always numerous in a little village wagging, and in order not to alert the Grandins, Vincent Champignol only consented to posse in the painter's studio. Although that decision only put a faint smile on Julien Tafforel's face, he submitted to it with the best grace in the world.

The handsome Félix, understanding that he was losing ground, also decided to take up angling, imagining that what had worked for his rival would similarly favor him. He set out of campaign immediately, and every time that he knew that Vincent Champignol was alone in his hiding-place, he hastened to take up a position alongside him.

He was an odd fisherman, though. Clad in a costume dazzling in its whiteness, dressed up to the nines, shod in highly-polished boots, his monocle in his eyes and his hands gloved, he brandished a magnificent cane purchased in Paris-and worth a good hundred francs—majestically. Needless to add, he was usually accompanied by a domestic specially charged with baiting and searching for insects, worms and maggots—in brief, all the vermin that every angler worthy of the name chooses attentively.

Having realized that white frightened the fish and that the illustrious chemist Humphry Davy, taking account of the principle of milieux, hunted in dark red garments and fished clad in green in order not to scare either the birds or the fish, he arrived one morning in a spinach-green suit that would have been the pride of the most original dandy of the Directoire. Nothing was lacking in it—not even the socks with a copper-sulfate tint and the satin-covered hat equipped with an immense veil in green gauze, like those that Englishmen on holiday suspend from their topis.

That ridicule kills is a verity as old as the world, and the handsome Félix was well and truly sunk!

On one fine day in the month of August, at about four o'clock in the afternoon, Vincent Champignol and the two suitors went down to the hiding-place and cast their lines in the water. Suddenly, a sharp cry rang out. Vincent Champignol had just been disarmed. A large carp had bitten and had been hooked, but before the angler had recovered his composure and consolidated his rod in his hand, it had applied two or three formidable thrusts of its tail and escaped, dragging the entire rod and line with it.

Still dragged by the crazed fish, the rod floated, describing the most fantastic swerves. It went out into the river, came back toward the bank, stopped abruptly, and set off again like an arrow, proving by that chaotic course how capable the carp was of towing an object that embarrassed it enormously.

As for Vincent Champignol, he stood there, open-mouthed and utterly disconcerted. He looked around in search of a boat in which he might embark. Then, finding none, he threw himself into the water fully dressed. At first he could set foot on the bed and was almost able to reach the line, but the carp, sensing that it was under threat, headed desperately out into mid-stream. Vincent Champignol bravely started to swim in pursuit.

In the blink of an eye, fearing for the life of his future father-in-law, Julien Tafforel kicked off his shoes, rid himself of his alpaca jacket and hurled himself into the river. In a few strokes, he arrived at the theater of the struggle…

At that exact moment Vincent Champignol seized the rod, and, slightly harassed by his clothing, turned over on to his back, flattening himself like a plank, and gave a few vigorous kicks in order to reach the bank. The carp too pulled with all its might, manifesting an intention to escape.

The sight of Julien Tafforel annoyed the former haberdasher, who wanted to keep for himself all the merit of the most glorious victory he had ever won. "I can swim," he said, "and I have no need of anyone to come to my aid."

The painter had one of those inspirations that one only finds in the crucial moments of life. "Who said anything about rescuing you?" he replied. "I'm only here to watch the carp and make sure that it doesn't escape."

Was that not the language of an angler? Champignol felt his entire body quiver.

"Oh, I recognize you in that! You're a true colleague. Make sure it doesn't unhook itself."

"I'm watching it."

One holding the rod and the other the line, the two men returned to the bank, bringing a superb carp, weighing, according to the estimate they had already made, nearly eight kilograms.

But they were dripping wet; their clothes were stuck to their bodies; various green algae were tangled in their hair. They looked something like those gods that painting and sculpture have imagined to represent rivers, only lacking the urns symbolizing their sources.

The handsome Félix could not keep a straight face; he burst out laughing. "Ha ha! What a mess you're in! You really are funny. You need to be hung upside down to drain you."

With an admirable presence of mind, Vincent Champignol shouted, in a severe tone: "You're laughing, Monsieur! You're laughing when we've just risked the greatest danger! Have you no heart, then?"

Then he threw himself into the arms of the astounded painter, crying: "Oh, my savior—but for you I'd be lost. How can so much courage and devotion be recognized? I'll never forget the service you're rendered me. My wife and daughter will bless you..."

To judge which of them was the most astonished—the handsome Félix or the painter—would have been impossible. As the latter was no fool, he quickly recovered his aplomb, kissed Vincent Champignol on both cheeks and said, with perfectly simulated emotion: "I only did my duty. Are you not already a father to me?"

"Oh, my dear friend, from this day on you are one of us—a member of the family."

That was an explicit consent to Laure's marriage to Julien Tafforel. Félix Grandin was under no illusion, for he did not pronounce a single word while the "drowning victim" and his savior congratulated one another in front of him.

Thus were concluded the hesitations and worries of Vincent Champignol—who could henceforth devote himself to his favorite pleasure without the slightest preoccupation. The Grandin family tried to resist and to launch a few malevolent insinuations, but public opinion loudly approved the former haberdasher for knowing how to show his gratitude and giving his only daughter to the man who had snatched him from certain death.

A few days after the celebration of the marriage, Vincent Champignol said to his son-in-law: "Admit that on the day you vanquished me in single combat you were experimenting with a new bait. Now, I hope that you won't have any more secrets from me, and that you'll let me have your marvelous recipe."

Julien Tafforel and his young bride exchanged knowing glances. Ought they to reveal the ruse or continue to dress in peacock feathers in order to retain forever the glorious title of "the finest angler of the era?"

The painter made the decision to confess, without naming me in order to avoid compromising me; he explained the stratagem that had succeeded so well, thanks to the connivance of Père Benamer.

Vincent Champignol did not harbor any resentment over the deception of which he had been the object, and was the first to laugh at it.

"When you go fishing," he said to his son-in-law, "one can't claim that your line has an idiot on both ends of it."

Camille Debans: *The Story of an Earthquake*
(1892)

On 18 November 1834, at 7.35 a.m., the ships at sea in
the Pacific Ocean off the coast of Chile experienced a violent
shock. Something like a terrible frisson ran through their hulls
from one end to the other, causing their timbers to creak and
their masts to groan; then, after five or six seconds of suspen-
sion, they resumed their progress, without anyone being able
to account for the strange phenomenon. They subsequently
learned that the shock had simply been the repercussion of the
Talcahuano earthquake—a repercussion felt more than three
hundred leagues away at sea.[14]

The mariners who put into Concepcion Bay a few days
later no longer found the town, and learned that the ships an-
chored in the harbor had almost all perished.

Concepcion Bay is one of the largest and most splendid
havens on the Pacific coast of South America. It is five
leagues across from north to south, and more than fifteen kilometers from east to west. Seen from anchorage, it appears
immense. With the naked eye, in clear weather, one can
scarcely make out the eastern and northern coasts, almost con-

---

[14] The earthquake whose devastation was still visible when *H.
M. S. Beagle* called in at Concepcion Bay in March 1834 and
was reported in Charles Darwin's journal to have destroyed
Talcahuano (not for the first or the last time), must have taken
place sometime before the date included in this story. Concepcion was itself devastated by a quake in February 1835, also
reported in Darwin's journal. Talcahuano was most recently
destroyed in the earthquake of February 2010, so the story has
not lost its timeliness.

tinually veiled by a light mist, which lends a mysterious charm to the horizon.

Talcahuano is a small town with white houses, distributed in a disorderly fashion over a peninsula in the south-east of the bay.

Behind Talcahuano, the foothills of the Cordilleras rise up immediately, covered by luxuriant vegetation and populated by innumerable herds of livestock. To the west, the principal hill of the town slopes down to fade away in a vast plain once occupied by the sea, extending between two mountains extending from the interior all the way to the town of Concepcion, which is the capital of the province.

Talcahuano no longer keeps count of earthquakes. Since its foundation—which was, parenthetically, due to French navigators—that small town has been destroyed at least fifteen times. Thus, its houses are constructed in anticipation of the frequent shocks to which it is subject. There are very few habitations of brick or stone, but in general, they are more or less spacious huts built in mud and supple wood. They have no foundations; the floorboards rest on enormous cylindrical logs, and the houses can, in consequence, move forwards and backwards without being damaged.

Experience has demonstrated that this plan is the most favorable in the event of volcanic eruptions, but from the point of view of road-building and the alignment of streets, that mode of construction offers inconveniences, the least of which is to annoy the Alcalde.

In fact, every inhabitant possesses a garden behind his house. When the requirements of cultivation cause him to feel the necessity of enlarging his garden, the proprietor contents himself with pushing his house, which slides over the logs and advances one, two or three meters toward the middle of the street. His garden therefore grows by as much on the side hidden from the public highway. This operation, repeated several time in accordance with need by each proprietor, ends up producing streets of microscopic width, whose irregular contours would make the most tortuous Flemish streets seem rectilinear by comparison.

When the encroachment reaches such proportions that the street is in danger of being replaced by a connecting wall, however, the Alcalde intervenes and lets it be known to the inhabitants, with a blast of his trumpet, that he is giving them twenty-four hours to readjust the alignment of their domiciles—and a pair of oxen harnessed to each house is sufficient to carry out the Alcalde's order.

Earthquakes are not rare events in Peru, and more especially in Chile. Valparaiso suffers fifteen earthquakes a year, but if these disquieting events are not the preliminary effects of volcanic eruptions in the Cordilleras, the inhabitants content themselves with coming out of their houses in order not to be crushed by collapsing ceilings.

In Copiapo, a small town in the north famous for its copper and silver mines, especially the Gallos family's silver mine, into the depths of which one goes down by means of a staircase carved in the silver mass, the earth is always quaking. The oscillations are not very obvious, but it is sufficient to lean on the wall of a hut to feel the perpetual trepidation of the ground immediately.

Thus, there are people in Chile who have been shaken by a hundred, a hundred and fifty, or even two hundred earthquakes.

For them, there are unequivocal signs by which one is able in advance to recognize the intensity of the terrible event: an increasingly heavy atmosphere, a sky veiled by hot vapors, nervous anxieties that extend in ascending progression from men to women, from women to animals, and from species to species thereafter, all the way to dogs, mules and horses, which are the most sensitive to the perturbations Thus, there are few examples of a mule or a horse continuing to walk during the five or six seconds preceding the subterranean noise and the trepidation of the earth.

Well, in spite of these premonitory symptoms, in spite of the habituation and in spite of everything, there is no Chilean who does not have an indescribable terror of earthquakes. Strangely enough, the older they get—which is to say, the more volcanic shocks they experience—the more fearful they become. I merely observe that; I shall not seek to explain it.

Now, toward the end of the month of October 1834, two volcanoes situated in the territory of Araucania, which were thought to have been extinct for half a century, vomited flame and a certain quantity of lava. On the other hand, it was learned that in San Carlos de Chiloé, in the archipelago of that name, three or four oscillations of a particular character had been felt.

People were, in consequence, expecting an imminent catastrophe. Every day they heard muffled detonations in the mountain, followed by long rumbles, as if thunder were growling. And the day after, they would hear from the vaqueros or the inhabitants of Concepcion that blocks of granite had been detached from the summits to tumble noisily into the precipices.

The old men who had escaped two or three destructions of their town felt gripped by fear and slept with one eye open, ready take up their families. Devoutly religious, like all Chileans, they implored the infinite mercy of God, and only found the appeasement for which they were avid in prayer.

The terror, which had been increasing since the beginning of the month, began to calm down after the twelfth of November. Alarming news became rarer, and it was thought that once again, they might get away with an alarm.

Talcahuano is an essentially joyful town. One could erect a temple to pleasure there. There is perhaps no country in the world, not forgetting Italy and Spain, where more effort is expended on follies, feasting, frantic dancing, guitar-music and egg punch. It seems that the poor Chileans and their amiable womenfolk are in haste to savor the fruits of life, and that tomorrow is, for them, the improbable date of an unhoped-for future.

Empedicles, I believe, reproached the inhabitants of Agrigentum for living life at a gallop, as if they were going to die the next day, and building their houses as if they were going to live forever. One might have made the same reproach to the Chileans of Talcahuano, except for the construction of the houses, for the dwellings and their inhabitants alike gave the appearance of awaiting the end of the world with a philosophy far more Christian that that of the vainglorious Sicilian rhetorician.

As soon as the inhabitants of Talcahuano were convinced that all danger had vanished, joy and feasting hastened to resume their empire over the light-hearted town.

A few *tertulias*—that being the name of the dances hosted in the region by people of certain importance—has taken place on the evening of the twelfth, and as no bad news came to subdue the town the following day, there was a big party at the home of one of the principal ship-suppliers. Naturally, almost all the captains and officers of the ships calling at Talcahuano were invited.

There was a considerable hotchpotch of nationalities—something akin to a miniature Tower of Babel—in the tradesman's drawing rooms, which did not prevent the young Chilean woman from being very amiable, and everyone was delighted.

The captains of the majority of the ships then got together to offer in their turn to throw an equally-fine party for their hosts, and the date of that maritime *tertulia* was fixed for 17 November.

A magnificent and spacious American whaler, a three-master, was chosen with common accord by the mariners as the least oily and most elegant venue that could be presented to Talcahuanan high society. All the sailors worked in shifts to scrub and polish the deck that was to serve as a dance-floor and the lower deck, where the gambling tables, boudoirs and sleeping quarters were set up. Flowers were brought aboard to surround and ornament the masts. The most delicate ear in the harbor was chosen and dispatched on reconnaissance to Concepcion, with instructions to bring back the best guitarpluckers in the town. A piano was unearthed, hoisted aboard, and thoroughly retuned for the occasion.

Finally, when the preparations were concluded, it was all so beautiful that the mariners dared not stroll on their own decks.

The great day arrived. The launches and dinghies from all the ships, graciously decked with flags, gathered almost simultaneously on what was known as Talcahuano pier. The guests embarked successively, and were ferried to the *Ocean Queen*, where the party was soon in full swing.

Oh, it was a beautiful ball! A magnificent and pictur-esque *tertulia!* Among the mariners there were no dress suits, but long the frock-coats that mariners call "mainsails." Every-one had gloves, of course, but in their pockets or clutched in the left hand, to show that they were familiar with society conventions. On the Chilean side, there was full European costume; for the ladies, that meant an overabundance of silk, feathers, velvet, ostrich-plumes and Chinese crepes.

They danced; they danced for a long time, and in every style: English jigs, boleros, tarantellas, waltzes, minuets, even quadrilles, not forgetting the Chilean *zamacueca* and the Peru-vian *refalosa*.

At midnight, everyone went down to the lower deck for supper. A few sleepy children were put to bed in the officer's cabins, and the party resumed more hectically and more noisi-ly than ever.

During that intermission, the sailors, who were wide-eyed with astonishment, having never seen such a hurly-burly before, performed all the dances they knew on the deck, with all the more enthusiasm because someone had broken open a barrel of rum in the *Ocean Queen*'s forecastle during the soci-ety supper.

The guests' supper was a true banquet. The men charged with serving at table had a great deal of difficulty satisfying the desires of senoritas who asked them to transport to some fortunate officer another the sparkling glasses in which they had dipped their red lips by way of a preliminary—a gracious custom of that liberal region.

In brief, by three o'clock in the morning, the stores being exhausted, and various groups experiencing the need to surrender their moist foreheads to the caresses of the open air, they left the table to return to the dances. On arriving on deck, however, they perceived that the sea had become choppy. The ship was pitching somewhat, although, strangely enough, there was no wind. It was, therefore, very difficult to dance. Anyone who had suggested bringing the party to an end at that point would, however, would have been very unpopular. What should they do, then? The young women's feet were twitching with impatience.

A local merchant offered to let the soirée continue on land at his house, and drink his cellar dry. The motion was welcome with an enthusiastic acclamation. They embarked at the double, and twenty minutes later, the *Ocean Queen* had become the most silent of whaling-ships. The only people still aboard were drowsy sailors, two or three weary officers no longer seduced by the splendors of society, and three or four sleeping children, whose mothers, avid to dance, had not wanted to burden themselves with them, and had confided them to the guard of the first mate when he took over the four o'clock watch.

In almost all the towns of South America, especially those on the Pacific coast, night-watchmen still exist whose functions, in addition to nocturnal policing, consist of crying the time every thirty minutes. For Europeans that custom has something primitive about it, which brings a smile to the lips, but in a land where, in spite of the luxury and the fêtes, the majority of the indigenes sweat in poverty, that fashion of substituting Christians for clocks testifies to a certain eccentric solicitude for the needs of the inhabitants.

Thus, the watchmen in question, who are known as *serenos* and perform their duties on horseback, are continually shouting, simultaneously: "*Son last tres!*" or "*Cuatro! Son las quarto y media!*"—and they add *lluvia*, rain, or *sereno*, fine weather, according to the circumstances. Finally, when five o'clock sounds, hey announce it and the sing a prayer, which begins: "*Ave, Maria, purissima, castissima, inviolatissima, etc.*"—a touching fashion of concluding their tiring work by actions of grace piously addressed to the mother of Our Savior. Then they go to bed, having been relieved of their service by the diurnal watchmen known as *vigilantes*.

That morning, well before the guests of the maritime *tertulia* had decided that they would go to finish their party on land, the *serenos* of Talcahuano had been exchanging anxious comments as they passed one another in the streets. The atmosphere was stifling in its heaviness, and the sea could be heard roaring in a lugubrious fashion in spite of the absence of a breeze.

On the mountain, five or six times, the dogs had uttered plaintive howls that put a chill in the bones. One of those landslides I mentioned had launched the echoes of its detonation into the precipices. In sum, for those experienced individuals, there was reason to fear an imminent catastrophe, and the best thing to do was prudently to seek shelter.

One old *sereno*, who heard five o'clock chime as he was going past the house where the ball had resumed at full tilt, uttered his call, muttered his prayer, and did not hesitate to add thereafter, to characterize the weather that was brewing, the terrible word *temblor*: earthquake.

The other *serenos* repeated it. Not one of the fanatical dancers heard that threat, but the other inhabitants leapt out of bed, as if the fatal word had been shouted over the town by the brazen breast of a giant taller than the mountain.

At six o'clock, all the inhabitants of Talcahuano were in the streets, in the squares, discussing what action they ought to take. A light tremor had already occurred. The old *sereno* had not been too quick off the mark.

The old people were interrogated; people ran home to gather up their most precious possessions; women and children were taken to places of safety.

The ball, however, was still in full swing. Too preoccupied with their own salvation, the fugitives had not thought to warn the dancers. One vigilante, however, who was passing by the house of the merchant where people were gorging themselves on pleasure with so much insouciance, knocked on a window, and when the window was opened, he uttered the frightful word: "*Temblor!*"

Pronounced by the policeman, it had the effect of the Biblical *Mene Mene Tekel Upharsin*. The guitars stopped dead, as if they had already been swallowed up; glasses fell from the hands of those who were completing their drunkenness, and who had sobered up on the spot. A livid pallor passed like a fog over all the faces that had been reddened by fatigue and sleeplessness an instant before. There was a redoubtable silence for a couple of minutes.

Then a voice cried: "*Fuera!*" Outside!

The *vigilante*, who had paused momentarily before that spectacle, tried to resume his course, but his horse refused to move, as if its four feet had been planted in the ground, and began to tremble in all its limbs. In the distance, already outside the town, the procession of Talcahuano's inhabitants was heading in haste toward the heights of Cap Estero, the culminating point of the peninsula separating Concepcion Bay from San Vicente Bay.

Scarcely had the word *fuera* been pronounced than the crowd of dancers poured out through the doors, windows and any other exists like a whirlwind. The Chileans, crazed by fear, no longer had any consciousness of their dignity, nor of the frailty of women and children. They crushed and trampled a fallen mass in order to get out more rapidly.

It must be said, in praise of the mariners, that not one of those rude whalers and not one of the other seafarers took a single step before the women and children were safe and sound.

But it was already too late. Scarcely twenty people made it out into the street before a frightful subterranean din was heard and the first shock was felt.

The house tottered; there were frightful cracks; the entire town was enveloped by dust—or smoke; who could tell?

Everyone fled as fast as possible.

Then, suddenly, the mountain began to roar violently; a second shock, which nothing could resist, was announced by a subterranean rumble of indescribable power.

Ordinarily, the oscillations of earthquakes are horizontal, passing from north to south or east to west. That day, at a few minutes to seven, the oscillations were produced vertically—which is to say, from bottom to top. It was as if a subterranean force wanted to lift up the terrestrial crust by battering it with repeated blows. As you can imagine, the houses, shaken in that terrible fashion, could not resist for long, and the entire town was reduced to a heap of rubble in a matter of seconds. Further abominable clouds of dust emerged from that mass, threatening to asphyxiate the fugitives and those trapped beneath the debris of the collapsed houses.

At every moment, the crowd gathered on Cap Estero saw terrified fugitives emerging from that dust and coming to join them, and fifteen minutes later, when a count was made, only a few people failed to respond to the roll-call.

By virtue of a kind of miracle, almost everyone had escaped. The houses were so lightly-built that their fall had only caused a few mishaps here and there, and there was still hope of finding a few bruised absentees, wounded but not dead.

In the bay, the sea was choppy without being menacing. All the ships at anchor were swaying gently, and among the unfortunates who had just witnessed the destruction of their homes, the young women in party dresses, the charming mothers whose sleeping children had remained aboard the *Ocean Queen*, rejoiced in the good fortune that had providentially kept their cherished infants away from the terrible danger; they wept with joy and delight for their miraculously-preserved sons.

Half an hour had gone by since the last terrible shock that had flattened the town; a rather benign tidal wave had arrived to lick the nearest debris after crossing the pier, and then everything had returned to its habitual order.

On the horizon to the west, the breaking clouds allowed the sight of a broad sheet of azure. The clouds of dust that had risen skywards at the moment of the catastrophe were now falling back slowly, taking on bizarre forms, over the rubble lying in the place where Talcahuano had been an hour before.

The unfortunate refugees on Cap Estero gazed at all that with bleak and desperate expressions, but as the loss of their little houses was, after all, the only misfortune they had to deplore, given that the merchandise and objects of value had been recovered before the collapse, a few people better tempered than the rest of the population were beginning to shake off their torpor.

On the other hand, the mariners who had mingled with the crowd pronounced reassuring words; people encouraged one another.

In a region where such dangers are constantly suspended over one's head, there are no long hours to devote to despair. In brief, there was a *sursum corda*, and the five or six thousand unfortunates sketched a movement toward their crumbled town.

But what had just happened was merely a preface. The drama was to be terrible, bloody, irremediable, and the unspeakable terror that the witnesses to that drama experience was such that several among them were aged by years in a matter of minutes. Two or three young women saw their hair turn white in an hour.

Just as the desolate caravan moved off in order to go take possession of the locations that had been their home, their domain and their fortune, the dogs resumed howling furiously, and the sky was suddenly covered by dense vapors.

From the direction of the mountains a ripping sound resounded. What a noise that must have been! The ripping of rocks!

And the earth, shaken again in a disorderly fashion, began to tremble beneath the feet of the poor Chileans, who fell to their knees and struck their breasts, confessing their sins.

The padres mingled with that frightened crowd, pale-faced and with trembling hands, also on their knees, distribute their blessings and murmured absolutions, which were divined rather than heard, through their taut lips and clenched teeth.

Suddenly, a man, his eyes horribly widened by fear, stood up to his full height and, without being conscious of what he was doing, extended his arms in the direction of the mountains. All gazes followed the indication, and they saw something that few people in the world can boast of having seen. A broad peak situated to the right of the plain that has been mentioned, on the far side of which Concepcion stood, had just split in two, and that was the ripping that had been heard. A precipice had opened up, of a depth as-yet-incalculable. To the right and left, walls of granite; in the depths, perhaps a new valley.

The padres, men, women, mariners—everybody— thought that it was all over, and that in five minutes they would be swallowed up by that frightful furnace; and yet, that was not the most horrible thing.

An unusual sound was produced in the middle of the bay; then the noise became a racket, and commanded the attention of a few wretches who still had the strength to look and listen. In the space of ten minutes they witnessed the most grandiose, and simultaneously the most infernal, spectacle that could ever be imagined.

This would be unbelievable were there not still, at the time of writing, people who were eye-witnesses of what I am relating. A crevasse had opened up in the sea, in the middle of the bay. The force of dislocation that had just acted upon the mountain was now exercising its limitless power on the rocks of the sea-bed, and suddenly, with a vertiginous rapidity, the entire bay emptied, as if by magic.

The stupor that overwhelmed the poor refugees on Cap Estero I shall not attempt to describe; but from the middle of that astounded crowd, three or four shrill screams rose up.

What am I saying?

They were the howls of lionesses rather than screams. There was nothing human about them: they were eruptions of savage voices.

And immediately, women richly clad in silk and velvet, with their feet elegantly shod, were seen to leap toward the shore, extending their writhing arms desperately, and then fall to the ground, inanimate, so suddenly had their strength abandoned them, unless they were caught by their companions. Those women were the young mothers who had been rejoicing a little while before at the idea that they had left their children asleep aboard the *Ocean Queen*.

What a horrible spectacle they beheld now! The waters, in retreating, had dragged with them the majority of the ships at anchor in the harbor. Those that had been unable to resist the terrible current of a sea that seemed to be taking flight had been dragged into the sheer depths and torn apart before anyone could ascertain how many men they were dragging to their doom.

In the middle of the bay, a mighty whirlpool, as horrible as the Maëlstrom, had formed in the blink of an eye and pitilessly swallowed up everything that the retreating waters had drawn into its funnel.

Ships of large dimension were seen entering the gyratory radius of the whirlpool and, launched like arrows, making five or six rotations on the rim of the gulf, then going to break up on the sharp points of rocks at the bottom.

In the rigging or on the decks, a few men clinging to ropes waited for a miracle. From afar, one could divine that they were uttering roars or sobs of despair.

That mass of water, twenty leagues square on the surface, drained away almost entirely. The bay was empty. About ten ships, among them the *Ocean Queen*, solidly moored by four anchors, had resisted the catastrophe. Tipped over on the bed of sand or mud, they were lying partly broken, for the majority, in colliding with rocky spurs, had lost part of their rigging by virtue of the violence of the impact.

The masses of water were finishing their disappearance into the bed of the bay when frightened me were seen appearing on the surviving ships. Their sole desire, spurred by folly or fear, it was easily divined, was to take refuge on land.

But where? And how?

To traverse the mud, where the low-lying areas were still full of water, seemed impossible, and in any case, the nearest of those stricken vessels was at least twelve hundred meters from Cap Estero.

Some appeared to resign themselves to waiting, but simultaneously, from the poop-decks of two ships, one of them English and the other French, mariners were seen letting themselves slide down broken masts and ropes that were hanging over the side. They had decided to cross the dried-up sea, without thinking that, in case the Ocean reclaimed its rights, it might be better to await the final result of the earthquake.

Those madmen, therefore, ventured on to the bed of the bay, precipitately fleeing their wrecked ships, thus setting a deadly example that was almost immediately followed by fearful members of other crews. That happened just at the moment when several further shocks, much less violent, came to presage the last convulsions of the ground.

As is readily understandable, however, the mass of the water of the Pacific Ocean, driven back momentarily by the volcanic commotion, and suspended by some unknown power, was soon precipitated into that harbor, which seemed to have attempted to escape its empire.

Concepcion Bay is, as it were, closed to the west by an island, Quiriquina, to the right and left of which are two channels, through which ships enter the port. With a frightful din, two liquid mountains raced through each issue toward the dried-up bay. After having passed Quiriquina, those two mountains joined up and formed a foaming mss of such elevation that the refugees on Cap Estero, the crown of which is more than two hundred meters above sea level, thought they would be reached, knocked down and dragged away.

But where the drama took on gigantic proportions was in the place where the stricken ships were awaiting their fate; it was from the rocks that the mariners attempting to reach land saw that mighty wall advancing with vertiginous rapidity, beneath the weight of which they were about to be crushed. In that supreme moment, they experienced such terror that, in order to hurl one last cry of despair at the heavens, the force of their lungs was multiplied tenfold—for, in spite of the roar of the immense wave, a clamor was heard.

Some lay down silently. Others turned intrepidly toward the wave and waited for it, folding their arms; then it was all over.

When the first mate of the *Ocean Queen* had anticipated the assault of that unique tidal wave, his first thought had been to shut the children confided to his care in their cabins. After that he had set about doing everything humanly possible to save them, and himself with them. A consummate mariner, sailing in the region for nearly twenty years and familiar with the maritime accidents that are the ordinary consequence of earthquakes, he had assumed that the greatest danger had not passed, and that the offensive return of the waves would be the solemn moment of life or death.

In a few words, too colorful, too technical and above all too strong for us to think of reporting them here, he had demonstrated to the few men who had remained aboard with him after the party that to flee across the bed of the bay would be to run to certain death. The sea would return with incalculable violence; if there as a means of salvation—and one alone—it lay in the absolute abandonment of the ship to the caprice of the advancing liquid mountain. In consequence, the four chains that retained the anchors were let loose, and when the *Ocean Queen*—which, moreover, had not suffered overmuch—was completely disengaged from anything that could offer resistance to the rushing water, they waited. Some other ships imitated the maneuver. A few preferred to trust to the force of their anchors and chains, and consolidated their moorings instead.

Moreover, when those brave seamen, in whom one would certainly have found the poet's triple bronze,[15] saw that frightful giant wall of water, white with foam and already laden with wrecks and corpses, racing across the bed of the bay, not one lost hope completely.

The mate retained his presence of mind; he ordered all his men below decks; all the hatches were hastily closed and everyone lay down, seeking a point of support so as not to be hurled against the walls of the hull. Who can ever know what a world of thought, what a poem of terror, despair and—who knows?—hope went through those men's heads during that solemn minute. Not one pronounced a word; only the cabin-boy was breathing loudly as he wrapped himself up in the captain's mattress, in accordance with the advice given to him by the boatswain. In one of the locked cabins a child was weeping and calling for his mother.

The noise suddenly redoubled, became horrible and made the ears bleed; a cold sweat streamed on the faces of all the men, and yet a single word was heard: "Ready!" It was the first mate again, whose composure had not deserted him.

What happened then? It seemed that the *Ocean Queen* was being crushed; a horrible cracking sound was heard; what remained of the masts was evidently torn away. The foot of the mizzen mast, which was supported on the bunk-room, splintered; a piece of wood struck the boatswain and killed him.

There was a frightful buzz; there was an irresistible surge; the beautiful ship, which handled like a dream at sea, was rolled over and over twenty times; the unfortunate mariners, thrown between the ceiling and the floor every time, re-

---

[15] The reference is to a phrase used by Horace; subsequent to this story's publication, it was borrowed by Robert Frost for the title of a poem that is nowadays more famous than the original reference.

ceived bruises or injuries every time, sometimes fatal. However, an oath, a sigh or a cry announced from time to time that it was not all over yet.

Those who were still alive were unaware of what had become of them. On every side the seething of the sea could still be heard; fortunately, they could also sense that the *Ocean Queen*, although rolled by the waves like an enormous ball thrown at top speed, was no longer on the bottom. In addition, it had not run into any obstacle since the moment when a submarine wave, perfectly appreciable, had snatched it from the rocks on which it lay.

Those who could still make these reflections did not have long to wait. There was a horrible jolt; the ship split open; several gaps were distinctly perceived in the sleeping quarters, and all noise ceased.

Elsewhere, for the poor Chilean refugees on the heights of Cap Estero, the splendor and the horror of the spectacle had been indescribable. At the sight of the immense sea hurtling toward the wrecked ships and the imprudent sailors who had ventured on to the bed of the bay, a horrible frisson had gripped the terrified spectators of the sinister drama. To the clamor raised by the mariners who were about to be swallowed up, a more compact and sonorous clamor replied. Everyone had extended their arms toward the unfortunates and uttered a cry that was a farewell.

Almost at the same moment, however, the attention of the refugees shifted to the ships thus far spared from the fury of nature. To begin with, there were many mariners in the crowd on Cap Estero, including almost all the captains in the association to whom the previous day's *tertulia* was due. In the midst of them was a young blond man with a distinguished physiognomy; he was the captain of the Ocean Queen.

After having examined attentively the various measures and precautions taken aboard the menaced vessels to escape the terrible danger of being crushed, the young mariner seemed content with what had been done aboard his ship and advanced toward the group where the young mothers whose children were aboard were standing, mad with grief and fear. In a calm, voice he sought to reassure them, affirming that his first mate was the one man who might save a ship in such circumstances. He explained what the mate had done, and that it was probable that there would only be unimportant misfortunes to regret. The children being placed in bunks and retained by pivoting planks, it was necessary, in his opinion, to retain hope.

The poor mothers wanted nothing more than to believe him. One of them gazed at him in desperate gratitude, in which one could read thanks for his generosity, but also an absolute incredulity with regard to what he had said. He turned round to hide the sentiment painted on his face, for he had les faith than anyone in the possibility of snatching any prey whatsoever from the advancing Ocean.

The moving liquid mountain, which everyone was following with their eyes, horribly sick at heart, soon came within a few meters of the first ship. That was a moment of terror, during which no one breathed. The poor vessel disappeared, swallowed up. The immense collapse of the breakers fell successively upon each ship. The *Ocean Queen*'s turn came. The whaler was drowned by the waves.

Then, continuing its frightful progress toward the shore, the gigantic wave, which seemed to be growing as it advanced, threatened the coast and passed over it, as if it were now going to cover the land that had attempted to dispute its empire. Finally, it rose so high that the unfortunates on Cap Estero, seeing it rising toward them, forgot Talcahuano, the *Ocean Queen* and everything else for a moment, in order to carry out a rapid retreat.

But that was the sea's final effort; it came to break at their feet, and then began to retreat slowly. In the direction of Talcahuano the wave had passed rapidly and noisily over the debris of the town, smashing everything in its path that the range of the earthquake had spared. Its momentum had carried it over the slopes of the mountain well beyond the town, to such a height that the voyagers to whom the story is told nowadays would not believe it if irrefutable evidence did not remain to prove the veracity of the fact.

A cry of agony, a further clamor of despair, escaped every mouth and the sight of that irremediable catastrophe.

This time, Talcahuano was completely destroyed, and everything that the unfortunate town still contained was lost forever, including the lives of the poor people who had been unable to flee or who were trapped beneath the debris of their houses. A horrible death! A horrible ruination!

Suddenly, an exclamation of timid joy rang out in the midst of the general stupor. The captain of the *Ocean Queen* shouted: "Look! Look!" And with his finger he pointed at the side of the mountain, on which the sea had finally stopped, and which it was abandoning quite rapidly. The breach full of a ship was stuck in the ground, and the mariner's eye had recognized the *Ocean Queen*.

Yes, the sea's momentum had been so powerful that the vessel had been transported over the town and well beyond, half way up the first of the foothills of the Cordilleras.

As I have said, no one would believe it if that extraordinary wreck were not still there as I write these lines, and were not the objective of curious excursions by all the travelers who visit Talcahuano.

Without wondering if the sequence of misfortunes was at an end, the crowd rushed toward the *Ocean Queen*. It was necessary to find out what had become of the men they had seen a short while before. Feeling a little hope reborn in their hearts, the young mothers took the lead, so rapidly that even the captain had difficulty keeping up with them.

Finally, they arrived. As the captain was figuring out what the easiest way would be to climb up on to the deck, and how he could maintain himself there, it became evident that efforts were being made inside to open the hatch to the bunkroom.

There was an indescribable excitement. Agile as a cat, the captain bounded to the hatch, and forced it open with impatient violence.

A blood-stained man with his head half-broken then appeared and tumbled into the arms of the young mariner, who embraced him enthusiastically without being able to suppress the sobs of joy that were tearing his breast. The man was the first mate, cruelly wounded but alive. Providence had owed him that.

"The others?" the captain interrogated.

"Dead!" the poor man replied, losing consciousness.

Fortunately, he was mistaken; for emotion, joy and dread were taking on superhuman proportions when the crying of a child as heard. In two bounds the captain was inside the bunkroom, opened the cabin from which the cried were coming, and picked up a pink baby boy, who did not have a scratch.

He was passed from hand to hand to his mother, who fled with him like a wounded lioness, while the other young women darted glances of hatred at her. When the other cabins were searched, one more wounded infant was found, dying. Two others were dead. The mother of one of them, suddenly afflicted with madness, went straight toward the sea and let herself fall into it from the height of a rock.

"I can't see the cabin-boy!" said the captain.

Scared, his hair bristling and his eyes wide, a child of about twelve appeared in his turn, and, realizing that he was safe, was seized by a frightful nervous fit.

While all this was happening, the sea had retreated, only leaving behind, in the place where Talcahuano had existed that morning, a sandy beach on which a few wrecks could be seen, and one or two corpses.

When the victims of the disaster redirected their gazes toward the sea, they perceived a few ships that had resisted the powerful effort of the sea. Two or three of those that had entrusted to the solidity of their chains and anchors were still struggling against the final convulsions of the Ocean. Others, which had been believed lost since the commencement of the earthquake, were visible on the horizon, coming back to their moorings.

In sum, in spite of the magnitude of the disaster, more ships had been saved than one would have dared to hope.

The *Ocean Queen* stayed on the mountain as a memorial of the earthquake of 18 November. For some time, the poor of Talcahuano went to take it apart in order to provide wood for their fires and salvage the ironwork, which sold at a high price, but a decree by the Alcalde issued in 1844 specified punishments for anyone who touch the wrecked vessel again. A cross was set up on its poop, and the *Ocean Queen* was considered henceforth as a kind of historic monument.

For the benefit of people naturally disposed to incredulity, we shall content ourselves with recalling that, in an earthquake in Peru, several ships experienced the same fate as the *Ocean Queen*. A Peruvian naval corvette was hurled a long way inland and a considerable number of men perished, but the most extraordinary of all was an American steamship which was carried by the sea eight hundred meters beyond the beach.

Finally, a circumstance even more astonishing was produced in Calcutta during the cyclone that cost the English so dear in 1864. A magnificent ship of three thousand tones was seized by the wind—you read that correctly, by the wind—and thrown a hundred meters inland, where it was embedded up to the gunwales. That one is also still there; it has been converted into a hospital.

Furthermore, all the details that we have just offered the reader have been furnished by Don Pedro B***, a resident of Conception. Don Pedro is none other than the *Ocean Queen*'s cabin-boy, who refused to allow himself to be repatriated— for, after the fright he had had, he would not consent to set foot on a ship again for a long time.

Emile Gautier: Le Désiré

The First Voyage of a Submarine Boat
(1893)

Jeanne de G*** to Hélène de B***
Dover, 25 July 1890

How busy I've been, my dear Hélène, since we last saw one another! So much has happened! What adventures!

Your little Jeanne is simply in the process of becoming a heroine, and if you read the newspapers you'd know that she has her place marked out henceforth in the gallery of famous travelers, alongside Miss Bly.[16] How many interviews we've given, Papa and I, since yesterday evening, you can't imagine. How many journalists we've seen—English, French, not to mention American, come from New York expressly to "have a talk." Papa hasn't calmed down. He's given the servants the strictest orders. But it does no good, and the journalists force their way in through the most tightly-sealed doors. More are arriving by the minute, pencil and notepad in hand, and they know how to manipulate Papa so that, while cursing them, he ends up telling them everything they want to know. They're so correct, so polite, so insinuating! Some of them are even very charming. One above all, a Parisian, tall, well-built, strong, very dark, with curly hair, a nice soft moustache and kind eyes, impertinent and cajoling at the same time, and a golden voice…but I'll stop there, or else I'll say something stupid and you'll make fun of me.

---

[16] "Nellie Bly" was the pseudonym of the famous American journalist Elizabeth Cochrane (1864-1922), who went around the world in 1888, attempting to beat Jules Verne's "record" of 80 days; she did it in 72.

Anyway, I'm rambling on and on, every which way, and I realized that I haven't even explaining the reason for all this commotion.

Oh, it's quite simple, my dear friend, and you'll see right away that we haven't usurped this unexpected glory. Can you imagine that it's underwater—*underwater*, you understand, like fish—that we've traveled from Calais to Dover? The day before yesterday, in fact, the submarine boat about which everyone was talking—do you remember?—at the last ball at the Ministry of Marine, has crossed the Channel for the fir time, and we made the crossing on board. They aren't numerous, people who can say that! At any rate, I'm the only woman who can say it, apart from one Spaniard, as pretty as a picture, who was going on honeymoon with her husband to Scotland. Since we landed, though, we haven't seen her again. Vanished, slipped away, evaporated, the young household! That's why all the glory is mine, without being shared. That's why I've had, on my own, he honor of being baptized "Amphitrite" by the Daily Telegraph. Amphitrite! Isn't that gallant! Oh, I was so frightened—but I'm very happy.

"In a submarine boat!" you'll say, with your severe little pout. "What an idea! But how was my little Jeannette, who is such a coward, able to do that?"

I am a coward, of course; in fact, that's why I preferred *Le Désiré*—that's the name of my fish-boat—to the ordinary ferry-boat that stupidly provides the service on the service. I was horribly afraid of sea-sickness. And on that day, the sea was choppy, swarming with white sheep. Now, I'd heard it said that submarine boats didn't roll or pitch, the agitation of the wav sot extending below a certain depth. That was tempting I can assure you, and in my place, Madame Grumpy, you'd have been seduced just like that little hothead Jeannette, for, if I'm not mistaken, you haven't been vaccinated against sea-sickness any more than I have.

Then again, it was funny to do what no one had done before and improvise the role of naiad. Indeed, at the end of the jetty one could read, in large letters, on a calico strip, the following notice: "Today, at noon precisely, the submarine boat *Le Désiré*, commanded by the inventor Claudius Bouget in person, will depart for Dover."

My decision was made. Following the example of Griboule, whose story amused us so much at school, for fear of the sea I went across the sea beneath the surface. It's the sea that would be taken by surprise. Oh yes!

What wasn't easy, of course, was to convince Papa. You know Papa, you know how stubborn he is. But this time, his stubbornness was complicated by a peculiar repugnance. He didn't believe in submarine navigation. When he was a naval construction engineer he had, it seems, been given the job of making a report on a submarine boat, which he had condemned "for mathematical reasons," as he put it, without even having consented to go down in it.

"But Papa," I asked him, "how did you know that the boat was worthless, since you hadn't tried it out?"

"What! What about algebra? And geometry? And physics? The sacred formulae. Remember what I told you: submarine navigation can only ever be a utopia or a paradox, a dream or a hoax."

"But Papa, people said the same about the phonograph. You told me a story yourself about a member of the Institut, a very learned scientist, who began by thumbing his nose at the man who presented the phonograph, on the fallacious pretext that he was a ventriloquist."

"But it's not the same thing." Hmm! Hmm! How tiresome they are these fin-de-siècle girls! "It's not the same. First of all, the phonograph wasn't invented by a Frenchman. He was some sort of Bohemian, a pillar of the brasseries, by the name of Charles Cros, I believe..."

"The author of *Le Coffret de santal*?"[17]

---

[17] The poet Charles Cros (1842-1888), the author of *Le Coffret de santal* (1873), perhaps best known for writing monologues for the comic actor Coquelin *cadet*, deposited a description of a sound-recording machine that he called a "palaeophone"

"Exactly. You see! A poet who had invented the phonograph! All right for the monologues, but the phonograph! Such machines, besides, could only be invented by Americans. You can't understand, my dear Jeanne, but listen to your father and believe me, for a French invention to be any good it needs to have gone via America, Is it Edison who's built it, this submarine boat? No, it isn't, is it? Well, they're trying to put one over us. Besides which, a phonograph doesn't take passengers and it doesn't travel underwater."

"No doubt, Father—but *Le Désiré* does travel underwater. Have you read the *Figaro?*"

"Get away! Journalists' stories! I know those soapboxes, It only works in the novels of Jules Verne. We naval engineers can't be made to swallow sea serpents of that size. A fish-boat! Ha ha—that's a joke. A fish, yes, but a drunken fish, a blind fish. Don't you know that three meters under the water you can't see a thing? It couldn't steer, your fish-boat. It would break its nose on the slightest obstacle."

"Even so, Papa, it's going to go. Read that notice. It's even taking passengers, who won't suffer from sea-sickness!"

"Yes, I've seen it. I don't understand why it hasn't been forbidden. Oh, if I were the government..."

Papa wants everything that annoys him forbidden, along with everything that disturbs his habits and everything that he doesn't understand.

In spite of everything, what a woman wants, God wills. You put the proverb into application with your husband; for want of anything better and until further instructions, I only apply it to Papa.

By dint of coaxing, I ended up, not without difficulty, in getting his consent—but I ought to add, to be frank, that he was utterly convinced that *Le Désiré* wouldn't be going anywhere. Perhaps he doubted its existence. He'd never have given in otherwise.

---

with the Académie des Science in 1877, a year before Edison patented the phonograph.

Le Désiré does exist, however—I can vouch for that. It has a very strange appearance, though. Imagine a monster of the apocalypse in the form of a flattened cigar, almost as long as your drawing room in Kermorvan—Papa says that's about fifteen meters—and about as large in the middle as the sidewalk in the Rue Auber, with a pointed muzzle, a shiny copper tail, ludicrous fins and large crystal portholes reminiscent of living eyes. On the top, about a meter fifty above the crests of the waves, there was a light canvas walkway supported by collapsible metal colonnettes, like telescope tubes, which reminded me of the elephants' palanquins in the Jardin d'Acclimatation. When the sea is calm and *Le Désiré* is sailing on the surface, the passengers can go up on that balcony, but when the sea becomes heavy and there's a danger of spray, the walkway is retracted, the hatches are hermetically battened down—see, I'm already talking like a sailor!—and the boat dives. You can't imagine how amusing it is!

As you can imagine, there was an enormous crowd to watch us leave. They clapped loudly as we went by.

"There's a little blonde who hasn't got cold feet! Bravo, bravo, little lady!"

It was almost in my ear that a tall young man dressed as a sailor, with a clue collar and a waxed cap, shouted that at me, as I was setting foot on the walkway. My God, it was a trifle familiar, but it gave me pleasure all the same. I looked at the sailor and smiled at him, to thank him. Was that naughty of me? He had such white teeth, and such a nice profile, like those one sees on old medals, with skin the color of a ripe orange.

Papa was in a terrible mood. He was walking stiffly without looking at anyone, with the clenched features he has at official ceremonies. It was only when we were about to embark that he relaxed. At the extremity of the breakwater we passed a little man with salt-and-pepper hair, very elegant, with long red-brown moustaches curled up at the ends, and disturbing eyes—my God what eyes!—as sharp as gimlets, that drilled into you. Papa knew him, for, after having saluted him, he went toward him with his hands extended. But the little man slipped away. He returned Papa's salute, winked at him, put his finger over his lips, and then, without saying a word, turned away and was lost in a group of unsavory-looking individuals.

"He's not very amiable, your friend," I said to Papa.

"That's Monsieur Marigron," he said.

"Who's Monsieur Marigron? An engineer?"

"No, no. Marigron, you know, is the head of the Sûreté."

"Oh! That doesn't prevent him from being polite, even if he is the head of the Sûreté."

"You don't get it, you silly girl," Papa said, impatiently. "Monsieur Marigron's on duty. He must be on the lookout for some criminal. I assume so…that's why he didn't want to be recognized."

It's possible, as father says, that I'm only a silly girl, but I think that when one doesn't want to be recognized one doesn't go out with eyes like that. At the very least, one does what General Boulanger does and puts dark glasses over them. Then again, I also think that when one is recognized, no duty, lookout or criminal ought to prevent you from having a little chat with friends, especially if there's a lady, who isn't yet, so far as I know, very frightening…

We haven't finished, anyway, with Monsieur Marigron. It's necessary, in fact, that I tell you…but let's not get ahead of ourselves, as your husband says all the time, in the Chambre, when he's talking to that old minister who's so angry and so ugly.

It was the inventor of the submarine boat, Claudius Bouget in person, who welcomed us on to the walkway and did us the honors.

I'll give you a sketch of the fellow in four strokes of the pen. Very tall, barrel-chested, neck like a bull, massive shoulders, a tumultuous face but full of energy, and an astonishingly square chin, planted vertically like a block of bronze; a solid chap, about thirty years old, giving the impression at first glance of a Hercules—the Farnèse Hercules, if the marble were made flesh. Certainly, with his broad cheeks, his moustache as stiff as a brush and his big head already going gray, his leonine silhouette, his rude jaw, his brick red complexion and his ruddy nose, he's not what we'd have called a handsome fellow when we were still in short skirts. On the other hand, thought, there's so much harmony in his lines, so much elegance in his gestures and his bearing, so much softness and pride in his gaze—the luminous gaze of a hypnotizer, tender and harsh by turns, flamboyant not moist, beneath bushy eyebrows—with his musketeer swagger and a certain chivalrous, determined, bold and cheerful air about him, frank and gracious at the same time, that his entire person radiates charm. He positively fascinates people around him, and even Papa was taken with him.

I confess that when we had to go down into the boat by means of the little iron spiral staircase as narrow as a ladder pierced in the rod, I felt a vague frisson, and a desire to run away crossed my mind—but the captain looked at me in such a fashion that I got my confidence and courage back immediately. He must be a magnetizer, that man, I'm sure of it, in his spare time. One senses that one would follow him to the ends of the Earth, and even further. Besides, Papa was grumbling; I didn't want to seem as if I was afraid, you see—so, bravely, I plunged into the hole. *All right!* As Miss Maud, our old English mistress use to say, when she finished her lesson.

"Well, Mademoiselle, here you are in the belly of the monster. It's not too bad, as you see."

The fact is that there was nothing disagreeable about the place.

We were in a little circular boudoir, with carpets, divans, curtains, electric lights, knickknacks and a piano. By way of windows, there were immense lumps of glass held in iron frames, through which one could see gray-green water, as in the aquarium tanks at the Trocadero. In the middle of the floor there was a big round bowl, like the bowls at the fair at Neuilly where the trained seals are shown, surrounded by a red velvet balustrade. At the bottom, there was another immense horizontal sheet of glass, through which the ocean bed was visible. In one corner, there was a kind of keyboard, with taps and handles, and little machines that looked like stout watches with needles running round graduated scales, which serve, apparently, to indicate depth, direction, air pressure, etc., and telephonic apparatus. That was the captain's post; it's from there that he directs the maneuvers, while chatting with his guests. As for the crew, one doesn't see them. In addition to the salon, in fact, *Le Désiré* has two other compartments: the forward chamber, where the lookout is stationed who lights the way ahead and signals obstacles, and the rear chamber, where the mechanics supervise the electric batteries and the engine.

No doors! One passes from one chamber to another with the aid of an extremely original system of communications, which I recommend. One gets into a sort of niche carved out in the wall, and presses a switch. Click! The niche pivots on itself and you find yourself, in the blink of an eye on the other side, without the bay having remained open for an instant. In a word, it's a kind of mobile sentry-box, like those double sea-shells one sometimes finds on beaches. You must have seemed rotating spy-holes in cloistered convents established on a similar model. It's like that, it appears, in case there's an accident in one of the compartment. The inventor explained it at length to Papa, who couldn't believe his ears.

"Do you understand, Monsieur? If a leak is produced, after a collision, in the pilot's post, or if, for some reason, the piles produce asphyxiating gases in the mechanics' post, or the engine is damaged, or the pumps swell up—any breakdown whatsoever, in brief—there's not the slightest danger. Not a drop of water or bubble of gas can filter through these doors, whose cracks are sealed automatically, as you can see, by rubber joints. You're as safe here as in an express train."

"Yes, yes," Papa replied, "I can see that. But if your apparatus breaks down, how can you get back to the surface, even if you're only four or five meters beneath it? What does it matter, in that case, that nothing can filter through the watertight doors, if we're obliged to stay there, in the middle of the Channel, under water, until someone comes to look for us."

"Well, Monsieur, you're forgetting the safety weight. Here, look at this button. It controls a lead weight of 12,000 kilograms suspended beneath the keel, and I only have to turn it—like this, see!—for the ballast to sink to the bottom, while the boat bobs up like a cork to the surface, where we can, without inconvenience or danger, open our hatches and await rescue. Believe me before taking aboard passengers, I've tested that emergency anchor thoroughly, at my own risk."

Personally, I was convinced. Papa was still kicking. When one has been a naval construction engineer, one doesn't like to admit—especially in front of civilians—that one is mistaken.

But that reminds me that I haven't introduced you to our traveling companions. Oh, it's soon done.

Firstly, there was the young Spanish bride with her lord and master; then two nasty-looking fellows with badly-dyed yellow beards and cloth caps—Englishmen, evidently—who never stopped playing cards, without unclenching their teeth, while drinking something colorless that smelt like varnish. Then a bald man, very wizened, wearing spectacles—at great scientist, it appears, a famous zoologist; Papa told me his name but I've forgotten it—who was taking notes all the time in a huge notebook and muttering gibberish.

That's all. Or, rather, that was all, until the moment of departure. At that moment, in fact, an incident occurred that almost degenerated into a tragedy. It's at this point that the plot thickens.

The captain had just given his men to prepare to cast off; the uprights of the walkway had already been retracted. A sailor was getting ready to lower the heavy lid of thick glass over the stairwell that serves as a kind of skylight for the submarine boat, when someone suddenly leapt from the quayside on to the boat, whose bronze hull resonated like a bell under his heels, squeezed through the half-open hatchway, and tumbled into the salon, at the risk of breaking his neck.

It was a man of about forty, vigorous, well-built, with regular features, but pale and weary, with a sharp gaze and a sly look about him; his lips were too red, his sideburns too black, his shirt too white and he had too many rings on his fingers, like those "posers" we saw once in the Plaza del Toros and whom your husband called, I think, "flashy foreigners."

"What does this mean?" exclaimed Claudius Bouget, launching himself toward the intruder with a menacing expression. "My boat isn't a circus, damn it! Why are you coming aboard with a perilous leap, without warning?"

"I beg your pardon, M'sieur," the flashy foreigner replied, with a pronounced Italian accent, "but I am in a great hurry. It's absolutely necessary that I reach London this evening, and I missed the ferry. If I hadn't leapt the way I did, I couldn't have got aboard. Besides, I am known. I am *il marchese* de Maltoti. Here are my papers. And this is to pay for my passage."

"Good, good!" said the captain, somewhat mollified. "As long as you have papers. It's already five past noon...but it doesn't matter. Next time, try to be a little less casual..."

"I beg your pardon," repeated the supposed marquis, who was becoming even paler, and whose entire body as gripped by a nervous tremor. "A thousand pardons! But I beg you, will we be leaving soon?"

"We are leaving," said Monsieur Bouget. "We've left."

In fact, a bizarre trepidation was beginning to make the floor and walls vibrate, while singular ripples of light were running over the windows. I wanted to cast one last glance at the world where one can breathe. It was then that I perceived the short gentleman with the salt-and-pepper hair, the long turned up brown moustaches and the eyes of an inquisitor standing on the last step of the landing stage, which was full of gendarmes, who was waving his arms and shaking a piece of paper. He was certainly signaling to *Le Désiré*, trying to stop her leaving. For sure, he had something to say to the captain, and as Monsieur Marigron was the head of the Sûreté it had to be something very important and very urgent. For sure, if I had told the captain, who was absorbed at that moment in the delicate operation of getting under way, what I alone had observed, he would immediately have stopped his boat...but I wasn't about to show any zeal on behalf of a keen-eyed magistrate who turns his back on people who salute him, under the shoddy pretext that he's on duty.

Anyway, two seconds later, the water passed over the boat and the land had disappeared. We were submerged, and I was entirely overwhelmed by the novelty of the experience.

My God, it's wonderful!

First of all, one can't hear anything, except for the purr of the electrical machinery, like the wing-beat of a giant fly, the creaking of the timbers and a continuous rustle, as if someone were crumpling silk in the next room, which is produced by the friction of the water. No shaking at all. Nothing resembling the swaying movement, so fatal to weak stomachs, of old-style ships, nor the enervating tremolo of railways. It's a gentle glide, like that of the blade of a knife cutting into butter.

But what a feast for the eyes! Green everywhere, more green and green forever! The entire spectrum of greens, with fugitive flickers of yellow and blue, from the tender green of newly-sprouting buds to the darkest bottle-green, passing through olive, apple-peel, dying frog, pear, ultramarine and goose-caca. There's a dazzling emerald. A greenish light inundates the interior of the boat, and as one could see clearly enough by it, without lighting the electric bulbs, the two Englishmen continued their game of cards imperturbably, while the wizened old scientist was feverishly taking notes and *il marchese* de Maltoti was no less feverishly examining papers that he took from a portfolio stuffed with banknotes. Our very faces were green; one might have thought that we were traveling inside an immense bottle, like the ones pharmacists mount, by way of a sign, over the gas-jets in their display-windows.

And all sorts of fantastic forms swim within it: bearded mushrooms like blocks of gelatin, nacreous, polychromatic and transparent, which are jellyfish; long silky ribbons, which are algae; then schools of fish of all sizes and colors. There are black ones, white ones, pink ones, blue ones and iridescent ones. There are yellow ones, which the wizened old scientist recognized, and named in Latin as they passed by. There are some that look as if they were made of gold, others of silver or copper. Some—rays, for example—resemble the gargoyles of Gothic cathedrals. Is it possible that there are so many differences between the free ray, seen as if at home, and the black butter ray?[18]

The boat doesn't seem to frighten the animals. On the contrary, they follow it, and flock toward it from all parts of the depths, like moths attracted by a candle. A few came to bump their noses into the windows, as if asking to come in. Doubtless we interest them as much as they interest us. The wizened old scientist was delighted—me too. Only Papa was pinching his lips, but I suppose that was to stop an exclamation of admiration slipping out.

When one looks up, through the glass in the ceiling, one perceives a large luminous circle through which one divines, rather than distinguishing, the sky and its clouds, as if one were at the bottom of an enormous funnel-shaped well. It makes a clear path, the moving borders of which are cut up by the splashing of the swell, and there the rays of sunlight dissolve, fragmented and tremulous, as if they were passing through lowered Venetian blinds.

When one looks down, through the glass in the seal-pool, one sees the sea bed fleeing underfoot. One might think that it's vast flat carpet, unrolled by invisible hands, without creases or fissures, and with no relief.

As I was marveling in astonished at that unexpected uniformity the captain suddenly said: "Don't be deceived, Mademoiselle, That's only an optical illusion, which arises from the fact that all the visible parts receive equal illumination, so that there are no shadows cast. In reality, the ground that seems

---

[18] Ray (i.e. skate wing) with black butter sauce is a standard French dish.

uniform to you is bristling with bizarre protrusions and clefts, some of which are very deep.

"Furthermore, nothing is easier than to demonstrate the fact. The spectacle's worth the trouble. We're just at the deepest point of the Channel. I'm going to stop the boat for a moment and go down fifty meters or so, almost to the bottom—you'll see!"

At this point Papa, who had been surreptitiously chewing his handkerchief for several minutes, could not contain himself any longer. "Are you mad?" he cried. "You want to stop the boat and go down fifty meters? But we'll no sooner have stopped than the boat will rise up—fffrrritt!—like a de-ballasted balloon. It won't be too soon, moreover. If you think I'm here for my pleasure…!"

"I beg your pardon," replied Claudius Bouget. "I'm going to stop *Le Désiré*, and, instead of rising up to the surface, it will not only descend fifty meters but remain there, stationary, without deviating from the horizontal, for as long as Mademoiselle pleases."

"Get away!" said Papa furiously. "That's contrary to all the laws of physics!"

"Monsieur," the captain riposted. "I never argue—I prove. Please pay attention."

Then, putting his mouth to the mouthpiece of the telephone, he gave his orders. Immediately, the purr of the engine stopped, while the gurgle of the water changed pitch, becoming higher and higher, and the darkness thickened around us, as if *Le Désiré* were sinking into a sea of ink.

"You haven't felt anything, Mademoiselle?" Monsieur Bouget went on. "Nevertheless, we've descended from ten meters to fifty-five—which is to say that we've fallen from the height of two six-story houses. Now, look!"

Abruptly, a powerful electric light lit up beneath the boat, illuminating the "landscape" all around. We were at the bottom of a submarine gorge, a kind of drowned street between two rows of high hills, bizarrely sculpted, velveted from top to bottom with giant fronds of wrack. In the midst of that chaos swarmed a host of monsters, to which the caprices of refraction and the blinking of the searchlight lent fabulous forms and implausible colorations, while down below, on the tormented floor, strewn with precipices and projections, were heaps of unidentifiable debris: broken pieces of wood half-buried in the mud, pieces of broken masts, rusty old cannons, twisted and broken anchors, and so on, like a demolition yard.

In truth, my dear, it's a cemetery of ships! How many unfortunate men are sleeping eternally there? In one gutted carcass caught between two spurs of rock as if between the jaws of a vice, almost entirely covered with parasitic vegetation, I could make out vague letters by the light of the diabolical reflector.

"The *Salut*," murmured the steward, at my side, "out of Saint-Malo. Twenty-five crewmen. It was returning from Norway, ten years ago, on a foggy night when it was rammed, holed and sunk by an English steamer. All hands lost."

The *Salut!* The homicidal fatality of these ironies! And there are perhaps a hundred in the same state, at the bottom of the Channel alone—one imperceptible point in the midst of the immensity of the oceans.

Le Désiré moved around slowly by means of its oars—for it's necessary to tell you that it can be moved by oars as well as electricity—scarcely a meter above that necropolis, almost touching the tips of masts, turning the corners of rocks, rising and falling in turn, sometimes pivoting on itself like a dog trying to catch its tail, or even coming to a dead stop.

"Are you convinced?" the captain asked Papa, abruptly. "Has this proof reckoned with your prejudices?"

Papa is obviously too honest to deny evidence, but he doesn't like being proved wrong…in public. He didn't reply, but, turning his back on Monsieur Bouget, and frowning, he went to drum his fingers on the windows while he watched dabs going by. Monsieur Bouget simply shrugged his shoulders, with a broad smile.

"Let's go back up," I said. "This hurts my heart and makes me feel ill."

"*A la disposicion de usted, señorita,*" the captain replied, switching off the searchlight. He speaks very good Castilian.

We arrived at the surface in one bound, in the splendor of the external light. We saw the sky again, the sun, the liquid plain, the vast horizon, limited in the distance to the north by a dark line—that was the English coast.

A few cables away from *Le Désiré*, to our right, was a little steamship displaying the French flag, coming straight for us at top speed.

"Why," said the captain, "it's the customs yacht from Calais. Why the devil is she traveling so fast? Do they take us for smugglers? He ha! We'll play a little game of hide and seek, Messieurs!"

And he made *Le Désiré* dive again.

"Aargh!" one of the Englishmen, suddenly, throwing away his cards. "What's that?"

"Aargh!" repeated the other, like an echo. "What is it?"

It was a shock, as you can well imagine. Those frightful islanders hadn't opened their mouths since we set off, except to pour in that colorless liquid that smelled like turpentine—so completely that I took them for deaf-mutes. To get them excited, something seriously extraordinary had to be happening.

Oh, my dear, what a fright you'd have had! Imagine a chimerical beast, the size of a man, a kind of octopus with a swollen skin, as if varnished, with a metallic gleam, full of big creases; four unequal tentacles like sacks, arranged like arms and legs; a huge round head with enormous bulging eyes as skinny as balls of glass; and a kind of spike, slender and pointed like an épée, sixty centimeters long, at the end of one of its twitching arms; lop-sided and thrashing around, pirouetting and tumbling in eccentric contortions, very close to us, tapping insistently on the window of the salon—which rendered a crystalline sound under its assaults.

"It's a swordfish!" cried the suspicious Italian.

"Never in this life," riposted the old scientist, adjusting his spectacles. "The swordfish doesn't carry its spur on the end of its flipper but on its nose. We are, Mesdames et Messieurs, in the presence of an unknown animal of which no zoologist has spoken thus far, and which, in consequence, we have the right to baptize, without anyone being able to say any different. It's evidently an unknown variety of cephalopod of colossal dimensions. I therefore propose to call it *Polypus quadrupes giganteus*, or simple *Polypus desirati*, in honor of the submarine boat that first discovered it. What luck, and what glory! That cephalopod will be the crowning glory of my life..."

"You might just as well baptize it *Polypus tricolor*," Papa interjected. "Look at that red, white and blue girdle of sorts around its torso. One might think that it's the sash of a Commissaire of Police."

"Commissaire of Police!" exclaimed Monsieur de Maltoti, in a changed voice. "Who said Commissaire of Police?"

But no one replied to the antipathetic foreigner, who collapsed like a wet rag on the divan, his eyes haggard and his mouth convulsed. The crowning glory of the decrepit scientist's life ended up hanging on to the starboard fin and trying to drive its sword into the joint of the hatchway.

"He's going to make us take on water, your accursed *Polypus!*" the captain cried, suddenly, in a tone of inexpressible fury. "Wait a minute, wretched cephalopod—we'll see if you like dynamite!"

And, opening a drawer, he took out a small cartridge as thick as a stick of asparagus, to which he hastened to fit a detonator, while explaining his hurried words to Papa what he was proposing to do.

"Look under that porthole," he said, "at that bronze conch. Two symmetrical tubes...same system as my doors...without a single drop of water being able to ooze through, I can put anything through it...a dispatch, a signal, a petard...I could out a man through it if the hold were big enough. This cartridge of dynamite, one electric spark...and the monster's thunderstruck!"

109

But there was no need to have recourse to that desperate means. Don't forget that we were still sinking. Suddenly, the *Polypus gianteus* let go of the fin, its body swelling up strangely, as if some mysterious ventilator had blown air between its hide and its flesh; it rotated on its axis momentarily and then, its flippers widespread, it rose up abruptly, head down, like a corpse being fished out with a rope. In the blink of an eye it had disappeared.

It was just as well! We had all—including the captain, who gave the impression of being inaccessible to terror—had five minutes of intense anguish: the kind of anguish of which one can die. Perhaps I would have died if the heady interior atmosphere of the submarine boat hadn't given me courage, tone and resilience. It's not ordinary air, in fact, that one breathes therein, but compressed oxygen…and that has an effect on you—oh, what an effect!—like two fingers of Roederer. Do you remember that story by Jules Verne, *Le Docteur Ox*, I think, that we read together at Cauterets last summer? You remember—it's the story of an Eiffel Tower that revolutionizes an entire town because the air one breathes at the top is so pure, so oxygenated, that everyone who goes up it feels cheered up, overexcited, galvanized, overflowing with energy, strength, courage, ardor and passion, while torpor and somnolence reign down below. Well, aboard *Le Désiré*, still thanks to oxygen, it's the same thing. How brave one feels inside! How much vigor, energy, faith and hope one feels— noble sentiments, hectic desires to embrace some holy cause...

But my letter is taking on the dimensions of a quarto volume. It's time I decided to get to the end...

We had been traveling all the while, so rapidly that we had reached Dover. Someone shouted: "Land!" in the forward chamber. A shadow fell across the windows, like the blurred profile of an immense scaffold. It was a boom, and a jetty. We came up, brushing the pillars; we were at the quay, level with the staircase to the wharf, where an enormous crowd had gathered, even denser than in Calais, howling "Hip, hip, hurray!" at the top of their voices.

I was nearly mad—mad with pride and joy...or, rather, as if I were drunk, drunk on intensive oxygen. Then I saw red. It appears that when one emerges from a green environment, it's a fatal effect. It's the law of complementary colors, formulated by the illustrious Chevreul.[19] Such, at least, was the explanation given gratis to Papa by the wrinkled scientist.

But what's all this tumult? The customs yacht that we saw at sea lands at the same time as us. A strange creature comes out of it, dragging his lead-soled feet painfully, dressed in waxed canvas, with a glass helmet tipped over his back, a tricolor belt around his waist and a bayonet in his fist—in brief, our *Polypus quadrupes giganteus desirati* in person, but with salt-and-pepper hair, long curled-up russet moustaches and the piercing eyes of Monsieur Marigron, the head of the Sûreté!

While the English mob carries Claudius Bouget away in triumph, Monsieur Marigron pounces on *il marchese* Maltoti. "You're the murderer of the Rue Vivienne!" *Tramp, tramp*, go the gendarmes, marking time with their big boots. "I arrest you in the name of the law!"

Well, yes, my dear Hélène, it was very simple. On the quay in Calais Monsieur Marigron was laying in wait for the murderer, knowing that he hadn't been able to catch the ferry *Empress Victoria*, which was too closely watched. That was why he hadn't greeted us more courteously, so keen was he to maintain his incognito until the last moment. When his prey, slightly by my fault—now I'm abetting the flight of malefactors!—had escaped him, he's jumped aboard the customs yacht in pursuit. Having perceived *Le Désiré en route*, he'd been unable to contain his impatience and, at the risk of his life he'd made a descent in a diving-suit. He was the unknown cephalopod that had tried to break in through our window, at

---

[19] Michel Eugène Chevreul (1786-1889), author of *De la loi du contraste simultané des couleurs et de l'assortiment des object colorés* (1839; tr. as *The Principles of Harmony and Contrast of Colors, and Their Applications to the Arts*).

the risk of sinking us, with his sash and his saber...borrowed from a gendarme. Except that, inexperienced in the diving business, once he arrived at a certain depth, disorientated by the excessive pressure, he hadn't been able to regulate the flow of air, which, blowing up his diving-suit excessively, had brought him back to the surface unexpectedly, feet first.

But he wasn't to be discouraged by such trivia, and we found him again at Dover, still in submarine costume, ready to do his duty no matter what the cost.

That audacity ought to reconcile me with him. How can one bear a grudge against a hero?

But you see, little Jeannette is something of one herself—a heroine, that is.

She could tell you a host of other things no less interesting, but it's necessary to know when to stop. I'll leave that for another time.

A thousand kisses.

Jeanne de G***

P.S. I can't, however, dispense with telling you that I'm getting married. I'm marrying the captain of *Le Désiré*. Papa is doubtless definitively converted to the cause of submarine navigation. How could it be otherwise?

Your Jeanne.

Camille Debans: *Fire Island*
(1893)

The little fort of Salem, in Brazil, is situated on the right bank of the river Amazon, almost directly opposite Para, a few leagues from the sea. It is the most boring place in the world, if you believe travelers' tales, and Dom Luiz Vagaërt had become the most splenetic officer in the Brazilian army since had been the deputy governor there.

The garrison comprised less than a hundred soldiers. Beneath the walls of the citadel vegetated a poor village sheltering a hundred negroes of both sexes, with whom a few Indians, former cannibals, came to mingle from time to time, in order to sell the produce of their hunting. There was not an intelligent face in the entire colony, and not a single white woman for five leagues around. The governor was married, it is true, but he was a Platonic governor who administered at a distance, because he lived in Bahia.

Dom Luiz Vagaërt therefore found himself the absolute master of the fort. In addition to his functions as deputy governor, he fulfilled those of magistrate, and rendered justice without appeal. Moreover, he was considered as an officer of the civil estate, and the local priest had asked him more than once to ring the bells and assist him at mass, to which he lent himself with a very good grace.

To combat the boredom Dom Luiz had, in the early days, devoted all his spare time to hunting. When he had a carpet in his bedroom made from the skins of twenty jaguars that he had killed, however, the poor deputy governor was obliged to admit that wild animals, dead or alive, no longer amused him. He went after caimans instead, but the caimans could not succeed in relieving the tedium.

Then he imagined that hunting snakes might procure him the distraction he needed, and, arming himself with a flask of ammonia, he went in search of rattlesnakes, vine snakes and all sorts of dangerous reptiles. He built up a fine collection. It was even said that a terrarium could be seen in his study in which fifty special flowers served as a residence for fifty living coral snakes. The coral snake is the most charming reptile in the world. Bright red, about as long as the penholder I have in my fingers at present, it lives in the calices of flowers, from which it gladly leaps out at humans, to whom its bite is fatal in less time than it takes a scientist to collect a prize.[20]

One day, Pedro Baçao, a simple soldier, and João, a sergeant, formulated a plan to go and see for themselves whether what was said was true. They climbed into the famous study through the window and searched for the terrarium with their eyes. It was set against the wall facing the door. The two soldiers approached, Pedro trembling and João negligently waving a little segment of a liana that he was holding.

It was an admirable spectacle that they beheld. In almost every flower, a coral snake was coiled up, seemingly nourishing itself on perfumes. Four or five hummingbirds were fluttering around the terrarium, and at intervals, one of the reptiles, weary of the sound of its wings, would brace itself and leap at a bird, which it never reached.

Suddenly, João's face took on an expression of sinister malice. Choosing a moment when Pedro, slightly reassured, was leaning over to see better, the sergeant—by way of a joke—slid his twig between the stems of the plants on which the frightful beasts were sleeping, and, with a slight movement, gave the flexible liana a vibrant impulsion that shook the receptacle of sudden death.

As rapid as thought, João then made his escape through the window. A hundred shrill hisses resounded in Pedro's

---

[20] Coral snakes are usually larger than this description and striped, but there are numerous species, so it might be overly hasty to reject this description out of hand as pure fantasy.

ears; he also tried to run away but collapsed as soon as he reached the courtyard. His brother, who was standing guard at the deputy governor's door, dropped his rifle in order to go to his aid, but it was too late. Five or six reptiles had bitten him. He went black, and scarcely had the strength to say what had happened.

Alfonso Baçao, the dead man's brother, leaned over the cadaver, kissed the forehead, went to pick up his rifle, and loaded it; a shot rang out and Sergeant João fell dead.

A few moments later, the deputy governor, on returning to the fort, discovered what had happened, had Alfonso arrested, and announced that a court martial would pass sentence on the murderer the next day. The latter was, indeed, brought before the Dom Luiz Vagaërt twenty-four hours later, and, as the deputy governor was even more bored that day than usual, he pronounced the death sentence in a perfectly calm voice.

The execution was to take place the following day, Thursday 16 September 1857.

Since the fort and the village of Salem had existed, no sentence of capital punishment had been pronounced, either on one of the inhabitants or one of the soldiers of the garrison. It was, in consequence, an event, and the deputy governor, who had doubtless judged Alfonso Baçao in accordance with his soul and his conscience, was not far from thinking that it might distract him slightly.

A crowd gathered on the ramparts at nine o'clock in the morning on that Thursday. The word "crowd" is perhaps ambitious, but everything is relative, and since the entire population of Salem was there, it would be ridiculous to remember that here at home, a hundred people do not constitute an assembly.

The entire garrison was under arms. The deputy governor, on horseback, was to preside over the execution, and while a picket of a dozen soldiers went to fetch the condemned man, Dom Luiz Vagaërt set himself at the head of his troop, who arranged themselves militarily in a square around the lace of execution.

Nine o'clock chimed on the deputy governor's watch. A frisson ran through the assembly. The condemned man had not yet appeared, however. Dom Luiz Vagaërt was very pale, and did not seem overly desirous of knowing the reason of a delay so little in harmony with military habits.

Finally, the sergeant in command of the execution detail arrived, out of breath, and, making expansive gestures before being able to speak, gave the deputy governor to understand that the prisoner had escaped.

At this news, Dom Luiz recovered his true colors, uttered a sigh of relief and murmured, in a low voice: "That Alfonso is not only a brave man but an intelligent fellow. His escape is the most unexpected and most agreeable thing that could have happened; we can spend at least a week searching for him. That will be seven days killed, and I hope that will be all, because we won't find him. All the more reason, though, to chase him."

"Comrades!" cried the deputy governor, from the back of his horse, "the guilty man has run away from the rigor of the law. Our duty is to do everything to ensure that Alfonso Baçao, condemned to be executed by firing squad by an authorized tribunal, is recaptured and shot as soon as possible. In consequence, we're going to set out on campaign right away, and a reward of twenty douros will be given to any soldier or sub-officer who brings him back, dead or alive. Forward march!"

And, continuing his monologue, Luiz said to himself: "He must have a good start. I could have promised a hundred thousand douros."

On the night that should have preceded his execution, Alfonso Baçao had received a visit from Salem's priest, to whom he had confessed his sins. Then, when he had been asked whether he had any last request before going to his death, he had asked for a bottle of eau-de-vie, which had been

116

brought to him, with the permission of the civil and military authorities—which is to say, Dom Luiz.

Half of that eau-de-vie had served to fill a gourd that the prisoner had in his cell, and the rest was generously offered to the sentinel charged with guarding him. The soldier had put up token resistance but Alfonso insisted so graciously that the other had not dared to offer a final insult to a comrade who was about to die by refusing. The sentinel had, therefore, accepted, out of a sense of propriety, drunk out of politeness and fallen asleep thanks to drunkenness. Baçao had then dragged the drunken man into his cell, and put himself on guard in his stead. It was then two o'clock in the morning.

Alfonso had not had time to get his bearings before a patrol was heard in the darkness. The sentinel was about to be relieved. The condemned man slapped his forehead in despair. When the password was exchanged he was sure to be recognized; he needed a miracle to save him. To take flight was impossible. Baçao waited.

The corporal in command of the patrol was some sort of half-breed who had come, no one knew why, from the Republic of Argentina, to which he had no desire to return. Fortunately, the man did not speak very good Portuguese, and Alfonso, realizing that, judged that it would not be difficult to deceive him. It was, however, the return to the guard-room that constituted the greatest danger. Until then, there was nothing to fear—the troopers and the half-breed were practically sleep-walking—but if, as always happens, there was a single insomniac among the soldiers at the post, all was lost.

Alfonso made a supreme resolution. The patrol was marching along the ramparts in a disorderly fashion. Fortunately, Fort Salem had never been besieged, and yet there was, in the eastern wall of the fortifications a kind of breach commenced by the sun and continued by that invincible enemy, time.

The ramparts, made of earth supported by bricks, had suffered a small landslip at that point, and although it was difficult to climb up into the citadel by that route, so steep was the slope, a desperate many might try to let himself roll down to the bottom, at the risk of breaking his neck.

In any other part of the fort Alfonso would have needed a stout rope to descend the rampart, but this was not the moment to go and look for one. As for the gates, they were well-guarded, for Dom Luiz Vagaërt had too little to do at Salem not to have introduced a very severe discipline in what he referred to as his army.

So, at the moment when the patrol arrived at the location of the breach, Alfonso, who was bringing up the rear, moved to the edge of the abyss and let himself roll down the rampart. The half-breed and his subordinates, hearing the noise, thought it had been made by some ferocious beast and went back to the guard-room at the double. A man was missing. Someone claimed to have seen a jaguar carry him away through the breach; a second contended that it was a caiman; a third declared that he had heard the cry of a famished boa, which resembles the sound of a saw cutting through rotten wood. That was quite sufficient to persuade the soldiers to barricade the guard-room, with the result that the sentinel was not relieved again before daybreak.

We know what happened after that. The escape was discovered at nine o'clock. The soldier found in the prison, sleeping off his eau-de-vie, was sentenced to a month in the cell. The half-breed guessed the cause of the noise he had heard at the breach, but refrained from mentioning it, and it was decided that after the siesta—which is to say, at the moment when human heads can tolerate the equatorial sun—between forty and fifty men set forth with weapons and kit to explore the forest, in which they were to camp throughout the duration of the expedition.

The fugitive, let us hasten to say, was already far away. His voluntary fall had been accomplished in excellent conditions: brambles, long grass and a few flexible lianas had deadened his impacts; even though he had felt empty space beneath him after rolling for a few seconds and had fallen from a

118

height of seven or eight meters, he had only sustained a few bruises.

When the dizziness that followed the vertiginous descend had passed, Alfonso got to his feet and marched northwards. That was not the direction he intended to take, but the village was east of the fort, and he did not want to be seen by anyone who might give the slightest indication of the direction in which he had gone.

What the reader had just learned is necessary to the understanding of the story, but Alonso's frightful story only really starts at this point. In three days, the man had seen his brother die, slain by the most terrible venom in the world, had been condemned to death himself without have had time to mourn, had been subjected to all the anguish of the night that was supposed to precede his execution, and by virtue of his self-composure in the midst of a thousand alarms he had escaped that ignominious death. He was saved. It seemed, therefore, that bad luck had relaxed its grip on him.

Well, all that was nothing by comparison with the alarms, anguish and torments that the man had prepared for himself by escaping.

The danger of being recaptured was, however, only apparent. He had gone into the forest after skirting the village of Salem. The paths used by the negroes and Indians were familiar to him up to a certain distance. He thought it best to head east, his intention being to go as far as possible toward the sea, then to cross the Amazon and reach Para.

Alfonso certainly knew what an equatorial virgin forest is like, since he had been garrisoned at Salem for a year, and, if he ventured thus into the bushy desert, it was not because he had any choice of paths. He marched vigorously until daybreak, following a path he knew well. He was, however, obliged to stop frequently and hide in a bush or climb a tree in order to let a hunting jaguar pass by or to avoid some other wild beast.

At seven o'clock the sun suddenly appeared on the horizon. Alfonso darted a glance around him. The part of the forest he had reached was unknown to him, and he had covered a formidable distance. Fear had given him the agility and instinct of an animal.

In sum, he was safe and on the right route, for the sun's rays, which were slanting through the dense foliage, indicated to him by their direction that he was still heading eastwards. He was exhausted, though. For three days the poor devil had been unvisited by slumber, and he needed sleep in order to recover the strength to continue on his way.

Two giant cedars rose up into the air to an incredible height, almost side by side. Fifteen or twenty meters from the ground, a tangle of enormous lianas formed a kind of bridge—or, if you prefer, a kind of enormous hammock—extended between them.

The interlacement of branches permitted him to climb fairly easily up to the lianas, and he found a peculiarly embalmed bed there, covered with flowers and green leaves, on which he lay down sensually, invisible to anyone except the birds and the squirrels. At the moment when Dom Luiz Vagaërt learned of his escape, he was sleeping the most profound and reparative of slumbers.

Meanwhile, he had already advanced well beyond the parts of the forest that the soldiers of Salem were accustomed to visiting. Alfonso was about to enter the heart of the virgin forest, and that merits description for several reasons. The first is that it will difficult to form any idea of the sufferings of the man if one does not know what obstacles he had to overcome; the second is that those immense woods, which extend from the Andes to the Atlantic Ocean, over an extent of twelve hundred leagues, has only been described by fantasists, whose endeavors are deeply dappled with poetry but of highly dubious exactitude.

The veritable virgin forest, seen from the Amazon, appears to the traveler to be a green wall. To penetrate into it seems as easy as plunging into the granite of a sheer mountain.

Whatever people say, an ax is utterly impotent to clear a path through that verdure. There is only one means of opening a way and that is fire—a means that is dangerous, when it is not impracticable

If, guided by an Indian, you penetrate into the forest by means of one of its paths, the spectacle that meets your eyes is initially sublime: gigantic trees, formidable lianas, unknown flowers, odorous bushes, grasses that grow to eight feet in height, and brambles, thorn-bushes and enormous cacti.

In the midst of all that, you sense that a population of bizarre beings exists, for every plant whose stem moves, every liana subjected to flexion, every leaf that stirs and every rustle that is heard—every movement, in sum—is produced by a living creature, charming or hideous, inoffensive or deadly: a snake, a crocodilian, a enormous batrachian, a bird, a quadrumane and all the intermediate species, whose appearance alone often causes suffering.

But that truly grandiose and seductive spectacle you only find at the edges of virgin forests, having marched for an hour at the most along frequented paths. And of hazard or necessity takes you further, that changes. The branches then become so dense that to get through them one lacerates one's hands and face on thorns that grow indefinitely. To be sure, you are still walking on a path, but it is necessary to be a jaguar or an Indian to know how to crawl along it.

The trunks of the trees sometimes accumulate across the route to considerable heights, and in between the trunks, vigorous bushes grow. Gradually, the thickness of the wood takes on terrible proportions. "The impenetrable horror" of the classics becomes an absolute verity. It is no longer merely a tangle of lianas, climbing and thorny bushes; it is like a fabric of incredible density, of which sufficiently large trees sometimes constitute the loom.

The life of the wood's interior then becomes a swarm. To the right, to the left, in front of you, under your feet, above your head, everything stirs, jumps, sings, whistles or roars. Everything there is alive, and everything kills. Oh, if one could see the scene from the stalls of a theater, what a marvel! Myriads of birds of all hues and all dimensions perch and call to one another: macaws, cardinals, squawking parrots and a thousand others; while an army of monkeys descends on four or five cacao-trees, omitting the one to which a jaguar has come to extend death with a thrust of its paw.

Along the trees, like living lianas, snakes of every side glide silently, and a ray of sunlight penetrates by chance through the foliage, all the way to the ground, which shines strangely. In fact, it is not the ground that shines like that, but water—running water, for beneath that framework of upright, curved and twisted living trunks, one perceives that a river is running, all the more evidently when the enormous maw of a crocodile appears at the surface.

Is there any need to add that Alfonso, once awake, understood the full horror of his situation? He had at least ten leagues to cover in such terrain, and he needed to reckon at least four days for that, for, in order to advance securely in that wall, it would be necessary not to place a foot without having carefully examined the place where it would fall. He would not be able to go past a tree before making sure that there was no enemy behind it—not to mention the Indians, whose taste for human flesh might not have disappeared entirely.

He also needed to eat. What? Fruits? They were not easy to gather, and might he not make a mistake and swallow poison? Fortunately for him, he found a few birds' nests and ate the eggs therefrom. His hammock of lianas housed a dozen parrots' nests. It was a true feast, washed down with two or three mouthfuls of eau-de-vie, because he had brought his gourd.

His fatigue had not been appeased, however. Baçao understood, therefore, that in order to bring his escape to a successful conclusion, he needed more strength that he had as yet, and resolved to spend the night on his bed of flowers. He had good lodgings there, eggs in quantity, and he was far enough away from Salem to have nothing to fear. It was, therefore, an idea to which a sage could not have raised any objection.

The end of the day he spent exploring the surroundings, and found, in case he had to make a rapid getaway, a passage through which, with the aid of a little gymnastics, he could cover half a league in half an hour.

The next morning, Alfonso was woken up by a gunshot.

He started, without being conscious of where he was— but reflection comes quickly to a man for whom everything is a danger.

With infinite care, without giving his hammock of lianas the slightest oscillation, he tried to turn round to see where the noise had come from. A savage could not have carried out the maneuver any better than he did. It took him a full minute.

Then, slowly and sagely, taking a thousand precautions, he parted a few lianas and saw the half-breed twenty or twenty five meters below, who, with his discharged weapon in his hand, was looking attentively in all directions and cocking his ear at the slightest murmur, while the smoke of his rifle-shot rose slowly and capriciously into the air.

Alfonso did not budge. The Argentinean then examined the path attentively, and seemed to reflect momentarily. He looked up at the lianas, but saw nothing. By the demon's pantomime, it was easy to understand what he was doing here. The deputy governor of Salem had been wrong to think that Baçao was out of reach and that he could have promised a hundred thousand douros as a reward. At the announcement of the twenty douros, the half-breed's eyes had taken on an expression of sanguinary avidity and he had said to himself: *I'll have them tomorrow.*

He probably knew about escapes, for he had only asked for four men to accompany him, swearing that he would not come back without the prisoner.

Dom Luiz Vagaërt had been on the point of not grating that request, but it was necessary not to appear to be hindering the action of the law, and in any case, he was still hoping that

Baçao was out of range. He had granted the corporal his four men, and left in the opposite direction with the remainder of his troop.

The half-breed had gone to explore the paths that led east into the forest, knowing from experience that an intelligent man was bound to think about fleeing seawards.

After an hour of searching, he had found fresh tracks, trodden grass, small broken branches and, here and there, bushes that had been disturbed. That was enough, and more than enough, for a man with the instincts of an executioner. He took his four soldiers along the path that Alonso had taken. Fortunately, night had fallen, and the man-hunters were obliged to make camp.

Before sunrise, the impatient half-breed had departed alone in the direction indicated by the increasingly visible tracks, for as the forest became denser, Alfonso had been obliged to break more branches and trample more long grass.

Carried away by his ardor, the corporal had moved far ahead of his men, and arrived at the place where Alfonso had stopped. Oh, if he had known that his prey was sleep twenty meters above his head!

But the fugitive, in order to reach his hammock, had climbed between sixty-five and a hundred meters over the trunks of fallen trees, on the thick bark of which he had naturally left no footprints, with the result that the half-breed had stopped in his turn, like a dog that has lost a trail, sniffing, listening, looking, and suspecting that the man he was looking far might be huddling only a few paces away.

Too accustomed to virgin forests and the ruses of wood-runners to take the trouble of searching for Alfonso's retreat, which might be in any one of a thousand equally-undetectable places, the corporal had thought of firing a rifle shot into the air, telling himself, with reason, that even if Baçao was two hundred paces meters away, he would think that it had been fired close at hand, because of the density of the forest echoes. That was perfectly concluded, all the more so as the fugitive, still asleep, had awoken with a start and might easily have committed the imprudence of showing himself in the first moment of alarm.

But Baçao had understood the wretch's ruse, and remained motionless. Meanwhile, he had made a decision. The half-breed would not be alone, and if his companions arrived, it would not be one enemy he had to fight but two, ten or perhaps twenty—for Alfonso had no ways of knowing whether or not the entire Salem garrison was on his heels.

He thought about all that while watching the Argentinean.

The latter seemed to have given up hope and to have decided to wait, for he leaned back against a tree and made as if to reload his rifle.

That was a ray of hope for the fugitive. He had one shot to fire himself, for he had not let go of the rifle with which he had mounted guard for a minute before his escape, and the half-breed, if he lost time, would never catch up with him.

Taking all possible precautions, placing his weapon over his shoulder, after having drunk a mouthful of eau-de-vie, Alfonso suspended himself from a strong branch, whose foliage shaded in bed, and with the agility of a monkey he leapt from branch to branch all the way to the passage he had explored and prepared the day before

That was not accomplished, of course, without the silence being troubled, however slightly.

The half-breed's ear seized a slight rustling of foliage. He stood up, without continuing to load his rifle, and looked sharply in the direction from which the sound had come. He distinctly saw Alfonso passing from tree to tree, and then disappearing behind a kind of natural palisade formed by immense bushes with giant thorns.

He launched himself in pursuit of the fugitive, and in order to gain ground, like the cunning savage he was, he climbed up on to the bridge of lianas in order to follow the same route as Baçao rather than run into the impenetrable bushes that stood between him and his prey.

He was agile too, that terrible man, and, in the blink of an eye, with a surety that Alonso did not have, he had divined, taken and followed the passage prepared by the latter. But there, once again, he found no further trace of the fugitive. He only heard, from time to time, and to his right, a few rustling sounds that indicated Alfonso's position. The latter was evidently trying to get closer to the river, in order to try to escape by swimming.

The half-breed soon made his decision then. He resolved to pursue Baçao through the heights of the forest, since the floor was impossible. Nothing, in fact, was easier that making progress toward a goal by passing from one branch to another.

He climbed into an ebony-tree, from there to the crown of a gigantic oak, and followed the man condemned to death, whom he could not see, but whose flight he could hear. The stubborn hunter, now sure of success, judged that it was no more than a matter of time.

Alfonso, gaining in skill, slid through the trees like a reptile, only passing via the leafiest branches. He held his rifle in one hand, now ready to make use of it against the tiger with the human face who was hunting him.

Suddenly, Baçao, who was also fleeing through the forest heights, uttered an involuntary cry of despair. There was a clearing ahead of him, rather narrow, in truth, but there was nevertheless a gap in the interlacing of the trees. The only possibility was to go around the obstacle. He veered to the left, making as much haste as possible, and found himself face to face with the half-breed. The latter was twenty paces away, standing on an enormous trunk.

At the sight of the condemned man, whose head first appeared in the foliage, the Argentinean uttered a sinister burst of laughter, which resembled a roar. But that ferocious joy was of short duration, for, on seeing Alfonso armed with a rifle, which he had not suspected, the fellow, who had all the ignominies of a torturer in his soul, went pale and began to tremble. In his haste to pursue Baçao he had neglected to reload his weapon, and the condemned man was now standing on a very large branch, with his back to the trunk, and taking aim at the half-breed.

The latter beat a prompt retreat and took cover behind his tree.

Alfonso had an impulse of generosity.

"Gregorio!" he shouted. "Give up chasing me. Let me escape, and you'll live—but if you don't give me your word of honor now, if you don't swear by the Virgin that you'll go back to Salem, I'll climb up to the top of this oak in a minute and from there I'll shoot you down like a parrot as soon as you emerge from your hiding-place.

There was a silence. The half-breed reflected.

"Do you swear?" shouted the condemned man in a tremulous voice.

"I swear!" replied the half-breed.

"On your honor?"

"On my honor."

"And by the Virgin?"

"By the Virgin."

"That's good. Go away," said Alfonso, in a calm voice, as if he had been completely reassured by the latter oath, which is rarely broken by Brazilians of the common people.

The Argentinean came out of hiding then, and showed himself to Alfonso, in whose word he knew that he could have confidence.

The two men looked at one another curiously without saying anything. At any other time they would hardly have recognized one another; with their faces and hands torn by thorns, their clothes in tatters, and their eyes shining with an atrocious fever, they were hideous.

Alfonso was almost naked; droplets of blood were visible on his torso, forming beads everywhere that a thorn had dug in. Horrible red and yellow mosquitoes as long as a little finger were buzzing around him and sticking to his open wounds, whose pain they multiplied tenfold. The skin swelled terribly under their bites, and they only quit the unfortunate's face to settle on his hands or his agonized legs. His feet, al-

127

most bare and covered with insects, were just bloody lumps. The half-breed had only fared slightly better, but seemed less bloody, evidently being more accustomed to the forest.

"Go away," the fugitive repeated. He raised his rifle again and insisted: "Get lost!"

Gregorio finally came to a decision. "I was carrying out the deputy governor's orders," he said, "but I've sworn. You can rest easy—I'm going." And he began to draw away.

"Make sure you stay in sight," Baçao shouted after him. "I need to be able to see you for as long as possible."

The half-breed obeyed. He made his retreat, keeping himself in view and turning round from time to time to dart the gaze of a panther at Alfonso. Finally, he disappeared into the depths of the forest.

Until that moment, the condemned man, overexcited by fear, the indescribable emotion of the hunt in which he had been the prey, had not felt the horrible pain of his wounds and he mosquito bites, but when he found himself alone, when he collapsed, streaming with sweat, on the enormous branch from which he had threatened Gregorio, hunger, thirst, an insurmountable lassitude and the frightful smarting that was devouring his entire body became a torture so frightful that he repented not having gone with the half-breed to die in Salem, and was even tempted to call him back in order to surrender to him.

Add to that the fact that it was already eleven o'clock. The unbearable heat of the region was, on that day—the twenty-first of September—more stifling than ever. Baçao felt gusts of wind reaching him that were literally fiery. He thought that he was about to die.

One last mouthful of eau-de-vie still remained in his gourd; avidly, he put it to his lips. That steadied him momentarily, and he thought about eating—but his wounds, in that heat, were becoming more burning by the minute. He searched with his eyes for a lemon-tress. He thought he had perceived one at the foot of tree he was in, and climbed down. Alas, it was an illusion. For more than a hundred meters the unfortunate was obliged to search the undergrowth, injuring himself further, without finding the bush in question, so common in those latitudes.

Finally, at the foot of a mahogany, a clump of orange-trees and lemon-trees attracted him by the perfume of its flowers and the brightness of its fruits. He bit into an orange avidly, then a second, and then a third, and eventually contrived to slake his thirst. That was the most urgent matter. Only then did he squeeze the citrus juice over his torso, his feet, his hands and his face. That was like taking a bath. He felt that he was returning to life.

As on the previous day, eggs stolen from parrots' nests furnished him with breakfast. He was getting ready to sleep for a while under the orange-trees when he heard a rustling overhead.

It was the half-breed, who was coming back surreptitiously. The monster's intention, in swearing to go back to Salem, was to gain the time necessary to load his rifle at his ease. Having done that, he had returned to Alfonso's pursuit.

The anger that the Brazilian felt accumulating in his head at the sight of Gregorio is indescribable. He picked up his weapon, slipped silently through the bushes without losing sight of his enemy, and started climbing a cedar, in such a way that he would find himself once again, and for the last time, face to face with the half-breed. It was necessary to finish it.

Meanwhile, the heat was becoming more terrible and oppressive by the minute. Thick black clouds were skimming the tops of the tall trees and darkening the forest, to the extent that one might have thought that night had suddenly fallen. Then the sun reappeared a moment later, even hotter.

The heavy atmosphere seemed to weigh upon the two men's shoulders like a lead weight. Alfonso, sweating copiously, reached the top of his cedar without being seen by the half-breed, who was searching all the nearby trees with his eyes.

"Gregorio," he shouted to him, "Don't search any longer. You're a perjurer and a coward. One of us is going to die."

On hearing the voice, the corporal prudently ducked out of sight. The two of them were then ten paces apart, with a tree-trunk between them, each waiting for an opportunity to shoot.

The condemned man was in haste to be alone. He took off his straw hat, put it on the barrel of his rifle, and, trying to imitate the moment of a prudent head, extended it gently from a clump of foliage, while he remained safely sheltered.

Gregorio was taken in. He promptly shouldered his rifle and fired. The hat, pierced by a bullet, fell. A cry of triumph emerged from the monster's throat and he emerged from cover. Alfonso appeared and said: "This time, you're going to die. Say your prayer."

A thunderclap of unusual violence resounded above their heads, shaking the entire forest. The clouds heaped up in no time at all and the storm burst with an inconceivable fury. The forest had plunged back into darkness.

Alfonso understood that the most urgent thing was to get away. Without attempting to accomplish another murder, he abandoned the half-breed, in order to head as rapidly as possible for the river, which could not be far away.

For his part, the half-breed, thinking that Alfonso was waiting for a clear shot in order to kill him, took advantage of the darkness and ran away in the opposite direction.

Ten minutes later, although the clouds were even blacker and more opaque, the two adversaries would have been able to continue their terrible duel, for the electrical discharges were succeeding one another so rapidly that bloody and unbearable flashes were incessantly replacing the sunlight.

Our Europeans storms are paltry events by comparison with tropical hurricanes. One hears something like continual artillery fire, accompanied by lightning-bolts that intersect and reinforce one another, multiplying tenfold with each passing second. They are all the more dangerous because all the clouds pass rapidly over the treetops without bursting, and the light-ning falls ten times a minute upon the tallest cedars.

The half-breed, as agile as a jaguar, fled with all the speed as he could contrive. His experience of tropical storms told him that the forest might catch fire in the blink of an eye. He also knew—and this is what sustained his courage—that tempests as furious as the one rumbling above his head do not last long.

The lightning-flashes were, however, succeeding one an-other with ever-increasing rage. Sometimes, a thunderclap was heard whose noise was deafening; then there was another roll more frightful still, and a third, and still more! In every direc-tion, formidable electric sparks were precipitating themselves into that sea of verdure, with crackles in the sky. Nature seemed to be in the process of an immense collapse.

Around the fugitives, the wild beasts and snakes were agitated, seeking salvation in flight.

Gregorio was beginning to lose his firmness of purpose. A dead squirrel had just fallen two paces away from him, but not a drop of rain. Gradually, however, the reiterated dis-charges of thunder seemed less continuous. The sky was start-ing to seem less black. The lightning was becoming less fre-quent. The storm was diminishing.

The half-breed breathed deeply. A cloud had just burst over the forest. A sheet of water descended as in a deluge—but that only lasted for a matter of seconds, after which the sun reappeared.

It might have been three o'clock in the afternoon. Mo-mentarily, the savage Gregorio started reflecting, wondering whether he ought to resume his pursuit of Alonso. This time, though, it was virtually impossible, so far had they drawn apart during the storm. He gave up, and headed back toward Salem.

He had not been walking for ten minutes, however, when he heard loud noises overhead. It was two jaguars fleeing in convoy, with plaintive howls.

Gregorio paid them no heed. He continued on his way, crawling through the thorn-bushes and climbing plants, suspending himself from branches in order to move more freely. He was in his element, and was perfectly sure of his route. However, a band of tiger-cats, leaping from tree to tree, came toward him like a whirlwind. He thought he was doomed. The felines were uttering frightful cries, mewling in terror.

Near to the ground, the long grass and the stunted trees were now agitating in a disquieting fashion. There was a hideous confusion. Gigantic boas momentarily displayed their shiny and viscous rumps, and then disappeared, heading eastwards. Enormous lizards were fleeing in the same direction; birds were passing over the forest in flocks. There was nothing, including the giant ants of the region, that was not hurrying in the same direction. It was as if all those monsters were going to some horrible sabbat.

Gregorio began to get anxious. The tiger-cats, still screeching, passed over his head urgently, without seeing him or without deigning to pay attention to him. That was strange. On the other hand, the emigration of the reptiles and other living things was becoming more compact.

The grass was collapsing as so many individuals passed through it, and snakes could now be seen moving in hissing troops toward the river; huge toads, disturbed in their philosophical apathy, were hastening slowly in the same direction. Then there were deer, wild boar, bears and tapirs—an interminable caravan of quadrupeds.

Something was definitely happening. Was it a flood? A dull noise was beginning to make itself heard toward the north.

A crocodile in a hurry ploughed through a thorny bush and passed by rapidly. It could not be a flood.

Gregorio climbed to the top of a tree, not daring to say to himself, as yet: *It must be a fire, then!*

There was no need to climb up to the highest branches to distinguish an immense flame rising up from the north to the west. The entire forest was burning. In falling five hundred times, the lightning had probably set fire to the dry branches of resinous trees. The conflagration had spread in no time, and now there was a flaming arc that was about to tighten, as if to encircle him and annihilate him.

Gregorio blasphemed, and made his decision. He followed the tigers, the birds and the reptiles and ran eastwards, not quitting for an instant the direction that the forest's inhabitants had taken, for he knew that their instinct would guide them infallibly toward the Amazon.

But there could not be too much haste. The fire, having burst forth and embraced the tall trees in its writhing grip, was advancing rapidly over the forest floor, where dead leaves and inflammable bushes flared up as if by enchantment, with the result that before having the first to dread and running the risk of being burned alive, there was the threat of asphyxia—for the smoke was already spreading almost beneath the corporal's feet, and raising opaquely toward the vault of the forest.

Mad with fear, Gregorio leapt from branch to branch without worrying about cuts and horrible stings, leaving shreds of his clothing or flesh behind at every step.

A band of crazed monkeys passed close to him, uttering squeals of terror and making the most frightful grimaces. For more than a quarter of an hour, he competed in agility with the quadrumanes, and covered as much ground as they did.

What a journey! The man needed an iron constitution to keep on finding the strength to flee after the incalculable fatigues he had experienced in the last twelve hours.

Finally, he sensed a hint of freshness in the atmosphere. The river could not be far away. At that moment, the man, bloody and covered in mosquitoes from head to toe, was frightful to behold. It would have been difficult for the most expert naturalist to decide whether he was a human or an ape. And yet he was still overcoming obstacles, as if fatigue was unknown to him. His arms and legs were stretching as if he had steel springs for muscles.

Finally, there was one last oak in front of him, and he perceived the immense river, whose current was already dragging a thousand fleeing animals heading for the other shore. At his feet a sandy beach twenty meters wide extended into the distance to either side.

But on that beach, reunited as if for a new Noah's ark, all the animals of the region, frantic with fear, were bounding, tearing one another apart, howling in a lamentable fashion, scraping the ground with their claws, and raising their noses into the wind to sniff the symptoms of the blaze. It was terrible!

To go down there, in order to jump into the river, would have been madness. Between the paws of jaguars, monkeys and all the other doomed creatures, an innumerable multitude of reptiles could be seen crawling, from vine snakes as slender as a willow-twig to enormous constrictors. All of them were swarming, writhing, hissing killing—and at intervals, driven by the mass of new arrivals as much as the survival instinct, the whole mass was thrust bodily into the river, where the crocodiles were having a feast.

Gregorio was trembling in every limb. Around him, the treetops were populated with monkeys, squirrels, scorpions, snakes and birds. The birds, rendered furious by the odor of the smoke that was reaching them, were carrying out a magnificent massacre of reptiles. And all around, a cloud of mosquitoes, thickening further with every passing moment, threatened to cut off the sunlight.

Suddenly the howling redoubled, the whistling became shriller, and there was a tremor in the entire mass. The squirrels launched themselves into the air without any objective; the snakes leapt sideways; the birds took off, and the cloud of mosquitoes advanced toward the middle of the stream. The place was clear. There was nothing left on the beach but the cadavers of the infernal sabbat.

The flow of the Amazon was instantaneously covered with a hundred thousand various creatures, swimming, drowning and tearing one another apart.

Gregorio thought that he was saved, but the foot of the oak in which he was situated was already beginning to burn, and all the way to the river's edge, where the water reddened by the caimans' feasting were lapping at the sand, all the thorn-bushes and all the dead leaves were on fire.

The half-breed, mad with desperation and blinded by the smoke, tried to resist asphyxia momentarily. Brief as that moment was, it was sufficient for the animals to draw away from the bank. Then, vanquished by the heat, he let himself fall into the flames and ran to the river, into which he hurled himself without worrying about anything else. Any death would have been mild compared with the one he had just avoided.

As he plunged into the cool water, the wretch, whose every pore was a burning wound, experienced a wonderful sensation of refreshment, and sensed that his strength was regenerated. He swam like a shark, and was able to avoid with marvelous skill the most dangerous of his companions in flight. For fear of caimans he headed for the middle of the river, whose current, unique in all the world, could carry him in a matter of hours either to Para or to some unknown island.

He gave no thought to reaching the opposite bank for several reasons. At that point, the Amazon was six kilometers wide, and he would have had to struggle for part of the night against the irresistible current. On the other hand, there was every reason to think that the fleeing animals would land on that shore, which would probably not be a good place to spent the night.

He therefore allowed himself to go with the current.

A few hundred meters further on, he felt something grab his hair, and something furry clung on to his shoulders. It was a poor little monkey, very pretty, that had been in the process of drowning and had grabbed hold of whatever it could. Gregorio tried to detach it and throw it back into the water, but the quadrumane dug its fingernails and teeth into the half-breed's flesh and it was necessary to tolerate and rescue the parasite.

The half-breed could still count on another three hours of daylight. He started swimming vigorously, still with his bur-

135

den, which was no longer biting him but was clinging to his bushy hair.

The river suddenly broadened out, and the Argentinean perceived the fortifications of Para. Alas, they were too far away for him to hope to reach it, all the more so as his strength was almost exhausted.

Gregorio had just passed the mouth of a small river when a canoe, paddled by an Indian, came into the Amazon. In the depths of the boat an inert mass was lying. That was poor Alfonso, who had also thrown himself into the first water he encountered, and who, by providential good fortune, had been rescued by an Indian to whom he had once rendered some service at Salem.

But let us return to the half-breed.

The current drew him on; he allowed himself to be drawn. In the distance, an island appeared. That was all that he needed in order to rest and wait for the next day. Thinking that he was saved, or nearly so, Gregorio mentally reviewed the day's events, and the monster uttered an infernal burst of laughter as he thought that Alfonso had probably been asphyxiated and burnt in the forest.

At about half past six, a quarter of an hour after sunset, the wretched Argentinean came ashore on the little island toward which he had been swimming for three hours. He was just in time. If he had had a thousand meters more to travel, his strength would have been insufficient.

He had scarcely set foot on land when he took hold of the monkey gently and drew it into his arms. The monkey let him do it. Then, either out of ferocity or foresight, the Argentinean seized the charming quadrumane by one foot, whirled it around his head four or five times and smashed its skull furiously on the ground. The poor little creature uttered a slight croak, and gave no further sign of life.

In spite of the hot climate, Gregorio felt his limbs stiffened slightly by cold; his long sojourn in the water had chilled him. He rolled in the dust with which the entire surface of the island was covered, which the sun's rays had warmed up almost all day long. That revitalized him somewhat, but his need for sleep was becoming more imperious by the minute.

He was also horribly tormented by hunger. He skinned the monkey with his teeth and fingernails, and gathered a few dead branches to which he set fire in order to cook his dinner.

The island on which Gregorio had found his salvation was absolutely deserted and very bare. That was extraordinary in such a location. Only the eastern tip, a rock on which a little fertile soil had accumulated, was sheltered by a handful of thorny stunted trees. With the exception of that rock, there was nothing to be seen on the islet's surface but the dust, the color of amadou, in which Gregorio had, so to speak, taken a bath when he landed.

Here and there, however, a pellitory or a spring of sunburned grass emerged from that dust. It seemed that nature had attempted to claim its rights even over this corner of the earth, and something must once had grown there, for in places one encountered branches that were fairly long, but devoid of foliage and absolutely try. It was with the aid of one of those sticks that Gregorio lit his fire, in the fashion of savages.

After having put the thigh of his monkey over the ardent embers, the half-bred sat down in front of his fire, with his knees tucked under his chin, with the intention of waiting until his supper was ready. Night had fallen. Exhausted, Gregorio felt his eyelids becoming heavy, and closing periodically; without the torment of his hunger, he would have fallen asleep in that posture.

For a while, vanquished by drowsiness, he dozed off—but he suddenly straightened up, as if a spring had been set beneath his feet, and uttered an indescribable scream, in which there was fury, anger, terror and despair.

He looked around, and thought he was the victim of a nightmare provoked by fatigue.

He rubbed his eyes feverishly with his agonized fists.

No, he was not asleep.

With an enormous bound he headed for the river. That first leap was followed by a second, then a third, and he ended up dancing like a terrified dervish, not knowing where to run, losing his head and tearing his hair.

What was happening, then? Something quite natural, but frightful: the island was burning.

It was being consumed in its entirety, and serpentine streaks of fire were running all along it, similar to those that run along papers that flames have quit.

The explanation of the horrible fact was simple. The surface on which Gregorio had landed was not an island; it was a mass of dead wood, the trunks of oaks, cedars, pines, palm-trees, coconut-palms and mahoganies that the Amazon had carried there from who knows where. The first trunks had been interrupted by the rick where the handful of trees grew; the others had accumulated in the tangle thereafter. Gradually, new arrivals had extended and lifted up the islet by passing underneath, and as that heaping up had continued for some three years, the upper layers of the pyre had been covered in dust—in a terrible, inflammable dust.

Gregorio understood everything. He tried to run toward the rock, but the soles of his feet were burned to the quick, and no human being can endure that suffering.

What could he do? Stay where he was? He would be roasted; he could already smell the odor of his own charred flesh, rising to his head.

He went mad.

In the darkness, he could make out all the ground of the island, which was reddening with frightful velocity. One might have thought that a subterranean bellows was exciting the furnace.

Gregorio fell, but got to his feet, and, making an extraordinary effort of will, launched himself toward the river.

He was stopped by another fall.

At that moment, the canoe carrying Alfonso went past the island. The soldier, who had recovered consciousness, saw that species of demon writhing in the fire, and proposed to the

Indian that they should go to his aid, without suspecting that he was talking about saving his tormentor. The Indian shook his head and paddled more vigorously.

Meanwhile, Gregorio roared.

His entire body was covered in hot ash. He was able to get up, but only to fall down again. Soon, Baçao saw him writhing in the midst of a blaze that was becoming increasingly intense. Digging his fingers into the embers, the half-breed was still dragging himself toward the river, with reptilian contortions. Momentarily, his spinal column flexed like an arch; then he collapsed, agitated feverishly, made one last effort, and remained immobile.

Then the flames burst forth.

The next day, the islet was no longer there. A few blackened tree-trunks, carried away by the current, were floating toward the open sea.

Aboard a steamer leaving for Europe, a man with a face reduced to pulp, wearily followed those wrecks with his eyes, with some slight interest. That was Alfonso Baçao, who, having arrived safe and sound in Para, had told his story to the captain of a ship about to sail, and had been granted a passage gratuitously.

Georges Price: *Springfield's Doubloons*
(1895)

Pierre Marsault came out of Monsieur Rivière's office with death in his soul and went mechanically into the labyrinth formed by the immense workshops, of which the great constructor's study was the center. He passed between the long rows of black buildings bristling with tall chimneys, shaken incessantly by the trepidation of machines, from which escaped, like the sound of monstrous respiration, a powerful and deafening concert: the roar of gigantic flywheels and the hiss of enormous ventilators, sometimes dominated by the ripping sound of a jet of steam or the shrill whistle of a boiler demanding water. He left behind the assembly shops on his right and arrived at a series of slipways set up on the bank of the Seine, where torpedo-boats and other small steam-powered vessels—in the construction of which the company of Rivière & Sons were specialists—were resting on their keel-blocks.

He stopped in front of the sixth slipway. He was very pale. Sat the top there was a placard: *La Flèche*. On the inclined plane there was an incomplete boat. The sheet-metal yacht, painted vermilion, had not yet entirely covered the delicate framework. For some unknown reason, no one was working at that moment on the other small boats, and beneath the grey October sky, in that silence and emptiness, always more sensible on the banks of great rivers, that red skeleton, reminiscent of the bloody carcass of a cetacean, seemed sinister and lamentable.

Pierre climbed the ladder and went down into the iron framework; there, putting his head in his hands, he wept.

His entire future had crumbled. This time, he was well and truly crushed. Everyone around him, except for his wife, had wearied of him. He owed money everywhere. Desperately committed to his scientific faith, clinging to the certainty of discovery, he had drained the cup of humiliation to the lees. Compensating himself for his shame with a glorious dream, as the ascetics of old paid with vile tasks for a future halo, he had abased himself, a scientist and an honest man, before shady wealth that sometimes sustained his work with a disdainful obol, and now, within sight of port, just as he was about to dazzle the detractors and the incredulous with the glare of a full-scale experiment, he had run out of support. He had been refused one final loan, and demands were being made for the settlement of previous debts, the advance payments for the work to be done.

Eighty thousand francs! He needed eighty thousand francs! The boat-builder had been inflexible. He had had enough of inventors. He had just lost thirty-thousand francs because of one of those dreamers who aren't as naïve as they seem to be and take a gamble, only risking the constructor's money, so he had decided to stop the funding. Certainly, he had deigned to add, he was not confusing Marsault with the mass, but the decision was general and irrevocable. And if the sum had not been paid in a week, the ship would be dismantled. He would be desolate, personally—oh, desolate!—all the more so because, he admitted, he had almost promised to extend the credit. Evidently, the invention was good—good enough for Pierre to find another constructor, he had added, ironically—but the disappointment that had just afflicted him had completed the measure; his resolution was definitively made, and nothing would make him deviate from it.

The fruit of twelve years' labor was lost. The fecund invention that, by giving a new form to ships, and by means of the double propeller with concentric and inverted blades that he had invented, would have revolutionized navigation and rendered previously-unknown speeds possible, would remain a dead letter. Deprived of aid, of the material means of execution, no longer having any associates, he would fall back definitively into the crowd of Platonic inventors, that somber phalanx of obscure strugglers of whom incredulity makes visionaries, who, every year, stifle beneath indifference the seeds of so many ingenious ideas, where so many treasures of labor, patience and effort melt and dissolve at the ardent contact of poverty.

Momentarily, a sinister and desperate thought came into his mind. The Seine was flowing close at hand...the Île de Billancourt was deserted...

But Pierre was not alone in the world. He had a wife and two small children. He glimpsed with agonizing lucidity the heart-rending image of the misery that would take possession of them on the day when their father was no longer there to bring the daily beak-full back to the poor nest, and he wanted to live—not out of courage, but duty.

The man went home, empty-headed, pausing for a few minutes in front of a shop-window containing nothing but bottles, symmetrically arranged, using up a quarter of an hour reading an advertisement for some patent medicine twenty times over. It was one o'clock when he reached his door.

He lived in a small house at the end of the Rue Vavin, behind which extended a large enclosure that had once been a garden. Nothing remained of its original destination, however, but a few flower-beds alongside the house, which Madame Marsault strove to maintain, where the long stems of yellow primroses and desiccated sunflowers, with their large faded hearts speckled with black dots, displayed their empty alveoli. One side was occupied by a large hangar, which could be closed by a tarpaulin sliding on a curtain-rod. Beneath that hangar, two model ships were visible, shiny and nickel-plated, resting on their blocks—two of those prized models that inventors construct with love, ornamenting and finishing off with minute care, fabricating them in precious wood and polished metal as if to favor sympathetic examination by making an agreeable impression at first glance.

At the back, in a corner, there was a small, very primitive brick construction surmounted by a long sheet-metal flue held in place by iron cables. Through the door, which had remained open, a little forge was visible, with its accessories.

In the remainder of the enclosure there were the thousand bizarre and inexplicable items that surround the existence of a researcher: buckets of water, doubtless for tempering metals, strange pieces of ironwork, barrels, rusty propeller-blades, an old anvil, yellow and cracked, cast-iron frames, broken piston-rods, fragments of wheels, an electric pile with thirty elements, deprived of its liquids, whose sandstone vessels were stained with the green leprosy of copper salts and whose broken electrodes were twisted in irregular spirals.

Pierre had come in by the small door to the garden. As he crossed that space, he turned his head in order not to see the models in the hangar, and, by means of a superhuman effort, attempted to assume an expression that was not so sad.

His wife was anxious. When she saw him, very pale, with dark circles around his eyes, his tread dispirited in spite of his determination to hide his despair, the worthy creature who shared his difficulties and his hopes came toward him and, without saying a word, hugged him and brought his children to him. She did not even ask him what blow had struck him. She knew that a further misfortune had fallen upon them, and, with her sagacious womanly instinct she had divined, without saying anything, the catastrophe in the letter that had summoned her husband to see the constructor.

In a few words that emerged with difficulty from his oppressed breast, he specified the extent of the disaster, the frightful simplicity of which did not demand a long explanation.

The valiant woman tried to summon up her courage. Perhaps, in fact, he might be able to find another boat-builder, more confident and more generous—but he closed her mouth with a word. How could they expect any such thing? On what resources would they live while they searched for an unknown savior? Until now, they had gone into debt, while depriving themselves. They had used up the humble credit of the neighborhood. Like Bernard Palissy, burning his furniture to heat his furnaces, they had sacrificed everything to gain a few days, to get through the hours, to reach, minute by minute, the moment of success when the invention, on which they had the right to count, would take form. But now? Now, it was necessary to live, to abandon definitively the dreams of modest happiness founded on the ship, and seek in consequence a job as an overseer, or even a workman, which he might not be able to find, having quit the workshops and factories years ago, taking with him the reputation of an irregular laborer.

Lunch had waited for the master of the house. The master of the house: a humble title, the attribute of the sovereignty of the hearth that raises a man by the holy exercise of his intimate royalty, and beneath the weight of which poor Pierre bowed his head, ashamed of being unable to fulfill the obligations that went with it.

After the frugal and silent meal, he went out into the enclosure and wandered amid the thousand items of debris heaped up by is laborious investigations. While walking slowly, his hands in his pockets, idly, he reviewed mentally his entire existence of labor and poverty: his brilliant graduation from the École des Arts-et-Métiers d'Angers, his first discovery working for Springfield, whose result had been a radical transformation, to the benefit of his employer, of the manufacture of steel, and an immense fortune for the Englishman. Then there were his successes at the Expositions, the gold medal awarded to his writing telegraph and the diploma of honor obtained by his recording photometer, which gave graphic form to light intensities: superb inventions, but unfruitful, which figured in the first rank of treasures of pure science, but which could not enter, by reason of their high price, into the domain of profitable application.

And, while thus rereading the melancholy story of his life, which nature always represents to us in great crises, often as remorse or regret, but sometimes also as consolation, Pierre headed instinctively for the little forge where, black with coal-dust and sweating, toiling away night and day, he had sung, in spite of past disappointments, the virile song of the laborer, the alleluia of hope.

Out of habit, he went into that narrow space. The furnace, under its sheet-metal mantle, was black. On the anvil was an incomplete model of a propeller, which he had constructed in wrought iron in order to be able to regulate and modify the curvature of the blades by degrees. He picked up the component, the blades of which were still straight. He looked at it for a long time, returning involuntarily to his idea, digging into it, allowing his mind to isolate itself from material anguish by an irresistible abstraction. His hand relit the extinct fire of its own accord. Soon, the resonant impacts of the hammer on the anvil rang out, and such is the divine power of labor, so great is the satisfaction that it produces, that the hot breath of the bellows and the rigorous and vibrant falls of the hammer had more effect of Pierre's mind, by virtue of their active harmony, than the consolations of devotion.

What morose philosopher made labor an eternal punishment supported by humankind to expiate original sin? It is, on the contrary, the sustenance, the supreme and sure remedy for the pains of life. It is, in its most humble creations, the fecund principle the raises human up and characterizes, but the faculty of production, the resemblance between the creature and the Creator. It is, ultimately, the dispenser of the freest enjoyments, those least submissive to exterior influences, for it shares with charity and honor the superb privilege of bearing its own recompense.

Absorbed in his labor, Pierre gradually found a less despairing state of mind. Then man who had abandoned himself a little while before, who had regarded his life as so completely finished that only the love of his nearest and dearest had prevented him from killing himself, contrived, not to conceive a hope, but once again to glimpse the possibility of hope. Immured in an inextricable situation as in a dark dungeon, he could not yet entertain the implausible thought of an escape, for a consoling aspiration for the future requires a glimmer of light, however feeble it might be, to serve as its guide—but if a ray of light were to appear through a crack in his prison he was ready to hurl himself toward the blessed fissure, to widen

145

it with his fingernails, and to recover, soon awakened the faith in better days that sometimes falls unconscious in bruised souls, but never dies.

At that moment, his wife came into the forge. She held out a specialist newspaper, the *Monde Industriel*, and showed him an article. He took the paper and read it.

Sir James Springfield, the great English scientist and manufacturer is in Paris at present; he has come to deliver in person to the Compagnie de Paris-Lyon-Méditerranée an experimentation carriage which, he claims, is a marvel. In our next issue we shall devote a special article to this magnificent apparatus, which contains all the instruments necessary to study the innumerable problems associated with traction. Several of these instruments are entirely new and extremely ingenious. Until now, nothing so complete has been seen, and we are obliged to think that science has no fatherland, in order not to regret that this first rate work is not due to a French company.

Sir James Springfield is staying at the Hôtel du Louvre.

The husband and wife looked at one another. The day before, Pierre had not thought of wondering what had become of his former employer, the man who had built his fortune on his overseer's invention without reserving him a share. Today, that name appeared to him to be a gleam of light that represented hope. Perhaps, in fact, Springfield would recall the original source of his wealth, and would consent to offer alms that would be a feeble restitution. If necessary, Pierre would give him a share—the majority shareholding, if he demanded it. He would only ask that his name, that of the creator, should not be excluded from the patents. And, with the particular enthusiasm of people in whom life is reborn, with the impulse of a reaction against the mortal void that had invaded him, he clung to that idea, looking at it from every angle, and eventually decided that it was practicable, probable and almost certain.

Pierre Marsault belonged to a modest family. His father, a simple foreman in the highways and bridges agency, had had considerable difficulty giving him the education necessary to enter an École d'Arts et Métiers. When he had graduated from the college, the young man, somewhat restless and vagabond by temperament, and desirous of seeing and learning about other countries, had made a kind of tour of France and had wandered from one city to another, one factory to another, for some years. He had eventually reached Calais, and, after the brief love affair of a worker who thinks too much to be able to dream, had married a pretty girl, Jeanne Brizzard, whose father was an overseer in the factory where Marsault was then employed in a similar capacity.

It had seemed that destiny had fixed him henceforth in Calais. His job was good and his superiors professed a particular esteem for him. Unfortunately, the company had been run by two brothers, one of whom occupied himself with the technical side of things while the other directed the commercial operations. The latter had allowed himself to be drawn into disastrous speculations that had ended in bankruptcy. The factory had been taken over, and the new owners had brought in their own managerial staff.

It is a short distance from Calais to London. In the former town, where our neighbors are considerable in number, Pierre had learned English. He gathered together his savings, departed for London, and found employment in Sir James Springfield's factory.

There, as elsewhere, his keen intelligence, his practical aptitude and, above all, his exceptional ability as a researcher and inventor had rapidly attracted the attention of the factory-owner. He had reached an exceptional position in a short time, and while keeping his modest title of overseer he had become Springfield's confidant and collaborator. Fortune appeared to be smiling on him, and it seemed that henceforth, in that solid, if not powerful company, his future ought to have been definitely assured.

Springfield, a member of the Royal Society, knighted by the queen, really was, as the *Monde Industriel* put it, a great scientist, but his vast intelligence was combined with a strange character and a mind devoid of all scruples. He fused, in the most bizarre confusion, the noble love of scientific investigation with the basest cupidity and the most intense avarice.

His harshness and pitiless rigor in business matters were proverbial throughout the United Kingdom. A perfect type-specimen of a man who succeeds in everything, served by faculties of genius, immense knowledge and a finesse all the more efficacious because it did not recoil before any means, however despicable, Springfield, unlike happy individuals, brooded leavens of envy and hatred that no one would have dared to suppose. A physician, chemist and engineer, he embraced the most various branches of science, and it seemed to him that he possessed the monopoly, that no one had the right to challenge him in any dispute regarding property or profit.

Like the other Englishman who, having tasted the water at the mouth of an African river and found it salty, said "We're in England," he would have immediately said, every time a discovery was announced: "That's in my domain."

And if, by chance a foreigner permitted himself to discover the fractionation of electric light, the liquefaction of oxygen or the direction of aerostats, he shrugged his shoulders like a Conservatoire prize-winner witnessing the performance of an amateur, but he felt invaded by the kind of cold rage that makes the jaundiced pallor of the bilious and malevolent whiten even further.

At the most, he professed a slight indulgence for his compatriots, but that concession, due to the most vivacious instinct that an Englishman bears within him, stopped at the limit traced by his self-interest. And if Stephenson or Séguin, returned to the world, had let some imprudent revelation of their discoveries to escape in his presence, he would have stolen Stephenson's idea with no more scruple than Séguin's.

As is often the case, the exterior of that complex individual did not betray his intimate instincts. Springfield was robust, very tall and wore lightly the vigorous old age for which the exercises of adolescence prepare the English. His face was bony and forceful. Two long white side-whiskers framed it, giving him the respectable air of an old mariner. His forehead, vast by virtue of its deeply receding hairline, was crowned by a gray crest, produced by the obstinate struggle of brushes against the rebellion of the sparse but strong hairs. His gray eyes, very pale, stared interlocutors in the face. One would prefer shrewd individuals to look away from eyes directed at one, but when cunning is combined with audacity, it does not show, and the apparent frankness of the gaze is merely one more aspect of shrewdness—whereas more than one honest gaze is lowered if timidity, either native or the daughter of deception, grips the heart.

With his inferiors, Springfield was cold and hard, but he remunerated them with a certain generosity. Very skeptical, he did not attach any importance to ties of sentiment, and thought that interest alone could assure him of the collaboration of the people he employed.

Thus, people in his entourage were very surprised to see the amicable way in which he treated his French overseer. Interested parties wanted to know the reason for that change in Springfield's manner. They questioned Marsault adroitly, and the latter had ingenuously admitted that he was on the track of a special method of manufacturing steel that would revolutionize the industry in question and reap enormous profits.

Everything was explained. Accustomed to speculate on the interests of others, Springfield was in it for his own self-interest.

The factory buildings were situated on one of the numerous lines radiating from Victoria Station, in the area where the ill-defined boundary between London and the countryside, which foreigners have difficulty grasping, is located. One suddenly ceases to see houses, but one still finds gas-lights on the roads, plaques indicating the names of streets, and even city policemen. Then, abruptly, one encounters an agglomeration of buildings, seven or eight rows of terraced houses, each with a matching garden, and ground blurred by fogs laden with the emanations of coal fires. Momentarily, one recovers the illusion of the city, and then one suddenly falls back into a vast flat and deserted expanse of countryside beneath the grey sky, bare in winter and green in spring, until one recovers the same rustic blocks of black or red back-to-back houses in their meager enclosures.

The factory and the lodgings of its workers constituted one of those agglomerations.

Marsault lodged in one of the rows of houses, occupying the one at the end of the terrace. Earning a sufficient income, he had furnished the interior comfortably, which Jeanne had decorated with the artistic instinct of Frenchwomen, especially those of the Midi.

Madame Marsault had, in fact, been born in Provence and had spent her childhood there. Her imagination had retained the sense of the beautiful that the spectacle of the splendors of nature, the memory of the powerful harmonies of the colors of sunrises over the infinite waves of the Mediterranean and the resplendent evenings over the violet mountains, leaves behind. Unlike her neighbors, the young woman did not consider her garden as an enclosure for hanging washing out to dry. She devoted to it all the time that she did not give to her house and child. She only had one son then, and, by dint of perseverance and care, she succeeded in creating in that narrow expanse a nest of verdure and flowers, into which she often came to sit down, to work or to watch her son play.

Jeanne was typical of those young women of the Midi for whom it seems that the expression "a beautiful girl" was invented. She was slightly above medium height, with an admirable figure. Her perfectly oval face was crowned with black hair, as lustrous as a raven's wing, very lush and thick, and her cherry-red lips were delicately shaded by two scarcely-visible hints of fine down. She dressed simply, as befitted a woman of her status, but with taste, although her southern temperament revealed itself in the choice of colors that were a trifle bright, which went well with her beauty.

Her marriage to Pierre had been a love-match, and since the day when it had been celebrated, their mutual affection had never wavered for a minute. It had only acquired, on the part of the young woman, a somewhat protective—one might almost say maternal—inclination. In consequence, Pierre's love for Jeanne, was not without a certain deference for the woman who was both a cherished creature and the worthy mother of a family. A constant spectator of her husband's labors, she had imposed on herself the law of facilitating his tasks, of permitting him to isolate himself from material cares in order to devote himself entirely to his studies and his toil. She realized miracles in order that her modest house should always present an appearance of the healthy cheerfulness, the offspring of order and care, that exercises such a strong and benevolent influence on certain speculative minds. And it required the final crush of imperious poverty in order for her to admit one day that she was impotent to fulfill the simple and sublime duty that she had mapped out for herself.

In the era about which we are talking, however, nothing had yet occurred to presage evil days, and every morning, after Pierre's departure for the factory, Jeanne took advantage of the first rays of the sun, which the fig comes to veil so rapidly in England, in order to enable her son to bathe luxuriously in the luminous fresh air on the garden lawn. Sitting in a pink dressing-gown under a little arbor, she devoted herself in the meantime to some needlework.

Every morning, Springfield, faithful to the precepts of sound hygiene, combated the evil influence of a sedentary life with an excursion on horseback. Because Pierre's house was at the end of the terrace, one side of its garden was on the edge of the road along which he passed, and on each excursion, he saw the young woman. She sometimes raised her lead on hearing the horse's hoof-beats on the hard soil of the road, and rapidly returned to her work, with the vaguely fearful sentiment that the sight of the man who holds their destiny in his hand communicates to the weak.

Every time that the hazard of his daily rides brought him thus to that cheerful depiction of intimate happiness, Springfield experienced an invincible sentiment of envy. A positive, ambitious, obstinate spirit, the man had lived, thus far, distanced from everything that he considered as human weakness. The idea of having a family, of supporting the sweet fragility of beloved beings on his strength, had always appeared to him unworthy of a well-tempered man, who pursues one aim with the firm determination to attain it. Among all the philosophers nourished by the strong sap of the University of Cambridge, who were counted among its most brilliant pupils, one alone had struck and convinced him: Hobbes, the rude thinker whose desperate and cold doctrine made egotism the basis of the social contract.

Glad to find in a powerful mind a reasoned and brilliantly deduced theory that responded to his own instincts, Springfield had extracted that body of doctrines from the domain of psychology to place it in that of casuistry, and had assimilated it to the extent of taking it as the primary rule of conduct and criterion of conscience. Thus, he had silenced within him anything even remotely resembling a sentiment.

And yet, while scorning the humble joys that simple people experienced in the accomplishment of the human mission that God has given us on earth; while mocking, internally, the serene luxuries of the modest that are the ransom of harsh duties and the relief of cruel labors, he could not prevent himself from envying them and resenting those who had fund them on their rugged path. Disdainful himself of the joys of the hearth, he could not bear the idea of seeing them savored by others. In the same way, the fallen angel who renounced heaven pursues his hatred of those who remain there.

Every day, that unadmitted but omnipotent jealousy increased in Springfield's soul. Circumstances, moreover, seemed to have adopted the task of favoring that monstrous expansion. Until then, the Englishman had only been witness by chance and at rare intervals of Pierre's intimate happiness. The sequence of events obliged him to see it at closer range, and to penetrate into the interstices of that blessed and placid dual existence.

On the day when the overseer revealed his ideas relating to the manufacture of steel, it was agreed that Pierre would do the bulk of the work at home. In fact, he had to draw up large-scale plans and prudence forbade their being executed in the design-studio adjacent to the factory. An indiscretion might have soon been committed. It was therefore agreed that Pierre would establish a drawing-room in his house, and that Springfield would come to monitor the work.

To explain the increasing frequency of Pierre's absences, it was said at the factory that he was busy examining and sorting through ancient accounts in order to bring together the documents necessary for the solution of a contentious matter. His wife had been glad of the scheme, which reduced the separation between her and her husband.

Fully occupied with his idea, dreaming of fame and fortune, the worthy fellow had set to work ardently. They had both collaborated in fitting out a large, well-lighted room under the roof. In the middle, on its high supports, stood a large white wood drawing-table laden with rolls of gummed paper, boxes of colors and boxes of drawing-instruments. The walls were lined with set-squares, T-squares, posterns and French curves—and in one corner, there was a little table supported a work-basket. Every day, while Pierre drew, Jeanne sat at that table, without saying a word, in order not to trouble his research, but glad to be there with him while their son took his daily nap in the next room.

Sometimes, when he had resolved one of the difficulties that loomed up before him at every step, Pierre put down his drawing-pen and walked back and forth in the room, rubbing his hands. Then, before getting back to work, he came to kiss his wife or even open the door to the next room and gaze at his son, placidly sleeping in his bed. Then, Jeanne broke the silence and they both made the beautiful plans that are both the bane and the consolation of all those who live in the imagination: inventors, those poets of matter, or poets, those inventors of ideas.

And as summer had come, the sun was in celebration, and threw over those dreams, through the large bay window, the transparent adornment of its bright rays.

In conformity with the adopted program, Springfield came frequently to follow the progress of Pierre's work. The hazard of these visits put him continually in the presence of these pleasant scenes, and gradually, his envious instincts were overexcited, and the factory-owner ended up conceiving a veritable hatred for his subordinate. He needed all his self-control to hide that sentiment, which took on the allure of an obsession and was often translated into bizarre manifestations that intrigued Monsieur and Madame Marsault considerably.

Sometimes, Springfield persistently fixed his eyes on Pierre's, and the latter felt a kind of frisson run over his skin as the bleak and penetrating gaze stared at him. Sometimes, the embarrassment he felt became so intense that he was on the point of asking Springfield why he was looking at him like that—but just as he was about to let the question escape, the Englishman would start speaking, generally about some technical question, and Marsault attributed the singular attitude to an absorbing distraction.

At other times, in mid-conversation, Springfield abruptly picked up his hat and left, scarcely stammering a word of excuse.

To be sure, he would have dispensed with Pierre's services long ago if he had not been dominated, above all, by the interest he had in keeping him close at hand. Springfield sensed in his overseer's brain a mine of ideas, crowded and somewhat confused, poorly disengaged from certain fields of ignorance, but of an inconceivable richness, and capable of moving worlds on the day when they were set to work by skillful hands like his own. He had resolved to exploit that brain as he would have exploited a coal-seam or a gold deposit. He experienced no more scruple in taking possession of that mine of ideas than in capping a well, channeling a river or domesticating any other natural resource.

Unfortunately for him, Springfield, who had never taken human sentiments into account, had competitors transformed into terrible enemies, who waged furious war on him at every opportunity, and were no more scrupulous than he was in the choice of the weapons they employed. Those adversaries had spies even in his factory, and strove to keep up to date with everything that happened there. They did not take long to discover the part that Marsault had played in various prior discoveries, and Springfield was severely judged for that dishonest conduct in English scientific and industrial society.

Naturally, Springfield was initially unaware of the rumors that were going round, but one day they were revealed to him in circumstances that inflicted a terrible wound on his self-respect. There was a meeting of the Royal Society in London; Springfield was to read a paper. As he made his entrance, he was welcomed with a marked chill, by which he understood immediately that his colleagues were suspicious of him. The Royal Society is extremely ticklish about everything touching the honorability of its members, and the honest gentleman in the chair, after having held a secret committee-meeting, declared that certain unfavorable rumors had taken on such a consistency that, in the interests of the organization, as in that of his colleagues, he was obliged to demand a few explanations.

The spies that were watching Springfield had kept their paymasters well-informed; nothing had passed unperceived, including, and above all, the mysterious meetings between Springfield and Marsault. Thus, it was thought that the factory-owner was preparing some great discovery, which he would owe, like its predecessors, to his overseer, the glory of which he would attribute to himself alone, as he had already done. Anterior patents were cited in which Marsault should have had the larger credit.

In brief, the truth had been glimpsed but considerably exaggerated. A note had been sent to the Royal Society by a group of Springfield's rivals. It was the very exaggeration of this document, which the president read out, that saved Springfield. The latter defended himself with disdainful skill, selected from the note two or three facts blown out of all proportion, and succeeded in convincing his colleagues.

The incident had no other consequences, but from that day on, Springfield's hatred for the man who had caused him to sustain that damage no longer knew any bounds. Even self-interest was impotent to sustain him in a longer dissimulation. Wanting, even so, to hold on to his "mine of ideas", he became more brutal with every passing day. He inflicted public humiliations on Marsault in front of his workers. He went so far as to hurl scornful epithets at him in the middle of the workshop—so effectively that the unhappy overseer understood one day that it was necessary for him to seek employment elsewhere.

Springfield strove to retain Marsault, but his decision was made and the two men separated with this remark from Springfield: "The day will come when you'll regret having left me."

A few days later the family left the little house that had been witness to so many beautiful dreams, and returned to France.

For his part, Springfield immediately set out to realize the threat contained in his final declaration. Marsault's work was sufficiently far advanced that nothing remained to do but take it to the final stage. So, a few weeks later, the famous new method of manufacturing steel was patented in every country in the world. Such was Marsault's character that he that when he read the details of the discovery in the technical journals and recognized his work, he waited for months, and then years, always hoping that Springfield would give him a share of the profits that would result from it. When he was finally convinced that his labor would be definitively sterile, he experienced some bitterness, but soon began to console himself, as a man who was rich enough in imagination to repair such a loss.

We know how the cruel realities of life had given the lie to that confidence in the future.

Springfield swore to prove that he was able to do without Pierre Marsault's work. He kept track of his industrial career step by step, spying on him, and every time he learned that his former subordinate was moving into a new area of research, he devoted himself to it furiously. He applied all his faculties to it, and all the resources put at his disposal by his fortune and the breadth of his means of execution, and he invented on his own behalf what Pierre found on his. It was thus that the Exposition Universelle of 1878 had two writing telegraphs, and that two recording photometers figured in the 1884 International Health Exhibition in London. In both competitions, Pierre's apparatus received the higher award, while Springfield's only received silver medals. As the moment when this story began, the English constructor was working to improve the propellers and the form of ships.

With his cold insular perseverance, which no defeat diminished, the hateful Iron Duke was attempting a third trial, dreaming of the voluptuous cruelties of a Hudson Lowe after one of Wellington's triumphs.[21]

On the day when Jeanne, in desperation, came into Pierre's workshop and handed him the newspaper that announced Springfield's arrival, years had passed over the memory of his crime. She had no idea of the hatred, still without effect, with which the man in question was pursuing Pierre. She believed, on the contrary, that the memory of the service extracted from her husband might dispose him to render one himself.

---

[21] Sir Hudson Lowe was the governor of Saint Helena who became Napoléon's custodian during the fallen emperor's final exile.

Everyone, in fact, generally judges others by making use of their own consciousness as a human dictionary. Eminently good and simple, almost always living on the serene heights of scientific speculation, pursuing his dreams of invention, nourished by the abstract and subtle algebra of seekers in the imagination, which draws the mind to a vague mysticism, Pierre had the ignorant indulgence of an apostle, and did not criticize people, of whom he knew very little; he only grasped facts and circumstances.

Pierre had never been convinced that Springfield's action in benefiting from his early research was a theft. With the noble blindness of pure souls, he had sought, in his sublime faith, to invent justifications for Springfield's conduct. At the very most, he had allowed himself to accuse him of parsimony in his regard. For in the end, he told himself, it was true that as an employee, he owed all of his work to his employer; but the latter might have taken account of the fact that the results of his labor had surpassed the ordinary limits.

As for the muted war of which he had been the object, Pierre had never had the slightest suspicion of it. The humble individual would never have been able to believe that the scientist had been traveling in his slipstream.

When the 1878 Exposition had been held he had been in Spain, and in 1884, he had been too poor to travel to London. He did not know that Springfield had exhibited apparatus analogous to his own, and he had learned of his two victories without knowing over which adversaries they had been won.

He arrived, therefore, at the Hôtel du Louvre almost with confidence—but when he went into the courtyard, a new reaction was produced in him. Suddenly, he found the hope that he had conceived absurd. He stopped, indecisively, on the threshold of the hotel lobby, ready to retrace his steps. A blond and neatly-clad clerk raised his eyes, paused momentarily in his work, and asked him what he wanted.

Then Pierre plucked up his courage. "Monsieur Springfield?" he asked.

"Room 239," replied the employee, after having checked the register. "But he only came in five minutes ago and picked up his correspondence; you'll doubtless find him at table."

"Thank you, Monsieur."

Pierre climbed the staircase of the inner courtyard and went into the waiting-room Around large tables covered in green baize, on which harsh gas-light fell, men and women were reading the newspapers and brochures that were distributed and replaced in an orderly manner by a grave and silent usher. As he penetrated into that vast room, tranquil in its banal luxury, and treading to the thick carpet, whose discreet pile muffled footsteps, he felt even more intimidated. Put off by the idle gazes that were raised curiously upon him, rotating his hand in his fingers, he searched with his eyes for a seat and sat down in a dark corner, glad to hide his blush in its protective gloom.

It seemed to him that his status as a beggar must be obvious in his attitude, in his face, in his costume and in his entire being. All those elegant men, and all those neatly-dressed women, seemed to him to be fortunate members of society. Their indolent poses, and the distractedly inquisitive gazes they cast in his direction justified that troubling humility. And yet, how many of those people had come in search of a refuge against the imperious dinner hour? How many had asked— and even those were the timid ones—for an imaginary name at the hotel reception-desk? How many of them were nursing stomachs that were empty, or ballasted by a two-sou loaf of bread, in favor of wagering the only louis they had in some shady lottery, until the hour when a man in a correct frock-cost could indulge, as if he were passing by after a good dinner, in a fantasy of losing his money in bad company? How many were riffling through a periodical, every meal reduced to the final toothpick that was waiting in their pocket for the moment to be triumphantly exhibited between two famished lips?

Parisian poverty has the sinister particularity that it crawls beneath gilded wainscots as well as the oozing vaults of catacombs, and that sometimes, the gentlemen in the black suit fills up on the ambassador's sandwiches, and laughs with his dancing partner at the dinner he has not had.

That comfortable and well-chosen room was not well-chosen to put hunger to sleep. At the back, two immense bay windows opened, through which appeared in all its splendor the sated placidity of exotic diners who come to Paris to dissipate piastres, pounds sterling, gold ounces and Hindu rupees. Through the transparencies of large arches, one could see small tables with dazzling white cloths and scintillating crystal, at which the gourmet appetites of the guests were blossoming. There were white-collared clergymen there, blonde English misses laden with silver jewelry, Spanish matrons in gaudy dresses and somber mantillas, gilded Mexican ladies with eyes of black diamond, savoring raw oysters, cutting up pheasants served in their plumage, sipping the cheerful foam of champagne, the gold of Sauternes and the ruby of old burgundies.

In that crowd, which was, at least, tasting the pleasures of the present moment, among those people to whom uniformed valets were bringing theater programs, Pierre sought the man on which his life depended. He suddenly caught sight of him at the back, at a solitary table. Next to him was a pile of newspapers and variegated brochures, whose pages he was cutting with a paper-knife, and which he was scanning while eating. The inventor, on suddenly seeing his arbiter, experienced an internal commotion, succeeded by a sensation of emptiness, a poignant anguish characterized by the slow, dull thuds with which his heart was beating in his breast. He waited, with the stoical determination to go on to the end, until Springfield's meal came to an end, and when he saw the scientist stand up and collect up his brochures, he went into the dining room and went over to him.

The Englishman did not appear any more surprised to see him than if they had parted company the previous day. He greeted him courteously and took him into a deserted corner of

160

the waiting room, suitable for a discreet conversation. They both sat down.

Suddenly, after the initial shock, the disturbance that had gripped Pierre had eased. He could no longer feel the beating of his heart. He had become, instantaneously, very calm and self-controlled; his mind was free, and in spite of the dryness of his mouth, which was still inhibiting his speech, he was able, after the obligatory preliminaries, to put his request as a man proposing a business deal, not a beggar requesting a service. That unexpected lucidity reassured him. On hearing himself speak, he gradually recovered his confidence, and it seemed to him that his arguments, neatly deduced and clearly expressed, were irrefutable.

Springfield listened to him without saying a word, leaning back in his armchair with his legs crossed, twisted the tip of one of his white side-whiskers with his fingers..

When Pierre had finished, the Englishman reflected momentarily, covering his interlocutor with a sphinx-like gaze. Curiously enough, that moment of uncertainty during which his destiny was being decided, did not seem as long to Pierre as one might have expected.

He waited calmly, even with tranquility, for the sentence that would be handed down. He waited, like a man who has played his last card, who has played it well, and who, sure of no longer being able to do anything for himself, places himself in the hands of God, saying: "I've done everything I can; the rest isn't up to me."

"My dear fellow," Springfield said, "I'm going to speak to you with an open heart. I have more than one reason to bear a grudge against you. You left me abruptly once, and since then, you've been an often annoying competitor. I could, therefore, reply to your proposals with a pure and simple refusal. But I know that you once judged my conduct in your regard severely, and I shall experience too much pleasure in proving that you were mistaken to use that right.

"I don't want to be either your associate or a shareholder with an interest in your discovery, because I've almost resolved the problem that you consider definitely clarified, by other means. But as it doesn't please me that my invention should benefit from your impotence, and as, on the other hand, I retain a good memory of the service you rendered to my company, I shall put at your disposal the eighty thousand francs that you need. They will be entirely yours. Now, if your pride finds it difficult to accept a gift, you may return them whenever you please, but I shall never demand them from you."

Pierre could not believe his ears. He was scarcely able to stammer a few words of gratitude.

"Don't thank me yet," the scientist said, "for there's one condition, which will be, at the same time, a service that you'll be rendering me and a small vengeance that is certainly due to me. Oh, don't be afraid; it's said that your king Henri IV, of whom the Duc de Mayenne had been the obstinate enemy, made him march very rapidly for two hours, and when he was sweating heavily, and ran out of breath, because he was very fat, the king said to him: 'Cousin, this is all the harm that I shall do to you in my life.' My vengeance is somewhat akin to that. You know that I've come here to deliver an experimentation carriage to the Paris-Lyon-Méditerranée. Before putting it at the disposition of the engineers I wanted to experiment on the line myself, to make sure that the journey hasn't disturbed any of its components. Tomorrow evening, I'm departing with the wagon for Marseilles, by the express. It's a matter of accompanying me, and verifying the efficacy of an apparatus that I've introduced into it, while I proceeded with other experiments."

"What is the apparatus?"

"It's simply a kilometric counter," Springfield replied, "but it needs to fulfill a dual objective: to mark the kilometers traveled and to emphasize each indication by means of a phenomenon that keeps the attention of the operators constantly alert. In certain experiments that the carriage will repeat frequently, since it's designed to study the traction on long and rapid journeys, the observation of the distance traveled is closely linked to other observations of regularity, force and direction. You know that, since you're a professional. It's therefore important that it can be followed without interruption , sometimes for long periods, by the engineer.

"To begin with I thought about incorporating a loud bell to resonate at every movement of the needle indicating a further thousand meters on the dials, but I thought that vibration might be insufficient in certain cases—during sleep, for instance. In fact, no matter how loud the bell is, the sound is always the same, the ear gets used to it, and after a short time that adaptation prevents the perception from reaching the brain; the proof is that one can sleep perfectly well in a room where there is a clock.

"I therefore imagined a simple modification of the counter, which consists of a metal box containing a large number of disks; at every kilometer a release-mechanisms causes one of the disks to fall into a sonorous bronze bowl situated a meter and a half below. According to the inclination of the disk in its fall, the impact varies in its intensity and tone; the result, in the sound produced, is an infinite variety that opposes any adaptation of the ear. Well, I want to see, by means of your example, if the apparatus really works in accordance with the idea I conceived."

"In sum," Pierre replied, smiling, "it's a matter of spending a single sleepless night."

"A sleepless night—that's exactly it," said Springfield. "It doesn't frighten you?"

Pierre shrugged his shoulders.

"So, let's settle our conditions. As I intend that my experiment should be thorough, I want a powerful interest to sustain you. That interest will be augmented for you by reason of a particular circumstance. I haven't yet received the necessary metallic disks. I'll replace them with hundred-franc doubloons, which I'll collect from the bank tomorrow morning. You've asked me for eighty thousand francs; I'll put eight hundred of those doubloons in the container of the apparatus. If you count the coins exactly in their kilometric fall, without

163

making any mistakes, all night long, until the last one, they'll be yours, and you'll thus have your eighty thousand francs. But I warn you that the slightest error—a moment of distraction, or two minutes of somnolence, during which you let a number escape—will take away any right you have to the accomplishment of my promise. You know me well enough to know that, in either case, I'll keep my word. Is that agreed?"

"Of course," said Pierre. "But your experiment, thus constituted, won't prove very much."

"Why is that?"

"Because I have such a strong interest in remaining awake and attentive that the strident fall of the doubloons won't have anything to do with the absence of sleep and distraction."

"Perhaps," replied the scientist, who was also a physician, with his indefinable smile.

Of that conversation and the bizarre clause added by Springfield to the service to be rendered, Pierre retained nothing but the dazzling and scarcely-believable material fact that he had succeeded.

He was almost staggering as he went downstairs, under the weight of an immense joy, with his forehead taut and blood pounding in his temples. The fresh air of the street gripped him and restored his physical and mental equilibrium.

The rendezvous was fixed for seven o'clock the following evening at the Gare de Lyon. Thus, the day after that, in forty-eight hours, he would have the sum that would henceforth give him independence, permit him to complete his work, to speak loudly and firmly to the constructor, and to acquire glory, renown and fortune for himself and his family.

In three days, he would return from Marseilles, and would go to line up the banknotes on the stupefied Monsieur Rivière's desk. He could already see himself in that vast dark office furnished with filing-cabinets, with its walls full of plans on gummed canvas, with the big window at the back looking out of the design studios where employees in their short-sleeves were toiling over high tables. He was already calculating the attitude he would take with regard to Monsieur Rivière: a correct, slightly frosty but very simple attitude, as if he had naturally satisfied the most natural demand in the world.

And he hurried through the foggy night, almost running, threading his way through the traffic, passing with the delight of a happy man through the tangle of vehicles in order to announce to his dear wife two minutes sooner the magnificent aid that Heaven had sent them. And in his joyful intoxication he felt surges of supreme gratitude for Springfield, the man he had so misjudged, who had never been able to do anything for him because nothing had ever been requested of him, and who was therefore seizing the first opportunity to prove, other than with words, that he had not forgotten the origin of his wealth..

That evening was one of those celebrations that destiny rarely offers human beings. One would never have believed that a sum of money, inert matter of varying shininess, struck into roundels, could exercise such an influence on the noble thinking substance known as the soul.

Cupidity is a word pronounced too hastily. It can be applied to two utterly different things, and embodies of those confusions of which more than one example impoverishes our language. There are two cupidities, as there are two idolatries. In the same way that a Russian muzhik, worshiping material images to which he attributes a divine influence, in more idolatrous in his Christian paganism than a Plato venerating a symbol in the gold and ivory statuary of the Parthenon, the man who, by a singular aberration, attaches himself to the materiality of metal money, is a despicable being, while one cannot have too much respect for the man who is able to see in the gold the keenly-desired means to enrich science or to sow happiness around him. And yet, there are not too words to characterize that striking opposition in the pursuit of the same goal.

Pierre did not mention the experiment imposed upon him to his wife. In keeping quiet he was obeying a sentiment that he could not define, a vague dread of seeing his wife found an apprehension, a doubt, on that trivial circumstance. He did not take account of the fact that, if he feared such an instinctive reaction in her, the seed of it must be in himself, still almost latent but already engendered.

He strode back and forth in the dining room, his cheeks pink, sketching project after project in gigantic dreams, seeing in the radiant limbo of a future what broadened immense and luminous horizons in his vision, a definitively smoothed road, staked out with all the discoveries that he had piled up in immense boxes during his happy, laborious hours, in an embryonic state.

And while sharing his joy, his wife, guided by her timidity, became frightened by those limitless planes, that immense, superhuman area that her husband was embracing while enjoying himself in the field of progress and genius, and which he seemed already to be seizing in the amplitude of the inspired gestures that accompanied his speech.

Pierre slept like a man exhausted, his slumber regular and calm.

That benevolent torpor mastered him for part of the night.

Suddenly, the big clock of a nearby factory slowly chimed five o'clock in the silent night. The complete annihilation of repose was dissipated. Sleep persisted, leaving the dormant senses more open. Those five sonorous bronze chimes penetrated his brain—and then occurred one of those strange phenomena of sleep that are as yet unexplained.

With the lightning rapidity that characterized the phases of a dream, a scene, a situation, was instantaneously designed in his overexcited mind at the first chime of the clock.

The carriage...the cold face of Springfield, the gold coins falling heavily, one by one, into the strident metal bowl, and himself, counting: one...two...three...four...five!

Then a frightful terror that was translated as a hoarse sigh, and the awakening, doom-laden, with the sweat of nightmare, which made him sit up in his bed, haggard, still in the grip of his dream, shouting in the darkness: "All is lost! I've been deceived!"

The dream left him a sinister impression that persisted even after daybreak. During the next twelve hours, which seemed to him to drag with desperate slowness, he was haunted by a somber presentiment, which he strove to combat with his reason, repeating to himself that the task that he had to fulfill the following night was mere child's play, and that he had often spent sleepless nights on calculations far more difficult than the simple enumeration of a succession of phenomena, each of which would noisily advertise its presence. To prove to himself how easy his task was, he tried to count, while marching up and down the corridor, the drops that were falling with a crystalline sound from a dripping tap into a basin.

He counted up to a thousand easily without making a mistake. He repeated the experiment with the hammer-blows of the stone-cutters working in a neighboring building and the plaintive creaks of a weather-vane turning incessantly in the autumn wind, with the same success. It was definitely child's play. And yet, an intimate emotion would not let him alone; he sensed the enthusiasm of the previous day ebbing away.

He asked himself questions that remained unanswered. He thought, involuntarily, that Springfield's response had been very prompt. He gradually began to wonder where the condition placed on his aid might conceal some trap, and whether it was really in order to carry out an experiment that the Englishman had imposed it on him.

In that clause, which was certainly strange but not alarming, he could not grasp the possibility of any ambush that human wisdom could foresee. At the very most, the obligation was the result of a caprice on the scientist's part, or perhaps a pretext for contriving a long tête-à-tête, in order to profit from it by extracting some secret from him.

Scarcely had he found that latter explanation that he reproached himself for it, as an act of ingratitude.

All that Pierre had told his wife was that Springfield had demanded his assistance in carrying out trials in his carriage during the journey from Paris to Marseilles, without being specific. He carefully concealed his anxious and agitated state of mind from her.

When the time came to take his leave of his beloved family, thinking that scarcely fifteen hours separated him from his goal, he recovered al his hopes, and the departure was almost cheerful.

The platform of the Gare de Lyon presented the animated aspect that the first chill gives to the departure-time of the express, when elegant people sensitive to the cold escape to the Mediterranean coast. Pierre made his way through those groups, looking for the experimental carriage.

He perceived it, magnificent in its new varnish, with its shiny copper ramps, the cupolas of its enormous lanterns, and the anemometers crowning its roof. It had been placed at the back of the train, where, for the first study, the accentuation of the various movements promised more numerous observations. He climbed aboard, and saw Springfield, who was making orderly notes on a tablet of polished oak.

The scientist bid him a brief *bonjour* and continued his work. At his invitation, Pierre sat down on a stool.

The interior of the carriage was brightly lit. The two Carcel lamps, in their crystal globes, illuminated the sparkling copper of numerous wires, which ended in a large central table with cylindrical recorders envelopes in graph-paper. Everywhere there were dials, bells, tables of figures under glass panels, where long needles were still dormant, of thermometers, hydrometers, etc.—an entire arsenal of science summarizing in a narrow space, by means of the most ingenious disposition, all the possible means of investigation.

At the back, at the top of the wall, was a large canister from which the disks would fall into the large copper basin, polished and shiny, held in place by strong iron clasps. In that canister, painted dark green, was the fortune, the eight hundred doubloons.

Not a word was exchanged until the moment when the train moved off. At that instant, Springfield reminded Pierre briefly of the terms of the agreement. The latter bowed.

Two minutes went by. Then there was a slight click. A golden glint appeared in the narrow iron mouth, and the coin—the first—fell noisily on to the angled wall of the basin, rebounding to the bottom. Pierre, in a firm voice, counted: "One!"

Springfield picked up a previously-prepared piece of paper, ticked off that number, and resumed his attentive study of a graph that was being slowly traced on one of the cylinders.

Pierre felt completely tranquil. In complete mental liberty, he examined the surrounding objects, several of which, although he was familiar with their usage and purpose, intrigued him by virtue of their new design. But his eyes frequently returned to the basin and, after about a minute and a half, as the train began to acquire its normal speed, he saw a second coin fall.

"Two," he said.

As on the first occasion, Springfield ticked off the number and resumed his observations.

For about an hour things continued thus. Pierre gradually became accustomed to his mechanical task, which seemed to him increasingly infantile. In any case, he had a guide, in the highly improbably eventuality that he forgot the last number announced: on the wall behind the canister there were three dials, the first indicating the units, the second the tens and the third the hundreds of kilometers. From where he sat he could not make out the graduations, but he could see the needles, and observe their positions changing. He got up and moved a little closer, in such a way as to look more closely at the dials without his companion noticing. When he was close enough he examined them, and suddenly stopped, nailed to the spot. The rim of each of the glass panels covering them had been covered with a strip of paper that masked the graduations.

When Pierre sat down again he looked at Springfield, and their eyes met. Springfield smiled ironically; the inventor blushed, and felt painfully impressed. It was definitely necessary that the trial be accomplished in its entirety.

He had now reached number sixty-three. Deeply troubled, he reflected on that sage precaution, which proved that Springfield was determined to carry out the treaty to which he had consented with pitiless rigor—and also, perhaps, that there was a mysterious hidden agenda, indistinct, but whose reality presented itself to his mind for the first time with certainty.

Suddenly the impact of a further coin resounded, Abruptly reminded of the situation. Pierre tried to count, and could not immediately find the next number in his head. It required a short, but sensible effort of memory to recall that the last number had been sixty-three. For a moment, in the presence of that temporary failure, he had the overwhelming impression of a complete collapse, or a mortal void. His companion had already raised his head, and was looking at him, when he said: "Sixty-four."

It was a terrible warning. When he had pronounced the savior number, the blood ran through his entire body, buzzing in his hears, as happens when life resumes its rights after the abrupt arrest of circulation that freezes you in moments of great danger.

To escape any further distraction, he resolved to have recourse to the natural method of children who do not want to forget the price of an item they have been sent to buy. He decided that he would repeat each number until the following fall, and, with all the power of his will, without allowing his mind to settle, even for a second on any thought or idea whatsoever, he maintained his concentration rigorously.

He got through another long phase in that fashion, and counted another 123 coins, recompensed for his stubborn mental tension by the absence of any hesitation.

The train flew through the night with vertiginous rapidity, only stopping at rare intervals to take on water for the engine. Springfield continued his various studies calmly, paying no heed to his companion except to tick off the numbers scrupulously at each call.

Sitting on a stool with his back to the wall, in the stiff attitude of an Egyptian statue, Pierre continued his mechanical mental repetition, fixing his wide-open eyes on the vast polished basin at the bottom of which the freshly-minted doubloons, newly emerged from the vaults of the bank, were forming a radiant heap with a thousand facets. His gaze attached itself, involuntarily, to a point inside the basin where the powerful and fixed flame of the Carcel lamp placed a superb luminous ray, a magnificent reflection that seemed to create an incandescent nucleus on the copper, and to escape from the metal in the thousand irradiations of its sparkling bouquet.

He experienced a kind of vague pleasure in gazing at that point. In being thus fixed, the fatigue determined in him by the rigid determination not to think about anything seemed to diminish. The result of that was a sensation of repose, a relative well-being that he did not seek to forbid himself, submitting to it almost unconsciously, and, above all, without linking the effect to the cause. He continued the monotonous operation that guaranteed him against any forgetfulness, and counted the kilometers regularly, each of which brought him, in sixty seconds, a fraction of his future, without any further hesitation coming to disturb him.

The long minutes went by—desperately long, in truth—but no obstacle emerged. And yet, the inventor was astonished to find himself devoid of strength to hope, when hope appeared to be permissible. He was invaded, unwillingly, by a very slow progressive paralysis of his faculties. Only the power of the enumeration, having taken on the force of a sort of instinct, still subsisted in the numbness that lulled him during each minute, the repetition of the same number, which, under the influence of the irresistible attraction of the brilliant spot in the vessel, was gradually augmenting to the extent of a blissful torpor, to the supreme peril, to slumber.

171

He murmured, in a voice that was still distinct, the number 495.

He began to recite it internally, but the ideally-articulated speech that designates a silent thought without the aid of the tongue gradually lost its clarity and was stifled in a sort of rhythm that only brought a distant cadence to the last glimmers of his perception, with which it was content.

Everything was conspiring against him: the fascination of the copper basin, his identical sense, devoid of meaning, of figures repeated sixty times over, fatigue and emotion, the alternations of despair and joy of the previous days, and even the movement of the train, rocked smoothly, like the maternal oscillations of a cradle, by the supple suspensions of the carriage.

He was asleep—what am I saying? He was dreaming!

His soul was traveling the immense space that dreams, liberated from the yoke of reason, open to the sleep of the unfortunate. The sky was radiant, illuminating the shimmering Seine. The bank was covered with people in their Sunday clothes. In the middle of the river was *La Flèche*, liberated from its stays, finished, painted white, decked with flags. He gave a signal. The ship slid along its slipway, in the midst of a slight puff of smoke. Its stern parted the tranquil waters, a joyous cheer rose up, and *La Flèche*, elegant and proud, swayed gently on the soft undulations, buoyed up by her majestic immersion.

All that, that entire triumphal scene, unfolded in the thirty seconds that separated him fatally from failure.

Springfield had straightened up, and was gazing at the individual overwhelmed by the absurd brutality of a natural need that seems so easy to vanquish. He gazed without his physiognomy expressing any sentiment of satisfied hatred or imperious pity, without anything being legible in his features but the curiosity of an observer. It was, in fact, at that moment, the physician alone who was following the phases of a natural phenomenon. And yet, the man had sought a vengeance. He knew full well to what ambushes he was exposing the unfortunate man he hated. He had calculated the power and the mode of action of all the bonds with which he had surrounded his mind. Was his vengeance not complete, then? Was there some chance that the fall of the doubloon would wake Pierre from his deep sleep, or that, if he did wake up, he would instantly find in his mind the exact figure to pronounce?

The scientist had taken out his chronometer. The speed being perceptibly constant, the coin ought to fall in ten seconds.

Seven went by. Then the eighth. Then the ninth...

Then, at the precise moment that the needle passed its zenith, Pierre said "Four hundred and ninety-six" in a firm voice—without ceasing to sleep.

At the instant when the second syllable vibrated, the doubloon fell.

The hypnotism that had brought Pierre his fatal slumber had also given him his lucidity.

Springfield had anticipated that effect, so he did not appear to be surprised. He remained motionless for three minutes, still gazing at the sleeper, who counted the successive kilometers without error at the very moment when the click was about to occur, as if he were able to see through the iron wall the play of the mechanism that produced it. Then he reached up to the window next to his head and opened it.

It was raining. The air came in through the opening in gusts, charged with cold raindrops. That sudden chill, falling on Pierre's head, gradually broke the charm.

Springfield had resumed his place and seemed to be absorbed more than ever in his calculations. But this time he was wearing his ironic and malevolent smile, ready to enjoy the mental torture that was about to assail the patient when he awoke.

The effect of the cold air and the rain was rapid. Pierre opened his eyes, looked around and sat up abruptly. He recovered consciousness of his situation, and formulated the desolating reality in a realization that summarized all his anguish:

I fell asleep!

Finding Springfield in the same attitude, however, he said to himself: *Perhaps I've only been asleep for a very short time; perhaps I simply lost consciousness. What was the last number? Four hundred and ninety-five. So it's four hundred and ninety-six that I have to count. Evidently, that must be the case, for if it were not, Springfield would have told me that I'd lost the game. And yet, it's not possible...I'm conscious of having slept for more than sixty seconds, and the coin hasn't fallen yet. I was doubtless only drowsy, while maintaining consciousness of what I had to do. But I was dreaming...no matter! Sometimes one walks in one's sleep, while dreaming, and yet avoiding obstacles. Then again, I have a vague memory of hearing my voice. Yes, I'm sure of it; I spoke. And since Springfield hasn't said anything to me, I was counting.*

Then, the question gripped him: *Where am I up to?*

He had scarcely arrived at the conclusion that all was not lost when that poignant interrogation loomed up before him.

If any element could permit him to solve the problem, it was necessary for him to extract it from his deductions in a matter of seconds. But what did time matter? What miraculous revelation could come to his aid to tell him how many numbers he had counted and fill in the gap that sleep had left in his memory. It was over: he would have to force himself to search, for a matter of seconds, for the solution of an insoluble difficulty.

Prey to a frightful constriction of the heart, his clenched fist on his breast, waiting for the moment when, the next coin having fallen, he would be obliged, in remaining silent, to admit defeat, the unfortunate man stared at the three mute dials, whose revelatory graduations were pitilessly masked by the circular screens that the atrocious hand of the far-sighted Englishman had placed there.

To think that salvation was there, behind that frail white paper, and that he could not tear away the obstacle and discover the saving secret!

Suddenly, a rush of blood rose to his face. For a few seconds, his eyes took on a frightful fixity, an indication of the rapid and superhuman work that his brain was doing.

Springfield had straightened up, directing his gaze at Pierre, hanging on his lips, certain that this time, the double vision of hypnosis would not come to his aid.

The patient was mentally calculating some mysterious equation. Suddenly, he straightened up, met the gaze of his sinister companion, in whom he now saw a torturer that it was necessary to battle to the end, and, at the moment when the strident vibration of the copper rang out, he cried, with a superb tone of challenge and victory: "Five hundred!"

The malevolent individual, beaten once again, stifled a cry of rage. Pierre was not mistaken!

What supernatural intuition, then, did he have at his disposal? The piece of paper on which the numbers had been ticked off was at the other end of the carriage. The annular masks on the dials were intact.

White with fury, he sat down, reproaching himself for having had the honesty, in the cruelty of his proof, not to abuse his victim's sleep by telling him, when he woke up, that he had stopped counting. Then, suddenly, he burst out laughing and shrugged his shoulders. He had found the only plausible explanation.

Pierre's sleep had been feigned.

Yes, obviously, the inventor had wanted to test his tormentor himself, and had thus defeated him with his own weapons. And on observing that fact, which seemed to him to be blindingly clear, Springfield sensed his inveterate and overexcited hatred boiling within him, and murmured; "Patience; the night is long, and there are still three hundred coins to fall."

The night was, indeed, long.

The explanation that Springfield had found was, of course, false.

Pierre with his investigative mind, had simply made the following observation:

On the three dials, he could only see the needles. Those three needles, like those of a compass, each extended across the entire diameter of the dial. They were all, at the present moment, identical in direction and rigorously parallel, except that the indicative painted tip of the dial indicating hundreds was pointing downwards while the other two were pointing upwards.

From that starting-point, by means of his habit of making deductions, he had reasoned as follows:

The graduation of the three dials is necessarily decimal. The vertical diameter of the dial indicating hundreds thus has the zero at the top and a hundred at the bottom. The indicator needle being very close to downward verticality, a century is about to be completed, but how close is it? Within ten kilometers, at the most, since the needle indicating tens is near its zero point and is separated from it by a graduation of ten. But as the needle indicating units is similarly close to its zero point, it indicates that nine kilometers out of the ten have been used up. Therefore, the next fall will mark a round hundred.

Which hundred? Before going to sleep I'd counted to 495. I'm conscious of having slept for a very short time. If the hundred that I'm expecting were the sixth, I would have slept for about an hour and forty-five minutes. I'm certain of the contrary, for, in addition to the approximate notion that I have of the duration of my sleep, I couldn't have counted more than four numbers in my sleep without making a mistake, and Springfield would already have told me if I had. The next number is, therefore, five hundred.

Another proof. The decimal apparatus is evidently conceived in such a manner as the register a round number of kilometers, a thousand or ten thousand; if it were ten thousand, the present position of the needle indicating hundreds would indicate a journey of five thousand kilometers traveled, half the total of the graduations of the dial. Now, it's only eight hundred from Paris to Marseilles. The dial therefore indicates a maximum of a thousand kilometers—which is perfectly logical, the first dial containing ten units, the second ten tens and the third ten hundreds. The figure at the base of the vertical diameter therefore marks half the thousand—which is to say, five hundred.

The gravity of the situation had given Pierre an ephemeral lucidity. After that immense effort, however, he experienced an unfamiliar sensation, a feverish and dolorous overexcitement, which was succeeded, without transition by periods of depression, mental anguish and exhaustion. When the overexcitement was dominant, he stood up and directed a savage glare at his torturer, even advancing toward him for the two or three paces that the narrow space permitted, clenching his fists and leaning on the large central oak table, as if he wanted to embed them in the hard wood. Then the invincible torpor followed, all the more terrible because he was conscious of it as it invaded and took possession of him, like a fainting-fit whose approach one senses and whose effect one anticipates. Stronger than the erethism and the numbness, however, the instinct of the numeration was stubbornly, almost mechanically, sustained by virtue of a kind of indestructible momentum: the strange force that, even in madmen, allows the obsession pursued in a time of sanity to subsist the midst of a general disruption of the faculties.

The time flew by. The kilometers elapsed. The sun rose, illuminating a misty and sinister daylight, rendered even paler by the alliance of the lamps, burning ruddily in the carriage, whose enormous dynamometers were bolted to the ceiling. And in that diffuse and dead light, which gave objects indecisive contours and fantastic reflections, Pierre, either braced like a tiger, his eyes launching flames from their reddened irises, or slumped on the stool with a corpse-like lividity, was still counting, counting, counting...

Springfield was afraid now. He had not foreseen such phases. He had counted on enjoying a fearful struggle, in which his hatred, his vengeance and the instincts of a cold and cruel observer would all find their aliment. He had triumphantly imagined an unfortunate supplicant, sobbing, bowed down by the humiliation of defeat, the fear of returning empty-

177

handed, under the annihilation of hopes already anticipated. But his physiological science had only calculated the first phases of that battle. The physician-engineer had not imagined the persistent victory, overcoming everything, leading his wretched victim to the intelligence of the web that had been spun, to the fury and exasperation of the whole organism, unbalanced by cerebral efforts, and alternatives capable of breaking any mental spring.

Yes, Springfield was afraid. His mask of impassivity had abandoned him. He was no longer pretending, now, to continue his experiments while the other struggled, and his hand trembled as he ticked off, by means of a last appeal to his self-composure, the numbers that Pierre uttered in a hoarse voice, the echoes of which made the copper vibrate..

He certainly felt vigorous and strong, capable of defending himself against an ordinary man, but not against an individual whose nervous system, thus overexcited, might triple his strength. And he watched, with his eyes dilated, all the movements of the companion who held his life in his crazed hands, with whom he was implacably trapped by the vertiginous rapidity of the express train.

The ordeal was approaching its end. The final hundred was already well advanced. Pierre had quit his seat. He had no more need, now, to look at the basin or listen carefully. The number emerged, with mathematical precision, as the coin fell through the air. The victim was three paces away from the torturer and seemed ready to exchange roles.

With his arms folded across his breast, Springfield, his hair bristling, his complexion pale, recoiled inch by inch—and Pierre, whose fits of prostration had ceased, advanced without saying anything, his lips contracted by a frightful rictus, his lips bloody from the bites he had inflicted on them.

The Englishman could feel the draught of his hot breath. Hideous, paralyzing terror took possession of him. His legs buckled. He was stammering now; he begged and pleaded with the man whose reason he had killed. He promised to help him, to support him. It was no longer a matter of eighty thou-

178

sand francs; he would give him half his fortune. His influence, his workshops, everything would be at his disposal.

But Pierre did not reply, and continued laughing, his breast rising with convulsive hiccups.

During this drama the doubloons continued to fall, each at the precise moment, into the bronze basin, immediately saluted by the exact figure that Pierre was now shouting in his enemy's face.

Then, suddenly, the inventor uttered a ferocious cry, the triumphant song of the brute that succeeded divine reason and howled, to the last ring of the last golden disk: "Eight hundred!"

At the same time he seized a lever and brandished it over Springfield's head.

During the entire duration of the struggle—the torture—a supreme glimmer of honesty had illuminated the ashes of that intelligence, which was consuming itself. Pierre had respected the life of his adversary while there remained a contract to execute. He wanted that gold, and he had the vague idea that it would not be his until he had counted it to the last doubloon in front of his torturer. Now, it was over; the conditions had been fulfilled. He was about to avenge himself.

But the train was reducing its velocity, approaching a station. Mad with fear, Springfield did not wait for it to stop. He opened the door with the rapidity of thought, and leapt on to the track.

Pierre remained where he was momentarily, amazed by that abrupt disappearance, like a Spanish bull that stops, bewildered, before the solid barrier behind which the agile toreador had disappeared. Then, seemingly forgetting the Englishman, he went back to the other end of the carriage.

The heap of gold was now complete, lying in the basin. He piled it into a large bag that he had brought and sat down until the train stopped at Miramas station. There, he lifted up the bag, which contained nearly sixty pounds of gold, like a father, got down, and calmly walked along the platform, repeating in a loud voice all the numbers that he had counted.

Springfield had fractured his skull when he jumped from the train. He died two days later. He had only recovered consciousness for a few minutes, and had not given any explanation of the mysterious drama of which the experimentation carriage had been the heater. He limited himself to saying, in answer to a question addressed to him by the local Maire, that the possession of the large sum carried by Pierre Marsault was the result of a contract made between them, and that the gold really did belong to his companion.

Six months later, Dr. G***, the illustrious alienist got down from his carriage at the door to a pretty house whose garden extended all the way to the Bassin d'Argenteuil. It was a beautiful sunny day in April. The trees were in bud and the birds were singing. In a warm corner brightened by sunlight, a man with a gentle and sad expression was sitting on a large armchair, contemplated by the gaze of a young woman with red eyelids, who was holding his hand, while two thoughtful children fixed their beautiful blue eyes upon him, charged with mute interrogation.

The doctor went to the man, whose lips were moving incessantly, as if he were muttering some mysterious prayer. He examined him, seemed satisfied, and said to the woman: "We can attempt the experiment now."

Half an hour later, they brought the invalid on to the little terrace that overlooked the basin, where a few white sails were gliding. Suddenly, there was a blast of a whistle, and a boat appeared, having been hidden until then on the section of the river that was masked by the wall of the property.

It was a steamboat, extremely elegant in form, its hull brightly painted white, which was cleaving through water with a rapidity that was almost prodigious.

The madman stood up, stared for a moment, with his eyes wide open and his finger extended, and then dissolved in tears, crying: "*La Flèche!*"

Pierre Marsault was saved.

Camille Debans: *A Steam Duel*
(1895)

Everyone knows this story, but no one has ever known the cause or the details. When a journalist runs short of sensational rumors and when the tide of news ebbs, far from hanging up his pen, the journalist searches old collections, finds the story of my duel, precedes it with the famous "from our New York correspondent," calmly inserts it and goes to lunch with a clear conscience.

The next day, the subscriber reads the article, smiles, and addresses an amicable salute to it, as if to an old friend. Then everyone is content.

The idea has occurred to me, given this state of affairs, of recounting the origin and denouement of the quarrel, out of pure philanthropy, for the journalists, having read me—if they ever read anything—will have the invaluable resource of adding fifty carefully-condensed lines to the narrative so frequently reproduced, and not yet outdated, of my duel. As for the subscribers—who read everything—it will replace for them the story of some stolen shoes or the hundred and twenty-seventh edition of a moldy pun.

One particularity among a thousand, of which no mention has ever been made, is that my adversary was none other than Tom Tompson, who is surely the most intrepid engine-driver in America—which I can proclaim without jealousy, since he usually maintains, when people pay him that compliment, that his son-in-law is the foremost engine-driver in the two worlds. And his son-in-law, Mesdames, is me, who will not hesitate to agree that Tom Tompson knows what he is talking about, for I am as devoid of false modesty as of real vanity.

Before he had the honor of becoming my father-in-law, Tom Tompson was ugly. I cannot say that old age and the mere fact of having granted me his daughter's hand have rendered him handsome; no, but everyone knows, in the vicinity of Thirty-second Avenue, that my wife's father was by far the ugliest of the Tompsons—and God knows, they were frightful!—whereas, since my entry thereinto, the family is almost tolerable.

Nature had afflicted him with a terrible nose. Thanks to that cartilaginous excrescence, his general appearance had take on, since infancy, incredible proportions; by virtue of a lugubrious farce of chance it was ornamented, at its extremity, by a huge, black, thick, hairy and greasy wart, which sometimes performed somersaults and agitated comically, according to the impressions experienced by its unfortunate owner.

What was terrible was that no one in the world, even by exerting himself, could look at Tom Tompson without laughing at his nose. And no expression was ever more exact than that, for, at the mere sight of the appendage in question, a burst of laughter took possession of you, without your being able to repress it. A fakir would have guffawed for at least an hour without giving a thought to his navel or to Brahma, and I've always thought that Democritus, if he had known Tom Tompson, would have found an opportunity at least once in his life to split his sides laughing, to the great amazement of his contemporaries.

Anyway, the first time I saw Tom Tompson—it was in Albany, in Hudson Street, outside number 9, as I shall remember all my life—he was advancing with a certain majesty, with his abdomen sticking out and his daughter Ellen on his arm.

I shall not permit either the old or the new world to dare to think that Miss Elen was not the most beautiful girl in the two Americas, the Antilles included. So, when I found myself in the presence of the couple, my gaze focused exclusively on the young woman. I had no suspicion of the incalculable gaiety of which I was depriving myself by not contemplating Tom Tompson, his nose and his wart first. But that pleasure was no less vivid for being delayed, for as soon as Ellen's admirable gaiety permitted me to redirect my gaze toward her companion, I was obliged to hold my sides and turn my eyes away, for if I had continued to look at him, I would certainly have been forced to roll around on the sidewalk in a crisis of laughter of which even the expression "Homeric" could only give a homeopathic—I might even say infinitesimal—idea.

"Tom Tompson! Tom Tompson!" I cried, as soon as my fit permitted me to speak. "Ha ha ha ha! Tom Tompson! I'll bet fifty dollars that you're Tom Tompson! Ha ha ha ha! Aaah, one shouldn't laugh like that! Aaah...ha ha! You're definitely Tom Tompson!"

I had been warned, though. In the railway workshops, in the stations, aboard the locomotives, Tom Tompson's nose and wart were famous, and I'd been warned that when I encountered him, I couldn't fail to recognize him and laugh till I cried, laugh till it hurt, and shout: "You're Tom Tompson!"—which I had not failed to do.

Unfortunately, it was the first time that Ellen's father had come to Albany, and, in consequence, he had never exhibited his disagreeably physiognomy there before. My infinite hilarity attracted the attention of passers-by; a crowd accumulated, whose members initially only paid attention to me and thought I was mad, but as soon as I had extended my arm toward the man with the nose and had launched at him my famous "You're Tom Tompson!" all gazes mechanically followed the direction I was indicating, and, at the sight of the wart and its owner, whose furious eyes were rolling to either side of that nose like two braziers on the edges of a double precipice, a clamor rose up, an inextinguishable laughter took hold of the crowd. Never, I'm certain, since Noah judged it appropriate to build his ark, had anyone laughed like that on this deplorably desolate earth.

Intimidated by the gazes that were being directed at him, singularly embarrassed by my exclamation, bewildered by the bursts of laughter that were shooting like rockets, the unfortunate Tom wore an expression that was becoming more comical by the minute. His wart, the object of general admiration, began to twitch, involuntarily, at the end of his nose, and struck poses, and did its utmost to merit the immense success of enthusiasm that it was obtaining at that moment. And the more Tom Tompson attempted to give his physiognomy the placidity of astonishment, the more than satanic wart, doubtless agitated by the interior stirring of a soul, danced on its promontory, placing itself in a new light from one moment to the next, with the result that the hilarity of the crowd, even though it seemed to have arrived at its apogee, increased further.

There were people sitting on the sidewalk, writhing in nervous laughter. Judge by that how much effect Tom Tompson's nose and the black pearl that was its ornament were having.

But everything has a limit, even Tom Tompson's patience. He had separated himself from his daughter Ellen to set himself at the center of the group whose joy he was providing. His furious eyes went from one laugher to another, doubtless seeking the one of which his powerful anger ought to fall.

It did not take him long, if my memory serves me right.

There were two of us standing closer to him than the other passers-by. He advanced straight toward my neighbor, and, folding his formidable middle finger over his thumb in order to give it the necessary spring, he administered a terrible flick to the nose of the young man, who stopped laughing.

It was evident that he wanted to attack the part of the face that every human being had more beautiful than him. The man with the bruised nose uttered a roar, and put his hand to his nose precipitately, as if he were no longer sure of finding it in place, so violent had the flick been.

The audience, who were expecting something and had begun to calm down, resumed laughing more loudly than before.

As for Tom Tompson, he turned toward me in order to take further vengeance. He was about to slap me in the face with a powerful backhander, and perhaps break two or three teeth, when I ducked rapidly, with the result that his blow struck someone else's face—but only after sending my hat flying twenty yards away.

It was then that the bursts of laughter took on crazy proportions. Hudson Street resembled a lunatic asylum. There were people there who ran away at top speed in order to cure themselves of such frenzy.

That last fit, even more astonishing than its predecessors, demands an explanation, and I shall give it with a good grace.

Since the age of twenty-two—I was twenty-seven then—I had lost the greater part of the hair that Mother Nature gave me. I was the victim of a baldness as absolute as possible. The word "victim" is not too strong, for in the epoch when I saw my hair begin to retreat—I dare not say one hair at a time, for they fell out in thousands every day—a protuberance was seem to appear on the summit of my head, which soon took on implausible proportions. It was a mole, but an unnaturally large mole, a giant mole, which affected bizarre forms into the bargain. You could see it from a long way away.

When I took my hat off voluntarily, an admirably-constructed wig hid my infirmity from the eyes of my contemporaries. But when I took off that warm dissimulation, my poor head looked like the peak of an arid and desolate mountain, at the summit of which the effort of a volcano had produced an immense bulge.

Now, Tom Tompson, in knocking off my hat, had also provoked the removal of my artificial hair, and the effect of my mole on the spectators of the scene was even more hilarious than the effect of the automaton wart of which Tom Tompson was so scantly proud.

Scarcely had I been decoiffed than my adversary's anger abated. He burst out laughing in his turn and held his sides until the moment when, having got his breath back, he cried: "You're William Turkey!"

I was amazed to hear my name pronounced like that, and didn't understand, so difficult do the people most inclined to laugh at others find it to imagine that others might mock them. I didn't understand how Tom Tompson had recognized me.

I've found out since that my mole was as famous in the stations and aboard the locomotives as my adversary's wart.

What a terrible invention of the Creator human nature is!

I'm not malicious, and while making fun of Tom Tompson, I thought that he would take it in good part and end up laughing like everyone else. Except that I hadn't thought of asking myself whether it would be equally agreeable to me to be ridiculed in front of everyone, and whether I had sufficient sense of humor to amuse myself, with the same gallantry, if I were the butt of the joke.

What I had hoped of Tom Tompson came to pass. Eventually, he started laughing with the mockers, finding the idea of his incomparable wart very droll himself. For myself, I hadn't reflected on the effect that the mockery I applied to others would have on me, and, like an imbecile, I became violently angry. I went pale, my eyes became bloodshot, and my entire face was hideous with fury. The crowd, when I insulted them, laughed more loudly at every insult my fury dictated to me.

The natural result of that was that I became even more enraged, and lashed out at two or three people. That irrational action might have earned me the scorn of Miss Ellen and the reprisals of the crowd, but I was no longer conscious of anything. We human beings are generally like that!

The audience had not taken the few blows I had distributed very well, and I sensed, in spite of my temporary insanity, that I was about to come to harm. However, Tom Tompson approached me, put his hand on my shoulder as if he were taking possession of something that belonged to him, and, turning to the crowd, he said: "Ladies and gentleman, this man belongs to me. I thought at first that he would laugh, as I have just done, at the disgrace with which nature has gratified him, but he has got annoyed, flown into a temper and lashed out right and left. He therefore thinks that we have insulted him.

Logically, he ought to agree that I have been insulted too, and by him, since he started it. Only a duel between the two of us can finish this quarrel, and I beg you to leave him entirely to me, in order that I shall have a man for an adversary and not an invalid."

That speech by Tom Tompson was an enormous success.

"He's right! He's right!" cried the crowd. "Hurrah for Tom Tompson! Hurrah for his wart! Hurrah for his nose! Hip, hip, hurray!"

I am now convinced that Tom Tompson had not the slightest intention of challenging me to single combat. His sole aim, in claiming me in that original fashion, was to get me away from a population who, after their fit of violent gaiety, might have finished up lynching me in the blink of an eye.

But I was too stupid to understand Ellen's father's generous gesture, and I should: "I accept! Let's go into a tavern and settle the conditions of the duel."

So Tom Tompson set about marching alongside me. The majority of the members of the crowd resumed their interrupted journeys, and only the curiosity-seekers followed us, in the hope of learning something interesting about the duel that had been announced to them.

We went into a bar. The cluster of indiscreet individuals who had attached themselves to us dispersed in all directions, except for two or three who would not let go as easily of the possible pleasure of seeing a man killed.

Although I was still intoxicated by resentment, I knew that it was customary to be very polite in the circumstances in which I found myself, and I offered my adversary a bottle of whisky.

We sat down—Miss Ellen had returned to her hotel—and drank prodigiously, getting so drunk that Tom Tompson, who had only wanted to save me in removing me from the crowd, could no longer remember anything except that I had insulted him, that he had insulted me, and that he was in perfect agreement with me as to the absolute necessity that one of us had to die, the earth being too narrow to accommodate two men, one of whom had a wart while the other had a mole.

"Oh, but think about it, my son!" exclaimed Tom Tompson, vigorously thumping the table. "Think about it! We need to fight a duel that people will still be talking about a hundred years from now."

"Tom, I'm your man!"

As I said that, I noticed his wart; it was standing up in a most bellicose fashion, which gave me pleasure.

"Your mole is twitching, my son," Tom replied, "and I'm sure that you're not afraid—so let's think of something that will be...hang on...there's a scholarly word that expresses it very well...hom...homily...Homeric! That's the word!"

"I don't know what it means, but I accept. Let's go for Homeric."

"Well, my son, what would you say to a duel swimming in the Hudson? We arm ourselves with daggers and...the rest speaks for itself."

"That's a nice suggestion, Tom, but it isn't practical. We'd start off on opposite banks, wouldn't we, and meet in the middle?"

"Naturally."

"Well, Tom, it might be the case that the current would drag one or other of us a few yards further on than we thought, and we'd be obliged to catch up with one another, wait for one another, and use up a lot of our strength swimming."

"That's true."

"With the result that when the real duel began, we'd no longer be vigorous enough for that critical moment—not to mention that whoever was upstream of the other would have an advantage."

"You're right. You're a good boy, my son. The chances have to be equal on both sides. Let's think of something else."

"We set about drinking more whisky, so much that Tom could no longer think of anything, there not being a single glimmer of reason in his poor head. As for me I'd already sketched out a few encounters with knives, rifles and even poisons, when a triumphant idea occurred to me.

"Search no further, Tom! I've got it!" I cried, with a radiant expression.

"You've got it! There's a scholarly word for that," murmured my adversary, his head swaying from side to side. "Let's hear what you've got."

"Here it is: One day, without saying anything. Tom Tompson climbs into his locomotive, staring from Washington. At the same time, William Turkey departs in his engine from New York. Tom Tompson and William Turkey will be on the same track, as if by chance. They'll be alone, and they'll give their mounts all possible speed, until they come together and both fly into the air."

"That's perfect," sighed Tom, downing a glass. "That's perfect."

"There's nothing more to arrange than landing on one's feet."

"On one's feet!" Tom Tompson mumbled, slowly, having difficulty articulating two syllables without a hiccup in between. "On one's feet! That's easy to say, my son. Land on one's feet! That might be quite difficult. On one's feet! Land on one's feet! A problem, that! No matter, my son—it's agreed. Your idea is superb. We'll do it the day after tomorrow. You can go, unless you'd like to accept a bottle of brandy in your turn."

When Tom Tompson tried to leave the tavern he no longer had any notion of the laws of equilibrium, and he lay down full length on the roadway, still murmuring: "On one's feet! A problem, that!"—which did not prevent the excellent man from remembering perfectly what had been agreed, while I, who seemed considerably more sober than he was, didn't remember anything, and when I left New York that day, it was to go for a walk in the country.

Tom Tompson, having covered three-quarters of the distance between Washington and New York, thought that I lacked urgency in coming to meet him, and when he came into the station in New York he was very surprised, not to say indignant, at my behavior. So he set out in search of your humble servant, in order to administer bloody reproaches for his conduct.

I was coming home—for it was already late—along the waterfront when a hand suddenly fell on my shoulder.

"I've been looking for you, my son," said Tom Tompson gravely, "to tell you that you're a disgrace to the railways."

"What!" I exclaimed, trying to recognize my interlocutor.

"I'm Tom Tompson, my son, and you were due to leave New York today to come and fly into the air with me and our two engines."

"That's true, Tom, that's true."

"Well, why didn't you come? You're not afraid, are you? Anyway, you ought to remember that it was you who challenged me."

"Well, Tom you have to believe me, because I'll tell you the simple truth; it's precisely the memory to which you refer that I'm completely lacking."

"I'd like to believe you," said Tom, in a mocking tone.

"You made me drink too much whisky, Tom, and I slept for forty-eight hours; after which I went out to get a little air, without giving a thought to you or our duel."

"So?"

"So, it's on for tomorrow, if you have nothing better to do."

"That's good, my son—it's on for tomorrow."

With that, we went our separate ways.

The next day, in fact, I got my locomotive ready as if I had some special job to do. In the midst of the hubbub at the station, no one paid any heed to me.

Tom Tompson hadn't gone back to Washington. He was due to have stopped in a small intermediary town that he's designated to me. At ten o'clock, his engine would set off too.

The only real difficulty in the execution of our plan consisted of being able to get ourselves on the same track without exciting the suspicion of the company's agents.

Fortunately, I knew a pointsman in a station situated about two-thirds of the way along my course. I told him that I was going to lend assistance on the track to Tom's engine, which was heading toward me at top speed. He believed me, switched the points and I went by.

To tell you that my heart wasn't beating a little faster when I found myself on that track, and when I thought about the imminent impact that awaited me, would be an infamous lie. So I set about accelerating my locomotive, in order that the intoxication of the speed wouldn't leave me any time to devote to reflection.

I could have derailed; I almost wanted to. It was, in fact, a frightful idea that I had had. Twice in my life I had seen locomotives run into one another, and I knew what terrible chaos it produces. With regard to the men on board, there could be no doubt about it: only a miracle—one of those miracles that even the imagination can't envisage, so improbable is it—could save them. Then again, it's a frightful contest; one of the machines gives the impression of trying to climb on top of the other and crush it, while the other rears up in its turn, making a terrible noise. The two monsters mate, uttering shrill and sinister cries with their whistles; the disordered respiration of the steam mingles with that confusion; one would swear that they were about to wrestle and try to throw one another. Then, often, a boiler bursts, the sound of shattering iron rings out, and the two adversaries, vanquished, broken and dead, fall back heavily to the ground, torn apart by that gigantic mortal embrace.

That memory came back to me perpetually, without my being able to drive it away, and that really annoyed me.

"Well then, William Turkey," I finally said to myself, "is it, by chance, that you're afraid? You've invented a duel such as no one has ever seen, and at the moment when the combat is about to take place, when, in dying, you'll frighten the uni-

191

verse with your glory, you start trembling and want to back out! More coal on the fire, William, and full speed ahead!"

That little speech rallied me somewhat. I put more coal on the fire, but as I raised my head, I felt a cold sweat invade my temples and my back. Tom Tompson was no more than a mile away from me, and we were heading toward one another at a hellish rate.

Do you want me to tell you everything? Well, I closed my eyes, with my back against my coal-bunker, and I waited.

A minute later, I perceived something like a gust of wind, I heard a rapid noise to me left…and my knees buckled.

Strangely, enough, though, I was still going, and the impact hadn't happened. That surprised me more than you might think. I opened my eyes. There was nothing in front of me any longer—no more Tom Tompson at all. I nearly fell over with astonishment. Where the devil had he gone? I darted a glance behind my engine, and then I saw my adversary drawing away from me.

It was enough to make one believe in magic. How had he gone past without smashing me, without smashing himself? Had he followed the example of those gentleman riders and trained his locomotive to leap over obstacles and run steeplechases?

It was scarcely probable—and yet there had to be a reason for it, and I racked my brains in vain trying to find it.

Deep down, although I wasn't sorry to have got out of that awkward spot, I ended up giving up in the face of such a puzzle, and slowed down in order to be able to retrace my steps placidly—which is what I did.

When I arrived at a little station on the edge of which I estimated that we should have collided, I saw Tom Tompson coming back too—but not on the same track as me, which surprised my somewhat.

We both stopped, and I realized then what I hadn't been able to see because my eyes had been closed while I waited stoically for death.

A pointsman, full of naivety and presence of mind—it's necessary to admit—having seen two locomotives advancing toward one another at fifty miles an hour, had initially uttered an exclamation of astonishment and then, as quick as thought, had thrown himself upon the lever and had pulled it in a desperate fashion, with the result that Tom Tompson, who had arrived level with the station in question first, had, involuntarily and for our common salvation, taken another track.

"Damn!" cried Tom Tompson, as soon as he could make himself heard. "That imbecile has spoiled our duel. We'll have to start again, my son."

Tom Tompson had the reputation of being extremely stubborn. I could see that he had not usurped that renown.

The next day, he presented himself at my home, very sprightly, offering a thousand excuses and compliments, calling the pointsman thanks to whom we were both still alive a double-dyed swine, an unregimented donkey, an obtuse ox and a hundred other appellations that ceded nothing in amenity to the first. If I were not sure of having a large number of female readers I would even transcribe the supreme insult that he addressed to him—an insult that has no equivalent in any language—but I know only too well what I owe to propriety, to my readers and to myself to take love of detail that far, even though I am fanatical regarding the scrupulous exactitude of the facts when I permit myself to write any narrative whatsoever.

After having stormed to his heart's content, and consequently caused his wart to strike all the poses that it affected in such instances, Tom Tompson held out his hand to me and said: "So, my son, it'll be the day after tomorrow."

"Agreed for the day after tomorrow, Tom."

"But this time, it's necessary not to miss our stroke. You'd be ridiculous forever, and so would I."

"God forbid, Tom, that that should happen."

"Good, my son. See you soon, then! See you soon!"

"See you soon, Tom."

Two days later, I set off as I had the previous time.

The weather was fine. I have no idea whether I ought to attribute my bravery to the atmospheric conditions, but it's certain that I was mettlesome that morning, to an incalculable degree. It has been remarked that revolutions are more often made and battles more often fought when the sky is cloudless, or at least when it isn't raining. Fog and rain cool human courage considerably, and no one likes to die in bad weather. Without discoursing any longer on the subject, I'll add one final proof: many, very many splenetic or desperate individuals have put off their suicidal plans indefinitely because the river into the depths of which they were about to throw themselves looked gray and cold.

At any rate, I was firmly decided to die like a hero, although several times already, even while putting on my shoes that same morning, I had told myself that I was about to get myself killed like an imbecile, without any profit to anyone, including myself.

At the end of the day, though, I had a mole, and Tom Tompson had a wart; it was necessary for us to submit to the consequences of that malevolence of Dame Nature.

In brief, once I was in the open air, traveling at a considerable number of miles an hour, I was no longer thinking about anything but crushing Tom, who seemed to be putting a singular obstinacy into crashing into me with his locomotive. Apparently, I didn't want to remember that it was me who had proposed the thing.

I had covered forty-eight miles—you won't demand the fractions, I suppose—and I was still seething with courage and impatience, when I was obliged to obey a signal that ordered me imperiously to stop.

A serious accident had taken place on the track. I wanted to get myself crushed by Tom Tompson, and to crush him myself at the same time, but I had no reason to go and crash into a bunch of derailed carriages and flattened passengers, so I slowed down—and just in time, for I came to a halt twenty-five yards from the site of the accident in question.

There was a frightful confusion of wagons, locomotives and merchandise of every sort: sugar, molasses, bales of cotton, casks of wine, barrels of whisky, etc., etc.

The train that had derailed hadn't been transporting passengers. By the first glance at the machine I knew which engineer had been driving it. That's always our first thought in such circumstances, because we know full well that engineers rarely come back from such experiments in ballistics.

Fortunately—if the word isn't too cruel—I acquired the certainty that the engineer and the stoker, who were probably lying dead a few yards away, were two of the most wretched, idle, drunken and intolerable scoundrels in America. I said a funeral prayer for them appropriate to their merit, and as short as my restricted esteem for their unfortunate carcasses. After having summarily accomplished that sacred duty, I got down in order to make a tour of the debris and lend my assistance to the clearance of the track, if necessary.

Imagine my shock, however, when I saw, running toward the train, the engineer that I had just mourned so briefly. People are right to say that death doesn't want good-for-nothings. The blackguard in question, launched into the air by the sudden arrest of his machine, had been precipitated, as if by a miracle, into a large deep pond, into the depths of which he had executed an incomparable dive, backwards. Thanks to that fortunate circumstance, his deadened fall had become a mere bath in dirty but protective water.

One saved, I said to myself. *So much the better; we don't want the sinner dead. As for the other, it's all right; the derailment will have saved him from that gallows.*

As I concluded this reflection, the stoker appeared in his turn. He was spry and cheerful, and when he was a few yards away from me I perceived that he was exhaling an agreeable and penetrating odor, of which his somersault was an insufficient explanation. It was, moreover, a strange contrast with the odor given off by the engineer, for the latter, steeped in stinking mud, would have made a manufacturer of asafetida run away.

Interrogated, the stoker recounted that, having been hurled into the air by acquired velocity, he wasn't thinking about anything but dying when he felt himself assailed in his parabola by little branches that were whipping his face. Then, as he was approaching the ground, a kind of hammock formed underneath him; he was half-supported by a very thick, very soft and highly perfumed clump of laurier-roses. He had slid for a few more seconds over that flower-bed, which deadened the momentum to which he was involuntarily obedient, and the scoundrel eventually found himself, covered in perfume, softly extended, without a scratch, on a thick and flowery lawn in the shade of the laurier-roses, two paces from a spring, like a demigod of antiquity at odds with Olympus.

Oh, if only those two fellows had been worth anything, like you or me!

As the stoker finished recounting his adventure, however, a voice was heard coming from the midst of the debris.

"Who's that?" we all cried.

"You might well say *who's that*, you frauds!" the voice replied.

I shivered and started running in the direction from which the calls were coming. They followed me. Imagine my astonishment when I ended up pulling out from underneath a veritable stew of merchandise…who? You've guessed it, but admit that it's a bit unlikely: Tom Tompson! Tom Tompson in person. His wart was intact, and so was he.

He perceived or divined my presence. "It's bad luck, my son—we'll have to start again. You didn't think my ideas were practical, but it seems to me that yours is giving a certain amount of trouble from the viewpoint of execution."

One thing I hadn't thought about was the cause of the accident. Now I had it before my eyes. Tom Tompson and his locomotive, coming toward me at top speed, had collided, after a bend in the track, with the train of which nothing remained but wreckage.

"How were you thrown under there, Tom?"

"In truth, my son, I have absolutely no idea. It knocked me unconscious. I only came round at the moment when you heard me shout.

"You were lucky!"

"You think so? William, my son, don't mock me. That's two days I've wasted, not to mention the locomotive, and that's a bad business. Next time, I'll wait for you at a location where it will be more certain, near the Black River Bridge."

"You're very determined to kill me."

"Me! Not at all—but since it's agreed. Do you, by chance, think me capable of backing out?"

"I didn't say that, Tom, I didn't say that."

"Well, my son, we'll do it Tuesday, if it's all right with you."

"No, not Tuesday. I have an invitation to Mrs. Tapeton's. Wednesday, Tom, Wednesday."

"Wednesday, my son, I shall be at your disposal. Come and have a drop of brandy—that'll get us back on our feet."

It was fated that we were never going to meet, and Tom Tompson was right: my idea wasn't practical at all.

To begin with, the company's supervisors were beginning to get suspicious, seeing both of us set off so often under futile pretexts—for it was, after all necessary to find pretexts. Secondly, we had observed that it was extremely difficult for us both to get on to the same track. There was always a pointsman there to put us back on the right track or an inspector to enquire about the reasons for our journey in such abnormal conditions.

At any rate, the following Wednesday, we were both faithful to our promise. Naturally, Tom Tompson was manning another locomotive, since his own had previously served to crash a train, give an engineer a bath and perfume a stoker, by means of previously-unknown methods that were impracticable in everyday life.

For myself, I still had the same machine. It seemed, though, that I had had a complete change of heart; the hesitations of the first day did not present themselves to my mind and I hastened the moment of impact as much as I could.

Did I have an intuition of the fecund outcome that the terrible new combat was to have? Who can tell? Perhaps, too, the spectacle of three enginemen saved in an encounter that should, according to all ordinary expectations, have cost them their lives ten times over, had made me think, unwittingly, that a man caught between two iron monsters might get away with it.

When I set off, I was not only serene and tranquil, but I had a hint of cheerfulness about me, whose veritable cause I would not have been able to identify. Tom Tompson, he told me later, was declaring incessantly to himself while letting off his steam in order to come and kill me, that my idea was utterly stupid, and that his duel in the river would have had much more class.

I still regret not having seen his wart at that moment, for it must have been, as you can have no doubt, particularly phenomenal; but happiness in this world is never complete.

You might think, readers, that I'm keeping you in suspense and not getting straight to the point. I'd like to see you do it, to see how much of a hurry you'd be in, in my place. As for the goal, the supreme goal, I can assure you that I was heading toward it with a rapidity that I judged entirely appropriate. Except that, at such moments, the mind has an excessively prompt faculty of reflection, and I'm only telling you the hundredth part of what I said to myself.

I was approaching Black River.

There are immense wooden bridges across which railways pass over many American rivers, but they're not fixed. The necessities of river navigation have obliged engineers to find systems that allow ships to pass. Thus, the bridges have to open; each half folds back toward the bank to allow the larger ships free passage. When the vessels have traversed that section of the river, the two halves of the bridge join up again, juxtaposing exactly, in order to let the fastest trains in the world cross the river and the gap.

There is a bridge of that kind on Black River. There further I went, the more certain I became that we would meet on the bridge, and that the impact would be frightful in its consequences.

By virtue of a rather sharp bend, neither Tom Tompson nor I could see the bridge, but as the iron track shorted the two opposed banks of Black River for several miles I perceived the fumes of his engine, and he must have been able to see my steam.

It was all set this time; there was no pointsman who could thwart our plan, no train with which we might collide before running into one another. The thermometer of my gaiety went down a few degrees, I must admit, but I didn't weaken. I stuffed my engine with coal, and planted myself upright on the tender.

It was certain that we would crash in the middle of the river.

Just as we were both about to move on to the bridge of doom, however, I heard a terrible crack on Tom Tompson's bank, and before I could form any idea of what was happening, another crack, even ore frightful, rang in my ears, and I perceived a void in front of me, to either side of me—everywhere...

"The bridge was open!" I cried, mechanically—and Tom Tompson must have said the same. Neither of us had thought, although it was quite natural, since we had chosen a moment when no train could get in our way and, in consequence, could not oblige the attendants to reunite the two fragments of the apron.

I had a vague idea that I had broken the barriers. I seemed to see something enormous on the other side of Black River take a mighty plunge, while a man spun in mid-air; then everything disappeared beneath my feet. I put out my arms, perceived the muffled sound of the fall of an enormous weight and the particular hiss of a fire being put out, and then felt myself going into the water, head first.

I ought to add that I must have penetrated the water with such impetuosity that not a drop of water splashed up around me. I disappeared to the bottom of the river like a bullet. If some unlucky shad had been passing the place where I fell at that moment, it's certain that I would have had the same effect as a cannonball on the unfortunate creature.

What happened next? Oh, my God, I could pretend not to know and take advantage of the opportunity to make you believe that I was saved by a miracle and an angel of the female sex—but as I know perfectly well how I got out of it, I'd rather tell you right away.

Tom Tompson really was an admirably constituted fellow. Allowing that my mole was a physical inconvenience comparable to his wart, it's certain that I was considerably inferior to him in every other respect.

He was, as you will understand, naturally a trifle stunned by the plunge to which he had just been subjected, but that concussion did not last long, and a few seconds after the fact, he was seen to reappear at the surface of Black River. His very first words were about me, for he muttered between his teeth: "This idea is truly impractical. Once again, we have to go back to square one. William Turkey, my son, you should have accepted my first proposal."

Having said that, while swimming, he darted a glance around him and started shouting to me at the top of his voice—but I was still deep under water, with no more suspicion that a world existed of bridges, warts, rivers, moles, Tom Tompson and locomotives.

"Dear God!" my adversary cried, then. "Has that imbecile been ill-mannered enough to drown here, with no thought for his honor and the promise we made me to crash into one another?" Then, having taken another breath, he added: "I'm not going to allow that. I don't want him to drown, until our duel achieves a satisfactory result."

That said, Tom Tompson dived like a porpoise, and started searching the river bed. He was obliged to return to the surface several times to draw breath, but he finally perceived me, dived one last time, grabbed me by the arm and dragged me to the bank, on which he deposited me, unconscious and half-asphyxiated.

After having made me return to the river a considerable part of the water that I'd just borrowed therefrom, Tom Tompson took me in his arms and carried me to a farm situated a short distance from the theater of our acrobatics.

All the noise we had made in falling into Black River having attracted a copious crowd of curiosity-seekers, they help my imperturbable adversary transport me. That did not, however, prevent those worthy people from enjoying themselves at the expense of Tom's nose and my head—but that could no longer disturb us.

I was laid on a bed; the farmer's wife set about making me a tisane, and someone went to fetch a surgeon to attend to me. Before the tisane as infused, or the doctor had arrived, however, I was on my feet, again thanks to that animal Tom, who, knowing my nature and judging me by himself, had been content to make me absorb half a liter of eau-de-vie.

Naturally we thought it inappropriate to remain at the farm any longer, and set off for a station, on order that we could each get home as soon as possible.

On the way, Tom Tompson said to me: "My son, we're certainly in an awkward position with regard to the company."

"Oh, certainly. As you say, Tom, certainly."

"That's three locomotives that your idea has cost, not to mention an entire train in which there was a great deal of molasses and brandy."

"It's probable," I said, "that they're going to demand explanations from us."

"And what will you say, my son, when they interrogate you?"

"I shall say, Tom…I shall say…in truth, I don't have the slightest idea. What about you?"

"Me? I shall tell the truth."

"Ah!"

"Yes, my son, and you'd do well to do likewise. If the gentlemen aren't content, we'll bid the company farewell. Young America, thank God, has no shortage of railways where they'll be happy to acquire and pay well for the two most intrepid engineers in the world, the day after they've attempted to make themselves immortal."

"Perhaps you're right, but..."

"I understand, my son, and like you, I think that there lies the difficulty. Will they let us start again? For it's necessary for us to start again."

"Tom, believe me, they won't let us start again."

"Well, my son, we'll do without the permission."

I told you that Tom Tompson was stubborn.

We got back home that same evening. We were summoned to company headquarters, as we had foreseen, and we were interrogated.

Without hesitation, Tom Tompson made a speech that lasted a good twenty minutes, in which he mingled a few Latin words with a great many unnecessary observations about honor, duty and glory. In brief, he talked like a book, to the great astonishment of the bosses and me; then he declared that, for the company, the glory of having two engineers as determined as us was more than adequate compensation for the trivial loss of four locomotives and twenty-five wagons, not to mention the merchandise.

They listened to him, they admired him, they admitted that he was right, and they even let us keep our jobs, but with the precaution of demanding our word of honor not to do it again.

"If it's only a matter of not doing it again on your company's lines, gentlemen, I'm ready to make that promise," I put in then, "but it can't prevent us from trying again on another railway."

"Other railways are none of our concern," the chairman of the board replied, with considerable sagacity.

When we were in the street, Tom Tompson said to me: "Listen, William—it's necessary not to let this little affair drag on."

"Certainly, Tom—I understand as well as you do the necessity of putting an end to it once and for all, but I confess that I'm a little discouraged."

"Discouraged, my son? What does that mean?"

"Don't get carried away, Tom. This is what I mean: my idea, that we thought so admirable at first sight, now seems to me to be impossible in the execution."

"I've already told you that a hundred times, my son, but you're obstinate. Me, you see, I'm always flexible, and provided that the duel takes place and our honor is preserved, I'll comply with your new opinion, if you have one."

"Alas, Tom, I don't."

"We need to rack our brains, then."

At that moment, I left Tom Tompson to go into a shop, in order to buy a new wig, because, as you can imagine, my old one had remained at the bottom of the river with the two locomotives.

When I came back, delighted to have covered up my capital protuberance again, my companion came toward me rapidly and said: "My son, I've got an idea that I think is both honorable and original."

"Speak, Tom, speak—I'm all ears."

"Tomorrow, we're going back to work. I consequence, we'll pass one another on the track at least twice a week."

"That's true, Tom."

"Well, my son, on the first journey in the course of which we'll encounter one another, we'll each carry a sturdy revolver, and we'll each fire six shots at the other with as much skill as possible."

"But what if we miss?"

"Then we'll find something else. But I advise you to take great care to aim true; I'll do my utmost, for my part, not to miss, for it's necessary to admit, my son, that we're wasting our time in a pitiful fashion."

Three days later, the passenger train that my locomotive was pulling was traveling at top speed on a straight line when I saw a plume of smoke on the horizon; it was Tom Tompson's train.

I asked my stoker politely to take cover, begging him in addition not to hold it against me if he got splashed, and I loaded my weapon.

I can assure you that my emotion, this time, was greater than before. Tom was advancing with lightning speed; he was already taking aim at me from afar, and I assumed my stance in order to take aim as best I could.

When I think about it now, I think it was excellent. Tom Tompson was definitely superior to me, and his idea was superb.

For a spectator, the scene could not have failed to be moving. The two trains fell upon one another like birds of prey; we were no more than a hundred yards apart, then fifty, then thirty; finally, we were level. I pressed the trigger twice, three times, six times.

Bang! bang! bang! It was a veritable fusillade. Bang! bang! bang! again, and we were already far away from one another. The terrified passengers put their noses to the windows. I had no idea what had become of Tom Tompson, of course, but I suddenly felt myself blinded by something warm that was running down my forehead over my nose and into my eyes.

"You're wounded!" cried the stoker.

"It's possible," I replied.

"It's certain," he said. "You're covered in blood."

In spite of the stoker's affirmation, I was in doubt. In fact, I didn't feel any pain, in fact, except for a slight prickling on my head, at the location of my mole, but that was all.

Eventually, when I arrived at my destination, I sought to discover the cause of my hemorrhage.

Without further delay, I took the return train and set off at full steam, trying to catch up with Tom Tompson's train, which was only twelve miles ahead of the one I was bringing back.

I made such good time that I arrived in the station almost at the same time as him. He had divined my intention, and, leaping down from his machine, he started running toward mine, on to which he leapt like a cat, crying: "O Providence! O Providence!"

"Tom, what's the matter with you?"

"What's the matter? Ask me, rather, what I no longer have. Look at me, my son, look at me. You've operated on me painlessly; you've operated and cauterized at the same stroke."

I stepped back, bewildered. Tom Tompson still had his nose, but he no longer had his wart. He seemed to me to be handsome.

It was a flash of enlightenment. I hurled my hat to the Devil and threw my bloody wig after it, twenty-five or thirty feet, and I showed my cranium to Tom Tompson.

"Like my hand! As smooth as the back of my hand! My son, we've invented the surgical duel. You no longer have a mole, I no longer have a wart. Only one thing worries me now."

"What's that?"

"I'm afraid of squinting when my eyes no longer encounter it at the end of my nose. That's all right, my son, come into my arms. You're handsome, I'm superb. We'll dine tonight at the Tompson residence, and we'll dine all night long. You've operated on me; I've operated on you. William, would you like to marry my daughter?"

"Miss Ellen doesn't know me very well and might not love me."

"She adores you! Imbecile steam-surgeon as you are, she adores you, and but for your mole, I'd have offered to you already. Now you resemble everybody else, I say to you: take her."

"That's sufficient, Tom. I'll take her tomorrow. The Reverend Smith can marry us in two hours.

Ellen is an angel; my hair has grown back and I have eleven children of both sexes, without a wart or mole among them.

Camille Debans: *The Conqueror of Death*
(1895)

In the early days of January 1999 the *Chicago Tribune* elected to celebrate solemnly the centenary of a discovery that had turned the world upside-down and produced ineradicable benefits, after having nearly brought about the most frightful catastrophes. The article in the American newspaper succinctly recalled the facts. Let us limit ourselves to reproducing the essential details.

You shall see, by virtue of the events that are recalled therein, and especially by virtue of the surprising conclusion, that it is worth the trouble.

The entire world, the *Tribune* said, ought to honor magnificently the man who, having dreamed of substituting himself for God in order to govern at his whim the rain, storms and fine weather, had the glory of finding the formula of his dream and putting it into practice. If statues are raised to the heroes of official massacres, what should be done for a man who endowed humankind with such a fecund prodigy?

It was on 24 June 1899, at four o'clock in the afternoon, that W. Benjamin Smithson created, in a plain on the Mexican frontier where no drop of rain had ever fallen, veritable cataracts in a serene sky, and became by virtue of that fact the dispenser of the abundance of harvests and the regulator of the Earth's wealth.

The enclosure in which the inventor of genius had to operate was in the middle of a plain, at the very place where a considerable city now stands: Smithstown, so named for the glory of Sir Benjamin. In those days, the country was desolate in its aridity. The immense crowd of people that had come to witness the meteorological phenomenon was primarily composed of local inhabitants for whom it represented sudden fortune, and had never grown any grain at all.

A cannon shot announced the beginning of the experiment. There were as many mockers as believers, and more. Two balloons with a capacity of about 6,000 cubic meters, one filled with oxygen and the other with hydrogen, rose slowly into the air, retained by powerful cables that only allowed them to rise up to a height of eight hundred meters. Beneath each aerostat there was a large gondola as voluminous as the balloon itself, oblong in shape and containing heaped-up bladders full to bursting, also containing hydrogen and oxygen, collected from the clouds of Illinois.

The two taffeta globs were linked together by a metallic device forming part of the apparatus, the principal wire of which unwound as the balloons drew away from the ground and maintained them in communication with a powerful electric pile installed in a vast cavern constructed for the purpose.

Floating with a serene majesty in the placid atmosphere—the sky was an implacable blue—the two aerial monsters rose up slowly. An embryonic sentiment of anxiety griped bosoms many lightly. Five minutes before, the quips had been raining.

"That's all that'll rain!" said one ferocious joker.

Now, that skepticism had evaporated. The imposing allure of the apparatus was intimidating the majority of the spectators.

Suddenly, the balloons stopped rising. The quadruple black mass stood out, bizarrely, against the intense azure of the sky. The chronometers marked four eleven and forty-three seconds—that historic detail in indisputable. W. Benjamin Smithson disappeared into the cavern from which he denouement would depart. There, he took hold of a little wheel, which he subjected to a dozen rapid turns, and then ran out to watch the aerostats. Two seconds went by; an enormous spark flashed, zigzagging between the ripping balloons, and a veritable clap of thunder was heard. Smithson maneuvered a little lever, and the nacelles burst in their turn.

Cruel black vapors formed, in the midst of which electricity raged. Lightning fell on a group of carriages and killed three people. Too bad! Then the cloud that had just formed by virtue of the condensation of the gas thickened so furiously and extended so rapidly toward all the points of the horizon that a fearful panic took hold of the crowd. People started fleeing in all directions, uttering screams of terror and desperate clamors.

"That man is the Devil himself!" howled the most terrorized.

Soon, large raindrops began to moisten the earth. The local inhabitants, ignorant of the use of umbrellas, ran away more rapidly than ever. Only a few fearless Yankees remained, mouths open, looking upwards, marveling at the miracle they were witnessing. And the miracle was completed, for within a few minutes, the rainfall had taken on the proportions of a tropical downpour.

And while the plain drank those benevolent sheets of water, Benjamin Smithson, opening a trap-door contrived in the vault of his cellar, sent into the air, to vertiginous heights, a series of bladders similar to the ones in the nacelles, propelled by powerful helices, which carried them up to the clouds, where they burst in their turn. The rumble of thunder was heard, and the rain increased in intensity.

The sensation that Sir Benjamin's success caused is easily imaginable. In a matter of hours, the entire world had heard the amazing news. Old Europe thought at first that it was a gigantic hoax, but explanatory details and extracts from newspapers were arriving by the minute, and it was necessary to yield to the evidence.

All these things are, of course, familiar to us today, and appear so simple, that it is as if they always existed. We regulate the weather in accordance with the general interest. The sky has no more caprices, and, in consequence, nor has the earth; its fecundity is regulated. At any rate, America went mad for a week. All the most improbable things one can imagine were done from New York to San Francisco and from the

St. Lawrence to the Mississippi in honor of Smithson, but still fell short of what that sublime genius deserved. European governments heaped him with honors. The inventor was celebrated in music, painting, sculpture, verse and prose.

Then, there was a sudden urgent alarm. In all the countries that had employed the Smithson method, conflicts of interest, and even of fantasy, were produced. Some people wanted rain and other wanted fine weather for the same day, some having need of water and others of sunshine. Civil wars broke out in weakly-governed countries. But those are no longer anything but memories. A long time ago, the executive powers to charge of the direction of the weather, and there are very few countries in which that management does not function to general satisfaction.

Sir Benjamin Smithson is, therefore, for all humankind, without distinction of races, a unique, incomparable benefactor. We would like the United States to celebrate the hundredth anniversary of his discovery in a fashion that will dazzle the world, and we are expressing the wish that the festivals that we are proposing will be the occasion for new benefits a hundred times more extraordinary, which W. Benjamin Smithson doubtless has in reserve for us after a hundred years.

For W. Benjamin Smithson—this might perhaps stupefy centuries to come or appear to be the most natural thing in the world, according to circumstances—is now a hundred and thirty-one years old. Everyone in the world knows that, but only those of his compatriots who know him personally know that he does not have the appearance of an old man, and that Mrs. Smithson, who became his wife thirty-nine years ago, appears today to be just as youthful, beautiful and as obviously young as on her wedding day.

We therefore dare to say, out loud, what has been repeated for forty years in American drawing rooms. W. Benjamin Smithson, after having discovered fifty secrets that have profited his fellow men, must have found, a long time ago, a means of conquering death and of maintaining himself in a state of eternal youth and virility. It is not longer permissible to doubt it. His worthy companion has, thanks to him, conserved the delightful figure and mental vigor that she had at twenty. Evidently, he knows the great secret. We affirm that with a profound conviction, with an emotion that makes all our muscles quiver and our souls float in the serene regions of a enormous hope. He knows the great secret!

But as he does not have the right to keep it for himself alone, we are convinced that the prodigious scientist wanted to wait for the moment of the centenary to which we have summoned all peoples in order to cause a frisson in human life that will endow it permanently with the most precious gift of all.

It is, therefore, on 24 June 1999 that America will have the immense pride of inaugurating, by virtue of the genius of its most illustrious son, the new era in which people will be able to say: "I shall no longer die."

Needless to say, this article was translated into all languages and commented on in every country. As with the power of making rain or good weather at will, a hundred years before, some people remained skeptical; others, secretly animated by a regrettable desire not to restore their souls to the Creator, did not hesitate to believe the promises of the American journalist.

The centenary, therefore, was awaited with a furious impatience. As the psychological moment approached, the Earth, from pole to pole, was gripped by a divine shiver—for no one was any longer incredulous.

On the eve of the great day, however, at the moment when humankind had nothing more to do than reach out a hand to see the supreme conquest fall into it, the joy, instead of turning to delirium, became anxiety, anguish and fever. What if, at the last moment, the certainty was acquired that the American newspapers were joking at the expense of the two worlds?

But no—W. Benjamin Smithson really was a hundred and thirty-one years old. He had been seen, in person, in Paris and London in 1992. He looked forty-five. His wife was a

211

sexagenarian; nothing was more certain—but ladies who had been her childhood friends, already wrinkled and decrepit, affirmed that Mrs. Smithson had not changed since the third year of her marriage. Thus, the great secret had been found.

"Hosannah!" sang the most convinced. "We shall be immortal!"

But the centenary celebrations, although worthy of the American people and the man they wanted to honor, went by without Sir Benjamin having spoken. Over the entire surface of the globe there was a disappointment that took on all the characteristics of despair.

In Europe, the disillusionment was so rude that the American journalists were held accountable for it; there was talk of making them expiate, by revolutionary means, the fraud of which they appeared to be the impudent inventors. But they defended themselves energetically. The *Chicago Tribune* even took the lead—as they say on racecourses—in crying more loudly than the rest and putting all the blame for what had happened on W. Benjamin Smithson himself. So when, all over the world, it was known that the American was refusing to prolong the lives of his fellows, sheltering his conduct under the pretext of philosophical scruples, an immense clamor of protest rose up from summits and abysms.

"What scandal! What infamy!" came the cry, from all directions. "What! Here's a man who holds our immortality in his hands, and he has the right to dispose of it as he wishes, even to deprive us of it if such is his pleasure? A thousand times no! It's necessary to force him, if you please. Let him be seized. A deep dungeon and, if necessary, torture in his honor, until he talks."

The most illustrious scientists wrote to Benjamin Smithson to demonstrate to him the meanness of his conduct. Some spoke of his duty, others of his glory, some of the rights of humankind, others of the will of God that had chosen him, Smithson, to bring the supreme news to his fellows...

A few, seeing that the objurgations were having absolutely no effect, went as far as insult, and finally, between the two extremes, there were vulgar reasoners who claimed that Smithson, driven by an extravagant ambition, wanted to be alone, with his wife, in possessing eternal youth, in order to hold the nations in a moral domination a hundred times worse than the most ferocious despotism.

In brief, people competed in irrationality. The entire world had lost its head, and yet, in sum, no one even knew whether the American scientist really possessed the talisman of long life.

The majority of European newspapers organized a conference in order to clarify that vital question. In the very first session, someone came forward to observe that a newspaper article is not an article of faith—even if the newspaper was from Chicago. No specific fact proved that Smithson was in possession of the secret that was attributed to him—in consequence of which, the conference ought to address itself to Smithson himself, in order to ask him whether there was any truth in the public rumor.

A letter was drafted in that same session, and three members of the conference were delegated to leave for America.

Smithson received them in the palace by means of which grateful agriculturalists had paid tribute to him a hundred years earlier, which was known as the Red House.

"Gentlemen," he said to them, without the slightest prevarication, "it's true. So, the time has come when it's necessary for me to explain myself. Yes, I have discovered the art of conserving youth—or, to put it better, of arresting the physical disorders produced by time on the human organism and, up to a point, of giving to those who employ my procedure an unalterable health. I was forty-eight years old when I made the discovery, and you can see that I haven't aged since. Mrs. Smithson is over sixty; I shall have the honor of introducing you to her, and you will take her for a young woman. But don't entertain any irrational illusions. I don't boast of having conquered death. In a brawl, in a battle, in consequence of a fall, people can die as before if they fracture their skulls, if they receive a rifle-bullet or a dagger in the heart..."

Smithson was interrupted by one of the three delegates.

"We shall not be so indiscreet as to ask for more details," he said. "Without judging your discovery *a priori*, we assume that it has not modified the economy of the human organism."

"Indeed; it only consolidates it."

"How long do you think that an individual might live by faithfully following your method and prescriptions?"

"I don't know—but I wouldn't be surprised if he could life for ten centuries, if not forever."

A smile slid over the lips of the three delegates, reflecting their interior joy. They had no doubt, after the prodigious Yankee's first declaration, that they would be returning to Europe with the secret of eternal youth.

"Well, Monsieur," said the most eloquent of the three, "we have come respectfully, in the names of the conference assembled in Paris, and, in consequence, on behalf of the City of Light in its entirety—in a word, on behalf of the whole world—to ask you to put the seal on your immense glory by finally unveiling the marvelous secret that will render us the terrestrial paradise..."

Benjamin Smithson replied, very gravely: "I'm flattered, Messieurs, that you have crossed the ocean to take that step, and I've given instructions that your stay should be made as agreeable as poor Americans can contrive—but with regard to my secret, I shall profit from our embassy to inform the world that I have decided never o reveal it."

As the three Frenchmen remained mute with stupefaction, Smithson went on: "After profound meditation, I have acquired he conviction that the indefinite prolongation of human existence would bring about, in a short time, an incomparable disaster more deadly than the benefit would be profitable. I shall therefore say nothing. Not because I want to keep the joy of living for myself alone—for, on the contrary, I have decided to suspend, at a given time, the measures to which I owe my incomparable old age. Whatever his genius might be, a human cannot encroach without folly on the attributions of God."

"What!" cried Pierre Seigreval, the most eminent of the three delegates. "You refuse…!"

"Believe that I'm very sorry—but you'll admit that, during my long life, when I have not lost the slightest fraction of my intellectual faculties, I have acquired an experience double that of other humans."

"So?"

"What I stands out most clearly from what I have learned," Smithson continued, "is that progress, whatever it might be, does not bring in its development any element of true happiness for humankind. The causes of human happiness: the passions, egotism, vices—in a word, moral maladies—have not changed."

"Oh!" said Seigreval, scandalized. "What you are saying is blasphemy."

"No," the old man replied, smiling. "How can you not see that truth? Evil people would have hundreds of years to wreak harm with the same fury. The good would be subject to their evildoing indefinitely. I tell you that it would be the triumph of malefactors and ingrates."

Having said that, Smithson made the gesture of someone who will not consent to hear further argument; he bowed gently, opening his arms in the fashion of Anglican pastors.

The three journalists protested in vain; he insisted on the unshakability of his resolution. No argument succeeded in influencing him, in making him soften the rigor of his sentence. Soon, he even changed the subject and invited his visitors to dinner.

It was as they were taking their places at the table that he introduced his wife to the delegates. Mrs. Smithson was a petite blonde woman with an amiable face. Her lips were incredibly fresh, her eyes extraordinarily limpid; one might have thought that she was eighteen.

Pierre Seigreval wondered whether he and his companions might be being taken for a ride. Anyone would have been able to believe, like him, that it was all an act, a comedy played for the simple objective of deception. During the meal, however, Mr. and Mrs. Smithson described events that they had witnessed with their own eyes fifty years earlier, and in a tone so sincere that their good faith could not be doubted.

Before leaving to return to France, the delegates made one last attempt.

"At least give us another reason," they said. "Just one."

"Gladly," said Smithson. "Suppose, then, that I deliver my secret to humankind. From that moment on, people no longer die, do they? Now, everyone knows that millions of people are born every year. A simple arithmetical calculation will then suffice to identify the precise moment at which the terrestrial globe would be too small to contain its immortal people. Then what will happen? The strong will do what they can to preserve their place; the weak will band together to defend themselves; there will be war—a universal, internecine war. People will kill one another, and my secret will no longer have any value. All the more reason to renounce it immediately."

What Smithson said was wisdom itself, but it did not succeed in convincing the delegates. They belonged to the species of deaf individuals who do not want to hear. Beside which, all their faculties were concentrated on one unique objective: to extract the divine secret from the American scientist. After that, they would see...

So, when they left the Red House to return to New York, the French journalists were more determined than ever not to abandon the game. At the railway station, a crowd was waiting for them, avid to know the results of their mission. Needless to say, they were all in accord in deploring Sir Benjamin's culpable obstinacy.

"He'll give in eventually, though," said the director of the American *Times*.

"He won't give in," replied Seigreval.

"Well, he has to give in," said a third person, with singular conviction.

216

There really never was such a burning question for the entire world. Since people had begun to hope for that almost complete attenuation of death, there had been no other topic of conversation, from one end of the Earth to the other. Old people, middle-aged people and the sick could not contain their impatience. They waited hour by hour for the news to arrive. Those who felt themselves close to falling into the great darkness of the tomb, those of whom it was said "He won't last the week," gripped by anguish, sought news incessantly of the state of the negotiations. More than one mother, leaning over the cradle of hr doomed child, demanded the miracle of which Smithson was capable—and who can tell whether it might not have been obtained from him by sending five or six desperate mothers as delegates?

When it was learned that Smithson was determinedly refusing to reveal his secret, there was a perfectly comprehensible explosion of anger. Meetings were organized everywhere; millions of indignant protesters condemned the conduct of the famous inventor without reserve.

It did not take long for them to be driven to extremes. What! There is a man who can prevent us from dying, and who is refusing to give us the supreme gift of unscathed life? But he does not have the right to rob us of that part of our heritage! It is necessary to force him, even if we have to inflict torture upon him to do so.

The most furious proposed locking Smithson up until he had responded to the world's demand.

But nothing prevailed against the obstinacy of the Yankee, to such an extent that the nations, in accordance with the customary course of events, became used to that disappointment, which was transformed into a vague hope. People continued to die. Disasters and wars occurred. People occupied themselves with other things, and the years went by, slow and exquisite for the young, rapid and ingrate for the mature and the old.

Smithson was still alive, and his wife too. Neither of them fell into decrepitude. Even better, the perpetual scientist, as he was now called, employed his genius—the greatest that had ever honored the human race—in performing new miracles, inventing improbably machines or processes.

Thanks to him, aerial transport became commonplace. For the old balloons, which no one had ever succeeded in steering, he substituted gigantic aeroplanes in the form of birds, to which electric piles of enormous power but small volume gave movement and life. To those who preferred something more rapid to that still rather slow means of locomotion—it took eight hours to go from Paris to New York—he offered a submarine tunnel, in which the trains traveled at the vertiginous speed of postal communications in pneumatic tubes. In fifteen minutes, passengers embarked at a station in New York were disembarking in the capital of France, on what was once the site of Les Halles.

Humankind, weary of so many marvels, no longer admired them. The means of production were so powerful that the workers, once so hasty to complain through the mouths of orators at public meetings, only worked for two hours a day. Work had become a distraction, a need, which caused Smithson to reflect, who remembered the noisy demands of old, the excessive programs now fallen into profound forgetfulness.

In the year 2073, he departed in a submarine, as a philosopher desirous of clarifying the mystery of the oceans, those of the land being almost entirely known. He admired the vegetation and the fauna of the submarine depths, and, after a few pauses in the most interesting locations, he landed in the vicinity of Bordeaux, where he was welcomed with all the demonstrations of crazed enthusiasm.

But the man was blasé with regard to honors. On the other hand, there was in that triumph, contrived by a slightly intoxicated crowd, something other than recognition. The cunning were trying to daze Smithson, to cover him with garlands, to conquer him so completely, in fact, that he would finally consent to release the secret of long life.

No man was ever subjected to such a diet of flattery and courteous temptation. For more than three months he was not allowed any rest. The Head of State visited him with great ostentation, as if he were the most powerful sovereign in the world. The Académie des Sciences offered him its homage in an extraordinary session, held outside the Institut in the old Galerie des Machines[22] on the Champ-de-Mars, which proved to be too small to contain a crowd avid to learn how death might be defeated. Smithson was proclaimed by acclamation the honorary president of all the scientific societies in the world. He was carried in triumph to his armchair. Then the most eloquent voice in Paris made a speech in which, after having heard himself compared to a god, he was invited to put an end to mortal anguish by revealing the mystery of his life.

He smiled impenetrably.

The orator, doubtless unfamiliar with that smile, which the delegates of the 1999 conference had seen flourish on the Yankee's lips, imagined that he had just caused conviction to enter into the softened spirit of the old man. He thought that by accumulating victorious arguments, he might strike the decisive blow, and launched forth into an admirable oration. Nothing more splendidly persuasive had ever been heard, anywhere, at any time. No one in the audience doubted that the advocate had won humankind's case.

Smithson rose to his feet. A tremor ran through the immense hall like a strange breeze. It was the fever of joy. People held their breath.

The scientist opened his mouth. There was an incredible silence, as if there were not a single one among the forty thousand people there who was not already counting on their relative eternity.

---

[22] The Galerie des Machines, a huge pavilion made of iron, steel and glass, was originally constructed as the Palais des Machines for the 1889 Exposition Universelle. When the exhibition ended, however, it was allowed to remain in place; it was used again for the 1900 Exposition, and then became a velodrome, but was eventually demolished in 1910.

"Messieurs et Mesdames," he said, in excellent French, "I thank you for the welcome that you have given me, which far surpasses my humble merit..."

And, continuing in that fashion, he responded to the compliments and flatteries that had been lavished upon him. He was eloquent, gracious and exquisite in his turn—but about his secret, there was not a word. The session ended without his having made any promise. Anger and disappointment might perhaps have been about to provoke some regrettable manifestation, and disquieting murmurs were already rumbling among certain groups.

Fortunately, skillful clamors of the lower orders circulated the suggestion that Smithson could not decently explain the affair to such an audience. Who could tell how long it might take him? Besides which, it was probably one of the most arduous problems of esoteric science, and no one would understand it. It was necessary to wait.

They did not, however, renounce the quest to make him confess. And as all the maneuvers had proved vain, they took advantage of a further celebration of which he was the hero to put him brutally in the necessity of replying. This time, he consented to do so.

"What you are asking," he said, "would be a hundred times worse than the death from which you want to be liberated. Take the trouble to look around you. By prolonging life you would be perpetuating vice, moral suffering, nameless unhappiness. Believe me, since I am the only man in a position to enlighten you on the matter, indefinite life—which is almost good as it is—would be a cruel torture. I won't tell you that a person would become blasé about everything and would become, after two or three hundred years, a stranger in the midst of younger generations, as old people between ninety and a hundred already are in many cases. That is obvious. But think about what one would become in the midst of unforgiving hatreds. Imagine what ingratitude alone would make of the unfortunate. If I could speak, you would now that I am a frightful example of that—but let's pass on

"Can you see drunkards, gamblers and malefactors renewing their crimes and infamies incessantly, sowing dolor and despair around them for centuries? Imagine certain spouses bound together forever—what am I saying, forever? Where are those who could live together for a hundred and fifty years? Once again, God has made things well. If I had not been frightened by what I foresaw, do you think that I would have hesitated for a moment to make my fellows happy, for whom I have toiled with such courage and obstinacy? Interrogate all those who are listening to me and ask them whether they would be delighted if three-quarters of their friends were immortal, and listen to their reply. And their relatives—that would be something else entirely.

"Oh, you can be sure that I've been on the point of saying everything a hundred times over, for the sake of a little peace—but a hundred times over, too, a secret voice had encouraged me to silence, and I have persisted in it. War, theft, pillage, and internecine massacres are formidable evils. It would not require two centuries, I repeat—and this is perhaps the hundredth time—for humankind, overcrowded, to arrive at those extremities, for want of room on this little round ball that is narrower than perhaps you believe."

He spoke thus for another hour, and concluded by saying: "If I gave in, Messieurs, in a very short time, there would no maledictions that would not be heaped upon my name and my person."

This time, there was an explosion of fury. The sage Yankee was insulted publicly. Newspapers published abominable diatribes against him. His caricature could be seen at every street-corner, accompanied by wounding captions.

"It's a practical joke," said the most earnest individuals, "and he hasn't lived for as long as people say. The Americans have deceived us in order to poke fun at Europe. If he had the power of which he boasts, would he hesitate? We ought to expel him shamefully."

And they provoked one another to lose their heads. It would not have taken much to pass from insults to acts of violence. Oh, if they had known how near the man, shaken in his resistance, had come to revealing everything! But when he saw that overflow of rage, he contented himself with shrugging his shoulders and murmuring; "There couldn't be any better justification of my resistance."

Before leaving Paris, he had the generosity to make a further gift to humankind, in the form of an inoffensive substance that suppressed almost all pain in all cases of physical suffering. After which he set off for America, and returned to his fatherland, where he was received almost as an enemy.

There, objurgations degenerated into insults. He and his wife were obliged to go into hiding, so to speak. Their dear children and their adorable grandchildren were subjected to base persecution.

Poor Smithson, desolate, sometimes said to his wife: "Who knows whether I might not be wrong. I have a strong temptation to give them what they want, and so much the worse for them."

One day, he saw one of his great-grand-daughters arrive at the Red House, carrying her only son in her arms, devoured by fever. She threw herself down at is knees, in tears, begging him, imploring him to save her child. Eventually she lay down at his feet, affirming that she would not get up again unless he rendered life to the suffering child.

How could he resist such a plea? He gave in. Smithson made the child drink a few drops of a golden liquid—and the mother, mad with joy, saw the fruit of her loins returned to life...

From that moment on, the perpetual scientist became less obstinate in his intransigence. The second centenary of his discovery of weather control drew near. He began to debate with himself as to whether, on that occasion, he ought not to yield.

That did not prevent him from contriving new marvels.

Thanks to the progress he made in telescopy, the great American brought the planets so close that it was possible to confirm the plurality of inhabited worlds. He pushed his irrefutable demonstrations far enough to establish that the worlds nearer to the sun sheltered beings more intelligent and more civilized than those of distant worlds. He was able to boast of establishing communication between Mars, Mercury and Earth.

But all that left people cold; they still wanted to know the great secret.

"That's not what we're asking of you."

In the meantime, he imagined a thousand improvements. He made a garden of the entire Earth. Unfortunately, humankind was no better. There were always further demands on the part of the human species. In many places, now, civil discord broke out in the matter of the weather. Some wanted rain, others serene skies. They tore one another limb from limb over that. On the other hand, nations had rapidly transformed aeroplanes into weapons of war. Frightful aerial battles took place in which the victors and the vanquished alike were almost certain to perish. These events caused him to despair. Extreme civilization seemed to be bringing humankind ever closer to black barbarism.

Human beings were scarcely obliged to work, technology having substituted for manual labor almost everywhere, but they were no happier. Everyone had too much time to think, to criticize, to desire enviously. The poor in spirit wanted to rise to the highest rank. The vicious demanded to share out the world to the detriment of the humble and the peaceful.

And yet, Smithson was still waiting for the great celebration that he assumed would be offered him in order to give his fellows the supreme benefit...

This time, however, there was no question of any such thing. The Americans, like everyone else, redoubled their acrimony against the scientist. At the moment when he was counting on a triumphant ovation, there was an upsurge of insults and sarcasm. With bloody unanimity, as if they had been driven by blind destiny, people competed in dragging him into ignominy. It went as far as threats. His house was

223

besieged. Inventions were demanded of him to meet all needs, and the satisfaction of all whims.

"How right I was!" he said, frightened.

And on 24 June 2100, when only three people came to compliment him on his anniversary, Smithson and his wife decided that they would stop drinking the elixir of life.

Within two days they aged through all the time that they had stolen from nature, and died disillusioned, without regret.

Paul Combes: *The Gold Mines of Bas-Meudon*
(1898)

I. In which Lauriane's Dream is Abruptly Interrupted

What was the brunette Lauriane dreaming about in her multicolored silk hammock in the warm and perfumed atmosphere of the greenhouse?

Around her, a thousand exotic plants deployed their green foliages or extended their spirals, constellated with flowers in sparkling colors, with bizarre forms and penetrating perfumes. Among them shone rare orchids, whose strange corollas were iridescent with marvelous tints. In a gilded aviary, a flock of brightly-plumaged birds perpetually in motion, mingled low notes and pearly modulations in a delicate chirping.

What was Lauriane dreaming about, and why was she sighing?

Many young women would have envied the calm and peaceful existence that she led in the elegant villa that her father, Monsieur Dumortier, possessed at Meudon at the entrance to the Pavé-des-Gardes. It is true that she had lost her mother, but a long interval of time had gone by since then, and the years, without leading to forgetfulness, had slowly filled in the dolorous void left by the departure of the beloved dead woman.

The father and daughter had felt their mutual affection increase after the cruel separation that had left them alone in the house, in the company of the maidservant who had seen Lauriane born. It is at such time that, in accordance with the poet's profound observation, "one perceives too late that one has not loved enough," and those who remain benefit from the retrospective tenderness that one regrets not having lavished on those one has lost.

Monsieur Dumortier and Lauriane were then, reciprocally, one another's entire universe, and for a long time, nothing entered their hearts to cause the slightest deviation of that affection—not even their common passion for rare flowers, a sentiment that, on the contrary, seemed to bring them even closer together.

Monsieur Dumortier was not exactly rich. The sole heir of the wealth of a family of moderate fortune, he had never made any effort to increase his wealth further, preferring the calm of a modest ease to the risks of the struggle for existence. His small income permitted him to live comfortably, without luxury, in the villa at Meudon, and to devote to his favorite passion what other inclinations might have expended in worldly pleasures.

Thus, the circle of his relationships was extremely restricted. He scarcely saw anyone else, on a regular basis, except the owner of the villa next door, Monsieur Roret, of whom forty years of neighborhood, since their early youth, had inevitably made a friend.

Then there were the lovers of exotic plants that he met at the merchants' establishments, with whom he was linked by common interests, and who occasionally traded their rarities with him.

It was thus that he made the acquaintance of Christian Norval, a young scientist whom a great Dutch horticultural firm had hired as a plant-hunter, and who had brought back incomparable orchids from the Dutch East Indies.

The modest Monsieur Dumortier was well-known to all orchid-lovers. Because Christian Norval needed, for his botanical identifications, to compare the types he possessed with those he lacked, he had asked to visit Lauriane's father's collection.

The day on which the young scientist was received for the first time in the Meudon villa, and allowed to admire the marvels of the greenhouse, was a memorable one. With what love Monsieur Dumortier was able to show off his *Dendrobiums*, his *Aerides*, his *Saccobiums*, his *Coelogynes*, his graceful Asian orchids, in parallel with his majestic American orchids, the *Stanhopeas*, the *Lycastes*, the *Cattleyas*, the *Laelias*, the *Miltonias* and, above all, the *Odontoglossums*, the *Cyrtochylums* and the *Oncidiums*, whose butterfly-flowers seemed to be fluttering in all directions on the branches of their panicles, capriciously fashioned and variegated.

Needless to say, however, of all the treasures that Monsieur Dumortier possessed, the one that charmed Christian the most was Lauriane, a living flower in all the freshness of her twenty years. So, he invented a thousand pretexts to return to Meudon and to insinuate himself into the intimacy of the residents of the villa. He succeeded in that without difficulty, as much by his gracious manners as his profound knowledge of living nature—knowledge that he was able to communicate with a marvelous artistry, without making it obvious. It was not only the world of plants that he had studied; he was fascinated by all the manifestations of the life of the globe, and was just as interested in birds and insects as in flowers.

While chatting, he touched on everything that nature contained, to such an extent that in order truly to know the beautiful flowers in the hothouse he also needed to know what birds, butterflies and bees lived in their locality in the countries that had given them birth. He was the one who populated Lauriane's aviary with birds like living gems. Monsieur Dumortier also owed to his generosity a superb *Coeologyne lowii* that Christian had brought back from Borneo.[23]

Thus, the young man became one of the best friends of the household, not without causing a certain displeasure to their neighbor, Roret.

Then, one day, at the request of the company in Amsterdam that had already sent him to Malaya, he departed for Surinam in Dutch Guiana, in search of new riches, after have

---

[23] The orchid called *Coelogyne lowii* by Paxton in 1849 is nowadays known as *Coelogyne asperata*.

227

said warm adieux to Monsieur Dumortier and Lauriane, and promised them a share to the discoveries that he was sure to make out there.

The young woman had not failed to notice the interest that she had inspired in Christian Nerval, and there was every reason to believe that, for her part, she had not remained indifferent to his attentions, for—it is futile to seek to dissimulate it any further—it was about the plant-hunter that she was thinking in her hammock suspended in the greenhouse, next to the brilliant songbirds that reminded her of the absentee. And she sighed as she thought that the enthusiastic scientist, in the bosom of the virgin forests of Guiana, passionately in love with nature, had doubtless forgotten all about her, entirely given over to his orchids, seductive flowers of which Lauriane was almost jealous.

In which she was wrong, as the continuation of this story will show.

At any rate, it was in America that her imagination was wandering when a ringing bell recalled her to reality.

She leapt nimbly out of her hammock in order to tell Marthe, the maidservant, that Monsieur Dumortier was taking his habitual siesta and that he should not be woken up unless the visit was so important as to render it absolutely necessary.

After a few moments, Marthe came to inform her young mistress that the visitor was none other than the owner of the villa next door, Monsieur Roret, who was asking to see Monsieur Dumortier immediately.

A cloud darkened Lauriane's forehead; her dark eyebrows frowned, giving her charming face a harsh expression that was certainly not habitual. However much displeasure Monsieur Roret's visit caused her, though, fearful of annoying her father, who appeared to have a weakness for the neighbor, she said to Marthe: "Tell Monsieur Roret to wait."

Then she went to awaken Monsieur Dumortier gently and inform him that their neighbor was waiting in the drawing room.

II. Monsieur Roret's Speculations

Monsieur Roret was the same age as Monsieur Dumortier. They had both been born in Meudon, in the neighboring villas in which they still lived. They had grown up together, and although they were far from having the same tastes, they had never lost touch with one another.

Monsieur Dumortier had married; Monsieur Roret had remained a bachelor.

As much as the former loved beautiful flowers and hated business, the second, a materialist disdainful of everything that did not have the objective of making money was relentlessly involved in variously fortunate speculations.

Monsieur Roret had succeeded, it was said, in making a fairly considerable fortune by means of property deals. He had exploited, in a rather intelligent manner, the expansive movement that carries Parisians avid for open air to take up residence in the suburbs—a movement facilitated day by day by the continuous improvement of means of locomotion.

Several times, he had been able to anticipate the direction in which the lovers of country life would go, and by buying up large tracts of land cheaply that he resold in plots at a handsome profit he had been able, in a relatively short time, to increase his capital considerably.

Encouraged by those initial successes, he had recently engaged in a much larger deal. It was a matter of acquiring, either by immediate purchase or by means of options that he had obtained for determined dates, all the building land situated in the commune of Meudon, especially the part known as "Bas-Meudon."

He had great expectations of the operation, being convinced that, out of all the places situated in the vicinity of Paris, Meudon was the one most attractive to the capital's inhabitants.

Perhaps he was right, in a way, but from the viewpoint of speculation, events were by no means in a hurry to justify his hopes. The plots of land he had bought at a fairly high price were hardly selling, or not at all; on the other hand, as the dates for the maturation of the options arrived in succession, Monsieur Roret was beginning to find himself short of disposable funds—and, in consequence, in a rather embarrassing situation.

That very day he had observed that one of his biggest options would fall due at the end of the month. It was time to take stock.

In that difficult situation, he had thought about his neighbor, Monsieur Dumortier.

Monsieur Dumortier was, undoubtedly, an inveterate enemy of business, because of the worries and annoyances that came with it. Perhaps, through, there would be a means of taking advantage of his one weakness, which was the affection he had for Lauriane. It would be easy to dangle before his eyes the sparkling possibility of easily realizing, in a short space of time, a superb dowry for Lauriane.

And, as he thought about Lauriane, Monsieur Roret sighed, in exactly the same way that the young woman had sighed in the greenhouse, when thinking about Christian Norval.

In the speculator there was never any considerable interval between conception and action. He went to his neighbor's house immediately.

"What's happening, then, my friend?" asked Monsieur Dumortier, "to make you interrupt my pleasant siesta. I was dreaming…"

"Dreams are what I want to talk about," the neighbor interjected. "I've just had some news of the utmost importance."

"What?" asked the orchid-lover, in a rather indifferent tone—for important things were the ones that interested him least.

"You know—or perhaps you don't, for these questions don't interest you—that until now, the government hasn't made a decision about the location of the Exposition Universelle of 1900. Should they use the Champ-de-Mars again? Should they transfer it outside Paris? They were hesitating. Now, I've just learned from a reliable source that the government intends to employ, for the 1900 Exposition, the vast spaces that the State domains of Meudon offer. What do you think of that?"

Monsieur Dumortier grimaced emphatically, and murmured: "The news is very disagreeable. I like Meudon a lot, because it's such a tranquil abode. If it's transformed into an international fair and invaded by crowds, it will become uninhabitable."

Monsieur Roret smiled and said: "Well, my friend, you're only considering the matter from the particular viewpoint of your tranquility. Personally, I see the circumstance as an opportunity for a superb speculation."

"Naturally."

"Yes, naturally! You know that I've recently acquired a good deal of land, especially in Bas-Meudon. Now, by virtue of the choice of Meudon as the location for the future Exposition, that land will soon increase in value tenfold, and I'll be able to make a huge profit."

"Then do so, my friend, do so. I wish you success with all my heart."

"But don't you, my dear Dumortier, want to take advantage of the opportunity to..."

"To do what, my God! You know how modest my tastes are. I'd rather not increase my small income than run the slightest risk."

"But there is no risk! It's mathematics. You buy a hundred thousand square meters of land at one franc apiece, you sell them at ten. It's a simple multiplication by ten."

"Indeed—and the product of the multiplication is tempting, but..."

"And then, my dear egotist, think about Lauriane. She's now at an age to marry. Think about the magnificent dowry you'd be able to give her!"

"Yes, but..."

"Besides which, it's not a matter for you of immediately disbursements. Look, I hold options on land. Their due dates are staged over various dates. I'll cede some of those options to you, on conditions we'll stipulate by agreement. That will permit me to extend my operations—and you'll gradually become a major landowner, without even noticing...I'll show you the land."

And Roret unrolled a large-scale map on which he pointed out to his friend the areas susceptible of being advantageously acquired. He accumulated certainties, juggled with figures, to such an extent and so cleverly, that Monsieur Dumortier, absolutely new to that sort of business, was completely dazzled and won over.

As for the reason alleged by the speculator to convince Monsieur Dumortier of the increased value that the land was certain to acquire—which is to say, the siting of the Exposition at Meudon—that had far less value than Monsieur Roret claimed. There had certainly been some talk, as our readers will remember, of installing the Exposition at Meudon, but the plan was far less advanced than Monsieur Roret had claimed.

Nevertheless, as it was in the order of possible eventualities, and as, if it came about, it would indeed give land in Meudon a massive increase in value, the speculator had conceived an ingenious plan permitting him to reserve those terrains and their increased value for himself in case of success, while leaving them to Monsieur Dumortier in the more probable event that their value did not increase.

To that effect, he had his friend sign a contract according to which Monsieur Dumortier would take an option on a certain quantity of land situated in Bas-Meudon, payable at a determined price at the end of a year, but Roret reserved the right not to deliver that land, in return for a payment of a forfeit of a hundred thousand francs. That clause permitted him to retain the land in case of a significant increase in value and to realize, even after paying the forfeit, a considerable profit.

In a year, in fact, the location of the future Exposition would be conclusively settled.

That scheme was, one might say, not entirely honest—and yet, Monsieur Roret was not, strictly speaking, a dishonest man. He was a speculator! Now, speculators—or certain speculators, at least—have granted themselves, in business matters, a very broad morality, which permits them to maneuver at their ease, by means of schemes that would shock contemporary ideas of delicacy, but which do not appear in any way incorrect to them.

Monsieur Roret did not want to ruin Monsieur Dumortier. He even had his interests at heart, and was very sincere in calling him his friend. But he did not see anything inappropriate in using that friend for the realization of his speculative schemes. Thanks to that friend, he could get over his temporary difficulties, safeguard the future, and perhaps bring off an excellent business deal.

Even if the speculation went seriously awry, looking at the worst possible case, the land could still be sold, little by little, without too great a loss, and no one would be ruined.

Finally, Monsieur Roret had a hidden agenda, which he scarcely dared admit to himself, but which was not, however, completely unconnected with the scheme into which he had drawn Monsieur Dumortier. Monsieur Roret, remaining a bachelor, had watched Lauriane grow up from infancy, and the entirely paternal amity that he had initially bestowed on her had been transformed some time ago, without him perceiving it, into a much more tender sentiment. The thought had occurred to him, very vaguely at first, of making her his wife, and as he saw more of her, the thought had taken on substance in his mind.

These things happen, even to speculators.

The first time that he took account of the phenomenon he was both astonished and frightened—astonished, because he had not believed himself capable of such a sentiment, which he considered as a weakness, and frightened because, being twenty-five years older than Lauriane, he could not believe in the possibility of the sentiment being returned.

Gradually, however, he had got used to the idea, had found it less and less baroque, and although he did not dare to manifest it overtly, his tenderness had given his behavior a gloss that Lauriane, a very sensitive person, had not taken long to notice. When the neighbor's tender gazes, long handclasps and sighs had revealed a very different state of mind in him, she had immediately observed an increasingly strict reserve, under the pretext that, having now become a "big girl," she could no longer indulge in childish games—and the familiarities of old had ceased completely.

Monsieur Roret, although smitten, was too intelligent to get carried away by stupidity. He no longer manifested his sentiments except in the form of an affectionate solicitude and waited for time and circumstance to provide him with an opportunity to please Lauriane. You can easily imagine the displeasure with which he saw young Christian Norval introduce himself into Monsieur Dumortier's home, and immediately conquer the manifest affection of the father and the daughter.

The scientist having gone away, however, the neighbor resumed hoping. Guiana is such an unhealthy country!

And in the speculation in which he had just proposed to Monsieur Dumortier, Monsieur Roret hoped, almost unconsciously, that he might find an opportunity to render himself useful, perhaps even indispensable, to such an extent that Lauriane, out of gratitude, might be led to accept him—a psychological phenomenon that occurs frequently enough for the speculator to have a definite chance of seeing his calculation justified by events.

At any rate, by virtue of these various considerations, Monsieur Roret thought it the most natural thing in the world, and even the most praiseworthy, to associate the fortune of his friend Dumortier with his speculations, even though they were causing him serious anxieties for the moment.

And that is how actions that are apparently villainous are, if not justified, at least susceptible to attenuating circumstances, when one takes account of the particular state of mind of those who commit them—that being said not to exonerate

Monsieur Roret, but to establish more accurately the true character of the individual in question.

III. Monsieur Roret Declares Himself

So, Monsieur Dumortier had let himself be drawn in. For the first time in his life, he had allowed himself to be tempted by the demon of speculation. It is true that it was, above all, out of consideration for his daughter.

The latter heard the news without enthusiasm. The prospect of a fortune left her absolutely cold. She was happy as she was, and since she had divined Monsieur Roret's secret thought, she did not trust the speculator. The operation in which he had just involved her father, although she did not understand it at all, inspired her with dread, and if there had still been time...

But it was too late. Roret had rushed the matter through. Everything was signed, countersigned and registered. There was no longer anything to do than await developments.

Developments were in no hurry.

Monsieur Dumortier, until then more assiduous in reading the *Orchidophile* than the political newspapers, sometimes surprised himself now by awaiting with impatience the arrival of *Le Temps*, to which he was a subscriber. But *Le Temps* remained obstinately mute in respect of the plan to install the 1900 Exposition Universelle at Meudon.

One day, however, a rather unclear article seemed to indicate that the question of the location of "the great international manifestation of the century's end" was on the brink of being definitively resolved. From then on, it was almost feverishly—and not without a certain anxiety—that Monsieur Dumortier waited for the appearance of the newspaper, for nothing seemed to indicate that the plan for the Meudon exhibition was in the offing. On the contrary, serious objections had been raised to that solution.

Monsieur Dumortier sighed, regretting his former quietude, anxiously interrogating Monsieur Roret regarding the chances of success in their speculation, becoming more impatient as the days went by with the menacing uncertainty in which he found himself and against which he struggled in vain.

Finally, the uncertainly was abruptly ended. The government had made a definitive decision. The Exposition of 1900 would be held on the Champ-de-Mars, with its usual annexes slightly enlarged, and a section at Vincennes. Meudon was completely abandoned and passed over in silence.

It was a rude blow for the two friends, but especially for Monsieur Dumortier, less used to the risks of speculation. Full of confidence in the knowledge of business that Roret possessed, he had conserved a tenacious hope along with his illusions, until the last moment.

He measured at a glance the consequences of the situation in which he found himself engaged with regard to Roret, and took account of the inevitable catastrophe that menaced him if his friend demanded the execution of the contract that linked them together.

On the expiration date of the options, it would be necessary to pay, to exchange his income bonds for land that was now devoid of any income, and difficult to sell. It meant ruination, embarrassment and poverty or himself and Lauriane; it meant the forced sale of his villa, his collections of flowers...

At that thought, a flood of tears rose to the eyes of the unhappy orchid-lover. He cursed his stupid ambition, his insane greed, his blind confidence in Roret, who called himself his friend...

In fact, though, if he really was a friend, he would not be so cruel as to cause his neighbor's ruination. He would doubtless consent to take on a part of the contract's burden...

Monsieur Dumortier clutched at that hope and, in order to transform it into a certainty, he wiped his eyes and immediately went, with his newspaper in his hand, to knock on Monsieur Roret's door.

"I've heard the news!" said the latter, with a dejected expression, as soon as he had let his neighbor in and before

Dumortier could say a word. "I was deceived...cruelly deceived!" He passed his hand over his brow and added: "In fact, though, a speculation is a lottery. To have the chance of winning, it's necessary to risk losing."

"Yes," murmured Monsieur Dumortier. "But look what terrible consequences that loss will have for me. I'm not rich, you know, and once I've honored my engagements, what will I have left—or, rather, what will my poor Lauriane have left?"

At that name, Monsieur Roret got up and shook his neighbor's hand, saying, emotionally: "Lauriane! Have no fear—she won't have to suffer from these events. Oh, you don't know how much I love her!"

"Yes, my friend, I know that you've always had a veritably paternal affection for her, and you've spoiled her a great deal."

"You don't understand," Roret interjected, who was still holding Dumortier's hand in his. "Yes, to begin with, I loved Lauriane like the child she was. An old bachelor, incapable of understanding the tender emotions of the family, I was, however, attached to her, and watched her grow up with the eyes of a father. Then, insensibly, I don't know how the transformation took place, but Lauriane caused me to experience very different feelings. Her beauty made an impression on me; the qualities of her mind and heart charmed me. She'll be an accomplished housekeeper; she's the ideal woman; she alone is capable and worthy of completing my happiness. I love your daughter Lauriane, my friend, and I'm asking for her hand in marriage!"

Astounded by this revelation, which he was far from expecting—because Lauriane had carefully kept Monsieur Roret's attentions in her regard secret from him—Monsieur Dumortier, thinking that he was dreaming, could only murmur: "You love Lauriane!"

And he fell silent, plunged in an abyss of reflections.

Monsieur Roret, who was watching him anxiously, went on, excitedly: "Well, yes, I love Lauriane. What's extraordinary about that? Isn't she adorable? How would I have been able to live constantly in her presence, so to speak, without falling in love with her? It was fated!"

"But no, my friend," Monsieur Dumortier was finally able to say. "There's such a disproportion of age between the two of you that I could never have imagined that such an affection might be born. Anyway, you love Lauriane, but does Lauriane love you? She's never said anything about it to me."

"Nor to me, and I don't know he nature of her sentiments in my regard, having never acquainted her clearly with mine. But that's not the question, for the moment. You fear, with reason, for Lauriane and for yourself, the disastrous consequences of your unfortunate speculation. Well, that disaster won't happen, since I'm offering Lauriane, along with my hand, my entire fortune. I'll help you to meet your engagements, and you'll conserve, along with your income, our villa and your flowers. The land of which we'll be the owners will eventually be sold, little by little, and perhaps the affair won't, in the end, be as bad as it seems."

Monsieur Dumortier remained silent momentarily. It appeared to him now, albeit in a manner that was still vague, that Monsieur Roret might have planned at long range the events that were now permitting him to ask for Lauriane's hand with some chance of success. Perhaps the speculation into which he had drawn his neighbor had had, in his eyes, the sole aim of driving Monsieur Dumortier and his daughter into a corner with no way out—a situation of which he, Roret, would be the master.

At that thought the honest orchid-lover felt the horror of his situation more profoundly, and in order to gain time and reflect, he murmured: "Listen, I need time to think about all this. It's worth taking the trouble. The house isn't in immediate danger. Give me a few days to look at your proposal from all the angles and to talk about it to Lauriane—then I'll come and tell you what we both think."

Monsieur Dumortier wanted to appear calmer than he was. It was with death in his soul that he returned to the villa. What was he going to say to Lauriane, who still did not know anything, about the ruination of their hopes and their neighbor's proposal?

The young woman had not failed to notice, some time ago, her father's preoccupations, and she had attempted to dissipate them by means of her perennial good humor. That very day, not suspecting anything, she ran to Monsieur Dumortier cheerfully to ask him why he had gone out.

Her father's grave expression wiped away her smile. "My God, what's wrong?" she exclaimed.

"Oh," said Monsieur Dumortier, making a superhuman effort to pull himself together, "I'm annoyed that the Exposition isn't going to be held at Meudon."

"But in that case," said Lauriane, who divined the gravity of that news, "the plots of land that were to increase in value so much, and which you've bought, are no longer worth anything..."

"Oh, they're worth the agreed price."

"Yes, but it won't be possible to sell them now."

"You're exaggerating. Difficult to sell, perhaps, but..."

"Father! Why won't you tell me the truth? When you've paid or the land—for it will be necessary to pay for it—we'll have nothing left, will we?"

"Nothing but this villa," Monsieur Dumortier admitted, dejectedly.

"And in order to live, it will be necessary to sell it?"

The poor man could only nod his head affirmatively, and Lauriane let her arms fall, lowering her eyes toward the ground.

"Oh, that Monsieur Roret!" she cried, in a moment of indignant revolt that she could not suppress.

"Do you know what Roret said to me?"

Lauriane looked up, interrogatively.

"Roret told me not to despair, because he loves you and wants to marry you. Did you know that?"

"I knew it."

"How? You never said anything about it to me."

239

"Monsieur Roret has made his sentiments manifest, but as I was unable to respond to them, I made him understand that; I thought there was no point in informing you of facts that might have troubled your friendship and which I considered, in any case, to be inconsequential."

"You can see, however, that it's serious, since Roret has asked me for your hand."

"And it's probably in order to do so that he pushed you into buying that land, which he knew to be valueless," said the young woman, angrily.

"The same suspicion has occurred to me."

"Well, he's mistaken if he thinks he'll get his way by that means. I prefer poverty."

"But my love…!"

"Yes, I understand, Father. I'm forgetful and ungrateful. At your age it will be hard to leave this villa, to abandon your flowers, to submit to privations…oh, why did you have to listen to that false friend? I had such a beautiful dream…! Alas yes, you're right. It's frightful, poverty."

And in a further surge of resentment, she cried, as she burst into sobs: "Oh, who will save me from this cruel alternative?"

A violent ring of the doorbell, which resounded at that moment, seemed to respond to that desperate appeal.

IV. Stanislas Borichevski

Marthe went to open the door, and the father and the daughter were able to hear a hoarse voice asking: "Is this really Monsieur Dumortier's house? There can't have been a mistake, though: the first house on the right, at the entrance to the Pavé-des-Gardes, Villa des Orchidées. That's here!"

"Yes, but what do you want?" said Marthe, in an ill-tempered voice.

"It's a message that I have to deliver to Monsieur Dumortier on behalf of Monsieur Christian Norval—a great character, believe me!"

"Christian Norval!" exclaimed Lauriane, involuntarily. "Marthe! Show him in!"

The individual that Marthe introduced to the drawing-room merits a detailed description.

It would have been difficult to determine his age. He was a tall, thin, stiff and angular man, with a sun-tanned face riddled with scars. Like chaotic brushwood, his hair, beard and moustache framed his peculiar physiognomy, at the center of which a red nose, striped with violet-tinted veins, testified to regrettable habits of intemperance on the part of its owner. The individual's costume corresponded in every respect with his physiognomy; it was made up of disparate garments, half-savage and half-civilized, including a deformed and discolored soft felt hat, a leather jacket, and velvet trousers engulfed by Mexican boots.

Not at all disconcerted by the expressions of astonishment that had greeted his entrance, the newcomer introduced himself.

"Monsieur! Mademoiselle! My name is Stanislas Borichevski, at your service. Here is a letter from Monsieur Christian Norval for Monsieur Dumortier."

And he held out to the latter an envelope that he had taken from beneath his felt hat, while bowing to the father and daughter.

"I also had something for Mademoiselle," he continued, ""but I had an accident. Instead of taking the boat that would have disembarked me at Bas-Meudon, I made a mistake and took the one that stopped at the Point-du-Jour. There I said to myself: *Meudon isn't much further away, I'll go on foot*…but it was much further than I thought. It was hot, the wind was raising dust, I was thirsty…

"In brief, I went into a wine-merchant's near the Pont de Billancourt, and drank a half-liter, another half-liter…as I was about to leave, I perceived that I didn't have enough money to pay my bill…the innkeeper made a fuss, called me a thief…

"Monsieur Christian had asked me to bring to Mademoiselle a whole packet of rare orchids that he had discovered out there in Guiana. I said to the fellow: 'There's more than a hundred francs' worth of flowers here; keep this package until I come back and pay you.' And they're back there..."

"Oh! Here!" cried Lauriane, giving Stanislas a two-franc piece. Take the boat there and back, and bring them to me!"

And while the singular messenger, very happy with this solution, hastened to carry out Lauriane's commission, the latter urged her father to read the young plant-hunter's missive.

The letter was only a few lines long.

Dear Monsieur Dumortier,

I have just arrived in Paris. Fortune has favored me. Not only have I gathered an ample harvest of flowers for the Van Houtten Company, which sent me to Surinam, but I have also found on my travels, if not wealth, at least the means to live independently henceforth.

Permit me to offer Mademoiselle Lauriane these few orchids, while awaiting something better.

After taking the time to settle my accounts with the Van Houtten Company, to which I am in haste to bid a definitive farewell, I will come to see you, and bring you a few curiosities, in Meudon, where I intend to take up residence myself, in your neighborhood.

Excuse the negligent appearance and manners of my envoy. I owe him a great deal and he is very devoted to me.

While awaiting the joy of seeing you again, I renew the assurance of my very sincere sentiments of affectionate respect, and beg you to present my best wishes to Mademoiselle Lauriane.

Your devoted friend,

Christian Norval.

Blushing with emotion, Lauriane could not hide the joy that this unexpected and, so to speak, providential return caused her, for she established a kind of mysterious connec-

242

tion between her supplication and the ringing of the bell that had immediately followed it.

In fact, nothing had changed in Monsieur Dumortier's situation, and yet Lauriane had begun to hope again—and that confidence even affected her father, for he smiled on seeing joy reborn on the young woman's face.

"Christian Norval's return gives you a great deal of pleasure, then?" he said, enveloping her with an attentive gaze.

"Oh, yes—a great deal."

Monsieur Dumortier became serious again, nodded his head several times, and simply murmured: "Who knows? Perhaps you're right."

And the father and daughter, forgetting Monsieur Roret, the speculation and its consequences, continued talking about Christian Norval while awaiting the return of his messenger.

Thus time, the latter did not dally on his route. In less than half an hour he returned to the villa, carefully carrying an enormous clump of orchids with numerous, rather large flowers, striped and spotted with brown on a lemon yellow background.

"But that is, indeed, a veritable rarity," said Monsieur Dumortier, filed with delight. "It's *Oncidium rigbyanum*, which I haven't yet been able to procure in Europe.[24] Oh, that dear Norval! He has no idea of the joy he's given me."

"On the contrary," said Lauriane, "he must have some idea, for it's certainly with that aim in mind that he's sent us these flowers."

"Well, my friend," Dumortier added, addressing Stanislas, who was wiping his brow, "are you still thirsty or hungry? Don't worry—I'll have you served anything you need. Monsieur Norval has said good things about you."

---

[24] The orchid called *Oncidium rigbyanum* by Paxton is nowadays known as *Oncidium sarcodes*.

"Monsieur Norval is very kind, and you too, Monsieur. At the moment, I have no need of anything. Do you have a reply to give me for my master?"

"Oh! You're in Monsieur Norval's service?"

"Which is to say that Monsieur Norval has been kind enough to take responsibility for me, although I'm not much good for anything; I try to make myself as useful as I can."

"And your master is well? The voyage hasn't overtaxed him?"

"He's marvelously well. Oh, he's strong, indefatigable—and often, out there although I'm an old hand, his resistance astonished me."

"You met him in Surinam, then?"

"No, it was in French Guiana—or, rather, in the contested territory between French Guiana and Brazil. You know that gold has been discovered there. It's always been my destiny to go from placer to placer. I was among the first in the Transvaal, Australia and Guiana, but it hasn't made me rich.

"To cut a long story short, I was prospecting for gold when Monsieur Norval, who was looking for flowers, met me in the upper reaches of the Carsewene river, just in time to prevent me from dying of starvation, for I hadn't had a bite to eat in two days.

"Since then, I've been attached to his fortune, and I've had the good luck to render him a small service. I'd found a tiny nugget in the alluvial mud of a river, and that permitted him, thanks to his mineralogical knowledge, to discover what I'd never have been able to find by myself—the original deposit.

"I was used to exploitations of that sort. We succeeded in hiring a hundred Indians to work it, and in a matter of months, Monsieur Norval had deposited a small fortune in ingots in the bank of Paramaribo.

"He gave me a generous share in his profits, but I could never hang on to it. I gambled, I drank…in brief, I'm still as poor as Job. I'm very glad that Monsieur Norval has consented to keep me on."

244

Monsieur Dumortier and his daughter had listened to Stanislas' story with interest, by virtue of the clarifications it gave them with regard to Christian's adventures in Guiana. He was obliged to do honor to a copious collation, while Monsieur Dumortier wrote a letter to the young plant-hunter.

My dear Monsieur Norval,

How many thanks we owe you, my daughter and I, for the superb orchids you have sent us. Thank you, above all, for having sent us news as soon as you arrived.

We learn with joy that you are in good health and in possession of an independent fortune, and we are looking forward to seeing you again as soon as you are free.

Since you are thinking of becoming our neighbor, we shall have more than one opportunity to talk at length about your voyage and our favorite flowers.

Your most grateful

Robert Dumortier

Stanislas did not want to stay at the villa any longer. He knew with what impatience Christian was waiting for the response to his letter and his gift, and although his master had not taken him into his confidence, he divined that the beautiful Lauriane was not unconnected with that impatience.

Monsieur Dumortier obliged him to accept a five-franc piece "to pay for his railway ticket" and permit him to arrive more rapidly at the hotel where the traveler was staying, but made him promise nevertheless not to stop on the way.

Then the father and the daughter went into the greenhouse, to install in the place of honor the magnificent *Oncidium rigbyanum*, which they never tired of admiring. There was no longer any question in their conversation of anything but orchids, Guiana and Christian Norval—as if Roret did not even exist, and the threat of imminent ruination were not hanging over their heads.

In the meantime, Roret was waiting anxiously for the response to his proposal, not daring to hurry matters along by an untimely visit, and astonished by the fact that his neighbors' reflections were so prolonged.

One day, he could no longer contain himself, and wrote a note to Monsieur Dumortier, which he sent via his housekeeper.

My dear friend,
You know that the first of the options you have contracted expires in forty-five days.
What are you going to do?
Yours,

Roret

Monsieur Dumortier, thus recalled to reality, hid that "reminder" from Lauriane, but set about study the means by which he could confront the situation without compromising his future, and that of his daughter, irremediably.

V. The Return of Christian Norval

It was a beautiful morning in May. In its frame of fresh verdure, Meudon was basking in the sunlight, with a festival air. The breeze, which was arriving from the woods in gusts, brought spring scents and birdsong.

Monsieur Dumortier, however—and consequently Lauriane—were very anxious. The future remained ominous, and the temporary brightness provoked by Christian Norval's letter had given way, in a matter of days, to bleak depression.

The father and daughter did not say much, having only sad ideas to exchange. Monsieur Dumortier had resumed reading the *Orchidophile*; Lauriane had returned to her watercolors, plants and birds.

Such were their occupations that morning, when the sound of a rumbling carriage that came to a stop outside the villa caused them to raise their heads. They looked at one another and smiled, having had the same thought at the same time.

Thus, it was without astonishment that they heard Marthe announce, as she opened the greenhouse door: "Monsieur Christian Norval."

The latter made his appearance almost immediately, followed by Stanislas Borichevski, carrying a large cage full of brightly-colored birds.

Tall, well-built, full of elegance and distinction, his face and hands bronzed by the tropical sun, Christian Norval bowed with ease and cordiality, as if he had only quit the father and daughter the day before. He took the cage from Stanislas' hand and signaled to the latter to withdraw.

Then, when the three of them were alone, he let loose all the emotion that he had suppressed until then and exclaimed: "Ah, Monsieur Dumortier! Ah, Mademoiselle Lauriane! How many times I thought of you, out there, lost in the bosom of the virgin forest!" He collected himself, and continued more calmly: "The proof is that I've brought you some of the charming birds whose song cradled my memories and my hopes."

"You're really too kind, Monsieur Norval," said Dumortier, pressing the young ma's hands in his. "These orchids, these graceful birds..."

"How can we thank you?" stammered Lauriane.

"I'm sufficiently recompensed," Christian put in, "by the fact that these flowers and birds have given you pleasure."

"They're truly extraordinary!" said the young woman, who could not weary of admiring the guests of the cage.

"One of them, especially," said the scientist, acquiescing to Monsieur Dumortier's gesture inviting him to sit down. "Look, that one, with the russet head, the black wings and the pale gray body. You can see that it's only ten inches long at the most, tail included. Well, of all the creatures living in Guiana and Brazil, that's the one with the most powerful voice. There's a humorous story told in the Brazilian interior about that subject, which I'll tell you some day."

"What is it called?"

"I'll tell you—but in order for you to understand, I'll tell you first how I made the acquaintance of the bird.

"At that time, I was traveling in the mountains where the river Maroni has its source. I had just met that eccentric Borichevski, whom you've seen, and had taken him into my service.

"One day, at about midday, exhausted by the heat, I was getting ready to take my siesta in my hammock, suspended between two palm trees. I was already beginning to doze off when, in the relative silence of the forest, I heard, quite clearly and quite distinctly, to sound of a bell.

"I sat up and pricked up my ears, quite astonished to see Stanislas continuing to stuff his pipe as if he hadn't heard anything. A minute went by, and then a second chime of the bell resounded in the depths of the forest.

"This time there was no doubt about it. Utterly astonished, I said to my companion: 'Is there a mission near here, then?'

"No, Monsieur," Borichevski replied, calmly lighting his pipe. It's the *Campanero*."

"What's the *Campanero?*" I asked.

"Eh? Yes—a bell-bird, the one the natives call *guira-punga*."

"*Guira-punga!* I get it! That's the name that travelers have corrupted into *araponga*. It's the Portuguese *ave de verano*—the summer bird—which Buffon renders as *averano*. Other naturalists call it the 'blacksmith,' the 'locksmith' or the 'field marshal,' while scientists know it as *Casmarhynchus variegatus*.[25]

"Then I got my bearings. I recalled that Marcgrave, in his *Histoire des Oiseaux*,[26] had commented on hat singular

---

[25] *Casmarhynchus vairegatus* is actually the name of one of "Darwin's finches." The bell-bird described by Christian is *Procnius averano*.

[26] The German naturalist Georg Marcgrave (1610-1644) co-authored with Willem Piso an eight-volume *Historia Naturalis*

song, sometimes similar to the sound of a hammer falling on an anvil, sometimes reminiscent of that of a cracked bell. And that curious bird was in the vicinity!

"When I say 'in the vicinity'…well, it was from four kilometers away that we had heard it singing. Judge the amplitude of its voice!"

"I couldn't rest until I'd captured one. It wasn't without difficulty—but there it is!"

"And which of its names should we conserve?" asked Lauriane.

"The bell-bird! That's the one that corresponds most closely to its strange particularity."

"Will it sing in the cage?"

"Undoubtedly. It's already done so."

"They're veritable rarities that you've brought us," said Monsieur Dumortier. "We're confused…"

Christian Norval avoided the thanks by hastening to name the other prisoners offered to Lauriane, and listing their qualities.

"But capturing all hose birds must have lost you a lot of time!" Lauriane exclaimed.

"Oh, Stanislas helped me," the young man said, smiling.

"So," said Dumortier, "you're thinking of taking up residence in Meudon?"

"I've decided to do that. Meudon is the point of the globe that pleases me most…probably because you live here."

"Oh, Monsieur Norval!" Dumortier protested, while Lauriane blushed deeply.

"And as I've made a small fortune from the gold mines in Guiana," the scientist continued, "I'm going to buy a villa near here, and like you, I'll devote myself to the cultivation of flowers and breeding birds. I hope you'll be willing to help me with your advice, in your capacity as a neighbor."

Brasiliae in 1648, from which the French translation cited might be a translated extract, although no such text is listed in the catalogue of the Bibliothèque Nationale.

Monsieur Dumortier could not help uttering a sigh, and murmuring: "Gladly—if I remain your neighbor."

"What!" Christian exclaimed, utterly astonished. "You're thinking of leaving Meudon, at the very moment when I want to set up home here! When I say set up home…nothing's settled as yet. Meudon pleases me, I repeat, because you're here…but if you weren't…"

Monsieur Dumortier's face and Lauriane's expressed such constraint that the young man trailed off. His interrogative, almost imploring, gaze went from the father to the daughter, trying to divine what their silence was hiding.

Finally, he could to longer contain himself, and he exclaimed: "Forgive my persistence, my indiscretion, but I beg you, if you consider me a friend, to confide to me, if it's possible, the reason that might oblige you to quit Meudon. What has happened since my departure for Guiana that could…?"

"Don't go on, my friend!" said Dumortier. "I'll explain to you briefly what had happened. I allowed myself to be tempted by my neighbor, Monsieur Roret, and entered into a speculation with him that has turned out badly. I might be obliged, in order to liquidate my position, to sell this villa…"

At the name of Roret, Christian Norval frowned. With the delicate sentiment of divination that jealousy gives to lovers, he had perceived the passion experienced by the neighbor for Lauriane, and had the presentiment that it had had a role to play in the circumstances that Monsieur Dumortier had just admitted to him.

Without seeking to delve into that question, for the moment, he insisted on having all the details of the speculative venture, and when he knew what it was amounted to, he was much less anxious, and strove to reassure his hosts.

"In your very natural inexperience in business," he said to Dumortier, "you're exaggerating the dangers of the situation. According to what you've told me, the due dates of the options are staggered over an interval of time, and in sum, although the value of the land hasn't increased, it won't be impossible to put them up for sale without too much loss…"

Christian interrupted himself, because an idea had suddenly occurred to him. "Oh, if we had auriferous alluvia in the vicinity, you'd see that land..." He stopped, and made as if to pick up his hat. "But I'm behind time," he said.

"Oh, but you're going to have lunch with us!" exclaimed Dumortier. "After such a long absence, we can't let you go so soon. Then again, you can give me your advice about this business with Roret..."

The cordiality of the invitation and Lauriane's gaze were irresistible. Christian accepted. "But first," he said, "I need to find out what has become of that good-for-nothing Borichevski and give him a few instructions."

Stanislas was in the kitchen, sat at the table with a bottle of wine that was already half empty, telling Marthe about his adventures with a brio that had won him the housekeeper's good graces.

"Pay attention," said Christian, taking him aside, "and try to follow my instructions to the letter. Listen carefully: first of all, I forbid you to drink to excess. You know that when you go over the limit, you become utterly incapable of rendering me the slightest service. You might even harm me by your unconscious chatter.

"In the second place, you're to go in search for a villa for sale or rent, preferably fully furnished, so that I can move in immediately, as close to here as possible. Come back in two hours to tell me the result of your enquiries. Here's enough to have lunch in some inn, but, I repeat, stay sober.

"Finally, I want you to let it be known that we've both spent our lives looking for gold mines all over the world, and that I've made a nice little fortune by so doing. Boast of being an expert in the profession of gold-prospecting—that should be easy enough, since it's true. Tell the story every time you have an opportunity to do so, everywhere."

Stanislas opened his eyes wide with astonishment at that instruction, and Christian added: "It will be very useful to me. I'll tell you why later. Go—and above all, don't forget my first recommendation."

VI. Christian Norval's Plan

That day, the hours went by lightly, joyfully and rapidly, before, during and after lunch.

Monsieur Dumortier felt reassured by his young friend's confidence in the future. Lauriane, entirely happy, reading in Christian Norval's eyes the profound affection that the scientist had for her, was now sure that, whatever happened, she would not be obliged to become Roret's wife.

Christian, no less certain that he pleased Lauriane, was mentally ruminating a plan that made him smile, without that internal labor showing externally except in a frank good humor.

He had had time to relate all the details of his travels: his fruitful quests for rare plants, birds, and even insects, of which he had brought back curious specimens for his personal collection; and, finally, the meeting with Stanislas, the discovery of an alluvial pocket filled with enormous nuggets of pure gold, the feverish exploitation of that deposit, the fortune and the return journey.

"And if I was so happy to be coming back with that fortune," he concluded, "it was because I thought that I was going to find friends here, who had welcomed me to their hearth one day without knowing me, by virtue of our common love of beautiful nature, and who had immediately become very dear to me. Remember that I'm absolutely alone in the world, with no family, and that your cordial welcome allowed me to find one.

"Oh, the beautiful dreams I had out there, in the midst of the most urgent activity. It wasn't the majestic virgin forest that I saw; it was a pretty quarter of Meudon, where I had decided to settle down for good as soon as fortune had smiled on me. There, we could live henceforth side by side, with our flowers, see one another every day, and..."

The young man sensed that he was about to say too much, and stopped. The arrival of Stanislas got him out of his embarrassment.

The gold-prospector, although having not stuck rigorously to his master's first instruction, had found what the latter desired; a small villa five hundred paces from the Pavé-des-Gardes, with a large garden and a greenhouse, for sale fully furnished—and very nicely furnished—where Christian could be in residence within a week.

"I know where it is!" exclaimed Monsieur Dumortier. "Indeed, nothing would be more suitable for you. It's one of the nicest villas in Meudon."

"I'll go and take a look at it, and come back to tell you if I make the purchase."

The villa suited Christian in every respect and it was so comfortably and so intelligently furnished that he scarcely had to do anything but have his luggage forwarded. Thus, he immediately went to the notary responsible for the sale, agreed the price and the terms of the contract, and ran to tell his friends that everything was settled.

Monsieur Dumortier and his daughter did not hide the joy that news caused them, but Monsieur Dumortier manifested the intention to accompany him as far as the station. He said that he needed to stretch his legs.

Christian and Lauriane exchanged one last gaze, and the two men took the road to the station. Stanislas had gone on ahead to buy the tickets.

Dumortier maintained silence.

"Do you have something particular to tell me?" Christian asked, having guessed everything.

"Yes. This is the last note that Roret has written to me, which I haven't mentioned to my daughter. What should I reply?"

And Dumortier shoed the young man the few lines with which our readers are already acquainted, reminding him that the first option expired in forty-five days and asking him what he was going to do.

"A fine question!" exclaimed the young man. "What are you going to do? Pay, since there's no means of doing otherwise. I don't understand this: 'What are you going to do?'"

"You don't understand, my dear friend, because I haven't yet told you everything—and I couldn't tell you in front of Lauriane, even though she knows everything. Monsieur Roret has offered to help me fulfill my obligations if Lauriane will consent to be his wife."

Christian did not bat an eyelid. "I suspected as much," he murmured. "at least, I suspected that the gentleman in question harbored tender sentiments toward your daughter, and his proposition doesn't astonish me. Well, Monsieur Roret is out of luck…for you've doubtless divined, similarly, that I love Mademoiselle Lauriane, and wouldn't have been long delayed in asking for her hand. You've given me the opportunity to bring forward the deadline that my discretion would have fixed. There—it's done."

"You can have no doubt, my dear Christian—permit me to address you thus—as to my response, nor that of my daughter, for our sentiments in your regard are all too evident."

"You fill me with joy—but I beg you, not a word to Mademoiselle Lauriane. I'd like to obtain her own admission."

"Understood. What should I reply to Roret?"

"Oh, that's right! Well, send him this reply: 'The affair seems better to me than I thought at first, and I shall keep all my engagements.'"

"Yes, but will I be able to?"

"You will—I'll answer for that. I have a plan."

"Well, my young friend, you've given me courage; and you'll make Lauriane very happy. Thank you, and *au revoir*."

"Within a week I'll be definitively installed in Meudon. *Au revoir!*"

As soon as he was alone with Borichevski, Christian Norval asked him whether he had found an opportunity to talk about gold mines.

"Several opportunities," the adventurer replied. "To begin with, in order to find out whether there were villas for

254

sale or rent in the neighborhood, I went into a wine merchant's..."

"Naturally!"

"There," Borichevski went on, without acknowledging
the interruption, "while drinking a glass, I asked for the information I needed, and insinuated that it was for a gold-
prospector with whom I'd run around all the places in the
world.

"Then I was bombarded by questions about gold mines.
It's odd how that metal interests everybody. And as you'd
instructed me to be loquacious, they didn't have to beg me.
You should have seen their eyes shine as they listened to it all.
They even bought me a few glasses."

"Well, well! You've found a new seam to exploit!" said
Christian, laughing. "That's very good, Stanislas. You'll have
to continue. You can go into Meudon every day, on the pretext
of attending to my villa, and go back to see the friends you've
made at the wine merchant's."

Stanislas was increasingly astonished by the manner in
which his master was taking things, but it did not displease
him at all. He therefore listened attentively to the further instructions that Christian gave him.

"Since gold interests them, tell them how it's found. Tell
them that you can recognize its presence in an area by means
of certain signs, and that you've observed those signs right
here in Bas-Meudon."

"In Bas-Meudon!" Borichevski exclaimed, astounded.

"Yes," Christian replied, "in Bas-Meudon. Don't go
shouting it from the rooftops. Adopt the most mysterious attitude, as if it were a great secret, and tell them that you're con-
fiding it to them as friends, on condition that they don't tell a
soul, that our presence in Meudon has no other objective than
to discover whether the land that we suspect to be gold-
bearing is capable of exploitation.

"Tell them, as mysteriously as possible, that it's me who
has secretly bought from Monsieur Dumortier the lands that I

had in mind, but that the entire hill of Meudon might also contain gold.

"In brief, this is what I want to do: to convince the inhabitants of Meudon that the subsoil of their commune enclose
auriferous wealth, and that it's sufficient to lay ones hands on
a good seam to become rich.

"You have only to support my plan devotedly, and you
won't have any complaint to make. Direct the covetousness of
your listeners primarily in the direction of Bas-Meudon.

"Know, moreover, that I'm not doing anything reprehensible, and that the ultimate objective I'm pursuing is entirely
legitimate. In consequence, you can go ahead with a clear conscience. It won't do anyone any harm."

The idea that had occurred to the young man is easily
deduced: to attract attention to the lands of Bas-Meudon and
give them, temporarily, sufficient value for Monsieur
Dumortier to be able to fulfill his obligations without any inconvenience. It was quite probable that Monsieur Roret,
caught in his own trap, would pull out of the bargain and take
on the land himself.

Stanislas complied with the program that his master had
sketched out for him all the more rigorously because it facilitated the absorption of a considerable number of "rounds" for
which his new friends competed with one another for the privilege of paying, in order to obtain further revelations from
him. The adventurer played his role so naturally that everyone
was taken in. His mysterious attitude lent credit to his tales,
and the secret—always communicated with the same mystery
from one person to another—was soon known to all the residents of Meudon.

A few welcomed the allegations with skepticism and
mockery, treating them as the ramblings of a drunkard—for
Borichevski was already beginning to acquire a well-deserved
reputation in that respect—but the majority accepted the plau-
sibility of the discovery, made by a man who really was a
gold-prospector by profession. Some even claimed, nodding
their heads, that they had already heard talk of something of

the sort, and that authorized scientists, first-rate mineralogists, had declared that there ought to be gold in Meudon or somewhere nearby.

Others resolved to seek information directly from Borichevski's master, and asked the latter when the scientist was due to arrive in Meudon.

Christian Norval laughed heartily at the success of his scheme, and was not at all surprised, on arriving in Meudon, to be stopped mysteriously at the corner of a street by a local landowner and asked: "Is it true, Monsieur, that there's gold in Meudon?"

"Who told you that?" Christian asked, simulating annoyance and surprise.

"But…your domestic, the gold-prospector."

"Oh, the accursed chatterbox! But after all, if he says so, perhaps it's true…he's the expert!"

VII. Washing out Gold in Meudon

That evasive confirmation of what Borichevski had said inflamed the imagination of the man who had provoked it. He immediately went in search of the adventurer and found him seated at a table in his favorite tavern, chatting about the current topic of all conversations in the midst of a circle of open-mouthed listeners.

"Gold," he was declaring, "can be found in nature in two quite distinct forms. Firstly, it's found in seams—which is to say, encased in rocks in which it's concreted, probably under the action of subterranean fire, although I've heard it said by some engineers that it might equally be the result of chemical action.

"At any rate, to extract it from that matrix, it's first necessary to pulverize it and then submit it to intelligent washing, which takes away the extraneous particles and lays the gold bare.

"In nature, that washing takes placed continually—hence the tiny pieces of gold and the gold dust that the Rhône, the

Rhine, the Durance, the Garonne and so on carry away with their sands..."

"What about the Seine?" asked one of the listeners, curiously.

"The Seine too; that's exactly what I was getting at. But I repeat, where does this gold debris come from? It's the disaggregation of rocks where gold is found in the form of seams—a disaggregation produced, either directly, by water, or under the action of other natural causes that it would take too long to list.

"Well, you see, nature has already done its work is subjecting that gold to a preliminary washing, and it's by meaning of a secondary washing that gold-prospectors exploit it."

"How?"

"Oh, it would take too long to describe in detail. We'll talk about that later. For the moment, you've asked me how there can be gold in Meudon. I'll explain. The sands that contain gold are deposited on the bed or on the banks of the watercourses that carry them, and that's how they form auriferous alluvial deposits of varying richness. As gold is heavier than the sand with which it's mixed, it's sometimes deposited in particular places, certain hollows, and forms what we call pockets, where it's more abundant. Sometimes, too, under the action of certain waters, it aggregates into fragments of varying sizes, called nuggets. You're not unaware of how variable the course and flow of a river is. For my part, I've heard it said more than a hundred times by knowledgeable engineers. And that's how one finds auriferous alluvial deposits at certain places where rivers have deposited them in the past, and have since changed their course or their circumstances.

"Well, I've heard my master say that, at one time, the Seine was an enormous river whose waters filled the whole of the valley between the heights of Meudon and those of Passy. It's then that small fragments of gold, contained and carried in gravel and sand, must have flowed from the mountains in which its source is located.

"In consequence, what's astonishing about one being able to find the gold in the alluvial mud that it deposited on the slopes of the hills of Meudon and Bas-Meudon?"

"That's true! That's true!" murmured the listeners. "But is there much of it, and how does one recognize the places? Can one see the tiny particles of gold?"

"It's difficult. There are sometimes—I found them myself elsewhere in France, in the rivers Cèze and Garonne—pieces large enough to be picked up; but generally, the particles are so small and so widely dispersed in the sand that they escape the most clear-sighted eyes."

"What can be done, then?"

"It's easy to recognize the places where the sand is red-tinted or black-tinted, and, in general, where it's a slightly different color from what can be seen elsewhere. If there's gold in the mud, that's where it's found most abundantly."

That indication had an unexpected effect on the audience. Each of its members offered the excuse of urgent business to hurry away and run as quickly as possible to examine the color of the sand, either on his own property or land that was up for sale in Bas-Meudon.

Even the tavern-owner went out by the back door to explore his garden, and Borichevski, who had not wavered in his seriousness, found himself alone with the last of the property-owners that had come in search of him.

"I'd be very glad to have a few words with you at my house," said the inhabitant of Meudon, in a mysterious tone.

"At your service," the adventurer declared, picking up his felt hat and getting to his feet to follow the property-owner.

"I'm Monsieur Pommeret," the latter said, in a low voice, as they went out. "I live not far from here near the Chapelle de Notre-Dame des Flammes. I have a big garden, whose subsoil is sandy, and the sand in question has the particular reddish color that you were just talking about. I'd be very glad to try washing the sand to see what quantity of gold it might contain. You are, I'm told, quite expert in these matters. Would you care to lend me your assistance? I'll give you a suitable remuneration."

"Monsieur Pommeret," Borichevski murmured, taking on an embarrassed expression, "I am, as you must be aware, in the service of Monsieur Christian Norval, and I could only place myself at your disposal during my leisure hours."

"That's understood! Can you come now?"

"Gladly."

Monsieur Pommeret hastened to conduct the adventurer to his house, showering him with kindness, playing to his weakness by inviting him to taste an old bottle behind the woodshed, and then dragging him feverishly to the bottom of his garden.

Having arrived there, the astonished Borichevski had to bite his lip in order to prevent himself from laughing. Monsieur Pommeret had destroyed a flower-bed of pansies and dug a kind of ditch sixty centimeters deep, laying bare a subsoil of yellow sand streaked with reddish-black lines, by courtesy of ferruginous infiltrations. It was a quartz-based sand including a rather abundant quantity of mica particles.

A geologist would immediately have linked that layer to the sandy ground and so-called Fontainebleau sandstone that make up almost all the summits of the buttes, plateaux and hills in the Parisian basin, as at Montmartre, Mont Valérien, Meudon, Fontainebleau and so on. There was, in consequence, no question of alluvial deposits.

But Borichevski, who was not a geologist and who was, in any case, carrying out the program designed by Christian Norval, examined the trench attentively, crumbled a handful of red sand in his palm, and affirmed with an irresistible conviction: "It's an auriferous sand."

Monsieur Pommeret, who could not contain his joy, exclaimed: "How does one proceed, then?"

"If you only want to carry out a trial, we can employ the prospectors' method."

"I do. What does it involve?"

"Of, a little simple apparatus will suffice. Give me *carte blanche* and a credit of twenty francs, and I'll assemble it for you."

Delighted, Monsieur Pommeret granted Borichevski everything he asked for.

The adventurer, having set to work, did not take long to return, carrying a set of equipment in a handcart: a trestle, two buckets, a sieve, two large wooden bowls and a plank that warrants detailed description. It was about 1.70 meters long, fifty centimeters wide and five centimeters thick. On one of its faces it was equipped, on both sides and one end, with a raised border between two and three centimeters deep. To that same face were nailed three pieces of coarse fabric as wide as the plank and thirty centimeters long, disposed at equal intervals.

All of that equipment was transported to vicinity of the garden pump, which seemed to Borichevski to be the most favorable place to proceed with the washing of the "auriferous sand."

The adventurer set up his plank with the end furnished with the border resting on the ground and the other on the trestle, with was about fifty centimeters high, thus constituting a gently inclined plane. The sieve was fitted to the upper extremity of the plank.

Having done that, Borichevski, aided by Monsieur Pommeret—who carried out all the prospector's instructions punctiliously—went to fill a wheelbarrow with reddish sand from the trench and take it to the washing apparatus. Then he explained to his host, speaking and acting at the same time, how to obtain the desired result.

"First one puts a quantity of the sand to be washed into the sieve, and one pours water on it, in moderation. The water draws away all the tiny particles capable of passing through the sieve—which, as I've told you, are generally minuscule. Only coarse matter remains in the sieve. We empty them out and we proceed, in the same fashion, to wash another quantity of sand."

"But the water is drawing all those fine particles to the end of the plank," said Monsieur Pommeret

"You're mistaken! It's carrying away the earth, the dust, but the particles of gold, although tiny, are heavy. As they run down they encounter the pieces of cloth and remain trapped there. For them, the cloth constitutes as many dikes arranged in series, which they don't have the strength to get over. If we didn't have the cloth, we'd be able to make transversal grooves in the plank that would have the same effect. That's how the gold-seekers of the Rhône used to proceed. Oh, I know my trade."

"But the cloth isn't just trapping gold. Look—this seems to me to be exclusively sand."

"Evidently. The cloth traps all the particles possessed of approximately the same density, and the gold is only there in infinitesimal quantities. But this permits us to reduce considerably the foreign matter with which it's mixed."

When the sieve had been filled, washed and emptied several times, Borichevski stopped.

"You can see," he said, "that the pieces of cloth are entirely covered and are no longer in a condition to stop any more. I take them off and I wash them in this bucket full of water, in which, you'll agree, we'll find sand richer in metal than that originally extracted from the trench.

"Now I'll show you how we treat this. Take one of those wooden bowls. Fill it, as I'm doing, from the bucket. That's it! Now take it in both hands, like this, and start moving it in a fashion similar to the movement of a winnowing-basket when winnowing grain. Not so fast—gently does it! See how I'm doing it.

"It's exactly like winnowing. The grain-winnower brings the lighter particles and straw to the surface. We're also bringing the lighter sand outwards, while the heaviest particles accumulate at the bottom of the bowl. It's winnowing water!

"And look, here in my bowl. It's obvious that it's the light articles that are at the top; their color is quite different from the others, considerably less dark. Look, if I tilt the vessel you can see, between the bottom and the edge, three or four bands of different color, which display the substances according to their density."

Monsieur Pommeret tried to achieve a similar result, but the work, although simple, requires the force of habit, a particular movement of the hand, skill and a great deal of patience. All that cannot be mastered at the first attempt. When he tried to eliminate the light sand, as Borichevski was doing, by stopping the rotary movement of the bowl, he spilled the entire contents of his own and murmured: "It's more difficult that I thought."

"Oh, you'll get there. Look, now. You can see that the sand I've brought outwards is slightly different from that which remains at the bottom. The work is concluded, and we have no more to do than take out the particles of gold.

"But I can't see any particles of gold."

"That's because they're too tiny, or confused with the sand."

"How do we get them out, then?"

"With mercury."

"Have you got any?"

"I couldn't find any in Meudon," said Borichevski, who was in no hurry to carry out the final test.

"Well, I'll go to Paris myself to fetch some. Leave all this where it is, and come to see me again tomorrow."

Monsieur Pommeret paid Borichevski generously; the latter withdrew, delighted with the result of his first washing of the auriferous sands of Meudon.

VIII. Gold and Happiness

In the meantime, Christian Norval had accepted Monsieur Dumortier's invitation to dinner.

"What do you have to tell me?" asked the latter, as he shook the young scientist's hand cordially. "Have you discovered gold in Meudon?"

"It's not me!" said Christian, smiling. "It appears that it's my man Borichevski."

"But…is it true? Is it even plausible?"

"It all depends what you mean. In fact, gold is extremely widespread in nature. It can be found everywhere, in greater or lesser quantities. Experiments were carried out on that subject forty years ago, at the Philadelphia Mint, by the late Jacob R. Eckfeldt.[27]

"That scientist obtained specimens of all the metals found in the various parts of the United States and submitted them to careful analysis with respect to gold. The result was that he found the precious metal everywhere, in varying abundance. All the metals he was able to acquire were slightly impure, and included a proportion of gold. It varied from one part in 440,000 for antimony and one part in 6,220,000 for galena."

"That's very little!"

"Yes, it's very little, but it's extremely interesting from the viewpoint of the universal diffusion of gold in nature. Those results encouraged Eckfeldt to carry out further research, and, in particular, he devoted himself to an attentive study of the clay in the environs of the city of Philadelphia. He collected clay from about four meters below the surface, and search it for gold. He found the metal in the proportion of one per 1,224,000 for completely dry clay.

"That's certainly very little, but as Philadelphia rests on a bed of clay measuring 4,180,000,000 cubic feet, it follows that the amount of gold contained in the subsoil of the city represents a value of more than six hundred million francs—and if the suburbs are included, five trillion francs.

"Then Meudon…"

"Just a moment…if my memory serves me right, ten or fifteen years ago, it was announced that certain geological

---

[27] Jacob Reese Eckfeldt (1803-1872) followed his equally-famous father Adam Eckfeldt into employment with the U. S. Mint in Philadelphia.

strata in the vicinity of Paris contain and appreciable proportion of gold. It's a matter, I believe, of supragypsous marls and
Montmorency millstone, which include a certain quantity of
clay. There's no reason why French clay shouldn't also contain gold."

"Exploitable?"

"That's the entire question! We aren't yet in possession
of methods capable of extracting that gold in an economical
fashion and permitting French or American clay to compete
with the Transvaal."

"Then your Borichevski...?"

"Might have found something better than those clays.
You're doubtless not unaware that Meudon has already attracted attention by virtue of the particularities it presents with
regard to gold?"

"I've never heard any mention of it."

"Well, the knowledgeable Professor Alexandre
Brongniart,[28] in his mineralogy course at the Museum, with
regard to sandy limonite, in sheets extended in the sandy
ground of Viroflay, near Meudon, remarked that people had
thought that they had found indications of the presence of
gold.

"That's not all: the sands that are used in making Sèvres
bottles come from Meudon. Well, when one breaks the glass
crucibles, one frequently encounters rather sizeable particles
of gold in the lower parts of their walls. Does that gold comes
from the refractory earthenware of the crucibles or from the
Meudon sand?[29]

---

[28] The chemist and naturalist Alexandre Brongniart (1770-
1847) collaborated with Georges Cuvier on a geological sur-
vey of the region around Paris.

[29] Author's note: "These authentic facts are reported in a work
by an inhabitant of Meudon, Dr. L.-E. Robert, *Histoire et description naturelle de la commune de Meudon*, p.297." The
text in question by Louis-Eugène Robert, published in 1843,
can now be read on-line

"As you can see, there is some evidence for the presence of gold at Meudon."

"You're convinced, then?" asked Monsieur Dumortier, smiling.

"No, but I wouldn't be sorry if it were to be generally believed for a while. You'll soon know why."

"All right. Here comes Lauriane!"

The young woman came into the room, wearing in a bright spring dress.

Although Monsieur Dumortier had not said anything to her about Christian Norval's official request, she had half-divined it from her father's attitude and implications in the daily conversations they had, in which the subject of the young scientist always came up. So she was slightly excited about this further meeting, which she sensed might be decisive.

And, indeed, scarcely had they embarked upon a banal conversation than Marthe came to announce an untimely visit from Monsieur Roret. Monsieur Dumortier asked the two young people to go into the hothouse while he received the neighbor, whom he had not seen for quite some time, in the drawing room.

Lauriane rested her slender white hand on the arm that Christian offered her, and they both went to sit down next to the aviary, beneath the high foliage of a date-palm.

"Monsieur Christian," the young woman said then, "we're in an entirely suitable setting for you to give me the details you promised me regarding your voyage to Guiana."

"Gladly, Mademoiselle," replied the scientist, bowing. "I would even add that I owe you an account of those memories, for you played a large role in them."

"How so?" she asked, blushing slightly.

"My God, Mademoiselle, I don't believe that it's necessary to beat around the bush between the two of us. I shall therefore be frank and honest, and you can tell me whether I'm right or wrong.

"When, in the course of my studies on orchids, I came here for the first time, I only had science in view. I had no suspicion that I would meet you here, and that from then on, it would no longer be science alone that would draw me to Meudon.

"There is no harm in telling you, Mademoiselle, that I experienced a cruel constriction of the heart in comparing the broad comfort in which you live with the slender resources of which I disposed, which obliged me to remain a modest plant-seeker and to live alone with my flowers and my beloved science. So it was with joy that I accepted the distant mission that, in taking me away from you, would perhaps put an end to my unrealizable dreams.

"Those dreams could not be destroyed. On the contrary, when I saw fortune smile on me, I began to believe that they might become a reality, and with every new ingot of gold that I deposited at the Bank of Paramaribo, it seemed to me that I was getting closer to the goal that, as yet, I only dared admit to myself.

"Even today, Mademoiselle, I would not dare admit it to you if I had not read in your eyes, and if I were not reading at this very moment, that you would permit me to do so.

"Mademoiselle, tell me whether you think me sufficiently worthy to be your husband and whether you would consent to be my wife?"

Lauriane had allowed the young man to speak without manifesting her sentiments other than by a benevolent smile.

"All that you have just told me," she said, "I have seen or divined, and if your plans had displeased me I would have cut the matter short, as I have done for Monsieur Roret's advances. In consequence, being as frank with you as you have been with me, I make you this reply: If my father has no objection, yes, Monsieur Christian, I would very much like to be your wife, for I'm sure that you would be an excellent husband for me."

"Have no doubt of that, Mademoiselle Lauriane! As for your father, I already have his consent."

267

"I suspected as much!" said the young woman, smiling. And she went on gaily, to hide the happiness that was filling her with emotion: "Oh, the villainous schemers who weave frightful conspiracies against a poor defenseless girl!"

"You don't hold it against us?"

"No, I thank you, for you're both good souls." This time, she could not hide the hears of joy that showed in her eyes.

"Lauriane!" exclaimed the young man, taking her by the hand.

But the terrible clang of a bell made them start in surprise.

It was the "campanero" from Guiana, which, for the fir time since it had been in the Meudon aviary, was giving voice to its singular call.

The two young people could not help laughing when they realized the cause of their alarm, while Monsieur Dumortier, who had finished with his visitor, also came to enquire about the origin of the sound.

Informed of its nature, he joined in with the gaiety of Christian and Lauriane, and then with their joy, when the young man told him the result of their conversation.

"Well, now let's go to dinner!" concluded Monsieur Dumortier. "Oh—do you know what Roret's just done? He came to beg me to ask Monsieur Norval whether there's any truth in the rumor that's going round relative to the presence of gold in Meudon."

"And?"

"I had your demonstration fresh in my memory. I made use of it—but, following the advice that you asked me to observe, I attenuated the weaker aspects and exaggerated the presumptions."

"Why?" asked Lauriane, astonished.

"Because," Christian replied, laughing, "it's necessary to return a little value to the lands that Monsieur Roret put into our hands, in order that he'll be the first in line to buy them back from you."

"Ah! I understand," said Monsieur Dumortier. "Yes, it's a good strategy—but will it work?"

"It will work—have no doubt about that. Borichevski is involved in it, and I'm convinced that he's already provoked searches in the commune."

"In that case, we'll open a bottle of champagne and drink to the gold-mines of Bas-Meudon!"

"And Lauriane's happiness!" added Christian.

"To everyone's happiness!" replied the young woman.

IX. The Discovery of a Nugget

Monsieur Pommeret was suspicious.

The particular filtrates obtained by Borichevski after the repeated washings that we have witnessed, did not display the slightest hint of gold. When they were dried out, they presented the appearance of a black dust, which Monsieur Pommeret carefully collected in a box and submitted to the analysis of a friend of his, a professor at the École des Mines.

"Where does it come from and what do you hope to find in it?" asked the scientist.

"My dear friend, permit me to remain silent on those matters for the moment," Monsieur Pommeret replied, "and simply give me an exact analysis of the specimen."

"As you wish. Come back in a week and you'll have the result."

A week later, Monsieur Pommeret received from is friend's hand a note indicating the following results:

```
Silica in the state of sand....................6.936
Manganese dioxide............................1.642
Iron peroxide....................................0.749
Cobalt oxide....................................0.008
Aluminum........................................0.202
Water............................................0.462
Traces of copper and arsenic..............--------
                                    Total ...9.999
```

"No trace of gold?" asked the inhabitant of Meudon, with an emphatic grimace.

"I didn't look for it," the professor relied, "but if there is any, it's in the trace category—which is to say, less than one part in ten thousand, and, in consequence, beyond any hope of possible exploitation. So you were hoping to find gold in the specimen?"

"I hoped so...I thought that it was an alluvial sand."

"Not at all. I don't know where you got it from, but it presents the appearance and composition of a sand formed by the disintegration of a manganesiferous sandstone of the kind that one finds in the vicinity of Paris—at Orsay, for instance, and above the sandstones of the Montagne de Train, near Moret."

"Well, that specimen comes purely and simply from my property in Meudon, with which you're familiar."

"Indeed. But who can have put such an idea into your head?"

"Oh, it's just an idea," Pommeret replied, evasively.

And in spite of the assurance of the knowledgeable professor of the École des Mines, he bought some mercury, and, on his return to Meudon, summoned Stanislas Borichevski to his house."

In fact, a new suspicion, in an inverse direction to the first, had occurred to him. Scientists are theoreticians, who do not have the experience of prospectors, and Borichevski seemed so sure of himself—and it does not cost very much to carry out a trial.

Without saying anything to the adventurer about the analysis he had commissioned. Monsieur Pommeret announced to him that he now had the mercury and that nothing was standing in the way of their pushing a further experiment in washing through to the conclusion.

Without the slightest embarrassment, Borichevski recommenced washing a new wheelbarrow-load of sand through the sieve. Then, Monsieur Pommeret felt that he was capable of continuing that work on his own, and asked the adventurer to do the washing with the bowl while he continued to pass sand through the sieve.

The two operations went marvelously, and were approaching their conclusion. Monsieur Pommeret was already talking about beginning the mercury treatment when all of a sudden, as he was emptying out the gravel left in the sieve, he uttered a loud cry that brought Borichevski running.

In the midst of the coarse gravel, sparkling in the sunlight, was a superb gold nugget, irregular in form, but almost having the size and rugged appearance of one of the semi-cotyledons of a walnut.

Monsieur Pommeret picked it up and, trembling with emotion, handed it to Borichevski, who could not believe his eyes. It really was, however, a nugget of gold, exhibiting traces of concretion or fusion, still enveloping a few particles of sand in its mass. It had the gleam and weight of gold; Borichevski could not be mistaken about that.

Thus, he backtracked, and wondered, in perfectly good faith, whether, by inventing a fable, he might not have put his hand on a reality. There really was alluvial gold at Meudon, then—in nuggets!"

That changed everything, completely, and it was a matter of warning Monsieur Norval as quickly as possible.

"It must be gold," he murmured, "but in order to be absolutely sure, I'd like to show this to my master."

"I'd like that," replied the property-owner, who could already see himself at the head of a gold mine, "but on the express condition that you and he maintain the strictest secrecy regarding this discovery."

"I promise you that." And, stretching his legs prodigiously, Borichevski ran to the Villa des Orchidées, clutching the precious nugget in his fist.

The adventurer had calculated correctly; his master was still there, glad to pass all his time with Monsieur Dumortier and Lauriane, with whom he was talking constantly about the past, the present and, most of all, the future.

Marthe told Monsieur Norval that Borichevski had an urgent communication to make to him, of the highest importune.

The young scientist hastened to go to his domestic, who placed the nugget in his hand, saying: "We've just found that at Monsieur Pommeret's."

"Impossible!" Christian exclaimed, weighing the object in his hand and turning it back and forth repeatedly.

"It's absolutely true—but I promised Monsieur Pommeret to keep it a secret."

"Oh, this is very curious!" said the young scientist, simultaneously smiling and pensive. Then, a sudden idea having crossed his mind he said: "Wait here and keep this. I'm going to make my excuses to Monsieur Dumortier and his daughter, and we'll go to my house, where I can submit the nugget to the touchstone. I want to make certain."

A few minutes later, Christian Norval tested the piece of gold found by Monsieur Pommeret with the touchstone and acid, and a smile spread over his lips at the same time that light dawned in his thoughts.

He did not let anything show, however, and he handed the nugget back to Borichevski, saying: "It really is gold. You can assure Monsieur Pommeret that we'll keep the secret."

It was, however, Monsieur Pommeret who did not keep it—or, at least, the comings and goings of Borichevski, and the earthworks that the property-owner was digging in his garden in the hope of finding more nuggets ended up attracting the attention of the neighbors. The latter, already put on the alert by the rumors that had been going round for several weeks, were on the lookout, and the rumor spread that Monsieur Pommeret had found a gold seam in his garden, that he was subjecting alluvial deposits to daily washing, and had already collected a great abundance of the precious metal.

That earned Monsieur Pommeret a visit from Monsieur Roret, who begged him, in his capacity as an old inhabitant of Meudon, like himself, to tell him the truth, promising to keep anything that was revealed to him secret.

Then Monsieur Pommeret showed him the nugget and recounted how he had found it,

It did not take much to inflame the speculator's imagination. He begged Monsieur Pommeret to sell the first fruit of his search, and, although the nugget only weighed eight and a quarter grams, he agreed to pay fifty francs for it. Then he returned home with the treasure and began to reflect. If the terrains of Meudon and Bas-Meudon contained gold, the value of those terrains was incalculable, and he, Roret, had made an error in getting rid of so much land in favor of his friend Dumortier.

Fortunately, he had the right to buy it back by paying a forfeit of a hundred thousand francs. The whole thing depended on whether, as he said to himself in his study, "the game was worth the candle," and whether the nugget found by Monsieur Pommeret had numerous sisters in Meudon. How could he make certain of that without giving too much away?

Monsieur Roret's decision was soon made. He had a correspondent in London to whom he wrote: *Find me, at my expense, an English engineer who has had experience in the gold mines of the Transvaal or Australia. Have him come to see me in Meudon* incognito. *I have important business to discuss with him.*

Having put that letter in the post, Monsieur Roret juggled with his nugget, murmuring: "We'll see! Perhaps I'll be able to do a superb deal!"

X. The Engineer and the Nuggets

Thus far, it was Borichevski who had benefited the most from the exploitation of the gold mines of Meudon; the unique nugget sold by Monsieur Pommeret for fifty francs had already cost the latter more than four times as much. Since fortune had smiled on him, though, Borichevski had resumed his deadly habits and had found it absolutely impossible on several occasions to assist Monsieur Pommeret in his search. That was all the more regrettable because the owners of neighboring properties had started digging on their own account, and had discovered several nuggets, which Monsieur Roret had similarly acquired.

The terrains of Meudon were definitely auriferous.

Everyone wanted to monopolize Borichevski in order to obtain initiation into the work of excavation and washing.

More or less secretly, large-scale excavations were effected behind the enclosing walls of various properties in Meudon, sometimes giving rise to bizarre finds of objects buried in various epochs.

Borichevski, pampered and spoiled, his pockets well-lined, yielded without restraint to his passion for alcoholic beverages and became more insolent by the day. The gold-seekers tolerated his eccentricities because they needed him, but Christian Norval, who did not have the same reasons to hold back, administered forceful reprimands on a daily basis.

One evening, the adventurer came back to his master's villa in an utterly lamentable state of drunkenness. Christian Norval, losing patience, gave him a thorough dressing-down and declared that he would to thrown him out if the present state of affairs continued.

Then Borichevski became high-handed with his master. "If you're not content with my services," he said. "You only had to say so. I can earn an honest living by my labor..."

"Your services!" Christian exclaimed. "Not only are you good for nothing, but you're compromising me. Everyone is astonished to see me tolerating a hardened drunkard..."

"That's sufficient!" Borichevski interjected. "You've had enough! Me too! Goodbye! I'll go elsewhere!"

And he went off, staggering, while the young man followed him with a compassionate gaze, ready to call him back—but the adventurer disappeared round a street corner, and Christian went back in, murmuring "Bah! We'll see!"

Once he had sobered up, Borichevski regretted his impetuosity. He had become veritably fond of his master, and he thought immediately of going to beg his pardon, but a kind of shame held him back and he began to wander through the streets of Meudon, like a soul in torment, his heart heavy, having no desire to go into a cabaret to drown his sorrows in the depths of a glass.

He arrived thus at the bank of the Seine, near the landing-stage of boats from Paris, following the ebb and flow of passengers with a dull gaze.

Suddenly, his eyes lit up. Among the travelers coming across the gangplank one by one he had just perceived a tall man whose physiognomy reminded him of an old acquaintance.

"Mr. Cowley!" he shouted.

The traveler stopped, examined Borichevski from head to toe with a rapid glance, and said in his turn: "Well, well! Stanislas Borichevski! By what chance...? Are we destined, then, to run into one another everywhere: Johannesburg, Coolgardie..."

"And Meudon!" concluded the adventurer. "But Mr. Engineer, have you come here to exploit placers, as in Johannesburg and Calgoorlie?"

"Perhaps. In any case, I beg you to keep my secret. I've come here *incognito*, summoned by a certain Monsieur Roret. You can take me to him—but don't let anyone know who I am."

"Understood, Master."

"But how do you come to be here? I left you in Calgoorlie!"

"From there I went to Guiana, and I came here with a young scientist who made a small fortune in the alluvial deposits out there."

"It's serious, then—the alluvial deposits of Guiana?"

"As serious as can be."

"And here? For after all, this Monsieur Roret, whom I don't know and who sent for me, asked for an engineer experienced in gold mining. Are there gold mines in Meudon, then?"

Borichevski was about to tell the engineer what he knew when he remembered, just in time, that the secret did not belong to him. For fear of harming Monsieur Norval, he contented himself with saying: "People are digging and washing, but…"

"Have they found gold, however little?"

"Yes, but..."

"Then take me to Monsieur Roret, quickly. There's something to be done."

When Borichevski had shown Mr. Cowley the engineer where Monsieur Roret's villa was, the Englishman said to him: "Where can I find you again? I might have need of you."

The adventurer indicated his favorite tavern, which made Mr. Cowley smile, the latter knowing all about the gold-seekers inveterate habits. Then, having rung the doorbell, the engineer was introduced to Monsieur Roret's house.

The latter had received a letter notifying him of the visit that very morning, so he had laid out in his study a map of Meudon, specimens of sand taken from various places, and the four nuggets discovered in the commune, all of which he had purchased.

"Monsieur Cowley," said the speculator, without wasting time in preliminaries, "my excellent friend Monsieur Bormann, in London, of whom I had requested an engineer experienced in gold mining, has recommended you too me and praised you very highly. You've been in the Transvaal, Australia—you're just the man I need."

Cowley bowed, without making any reply.

"Know, then," Monsieur Roret continued, "that very recently, a young scientist has come to live in Guiana who has come back from Guiana with a rather nice fortune made in the gold mines of that country. He had with him, as a domestic, an adventurer, a former prospector, who examined the terrains of Meudon and declared them to be auriferous.

"Oh!" exclaimed Cowley, amazed. "It's that adventurer..."

"Yes. And I certainly wouldn't have attached any great importance to what he said if the inhabitants of Meudon, having carried out diggings and washing on their property, hadn't found, successively, these four nuggets, which are indisputably gold."

Cowley, whose astonishment and curiosity were excited to the highest degree, examined the four nuggets one after another with minute attention, and remained plunged in profound reflection.

"Well?" demanded Roret.

"Well, it's certainly gold—but those nuggets present a particular physiognomy that throws all my ideas into confusion, and prevents me from arriving at a firm conclusion on the subject. I've never seen anything like them..."

"What's so peculiar about them, then?"

"Oh, at first glance they're nuggets like any others, but when like me, one is habituated to the appearance of gold debris, one finds an appearance of fusion in them that isn't ordinary. If you want my honest opinion, in brief, one might think that they were artificial nuggets..."

"Aha! Then, you believe..."

"I don't believe anything at all. I'm only giving you my initial impression. It's necessary not to jump to any conclusions. First, I need to see the soil where these nuggets were found."

"Here are specimens identical to the sands that were washed," said Roret, presenting the engineer with some little bags of cloth containing extracts made from several excavations.

Cowley submitted them to careful examination, and concluded: "These sands have very little chance of being auriferous. Nevertheless, I need to see them in location and in their relationship to other strata. In sum, what do you want from me?"

"I want to know whether the land situated in the commune of Meudon can be fruitfully exploited from the viewpoint of gold, because I possess a considerable quantity of that land." And Roret, using his map, showed the engineer the location of all the parcels of land that he had acquired, especially in Bas-Meudon, as many on his own account as with Monsieur Dumortier's conditional option.

"Right!" said Cowley. "I understand perfectly. At present, these plots of land have no value, but if they're auriferous, or reputed to be auriferous, they might acquire a very great value. In consequence, what you want me to tell you is whether these terrains really are auriferous?"

"Exactly."

"First, it's necessary for me to reach a conviction with regard to these singular nuggets. Do you have a touchstone, nitric acid and a little saw?"

"I have all of that," said Roret, swiftly.

Firstly, Cowley tested the various nuggets with the touchstone and the acid.

"I suspected as much," he said, when he had concluded the trials. "These nuggets aren't pure gold. They have exactly the same composition as first-rate French gold jewelry; one might therefore think that they've been produced by melting down jewelry. But let's have a look at their internal texture.

Skillfully using the little fretsaw that Roret occasionally used to cut wood, Cowly set about sawing the largest of the nuggets in two. The fine steel blade sliced rapidly through the metal, and the operation was almost complete when the saw came to a abrupt stop and the blade snapped.

The section of the nugget was sufficiently extensive for it to be possible to separate the piece of gold into two with the aid of a steel chisel. Then, the obstacle that had broken the saw became visible: it was a little diamond, cut in rose fashion, completely embedded in the gold of the nugget.

The two experimenters gazed at it, astonished but convinced. It really was a matter of artificial nuggets resulting from the melting off jewelry, from which someone had not even bothered to remove the precious stones.

"From whom did you acquire these nuggets, then?" Cowley asked.

Roret explained how he had obtained them.

"Then it must be the prospector you mentioned who has made them. But why? First of all, that needs clarification."

Cowley took his leave of Monsieur Roret, telling him that the first necessary step was to question Borichevski in order to discover the true origin of the nuggets. Without mentioning that he had known the man in question for a long time, he declared that he would take charge of the enquiry personally and would come back to see the landowner when he knew something.

XI. How Monsieur Dumortier's speculation in Meudon earned him a hundred thousand francs

Cowley set off in search of the adventurer and found him, as he had expected, in the tavern.

"Aha!" he said, sitting down opposite him. "You haven't been entirely frank with me, Mr. Borichevski. You talked to me vaguely about gold-washing carried out in Meudon, when you are, in reality, the initiating mainspring of all that work. You've even fabricated nuggets that might have fooled anyone but me. With what aim?"

"Me!" exclaimed Borichevski. "I've fabricated nuggets?"

There was such a note of sincerity in his protest that Cowley added: "Who, then? For those nuggets are artificial."

"Are you sure?"

"Quite sure—and you know that I can't be mistaken."

"In that case, their discovery is even more extraordinary than if they were natural, for it's certain that no one put them there intentionally." And Borichevski recounted the naïve fashion in which a few property-owners had dug in their gardens and found the nuggets.

"According to what you've told me," the engineer concluded, "I believe I understand that the various finds were made not far from one another."

"Indeed."

"Well then, take me to the place in question."

Borichevski complied with a good grace and showed Cowley, in succession, Monsieur Pommeret's villa and the neighboring villas where the nuggets had been found.

Suddenly, the engineer's attention was attracted by the Chapelle de Notre-Dame-des-Flammes, which was adjacent to the villas in question. "What is that building?" he asked.

Borichevski satisfied his curiosity, explaining that the chapel had been built on the spot where the terrible Versailles railway disaster of 8 May 1842 had occurred, when so many people had perished, burned to a crisp by the conflagration that the locomotive's coal had communicated to the wagons.[30]

"Yes, I've heard mention of that events," murmured the engineer, "and now I know all that I wanted to know. But to get back to our nuggets, who gave these worthy people the idea of digging for gold in their gardens?"

Borichevski understood that he ought not to tell the whole truth, and he attributed the initiative to what he called a hoax: a hoax that had been more successful than he had anticipated.

Cowley reflected for a few moments, and finally said: "And what does your master, the young scientist Roret mentioned to me, think about all this?"

"My master, discontented with me, has thrown me out."

"Oh, really? And how are you making a living?"

"I render a few services to the people looking for gold."

"Well, I like you, and I too want to do something for you. I know where to find you, and when I need your services, I'll pay you well."

Cowley immediately went back to Monsieur Roret's house.

---

[30] The Chapelle de Notre-Dame-des-Flammes, built in Meudon to commemorate the victims of France's first great railway disaster—the number of dead was never accurately ascertained because the bodies were so completely burned—was listed as a historic monument in 1938, but that did not prevent it from being demolished in the early 1960s.

"Well," said the latter, "how is your investigation going?"

"It's concluded. It wasn't Borichevski who fabricated the nuggets. They weren't even fabricated intentionally."

"What is their origin, then?"

"They simply come from the Versailles railway disaster of 1842."

"I don't understand."

"You will. You're not unaware that the majority of the bodies of the victims of the catastrophe were entirely burned up, and that the jewelry they were wearing was melted. It's that melted jewelry that constitutes the nuggets found in the vicinity of the Chapelle de Notre-Dame-des-Flames, on the location of the catastrophe. There's no other plausible explanation."

"So," said Roret, with a expression of disappointment, "if all the gold that can be found in Meudon is there, there's no reason to take the affair any further."

"You're mistaken, my dear Monsieur!" said the engineer, swiftly.

"What do you mean? Is there or is there not exploitable gold in Meudon? That's the whole question."

"I don't believe there's exploitable gold in Meudon—but that isn't the whole question."

"Explain yourself!"

"It's quite simple. At this moment, almost all the inhabitants of Meudon are convinced that there's gold in their commune. They haven't found any before because they haven't taken the trouble to look for it, but they'll do so a lot more now that they've found some, without being aware of the true origin of these nuggets. Now, it isn't you or me who will disabuse them on that subject."

"What are you getting at?"

"This: you've made a speculation in Meudon land; you've shown me the plans; you have an enormous quantity of it to hand. It's necessary for you to dispose of those plots of land as fruitfully as possible. If they were auriferous, that would be extremely easy."

"But since they aren't."

"Although they aren't…as everyone believes that they are, it comes to the same thing, and remains extremely easy…oh, my dear Monsieur Roret, do you believe that in the Transvaal, in Australia, all the plots of land—all the 'claims,' to employ the technical expression—are auriferous? Not in the least! There are good ones, there are passable ones, and there are bad ones. When claims have been celebrated for their production one sells them on again, even after they've been exhausted. There are superb speculations to be made in that fashion. It's not the prospectors who get rich—it's the people who speculate on the land, on the entitlements, on shares in gold mines."

Talking about speculation to Roret was placing oneself on his favorite terrain. "You're right!" he exclaimed. "Here, near Paris, the situation is magnificent. The incontestable discovery of nuggets whose true origin no one suspects has set the whole area seething. People are already asking me about buying land…"

"Well, to speak in proverbial terms, it's necessary to strike while the iron's hot. It's necessary to create and launch, without losing a moment, the Societé des Mines d'or de Bas-Meudon—and you'll see your land take off. If you care to give me *carte blanche*, I'll commit myself to your affair."

"Gladly. But first, a piece of advice? I've passed on a considerable number of my options to my neighbor, Monsieur Dumortier, but I've reserved the possibility of getting them back by paying a forfeit of a hundred thousand francs. What should I do? Let Dumortier benefit from the increased value of the land, or pay the forfeit and take back my options?"

"Don't hesitate—pay the forfeit. Take back the options for yourself. You're sure to make an enormous profit."

And that is why, the following morning, Monsieur Dumortier was informed that Monsieur Roret, in accordance with the clause in their contract, was taking back the options he had ceded, and was placing at the disposition of his neighbor the stipulated forfeit comprising the sum of a hundred thousand francs.

On reading the letter that brought the good news, Dumortier leapt for joy. To be free of his engagements and make a hundred thousand francs without opening his purse! He had never expected so much happiness. He decided that he had definitely made a good speculation, precisely because it had not been carried through to its conclusion.

"Lauriane! Lauriane!" he cried. "Not only are we not ruined, but our fortune has increased by a hundred thousand francs."

"Should we accept them?" asked the young woman, brought running by these enthusiastic exclamations.

"But of course, my dear! With pleasure and without the slightest scruple. It will be your dowry. *Sapristi!* What disagreeable emotions I had before this joy—we've certainly earned them! Besides which, if Roret is offering them in breaking our contract, it's because he's expecting to make a profit thereby. So I'm going to put them in the bank right away, and invest them in nice safe bonds…and no one will ever tempt me to speculate in land again!"

That was what he did, and when Christian came to visit his friends, he was told the good news.

The young scientist smiled in satisfaction, for he felt that he was the original artisan of that joy, and simply murmured: "You see that it's necessary never to despair."

"But what is Roret hoping to do?"

"Don't worry about that. He's glimpsed a means of making a big profit on his land; otherwise, he'd never have taken that thorn out of your foot."

"What if they're auriferous?"

Christian smiled again, and said: "They already have been, for you, my dear hosts—that's the main thing. As for Monsieur Roret, time will tell. Don't forget that it's the housewarming tomorrow. You'll be able, my dear Lauriane, to inaugurate your future home."

XII. Christian Norval's Villa

The next day was Sunday.

Since he had taken possession on the villa in Meudon Christian Norval had not wasted a minute in fitting it out in accordance with his tastes and Lauriane's, which scarcely differed from his own.

He had used Monsieur Dumortier's villa as a model, to such an extent that when Lauriane entered his home for the first time that evening, on her father's arm, she could not repress an exclamation of astonishment. Everything, down to the slightest detail, reminded her of the paternal house.

Christian, estimating that he had produced the desired effect, bowed and said: "This way, you'll hardly noticed that you've changed residence; all the more so as Monsieur Dumortier will want to spend as much time here as possible. I know his habits; he'll feel quite at home here.

"Indeed," said Monsieur Dumortier, who found objects familiar to him in the same places as in his own house. "You're a skillful sorcerer, my dear Christian. You know how to capture people by means of their weaknesses...their cherished habits. Look! Here's the latest issue of the *Orchidophile*, on a lacquered side-table, next to a low armchair, by the window, just like home...oh, Christian, Christian!"

The young scientist showed them around the house. Monsieur Dumortier and is daughter went through the various rooms, moving from one astonishment to another, so great was the resemblance between the arrangements and fittings of the two villas. They ended up in the greenhouse, where Christian had accumulated veritable treasures, as many in the form of plants as birds, which he had collected in the course of his various voyages, placed in the care of his friends and finally reassembled in the definitive abode that he had chosen.

The young man's guests, passionate about such beautiful things themselves, appreciated them for their full worth, and listened delightedly to the details the traveler gave them regarding the circumstances in which he had discovered them.

It was there, in the midst of those marvels of nature, which they never wearied of admiring, that they spent much of the day, finding that the hours passed too rapidly. So, when Marthe, who had come to lend a hand to his housekeeper, announced that the meal was served, Christian exclaimed regretfully: "Already! I thought I was in paradise, and no longer had any need to eat or drink!"

"Well, for myself," said Monsieur Dumortier, "I confess that I have a great appetite."

"Me too!" said Lauriane, gaily, leaning on the arm that Christian offered her in order to escort her to the dining room.

"And now we've descended from the clouds," Monsieur Dumortier said, as they sat down at table, "I'll tell you something that you doubtless don't know yet, my dear Christian, since I only learned it myself this morning."

"What's that?"

"This is it! This morning, when I got up—I'd scarcely finished getting dressed—I hear my doorbell ring, and Marthe comes to tell me that Monsieur Pommeret wanted to talk to me."

"Oh, yes: Monsieur Pommeret—the man with the nugget."

"Exactly. I go down to the drawing room and Monsieur Pommeret tells me that, not having found anything more in his garden, he wants to buy one of the plots of land that I own in Bas-Meudon, which have been recognized as auriferous. I reply to him that, in the first place, I no longer possess a singly inch of land in Bas-Meudon, having reverted everything to Monsieur Roret, and that, in the second place, I don't know whether the land has been recognized as auriferous. Then Monsieur Pommeret tells me that Roret has brought an English engineer from London, named Cowley, an expert proven in the Transvaal and Australia, and that the aforesaid Cowley has recognized the auriferous nature of the land in Bas-Meudon."

"Cowley!" murmured Christian. "Where have I heard that name before?"

"That explains, my dear Christian, Roret's sudden change of mind and repossession of my land. The land is auriferous, and he expects to make a big profit on their sale."

"Are you regretting their loss?" asked the young man, smiling.

"Oh, not in the least. I've had too much worry. If I learned that they were shifting gold from them by the spadeful, it wouldn't bother me in the least. For once in my life I had a crazy fit of ambition, but that's over now."

"You're right. Besides which, I can guarantee that they'll never be digging up gold by the spadeful in Bas-Meudon."

"You have no confidence in the engineer Cowley, then? But you, yourself..."

"Oh, my dear Monsieur Dumortier, I've told you in what proportion I believe that there's gold everywhere."

"But I haven't finished my story. Monsieur Pommeret goes away, saying that he'll address himself to Roret in order to get a 'claim'—that's the technical expression he used—and I escort him back to the threshold of my abode. What do I see? Your Borichevski, at the corner of the Pavé-des-Gardes, talking in a low voice, but animatedly, to an unknown man of foreign appearance. And Pommeret says, as he leaves me: 'There's Mr. Cowley now!'"

"Aha!" Christian exclaimed. "I've got it. It was Borichevski who mentioned this Cowley to me, as an exceptional engineer."

"You see!"

"And what's become of your domestic," Lauriane put in. "He's no longer to be seen in your house."

"Oh, for some time he's been doing the same as the other inhabitants of Meudon: looking for gold. Anyway, I don't need him. As for Mr. Cowley, whom Borichevski had mentioned to me as a good engineer, I have reason to suppose that in the gold mining business, he acts first and foremost as a

286

speculator. For the gold mines of Bas-Meudon, that's entirely the case."

"So you don't believe in them?"

"Not in the least—and today, I can admit to you frankly, just between us, that if I pretended to believe in them, just a little, or if I wanted to let them be believed, it was precisely because I hoped that Roret would let himself be caught up in the affair and buy back your land."

"My dear Christian!"

"My little scheme having succeeded, I no longer have to conceal my true opinion, and I'd even be annoyed if worthy people are about to risk their money in this bad business. With Roret, it was fair tactics, but I don't want anyone to make use of my opinion to make honest people chase after a chimera..."

"Are you going to disabuse Monsieur Pommeret, then?" asked Lauriane.

"Oh, Monsieur Pommeret has the means to pay for a little claim in Bas-Meudon. He really is too credulous. He won't find anything, and it will all end there…it's only if things take a serious turn that I'll think it my duty to intervene, since I'm the original cause of all this fuss. Ha ha! What a curious example of public credulity! But let's talk about something else. It's today that I've resolved to ask you to specify precisely a point on which we're all in agreement...

"You've been kind enough, Monsieur, to grant me the hand of your daughter, and Lauriane has told me that the union in question is her dearest wish—so, when will the marriage take place? There's no reason for any further delay. The future spouses' dwelling is ready..."

"And Roret has furnished the dowry," Monsieur Dumortier concluded, laughing. "Well, my children, you can marry whenever you wish. No prevarications, now! Let's fix the date for a month from today. That will leave the time necessary for the formalities, the dress, and so on."

"That's it—next month!" exclaimed Christian, joyfully. "Is that agreeable to you, my dear Lauriane?"

"I have too much respect for my father's wise advice not to accept it," she replied, smiling.

"And then," said the young scientist, "we'll take a little trip to Switzerland, or Italy, and we'll come back to Meudon to cultivate our orchids."

"Admit," concluded Monsieur Dumortier, "that there's no more agreeable occupation, and that it's far better than speculating or searching for gold."

"I admit it," said Christian. "But if I hadn't started out by finding gold in Guiana, I wouldn't have been able to cultivate orchids tranquilly with you and Lauriane."

XIII. Gold Fever

The month went by rapidly, and Christian and Lauriane were married in Meudon, without any ostentation, among an intimate circle of relatives and friends. Then the newlyweds departed for Italy, leaving Monsieur Dumortier to look after the two greenhouses and the two aviaries. That excess of occupation did not prevent the excellent man from sighing as he thought about the absentees, but he consoled himself with the thought that they would soon return and that nothing would separate them from him in future.

While these happy events were taking place, Monsieur Roret and his collaborator, Mr. Cowley, entirely devoted to their speculation, had not wasted any time.

Borichevski, duly schooled by the engineer, had channeled the enthusiasm of the gold-seekers toward the terrains of Bas-Meudon. As it was necessary to deceive the analyses that certain acquirers if claims might have been tempted to carry out, however, Mr. Cowley had proceeded to "salt" the land.

Monsieur Roret, after having protested against this operation, which was both costly and compromising, had finally allowed himself to be convinced by the engineer's arguments.

"Remember," said the latter, "that it's common practice everywhere—Transvaal, Australia, etc. Gold seams are extremely capricious, and some rich claims are surrounded by other plots that don't contain an atom of gold. Do you think people resign themselves to taking a loss on that land? Do you think that anyone admits it when a claim is exhausted? Not at all. One can always find buyers for land that's supposedly auriferous, and when there isn't any gold, one puts some in. One salts them with gold dust, so that the analysis of specimens taken from them aren't too discouraging. That's what it's necessary to do here."

"But it's horribly expensive!"

"Not as much as all that. A few grams of gold dust, intelligently distributed, will suffice for each claim. Let me take care of it."

"But who'll do the work? If anyone found out..."

"Have no fear. I have the very man."

"Who? A local man?"

"No, on the contrary—a foreigner: Stanislas Borichevski."

"But that's the faithful factotum of Christian Norval, whom I have no reason to number among my friends..."

"He was, yes, but not anymore. They parted on bad terms. Besides which, I met Borichevski in the placers a long time before he made Monsieur Norval's acquaintance, and he trusts me completely…just as I trust him. I repeat, he's the very man we need. Remember that, consciously or not, he was the one who started this whole business. Here in Meudon, they swear by him, they consult him about everything; he renders the naïve gold-seekers continual services. He knows their weaknesses, their passions. He can make them do whatever he wants. Furthermore, he really is an expert in all matters pertaining to gold mining. He'll apply that expertise to the salting."

"Without anyone seeing him?"

"He'll operate by night, in good places, taking all the necessary precautions."

And that is how Stanislas Borichevski, equipped with a lather satchel full of gold dust that the engineer had procured for him, came to be given the job of salting the claims that had been sold the previous day.

As the prudent Mr. Cowley had anticipated, analyses were carried out, and gave results that, if not very encouraging, were at least of a nature to justify further research, and to maintain the ardor of the buyers of claims.

Thus, Monsieur Roret's business affairs made very good progress.

Monsieur Pommeret, the first in line, had given the lead, and had bought a large plot, where, aided by Borichevski, he had set up an improved washing facility. That worksite, after treating sixty cubic meters of sand, had produced 1.36 grams of gold. It was very little, but it was necessary to persevere in order to find more—that was Borichevski's opinion, and also Mr. Cowley's.

Monsieur Pommeret was an important person in Meudon. He was known as a man of good sense, who certainly would not have launched himself into the business of washing for gold if there has not been a serious chance of success. People remembered the finding of the nuggets, the sand-analyses, the results obtained here and there, and those that certain inhabitants of Meudon were said to be hiding, in order not to attract the attention of the government to the wealth that their land contained.

In brief, Monsieur Pommeret's example was contagious. At first, a trickle of buyers approached Monsieur Roret; then their number increased; and finally, everyone started to go with the flow. There were people who spent their life savings to buy a few square meters of auriferous land in Bas-Meudon. Buyers even started coming to neighboring communes: Issy, Sèvres, Chaville, etc.

On seeing that, the engineer said one morning to Monsieur Roret: "We're there! The business is launched, the public is excited. It's time to create the Societé des Mines d'or du Bas-Meudon."

"What's the point, since we can sell the land?"

"Sell the land! A fine business! Your profits won't be anything extraordinary. It's paper that it's necessary to sell: gold mining shares. That's a superb business."

"But dangerous!" murmured Roret, who was suspicious of the hazardous speculation in question.

"Not in the least! There's gold at Meudon—that's proven. We're creating a company to exploit it. Where's the harm? The mines exist. They're there, ready to hand. Everyone can see that. Well, we want to exploit a part of our land ourselves. Truly, I don't see anything reprehensible about that."

Roret allowed himself to be persuaded by this reasoning, and there was son o other topic of conversation in Meudon but the imminent creation of the Societé des Mines d'or du Bas-Meudon, whose initial shareholders were Monsieur Roret, Mr. Cowley and Stanislas Borichevski.

The English engineer then made the supremely clever move of recruiting the worthy Monsieur Pommeret into the group, by persuading him that the company would give him better results than his own exploitation.

As soon as the news became common knowledge—and the three associates spared no effort in spreading it—other inhabitants of Meudon asked to join the Societé. Only a small number of specially selected individuals were admitted as founder members, and the others were promised shares.

They were already at a premium.

While Monsieur Roret occupied himself with the constitution of the Societé, land-buyers continued to approach him. They were made to pay dearly, and it was only with great difficulty that small claims were ceded to them, the Societé, it was said, intending to reserve the bulk of the auriferous terrains.

That small corner of Bas-Meudon had taken on a very animated appearance. There was a constant coming and going of improvised diggers carrying barrow-loads of tools, sieves and washing-bowls. The claims were minutely delimited and carefully surrounded by fences. Within these enclosures the soil was dug up, and the washed sand piled up in artificial mounds.

From dawn onwards, the gold-seekers were at work, and they did not leave until nightfall. They ate lunch and dinner while they worked. Some fanatics even camped on their plots and spent the night there.

And yet, the harvests of gold were either non-existent or ridiculously small. Strangely enough, in spite of the feeble results that each prospector observed on his own claim, and admitted, he imagined that his neighbor had achieved superb results, and was deliberately concealing them—and the hope of a similar success drive him to continue his endeavors.

XIV. Mr. Cowley Prepares a Major Coup

Everything was ready, definitively, for the launch of the Societé des Mines d'or du Bas-Meudon. Only one formality remained to be fulfilled: to give absolute confidence to the future share-buyers, it was necessary that the enterprise should be based on an absolutely irrefutable analysis of the terrain. Those of Mr. Cowley, the Societé's own engineer, might be open to criticism on the grounds of partiality.

In order to cut that objection short, he suggested to Monsieur Roret the idea of having a public and solemn expert examination carried out, combining all possible guarantees of sincerity and exactitude.

That proposition frightened the speculator somewhat.

"Hmm!" he said. "I can't see how you're going to ensure that gold is actually found in terrain that hasn't been prepared for that purpose."

"That's why," Mr. Cowley replied, "I'm going to prepare it in advance."

"Still by means of the same method?"

"Indeed, and by means of the skill of Borichevski."

"It's very delicate, for, after all, how can you make use of the accurate deployment of that expertise?"

"It's very simple. We'll invite all our friends and all the people interested in our enterprise to come to Bas-Meudon on a particular day. There, having previously taken specimens publicly from the terrain in order that they can be subjected to a minute analysis, we'll invite our guests to bring with them, if they wish, their own assayers or mineralogists, inspiring complete confidence in them."

"They won't fail to do so!"

"I hope so! On the terrain, in a place chosen by me, I'll install in advance everything necessary to carry out several washings simultaneously, and I'll have a trench dug where the specimens have been planted in advance. It's a forced move, but it's indispensable to the success of the operation. It's at the bottom of the trench, at the place where I'll instruct Borichevski to plant the specimens, that our excellent collaborator will proceed with an energetic salting—with the result that at assay, our land will yield an entirely encouraging proportion of gold. Is that simple enough? Can you see any objection to it?"

"I can't see any—but some hitch might crop up."

"Don't indulge in needless hypotheses. I'll arrange everything so that the operation goes as desired. If a hitch crops up, I suppose I'll have to remedy it, in such a fashion that nothing unfortunate happens. So it's settled. Send out your invitations. I'll go brief Borichevski."

Indeed, while Monsieur Roret informed his friends about the great public experiment to be carried out the following Sunday, the engineer took the adventurer to one side and gave him a detailed account of the program that he would have to carry out.

In the very middle of the land, Borichevski was to set up a series of washing apparatus surrounding a vast circular space, at the center of which he was to fig a trench ten meters long and fifty centimeters deep, and when Saturday came, he was to sow the entire surface of the bottom of the ditch with a quantity of gold dust, and then cover it with a few centimeters of sand.

Mr. Cowley made sure that the prospector had understood his instructions fully, and gave him the funds necessary for him to make an immediate start on the washing apparatus.

The news of the great experiment that was to take place the following Sunday soon spread throughout Meudon. A large number of curiosity-seekers went to the place where Borichevski was working, following the details of his installations carefully. The adventurer even began to find them annoying, and wondered how he could proceed with the salting unobserved.

He imparted that anxiety to the engineer, who replied: "You'll only operate in pitch darkness."

At six o'clock in the evening the trench was finished. Seeing that the idlers were stubbornly remaining there, Borichevski decided to leave them to it, and went back to Meudon. He was due to meet Cowley after dinner, so that the latter could give him the gold dust destined for the trench.

He therefore presented himself at Roret's villa at eight o'clock, and the engineer, as he handed him the packet of gold dust, gave him his final instructions.

"Above all," he said, "be prudent—and don't get pinched!"

"What time should I go out here?"

"The more advanced the night is, the better it will be. It's necessary to avoid, as much as possible, being seen by belated passers-by."

"I won't go until after midnight, then."

"That's good. Until tomorrow!"

To kill time, while waiting to set forth on his nocturnal expedition, Borichevski went to his favorite tavern, where he was well known. As it was a Saturday—pay day—the tavern was full. Borichevski's arrival was greeted by a thousand varied interjections.

"Aha! here's the prospector!"

"Tomorrow's the great day!"

"Well, will they find any nuggets out there?"

Borichevski sat down in the midst of the customers, lit his pipe, ordered a rather complicated American cocktail, and started recounting, with his habitual verve, a series of fanciful stories."

"Yes, but in sum," one of his listeners concluded, "thus far, the gold harvest hereabouts hasn't been great, and people have spent far more than they've earned."

"Well," cried he adventurer, who was beginning to get tipsy, "you'll see tomorrow. I've opened a trench at random—absolutely at random. What have I found? A superb sand, very rich! You'll see at the analysis. Gold is very irregularly deposited in alluvia, a little here and a lot there. It's all a matter of putting your hand on a good location, and I think I have, this time."

"It's a good spot, then?" someone is the audience asked, curiously.

"Excellent! One could pick up a nice weight of gold there, quickly. Anyway, tomorrow, you'll see!"

Without changing its theme considerably, the conversation continued well into the evening. Borichevski, who was well-supplied with funds, thanks to Monsieur Roret, multiplied the cocktails without counting them, so that his loquacity continued to increase. He treated his listeners as comrades, and made them a thousand confidences about his past adventures, about gold prospecting, the life that one led in the lacers, and so on.

He ended up completely forgetting his program, and started denigrating the Meudon terrains, declaring that they weren't worth a farthing—to the great amazement of the customers, who were unable to explain that sudden change of tack. They agreed, however, to attribute it to the amount that the prospector had had to drink, and advised him to go to bed.

"Me, go to bed!" he exclaimed, looking at the clock set above the counter. "Oh no—I've got better things to do."

These imprudent words passed unnoticed by everyone, except for the tavern-keeper, who still had a clear head and had followed Borichevski's divagations with the keenest interest.

It is necessary to say that the worthy businessman was the proud owner of one of the claims that was closest to the spot where the adventurer had dug his trench, and he told himself, with some reason, that if the trench was on rich ground, his own had every chance of containing a similar quantity of gold.

Now, he had noticed that, in spite of his frequent libations, Borichevski had kept an attentive eye on the progress of the hands of the clock, and that preoccupation had intrigued him considerably. So he was struck by the final words that the prospector pronounced, and when the latter had succeeded in getting to his feet and heading for the door, stretching his limb, the innkeeper said a few rapid words in a low voice to his wife, who replaced him at the counter, while he slipped out of the back door.

No one noticed the simultaneous exit of Borichevski and the owner of the establishment, the conversation having resumed noisily.

XV. Nocturnal Adventures

The night was clear but moonless—a favorable circumstance for the adventurer's expedition. The freshness of the air, abruptly succeeding the overheated and smoky atmosphere of the tavern, caused Borichevski to become dizzy temporarily, and he felt the need to stop in order to become steady on his feet again.

Then he gathered his scattered wits, got his bearings, and headed at a slow pace toward the road leading downhill to Bas-Meudon.

The innkeeper, as we have said, had left the tavern at almost the same time as the prospector. Taking off his apron and putting on a soft felt hat, he went through the garden and cautiously opened the lattice-work gate, above which could be read, on a semicircular sign: BOOTHS AND ARBORS.

His intention was simply to see whether Borichevski was going to bed—which was easy, for since the adventurer was no longer in Christian Norval's service, he had taken furnished lodgings near the tavern.

When, on the contrary, he went in the direction of Bas-Meudon, the man who was observing him unobtrusively murmured: "Eh! Where's he going, then? I need to see."

And, closing the gate behind him, he started following Borichevski, while carefully avoiding letting the other see him.

That precaution was not unnecessary, because it was evident that the prospector, desirous of being unobserved, was only advancing with suspicion, turning round from time to time to check that no one was following him.

At that late hour, however, no one was about in the streets of Meudon, and the adventurer arrived at the bottom of the slope in the most complete solitude and silence.

The innkeeper had followed at a distance, imitating the precautions taken by the man preceding him—which is to say, waking at the very edge of the road, where the grass grew densely, in order to stifle the sound of footfalls.

Borichevski continued moving forward, multiplying his precautions, for he was approaching the claims surrounded by fences, some of which were guarded by dogs, while others, as we have already said, were occupied by their owners in person.

He did so well that he arrived without any mishap at the gate of the enclosure of the Societé's terrains, which had been left open during the day to permit the public to enter and monitor the prospector's preparatory labors, but which was locked by night.

Borichevski had the key; he opened the gate, went into the enclosure, and closed it behind him.

Having drawn closer, the innkeeper observed that the adventurer had turned the key on the inside, which was a great disappointment for his curiosity. There were a good many gaps in the fence, but the night was too dark for anyone to distinguish through those narrow fissures what was happening beyond a certain distance.

Very disappointed by this inconvenience, the wine-merchant reflected, and got an idea. His own claim was adjacent to the Societé's enclosure, and from his claim, by improvising a ladder with the washing apparatus he had stockpiled there, he would be able to look over the fence.

Unfortunately, he did not have the key to his own enclosure on him. In the time that he would need to go and fetch it from Meudon and come back, interesting things would surely be happening that he would be unable to witness.

What should he do?

The innkeeper decided to climb over the fence. There was no crime in introducing himself by climbing into his own property.

He immediately set about attempting the operation. Having gathered a few stones and bricks at the foot of the enclosure, he succeeded in getting hold of the top of the fence with both hands, and tried to hoist himself up by the strength of his wrists. Unfortunately, the wine merchant, already mature in years and beginning to run to fat, had no aptitude for that gymnastic exercise. His shoes scraped the planks noisily, which started several dogs in the vicinity barking.

Frightened, the man let go, while the pyramid of stones that had served him as a ladder collapsed noisily, dragging him down with it. Before he could get to his feet, two men had surged forth, equipped with lanterns, and grabbed him by the collar, saying: "Who are you? What are you doing here?"

"I'm Jean Graves, the wine-merchant from Meudon," he replied, standing up. "Look at me—you'll recognize me."

The two men illuminated the innkeeper's face with their lanterns, and did indeed recognize him. Still suspicious, however, they demanded: "What are you doing here at this hour, Monsieur Graves? It's not normal!"

"I was coming to my enclosure. And then, in fact, I can tell you that I was following a suspicious individual that I saw prowling around near here.

"Oh! Where is he?"

"In there, in the Societé's enclosure." In order not to compromise himself, Jean Graves judged it appropriate to disguise the truth.

"We'll go take a look!" said the two men, heading for the gate by which Borichevski had entered.

The latter, having heard the noise and perceived the lights, did not think about the fact that the gate was locked, and, fear that he might be caught, ran precipitately to the other side of the enclosure, which he scaled without difficulty and leapt down on the other side.

As ill-luck would have it, though, he fell into a claim where the proprietor was camped in an improvised tent. In addition, the latter had a dog, which hurtled toward the adventurer, barking furiously.

The owner of the claim, woken up with a start, threw himself on Borichevski, shouting for help. All the neighbors came running, including the two men who were with the innkeeper. The prospector found himself captured, and took on a piteous aspect, not knowing how to explain his presence in the place in the middle of the night and his climb over the wall. He wondered how it would all finish.

He had, moreover, been immediately recognized, and everyone was astonished to find him there—so he was pressed with questions, which Borichevski, in spite of all his cunning, found it very difficult to answer, all the more so as his head was obscured by alcohol fumes.

Jean Graves, still scenting a mystery, refrained from intervening to get him out of the awkward situation; on the contrary, he would have liked to see the situation clarified.

"It's not normal," he repeated, in a low voice, to his neighbors.

"Well, what are you doing here?" Borichevski was asked, from all directions.

"I was on sentry duty! I was taking my turn, on the engineer's orders."

"But why did you climb into your neighbor's enclosure?"

"I made a mistake, I couldn't find the gate. You can see that I've had one too many."

"Right! We'll let you sleep it off in our neighbor's tent, but keeping you in sight, and at daybreak we'll take you to the Commissaire. He'll get an explanation!"

"That's right—to the Commissaire," said Jean Graves, supportively. And he went away, regretfully, to go and reassure his wife, promising himself to come back bright and early.

Indeed, at dawn, he went back to the place where Borichevski had been caught and had spent the night.

Somewhat sobered up by his slumber, the adventurer tried to think of a way of getting out of trouble without compromising himself, but could not find one.

He was not given the time for lengthy reflection. Interrogated again and unable to provide satisfactory answers, he was taken to the Commissaire of Police in Meudon, escorted by a troop of local inhabitants already informed of the night's events.

The Commissaire, who was still in bed, got up grumbling, interrogated the adventurer in his turn about his singular nocturnal excursion through the claims, and, similarly unsatisfied by Borichevski's confused explanation, had him searched.

The prospector had not even had the presence of mind to get rid of the bag gold dust, which he had hardly begun to sprinkle when his nocturnal operation had been disturbed. The bag was seized and handed to the Commissaire, who, having weighed it in his hand and opened it, exclaimed: "But this is gold dust! Where does it come from? Is it to collect this that you introduce yourself into the claims by night? Are you a thief, then?"

"Me, a thief!" cried Borichevski, exasperated. "No, of course not! It's too bad—but I don't want to be taken for a thief or to be treated as one. Send all these people away and I'll tell you the truth."

The people who had brought the adventurer would have preferred to stay, but he Commissaire, desirous of getting to the bottom of the affair, ceded to Borichevski's request and had the room cleared.

When they were alone, the prospector did, in fact, tell him a part of the truth, declaring that he had introduced himself by night into the Societé's land, not to harvest gold, but to sow it there. Surprised in the middle of that operation, he had wanted to slip away unperceived and had gone to throw himself into the neighboring claim, where he had been captured, people right judging that his presence and his climb over the wall were suspicious. Pressed with questions, he was obliged to admit that it was according to the orders and on behalf of Mr. Cowley and Monsieur Roret that he had undertaken the maneuvers in question, with the aim of giving the terrains of Bas-Meudon a value that they were far from having naturally.

The Commissaire, completely edified on the subject, retained Borichevski temporarily at his disposal, and submitted a report to the court.

XVI. To Each According to his Actions

Since Mr. Cowley had arrived in Meudon, Monsieur Roret, in order always to have him close at hand, had offered him a room in his own home and a place at his table. The engineer had thus become a permanent house-guest of the speculator, and was hardly ever apart from him.

That day, Roret, having slept late, did not come down to the dining room until nine o'clock. Mr. Cowley had been occupied for a long time in religiously taking tea and sandwiches.

"Well?" Roret asked. "How did Borichevski get on?"

"I haven't seen him yet," the engineer replied. "Undoubtedly, having stayed awake half the night, he felt the need to rest. Hold on—that's doubtless him!"

Someone had just rung the doorbell. It was not the adventurer who came in, though; it was Monsieur Pommeret, greatly alarmed, who exclaimed: "What does it mean? Borichevski was arrested last night climbing over the fences of the claims. He was found to be carrying gold dust, but he declared energetically to the Commissaire that he wasn't a thief. I don't understand any of it!"

Roret and Cowley were dumbfounded, and looked at one another anxiously.

"Nor do we," said the engineer. "We don't understand it either. You're a local man—can you obtain some enlightenment from the Commissaire on the matter?"

"I'll try," declared the honest Monsieur Pommeret, who went to the Commissariat forthwith.

When the two accomplices were alone, understanding the gravity of the situation, they remained silent momentarily, and then Roret murmured: "If Borichevski has denied being a thief, he must have given the Commissaire explanations capable of getting himself out of trouble, but getting us into it. I had a presentiment that something like this would happen, you know. I was uneasy, and I begged you to be prudent. You were wrong to take things so far!"

"It's that Borichevski who's an incompetent and a traitor!" exclaimed the engineer, angrily. "Anyway, before rushing to judgment, let's try to find out exactly what's happened."

The two associates went out in search of news, each in a different direction, and soon had no doubt about the situation. All that they did not know was exactly what information Borichevski had given the Commissaire. The latter, refusing to yield to the insistence of Monsieur Pommeret, had maintained he most absolute silence in that regard.

Needless to say, the public experiment advertised so loudly did not take place, and was postponed until an indeterminate date under some pretext or other. All Meudon was seething; everyone was commenting in various ways on the events that had just taken place, and people were even beginning to insinuate hypotheses in whispers that were not far removed from the truth. Everyone, moreover, was astonished by the silence and inaction of the Commissaire, who was keeping Borichevski in prison without following up the affair.

Roret and Cowley were most intrigued by that inaction, and wondered what course of action they ought to adopt.

Their uncertainty did not last long.

One morning, they were summoned to the court in Versailles, went there, and were confronted with Borichevski. It was necessary to confess everything.

The magistrate charged with the investigation, after a severe admonition, concluded by saying: "Needless to add, in the circumstances, the Societé des Mines d'or du Bas-Meudon appears to me to be a simple fraud. I therefore invite you, not only not to take things any further, but to compensate the people who have been taken in by your promises, even before they decide to lodge complaints against you. I won't hide it from you that, in the latter case, I shall consider it my duty to pursue you with the utmost rigor.

"I suggest that you, Mr. Cowley, should leave the country and return to England, and that you, Monsieur Roret, should liquidate this affair as rapidly as possible if you don't want it publicized, to your great prejudice."

"What about me?" asked Borichevski, who seemed to have been forgotten.

"You! According to the investigation made yon your count, you're a foreigner with no resources, no profession and no dependents, given to inveterate habits of drunkenness, and you've made yourself an accomplice of an indelicate operation. In those conditions, it's very probable that an expulsion order will be issued against you."

That eventuality was not calculated to frighten the adventurer unduly; he had been the victim of many others. What did it matter to him whether he was here or somewhere else? He pronounced a philosophical "So be it!" and left, to be returned temporarily to prison.

Having returned to Meudon, Roret and Cowley had a terrible argument, blaming one another for the crime, and it would not have taken much for the settlement of their account, which was very arduous, to have degenerated into pugilism.

Finally, the engineer, having succeeded in making the speculator part with a rather large sum, packed his bags, left the country, and no more was heard of him. It did not take long for Roret to see the people who had bought land from him flooding back to demand, one after another, the annulment of their purchase on the grounds of deceit regarding the quality of the merchandise.

The speculator protested with all his might, and tore out his hair, but was finally obliged to reimburse the money unduly received, and saw his liquid resources dwindling visibly.

In the meantime Christian and Lauriane returned from their honeymoon voyage; their first visit was to Monsieur Dumortier, whom they had alerted by telegram.

"It's high time!" the latter cried, when his two children threw their arms around him. "I'm visibly getting thinner. And since you've arrived just in time for dinner, let's go to the table! Marthe, serve it hot!"

The excellent man could not contain his exuberant joy.

When the first effusions had calmed down, Christian asked what had happened in his absence. "How's Monsieur Roret? And the gold mines of Bas Meudon? And Borichevski?"

"Monsieur Dumortier told them everything he knew.

"Borichevski arrested!" Christian exclaimed, on hearing that news. "In spite of all his faults, though, he's no thief!"

"That's what he said."

"It's evidently a misunderstanding. My guess is that he was acting on behalf of Roret and Cowley."

"Probably. In any case, he's been kept in prison, and, according to what I hear, he's going to be expelled from France as a foreigner."

"Oh, I'll go claim him and answer for him. He's committed wrongs in my regard, but on the other hand, I owe him too much to abandon him."

And, indeed, the following day, Christian Norval took the necessary steps to have Borichevski set free, declaring that he would take him into his service and thus assure him of means of existence. He was just in time. Forty-eight hours later, Borichevski would have been taken to the frontier.

The adventurer, duly appreciative of the step taken by his former employer, dissolved in apologies for the past and solemn promises for the future. Extraordinarily enough, appointed as gardener for Monsieur Norval's and Monsieur Dumortier' villas, he kept his promises much better than one might have expected. In fact, he abstained from frequenting the tavern, where he was not spared mockery regarding his washing for old.

Happy individuals, like happy peoples, have no history. Such is the case with Monsieur Dumortier, Christian Norval and Lauriane. Nothing ever comes to trouble the calm and peaceful existence they are now leading in Meudon as I write these lines. The only notable event that has taken place since the two newlyweds returned from Italy is the birth of a son, as handsome as his father and mother and "as indolent as his grandfather," at least according to Monsieur Dumortier, who is delighted that his grandson has something in common with him.

As for Monsieur Roret, almost ruined and completely discredited, he has sold everything he possessed in the locality as best he could, and nothing more has been heard about him, or of the gold mines of Bas-Meudon.

www.ingramcontent.com/pod-product-compliance
Lightning Source LLC
Chambersburg PA
CBHW030343020726
47493CB00003B/668